MW00427284

The Gryphon Generation
Book 2

A New Era

By Alexander Bizzell

Acknowledgements

Doing the traditional thing this time around and personally thanking my mom and dad for supporting me through this novel.

A huge thank you to all my fans, friends, and Kickstarter backers alike that made book 2 possible.

Again, I want to thank Trevor Cooley for his constant mentorship, hours upon hours on the phone, and his extreme dedication to making this book the best it could be. He has no reason to go above and beyond like he does besides being a genuinely good dude.

I still find myself wanting to thank Jess E. Owen and Larry Dixon personally for getting me into writing. Even the third and fourth time through their novels, they are still as captivating and inspirational as the first read through.

Yet another incredible cover done by Cyfrowa "Red-Izak" Izabela that really ties the whole book together. With her image, you can truly judge a book by its cover and hope my quality of work is on par with her own.

The other gorgeous interior images you will come across were done by Chantel Hale and Kaja "Blajn" Sztajnkier.

And last but not least, front and rear cover layout was done by my man, Scott Ford.

Kickstarter backers

Jedidiah "Kalenai" Davis

ScaniGryph

Jay Doran

Birdghost

"Forest Wells"-From one indie author to another, keep up the good work!

Henrique Andrade

Gawain "Gryphon at heart"

Tory Chang

Henrique “Loggor” Andrade

Shawn Dean

Tucakeane

Jere Edwards

Der the Gryphon

Carole Axium

Saylor

Matee Mana

A. L. Freeman

Peter Caulfield

Taran the Gryphon

Jeremy Hillis

Ulysses

Bryan

Siren Griffon Glück

Aaron Garrett

Roz Gibson

Jay Doran

Onix331

Taz

Philipp Haeuser

TaranGryphon

MaraSabot

Nivatus

Tucakeane

Kitt

Christian Largent

Andrew Armstrong

A New Era

John Miyasato

Gawain Doell

Stormdancer

Jennifer Priester

Justin Ellison

Emilie Rose

Mark Grandi

Carly Pope

Table of Contents

Chapter 1 Hit The Bricks

A loud whistle rang out. Thyra stopped sprinting, foreclaws digging into the soft grass, and immediately turned around to head the opposite direction. Her chest heaved and burned. Her legs felt like they would give out at any moment. Blood pumped in her ears, dulling the sound of another loud whistle.

"Red-tail! Pick up the pace!" Coach Victor shouted from the sidelines.

The harpy eagle's gray facial feathers blew in the gentle breeze as he sat comfortably and drank from his paper coffee cup. The massive gryphon seemed to sit still as a statue on the sidelines. He was possibly the largest gryphon in all of gryphball, besides Aadhya. His size made sense, seeing how Harpy Eagles are the strongest eagles on earth. Thyra could see the steam coming off his cup in the cool morning air. He brought the container to his great curved beak and sipped, watching her sprint across the field with his black eyes.

Thyra pressed on, running the full length of the field now in a full sprint. Rachel quickly caught up to Thyra. The much smaller kestrel gryphoness with a body the size of a housecat managed to keep pace with her. The cold air burned in their lungs, hot vapor clouding in front of their faces with each labored expiration. They shared a glance, but were unable to utter a word to one another.

Thyra's foreclaws and hindpaws dug into the earth with each leap. Then came another whistle blow. Thyra and Rachel stopped together and turned again. She could see that her other teammates Aadhya and Antonio, who had been trailing behind in the beginning, were now in the lead.

"Push! Red-tail, Kestrel! Push!" came Victor's booming voice once again.

Thyra cried out in frustration and used every last bit of her energy to sprint once again. Her eyesight began to fade. Her lungs felt as if they were about to explode, but she pressed on. She passed the two larger teammates in front of her and, with Rachel right beside her, continued towards the opposite end of the field. Three quick whistle blows finally came, signaling the end of their bouts.

Thyra's legs gave out and she collapsed on the ground, rolling on her back and staring up into the golden orange morning sky. She wheezed, trying to catch her breath as her friends collapsed beside her.

"Not bad," Victor said and walked up in front of the exhausted group, towering over them. "Take a fifteen-minute break before the rest of the team gets here, but report for the morning meeting at eight." His dark gray crest feathers roused as he stared down at them. "Understood?"

They all gave a nod. The coach turned tail and left, heading towards the locker rooms. Thyra let out an exhausted moan, still lying on her back as she finally caught her breath enough to speak.

"I don't know what aches more! My wings or my legs," she complained. Between the long flight from home to the stadium, and having to do the early morning sprints as punishment for leaving early the previous day, she was sore all over.

"It will become easier over time." Antonio assured her. The harris hawk stood and ruffled his deep brown chest feathers, then turned his yellow face to watch Victor leave. He readjusted his burnt orange wing shoulders and stood to walk towards the dugout.

Aadhya gave her a reassuring beak smile and reached out with a giant white-feathered foreclaw. "Running is something I do not do well, but as Antonio said, it will become easier as the training proceeds." The bearded vulture was every bit as large as Antonio, and easily helped Thyra up onto her feet.

Thyra shook herself off before looking into Aadhya's red and yellow eyes. The eyes stood out in sharp contrast to the black band across the eyes and white facial feathers. "Yeah, yeah, I know. It just sucks getting there."

They all followed Antonio back to the sidelines and grabbed their water bottles. Thyra raised the bottle upside down and squeezed, the cool liquid parching the desert in her beak.

"I don't know what everyone's complaining about! I can run for days. I love running and flying," Rachel chirped and ruffled her cream-colored chest feathers, not even out of breath anymore. "There was this one time that I ran all the way here from Chattanooga just because I felt like running! I mean it took a lot longer than flying, but it was still fun!"

Thyra glared down at her, which caused Rachel to chuckle. The tiny kestrel turned her bluish-grey topped head up to look at Thyra. Rachel's big black eyes almost seemed to extend down due to the black spots underneath the oculars.

"Not everyone has racing fuel pumping through their veins like you do." Thyra retorted. Having emptied the water bottle, she placed it back on the bench and went to lie back down on the soft grass once again. She sighed and closed her eyes. Her stomach chose that moment to audibly complain.

"Did you not eat this morning?" Aadhya asked, and reached into her pouch, which was sitting on the bench next to her.

"Besides a banana I ate on wing, no," Thyra replied. "I had to get up really early to fly here from Macon."

Aadhya dug around for a minute before pulling out an aluminum foil wrap. She opened it up and handed Thyra a wholegrain pita. "That will not do. You need to eat plenty of good carbohydrates before practice, or you will run out of energy."

Thyra sat up again and took the pita from Aadhya. "I usually eat well before practice, but I guess I do have some time before we start once again." Thyra nodded and tore chunks out of the pita.

"Well, well, you ladies look lovely this morning," came a mocking voice from behind them.

Nathanial walked out onto the field with head held high, dark brown feathers preened perfectly. The striated caracara sat and ran his talons through his neck feathers, flecks of gray and orange showing off in the light. He glared at the group of disheveled gryphons and opened his silver beak to cackle. “It looks like you birds got tossed around by a housecat! What’s the matter, already tired? And here I thought I was going to have some competition today.”

Rachel stepped forward with a scowl. “Shut your beak, dirty caracara! We will still kick your tailfeathers up and down this field today.” She poked a little talon against his peanutbutter-brown spotted chest to drive the point home.

Nathanial stared down with his yellow face and pushed her tiny foretalons away. “Is that what you think, runt? I’m the best player here! I would like to see you try, but by the looks of it, you couldn’t even best a gryphlet. Not even on your best of days.”

Rachel ground her beak and ruffled her feathers. “Listen here, assfeathers! Today I’m going to push your beak down into the dirt! I’m going to clean house with your…”

A large gray talon rested on Rachel’s wingshoulder. Aadhya stood next to her now, towering over Nathanial, and said in a calm voice, “Nathanial, we have no quarrel with you. Perhaps you could take leave for the time being.”

Nathanial frowned and raised his head up high, trying futilely to match her own height. He met her gaze with his pure black eyes, almost challenging her right then and there. “This is as much my field as it yours, Vulture. I suggest you keep your friends in check if you don’t want me to send them to the infirmary.”

Aadhya shifted her great peppered wings and roused her angel white crest feathers. She pushed tiny

Rachel back behind herself and stared back into his eyes for another second.

"It would be in your best interest that you not threaten my friends again," Aadhya warned him in a gentle voice. Thyra and Antonio stood a distance away but could tell by her body language that Aadhya was angry.

Nathanial snorted through his nares and backed down, waving a claw like it was nothing. "My best interest? Whatever, I don't have time for your shit anyways." He walked past Aadhya, giving her a hard shove as he did.

Aadhya did not move and remained steadfast, only turning her head to watch him walk to the other side of the dugout.

"Is he always going to be like that?" Thyra approached and asked the two.

"You mean a complete seagull's cloaca?!" Rachel yelled out loud, letting out some steam. Her wings twitched and all her feathers stood on end. "Yes! He's always like that. Thinks he's so great. I outta knock him down a few pegs myself! Teach that Caracara a lesion he won't forget!"

Nathanial looked back and grinned Rachel frustrations, which through her into another grumbling fit of rage.

"If I may, perhaps he teases you so because you give him the reaction he wants." Antonio pointed out.

Other gryphons were beginning to gather around the dugout now, preparing for the morning meeting. Rachel took a deep breath and let out a sigh. "I know it is. I've had people tell me that all the time. I always got poked at and laughed at when I was a gryphlet because I was so small. And they knew I would always explode in their face. I just can't help it."

"Well you're better than him. Just remember that next time he tries to tease you," Thyra said as the area became more crowded with chatting gryphons.

A pair of identical corvids walked up to the group with a curious look in their eyes. They looked Thyra over. One of them spoke, his yellow eyes shining brightly in the morning sun. "Hey, we saw you all leave early yesterday from practice, and then we saw you on the news. Is everything all right?".

"It was something about that anti-gryphon church rally, I think," the other corvid added. This one had blue eyes, but their voices sounded the same.

Thyra had to look between the two for a second. "Well, everything isn't all right. One of my friends ended up in the hospital with a broken wing, and it looks like there hasn't been any repercussion yet," she admitted.

The news reports had slightly favored the actions of the Gathering, making it look like the group was not completely at fault for the sudden riot, and it angered Thyra to no end. The Gathering hadn't been there to have a peaceful sermon in the park, they had been there to start a fascist protest. It had ended poorly when the Gathering formed a riot against the counter-protesters, and during the violence, her friend Isabell had gotten put in the hospital.

The blue-eyed corvid nodded in response. "Sorry to hear about that. I've read about that church before, but we don't live near Macon so we don't have much experience with them."

“They don’t sound like good people,” the yellow-eyed corvid added in. “Oh! I’m Brandon, and this is my twin brother, Braden.” He reached out to shake Thyra’s foreclaws.

“Sorry we didn’t get the opportunity to talk much yesterday. It was a busy day and you all left early,” blue-eyed Braden added and reached out to shake as well.

“It’s fine. I’m sure we will get to know each other as time goes on,” Thyra responded just as Victor stepped onto the field.

Everyone fell silent as the great Harpy eagle gryphon walked out in front of the team. He looked over them with his black eyes and waited for everyone to sit in a neat row before him.

“Morning team. Today, we will scrimmage against one another. Two teams of four will play at a time. I will divide you into these groups, and the rest will hit the weight room. Am I clear?” Everyone nodded in response. “Good. First I will divide the forewords. Kestrel and Red Tail will be group one.”

Thyra and Rachel looked at each other and smiled before stepping forward.

“Next group will be Caracara and Harris.”

Nathanial glanced over to Antonio and snorted.

“And the defenders for group one will be the Corvid twins.”

Brandon and Braden joined Thyra and Rachel.

“Then the defenders for group two will be Seahawk and Eagle.”

Thyra looked over to the other gryphons she had not met yet. An osprey gryphon joined with Antonio and Nathanial, closely followed by a golden eagle. Antonio seemed to know them and shared a couple words with the new gryphons.

"As for the rest, to the weight room. I will come get you when it's time to switch," Victor concluded.

The now-thinned-out group of gryphons turned and headed towards the exit of the field, leaving the eight standing before Victor. Aadhya whispered 'good luck' to the group and left the field with them.

Victor stared at the two teams for a minute, almost as if he was judging them. "I have chosen to separate you into these small groups because I want one defender and one forward from each team on the ground the entire time. You will switch later in the day to get a better feeling for both air and land positions. You will have no goalkeeper, and group one will possess the ball first. Are there any questions?"

The groups remained silent, and Thyra looked over to Antonio. He did not break his concentration from Victor and seemed to be calm despite being put on Nathanial's team.

"To your positions, then." Everyone stood up and began to walk towards the center of the field.

Nathanial shoved Antonio with a wing. "Just stay out of my way, Harris. Maybe you will learn something if you watch me." With that, he took off to the skies, pushing himself into the air without even discussing their strategy. Antonio sighed and walked out to the opposite side of the field from Thyra and Rachel.

Rachel glared at Nathanial turning circles in the air and looked up to Thyra with fierce burning eyes. “Let me have the skies, Thyra. I want to take down that Caracara with my own claws. I told him I was going to shove his beak into the ground, and by God I’m going to do it!”

Thyra chuckled and looked down at the excited Kestrel. “Go get him. I think I’ll be fine on the ground.”

That was all the response Rachel needed and, in a flash, she took to the air. The yellow-eyed corvid gryphon, Brandon, went to join Rachel as the air defender as his brother walked up beside Thyra.

“I understand you haven’t played much professional gryphball,” Braden, said to her. “If you need any extra help, I’ll be right here behind you.”

“Thanks. I’ll try my best.” Thyra replied.

Braden smiled and backed up closer to the ground goal. Both teams readied themselves and Victor took the whistle in his claws. Thyra’s heart thumped fast in her chest; excitement taking over as she faced her friend, Antonio on the other side of the field.

He crouched down and opened his wings slightly. Above, Rachel was hovering in the air right above Thyra, staring at Nathanial with intent to kill. Everyone was lost in the moment, time standing still.

A whistle blew and Thyra was brought back to reality as the sound of an air cannon behind her fired off, sending the gryphball into the air. She took off sprinting straight towards Antonio and looked above her to watch Rachel catch the white gryphball with ease.

Nathanial screeched out and beat his wings hard, heading straight for Rachel. She dove at the last second to avoid Nathanial's tackle, and flapped her small wings hard, gaining more speed.

The golden eagle defender dove towards Rachel next, and Rachel screeched out at Thrya to get open. By then, Antonio was on top of Thyra, running right along her side. Thyra sprinted faster and managed to outrun him by a gryphon length.

Rachel tossed the gryphball down to her before maneuvering up and away from the large defender in her path. Thyra's eyes opened wide as she jumped to catch the ball in her foretalons. She landed on three feet and went to tuck the ball away under a wing just as Antonio slammed into her side. She squawked and hit the ground on her side, sliding along the grass. The ball rolled across the ground and Antonio quickly grabbed it before throwing it back into the air. Nathanial caught the white ball and made haste towards the opposite end of the field.

"Sorry." Antonio replied and reached out with a foretalon to help Thyra back up. She grabbed it and stood back on all fours with a cough, holding her side.

"Did you have to hit me that hard!" she squawked in surprise. "This is practice."

He folded his ears back in response. "Yes, I did. Forgive me, but the opposing team will not be so gentle as I. Do remember this."

With that, Antonio took off towards the opposite side of the field. Thyra took off after the gryphon, trying to keep pace with him. Every breath made her wince as sharp pain lanced through her side. The hit from Antonio had made her realize she was going to have to toughen up.

Above, Nathanial flew straight as an arrow towards Rachel. They played chicken, neither one of them banking to one side or the other. At the last second, Rachel dropped slightly to let Nathanial pass. At her smaller size, she knew hitting him head on was a stupid decision, but her real intention had been to distract Nathanial from paying attention to Braden, who was coming in from the side.

By the time Nathanial noticed the corvid gryphon, it was too late. Braden hit Nathanial like a semi-truck. Nathanial squawked out in pain and rolled in the air, dropping the ball in the process. Rachel swooped in fast, and caught the ball midair as Nathanial flung his wings out to catch himself into a steady glide. He mumbled and cursed under his breath, turning his head to watch Rachel speed off towards the opposite end of the field.

Thyra forgot her own discomfort and could not help but chuckle a little at seeing Nathanial hit so hard. She wished it had been her tackling him like that.

The golden eagle gryphon back-winged towards the great circular air goal to defend it from the fast approaching Rachel. He hovered in place and readied himself, but it did him no good. Rachel rolled to the side and tossed the gryphball right past him, sending it soaring into the open goal.

Thyra screeched happily for her friend and the piercing sound of Victor's whistle filled the field once more.

"Very good, Kestrel!" Victor said while walking into the middle of the field. All of the eight gryphons came in to the center to hear Victor. "There was some good defense played by both sides, but you need to open your eyes, Caracara." Victor's black eyes settled on Nathanial, who quickly looked away and snorted angrily through his nares. "You were so fixated on the grudge you have with the Kestrel that you didn't even see Braden coming in from the side. I won't tolerate that again, do you understand?"

Nathanial grumbled under his breath and flattened his feathers.

Victor's eyes narrowed. "I didn't hear you. Understood?"

"Yes sir," Nathanial replied, ears folding back. His beak ground in agitation and no one dared look at him besides Victor.

"Good. Alright, switch positions and go again."

Everyone nodded and Victor turned to leave the field. Rachel fixed her gaze on Nathanial and when he made eye contact, she stuck her tongue out at him.

His feathers roused and he growled loudly. "You'll pay for that." Nathanial threatened which only earned a chuckle from Rachel.

"Hey, it's not my fault you have the brain of a seagull!" Rachel grinned even more as Nathanial's eyes widened at the quick retort.

Thyra could not help but chuckle a little. It only made Nathanial even angrier.

"I…I'll show the both of you! You better say your prayers! Y…you…you"

"T-t-t-today Junior!" Rachel mocked even louder and turned tail to walk to her side of the field.

Nathanial squawked and walked away, mumbling under his breath. Antonio walked up besides the furious bird. "I need you with a level head on the playing field."

Nathanial quickly turned his head to glare at Antonio, fire burning in his eyes. "And I need you to shut that ugly beak, old man! I'll kick that hen's ass!" He took off into the air once again, leaving Antonio behind.

The golden eagle gryphon walked up beside Antonio and sighed. "Young love is a crazy thing, isn't it?"

Antonio grinned in response. "Yes, it is. Jason, see if you can calm him down."

With a nod, the golden eagle gryphon was off into the air to chase after Nathanial. Antonio turned to look across the field, watching Thyra and Rachel laugh and carry on for a minute before taking their positions.

"Ready?!" Victor shouted across the field, and then the whistle blew once again.

Chapter 2 Check Up

Johnathen shut the door to his white station wagon, adjusted his casual dark brown blazer, and approached the large metal pavilion in front of him. It had been a while since he had last gone to the Macon Farmer's market, and had decided it was a good day to go for a visit. The market was the local hub for fresh goods, but the parking lot was less crowded in the fall months than it was during the summer.

He walked across the parking lot, his black leather shoes clicking against the concrete, and into one of the entrances. The inside was packed with various vendor stands. He never got tired of the smells of fresh baked goods, flowers, and handmade scented candles.

Johnathen moved through the spacious pavilion, stopping briefly at one vendor to purchase a blueberry muffin, and found what he was looking for, a flower vendor. He approached the stand and looked over the eye-catching arrangements of flowers before a blond-haired woman turned to greet him.

"Hello, Sir! Can I help you with something?" she asked politely.

"Yes! I'm looking for some flowers for a friend."

"Well you can never go wrong with a bouquet of roses for that special someone," she said with a little smile.

Johnathen laughed and shook his head. "No, no. These aren't for my wife. I have a friend in the hospital."

"Oh, I'm sorry to hear that. Well, I do have an arrangement of bright daisies and white daffodils that would be perfect for a get well soon card. Why don't you pick one out?"

Johnathen shrugged his shoulders. "Well, I haven't bought many flowers before, so I really don't know which are which."

The woman chuckled and walked over to a row of assorted vases, each one containing multiples of the same flowers. "I'll teach you then! These right here are the daisies." She picked one up to show him. "You can tell by the yellow center and the multiple thin white petals coming from it." She handed it over to Johnathen and as he brought it to his nose to smell it, she picked up another flower. The woman caressed the yellow cone in the middle and held it up for him. "And these are the daffodils. You can tell by the frilly bulb cone in the center and the big leaf like petals coming from it." She handed that one to Johnathen and he smelled it too.

"They look nice and smell good. I'll take them. Do you put them in a vase of some sort?"

"Of course. I can make you an arrangement with a vase for thirty dollars."

"Sounds good. I'll take it." Johnathen said.

The blonde woman smiled and pulled out a receipt book. “Great! Well give me ten minutes and come back by. I’ll have it done by then. Your name?”

“Johnathen,” he said putting emphasis on the E.

She scribbled down “Jonathan”, which made him sigh, but he didn’t bother correcting her. This always happened. He would never forgive his parents for misspelling his name on his birth certificate.

“I’ll be back in a bit, then,” he told her. Satisfied, he turned around and spotted the produce stand that Thyra used to work at, Jimmie’s stand.

The old man was busy as ever, talking to another customer and ringing them up for their purchase. Johnathen walked past a couple other venders and picked up one of the tomatoes from the stand. He placed the tomato on the counter just as the other customers walked away with a brown paper sack full of vegetables.

“What can I do for you today, young man?” Jimmie asked, still keying away at the register. The register made a loud ding and the cash drawer opened up.

“I think I’ll take a couple tomatoes, and some zucchini. I doubt Thyra will eat any of it, though.” Johnathen responded. Jimmie stopped putting his money away and looked up, his wrinkled face turning into a big smile.

“Well I’ll be damned. If it ain’t Johnny. How have you been?” Jimmie reached over the counter and took Johnathen’s hand in a firm handshake. Jimmies skin was callused and rugged, feeling like sandpaper in Johnathen’s smooth hands.

"Well enough. Mainly wondering what I should be doing with all this free time." Johnathen pulled his hand back and picked out a couple more bright red tomatoes.

"Looks like you've let yourself go a bit. Ain't seen you with a scruffy face or long hair before. Didn't even recognize you at first." Jimmie pointed out with a slight grin.

Johnathen pulled his long black hair back with his hands, and tucked it behind his ears. He had been letting it grow. It almost touched his shoulders by now. "Yeah, I haven't had hair this long since high school. Thyra says she likes it, though."

"So I take it ya still ain't been back to work?" Jimmie asked politely, pulling out a brown paper sack.

"Not yet, but I think with what happened yesterday, I'll probably be back to work soon." Johnathen placed the tomatoes and zucchini on the wooden countertop.

Jimmie ticked away at the register for a second and sighed. "I heard the news. I was worried after I got word of a hospitalized gryphon, but then I saw the interview with Thyra and those other gryphon friends of hers. She did a courageous thing, you know. Standing up like that for others like her."

"That's just the type of person she is," Johnathen responded.

Jimmie filled the brown paper bag with the vegetables and looked at Johnathen. "We need more like her. 'All that is necessary for the triumph of evil is for good men to do nothing'."

"Edmund Burke," Johnathen said with an impressed nod. "I didn't know you studied philosophy."

"We all had to study philosophy in high school. That's just one of them things I remember most." Jimmie turned back to his register and tallied up the total. "Four seventy-two, please."

Johnathen pulled out his wallet and handed him a twenty-dollar bill. "Keep the change. Buy yourself a case of beer or something. It's the least I can do for you taking care of Thyra all these years."

Jimmie took it out of Johnathen's hand and stuck it in the register. "Much obliged. Trust me, Thyra took care of me more than anything else. I had to hire three delivery guys just to do what she did in a day!" Jimmie laughed and sat down in his ragged lawn chair, pulling out a Coke from a mini-fridge next to him. He cracked the can open and took a sip. "How's that young gal doing anyways? I haven't seen her in a couple weeks now."

"She's a little stirred up from yesterday. With what all happened with the Gathering, and just starting her gryphball practice, she has a lot on her plate," Johnathen explained. "She had to fly out very early this morning to Athens so she would make it to practice on time. I'm sure she is exhausted, and I probably won't see her again until the weekend."

"She ain't been flying back to Macon after practice?" Jimmie asked.

"No, it's a long flight and the practices have been tiring her out. She's been staying with a new friend, a bearded vulture gryphoness named A...Ad...Ad something." Johnathen rubbed his forehead, trying to remember her name.

"Oh yeah, I remember seeing her with Thyra on the interview from yesterday. I ain't never seen another gryphon in person besides Thyra, but that vulture girl was twice as big as she was. I can't imagine a creature that big flying in the air."

"She's a bit intimidating for sure, but she's very kind." Johnathen remembered her sitting in the corner of the hospital room when he arrived and just how gigantic she looked in the cramped room. Her yellow and red eyes had given him a bit of a startle at first, but she was so calm and poised that he had been put at ease quickly.

"Well, you tell that vulture gal if she needs a job, I could sure use her. I'm sure she could haul all the deliveries in one go, even on our busiest of days." Jimmie pointed out and took another sip from the can.

Johnathen nodded and picked up the brown paper sack full of vegetables. It wasn't likely that a professional gryphball player would want to take a side job, but he did not want to be rude by pointing it out. "I'll make sure to pass on the invitation, and I'll tell Thyra that you said hello."

"Please do, and tell her to come by for a visit soon!" Jimmie waved goodbye as Johnathen turned and left.

He walked by a couple of other vendors and approached the florist. She was busy making the final touches to his bouquet, arranging the brightly colored flowers to contrast the white ones. Johnathen sat the bag of vegetables on the counter and cleared his throat, causing the florist to spin around.

"Oh! Just in time. I was just finishing it up." She picked up the clear glass vase and set it on the counter to present it to him. "What do you think?"

"I think it looks perfect." Johnathen said with a smile. He reached into his pocket and pulled out two twenty-dollar bills. "Here you go, no change."

Johnathen picked up the vase with one hand and the paper bag with the other. The blond woman smiled and thanked him before he made his exit.

It was a little cumbersome to carry both large objects, but he managed to make it back to his Volvo wagon without dropping anything. He placed the vase in the front seat and buckled it in so it would not move. The last thing he wanted was water all over the interior of his nice car.

Johnathen got into the driver's seat and pushed the start button. The Volvo hummed to life and he sat for a second before remembering the card. He opened up the glove box and pulled out the get well soon card. The front of it depicted a cartoon chickadee with a cast on its leg and a smile on its beak. He had thought it somewhat humorous at the store, and still grinned at the sight of it.

"Hopefully it's not in poor taste…" He second guessed himself for a minute, but signed the inside of the card anyway. He signed it both for him and Thyra, since she had forgotten to sign it before leaving that morning.

Johnathen put the card in the envelope, sealed it shut, and placed it in the forest of flowers. He put the car into drive and exited the parking lot before turning on the radio to an Atlanta talk show. The conversation piqued his interest, and he turned up the volume to listen to what they were saying.

"*...and apparently the police released everyone that was arrested during the violence at yesterday's rally*," one of the male talk show hosts said.

"*Really? I thought that they were pending trial for the fight that they started*," a female replied.

"*Apparently, one of the members from The Gathering paid the bail for all of them. I don't know about you, but that sounds a little fishy to me*."

The female scoffed. "*I don't see why the church would have anything to do with them, especially after they acted out against the protestors like they did. I say let them face time for what they did. Especially after injuring a good number of people and putting that one gryphon in the hospital*."

"*That's just it*," the man replied. "*We actually have a source that said they heard the preacher from the rally encouraging violence against gryphons and preaching other fascist beliefs*."

"*I'll believe that. There's always been something wrong with that church and all its members. I heard that an African American couple tried to go to the church and they were turned away at the door*."

"*And that's not all either. Did you see that local gryphoness on the news last night? She was talking like they were some sorts of alt-right group. At first, I didn't know what to think, but already today we've had a couple callers confirming what she was saying. It sounds like there's more that meets the eye with this Gathering church.*"

"*Well folks, if you want to call in and add anything else, we will open the lines up after a quick commercial break.*"

The radio switched over to advertisements about the local Ford dealer, and Johnathen switched the radio off. He took a deep breath and gripped the steering wheel as he drove.

"Looks like Matthew messed up big time. Finally people are starting to take notice." He put his hand into his blazer pocket and gripped the thumb drive that was inside.

It contained a copy of the footage that Isabell had caught at the rally. It confirmed everything the radio talk show hosts were talking about, and it would prove the truth of all the anonymous tips they received. This was hard evidence against The Gathering, something that Johnathen himself had not been able to obtain in all these years. Matthew and his congregation were meticulous and covered their tracks well, but their luck had finally run out. After he was done visiting Isabell, he planned to pay a visit to the news station.

The hospital came into view and he pulled into the parking lot. He grabbed the flowers and exited the car, careful not to spill any water. The sliding glass doors of the hospital opened automatically as he walked in and approached the elderly nurse at the front desk. "Hey, I'm looking for Isabell's room. She's the gryphoness. I was here yesterday, but I forgot the room number."

"Oh the gryphoness. She's in two-o-two," the nurse replied without even looking at the computer. "Elevator is down the hall and to your left."

Johnathen thanked her and entered the elevator. Once on the second floor, it was a short walk to her room, and the door was wide open. He knocked on the door anyway and peeked inside.

Isabell turned her head and perked her black eartufts. "Johnathen! I didn't know you were coming by." She used the remote to turn down the volume on the television. She had been watching a re-run of an older nineties sitcom. The laugh track played in the background of the show, but the mood in the room was far from joyous.

"Hope I'm not interrupting anything." He walked in and placed the vase on the table next to her bed.

"Not a damn thing," Isabell replied, now turning her attention to the flowers. She snorted through her nares. "I don't understand you humans and the infatuation with flowers, but it's a nice gesture."

Johnathen shrugged his shoulders and grinned. "It's just something we do."

Johnathen looked her over. She was in the same position as yesterday, her wounded wing outstretched and wrapped in a cast. Multiple wires kept it suspended from a rig attached to the bed. She was reclining on her side, her body covered with a white blanket.

"How are you feeling?" he asked in a polite matter as he sat down in the recliner next to the bed.

"What the hell do you think?" Isabell replied sternly. Her eartufts folded back against her head and she turned her attention to the television once again.

Johnathen sighed and fell silent, trying to think of what to say next.

She grunted. “I’m stuck in this bed for the next three weeks, they said. I won’t start therapy until the fifth week, and they said if I make a full recovery, I won’t be able to fly for over a year.”

“But they did remain optimistic you would make a full recovery?” Johnathen pointed out.

“Well, they seemed positive, but I know it will never be the same.” The room feel silent once again besides the chatter from the television. “And the food is terrible.” She added jokingly to lighten up the mood a bit.

Johnathen chuckled and looked over to the half-eaten turkey sandwich on the plastic hospital tray. The rest of the sides were untouched.

He gestured at an untouched container. “Try the cinnamon apples. They aren’t half bad.” He leaned back in the chair and glanced up at the television, memories starting to come back to him. “When my mom was really sick, I would spend days at a time here. After hours I lived off vending machine food and it got to the point where I would look forward to the awful biscuits and gravy in the morning.”

Isabell turned her slender black beak to look at Johnathen as he continued his story.

“They would serve country fried steak on Tuesdays, which was the best thing they have. Well, second best thing. The first being those cinnamon apples. My Mom didn’t like them at all, never did. So I always ate them for her.” Johnathen took a deep breath and looked over to Isabell. Her blue eyes stared back at him. "But, yeah, everything else is pretty terrible."

"You can have them if you want," she said and cocked her head curiously. "What happened to your mother?"

"Passed away. Liver disease," he replied and took the tray off of the table.

Isabell's eartufts and scarlet-colored feathers flattened against her body. "I'm sorry to hear that."

Johnathen picked up the metal fork and speared an apple slice. "It was a long time ago, so no worries." He put the apple slice in his mouth and chewed on the squishy slice. He shrugged. "Yeah, I guess they're not that great, but they do in a pinch. Much better when they're hot."

He swallowed and forked another piece. "Enough about my sad history. What about you? Do you keep contact with your adoptive family?"

"How did you know I had one?"

"Well, just going from what Thyra has told me, all the gryphons were adopted when the labs closed. Well, at least at the lab she was at. So, I just assumed it was the same for you too."

Isabell looked out the window, blue sky and sun shining through the large bay windows. "Yeah, it was the same way in Africa. But no, I don't keep in contact with them. I wasn't with them for long before I went out on my own. They were pretty poor and the only reason they took me in was the grants the government gave them for housing me." She snorted. "They treated me like a dog; giving me whatever scraps they had left over, ordering me around, and refusing to give me any education. So I said screw them and flew off one day. Haven't seen them since and probably never will."

Johnathen finished the apples and put the tray down, staring blankly at Isabell.

She turned her head to look back at him, confused by his staring. "What?"

"I'm sorry to hear that. All of it really." Johnathen replied.

Isabell snorted through her nares again. "It's alright. As you said, it was a while ago. Ten years, give or take."

"We humans say it's rude to ask a woman's age, but I hope you don't mind me asking. How old are you exactly?" Johnathen asked.

"I'll be thirteen in November."

"Didn't know you were so young. Thyra just turned nineteen." He said. He knew gryphons aged much quicker than humans but thirteen still seemed young to him for someone who had gone through so much.

"Young? I was fully matured at four. In relative terms, I'm almost as old as you are," Isabell finally gave a small smile to Johnathen, "And a hell of a lot better looking."

He smiled back. "You got a point. Sorry, you know how slow we age."

Isabell's eyes squinted in thought for a second. "You said Thyra just turned nineteen, right?" Johnathen confirmed with a nod. "Wouldn't that make her one of the first gryphons?"

Just then, Johnathen's pocket vibrated. He withdrew his smartphone and smiled as he looked down to see a text from Thyra. "Speak of the devil."

Isabell perked her eartufts with new life. "Thyra?"

Johnathen nodded. "She's asking how you are." His thumbs typed on the digital keyboard while he wrote out a message in reply.

"Tell her to bring me some damn cigarettes when she visits. I need one more than anything else right now."

He laughed and put his smartphone away. "Yeah, no way Thyra would do that. But I'll see what I can do next time."

Johnathen stood up and pulled the card out of the bouquet. He handed it over to her free foreclaw. "Let me know if there's anything else you need, but I've got some errands to run."

Isabell took the card in her foreclaw and set it down on her chest. "Gee, a card. Thanks, I needed another one of those. What's on it? A bird?" She said a little sarcastically.

He let out an embarrassed laugh and waved goodbye on his way out the door.

"H...hey John." Isabell called out at the last second, causing Johnathen to stop and turn to look at her. "Come back soon, please." Her expression had changed from her normal stuck up self to one of loneliness.

"I'll come bring you some dinner." He promised with a smile and turned to walk down the hall.

She sighed and looked down at the card. The laugh track and clapping on the television played once again as the episode ended. She took the envelope in her beak and tore it open with a talon. Isabell looked at the cartoon chickadee printed on the front of the card and grinned. “Jackass.”

Chapter 3 Grasping At Straws

Stained glass windows filtered the morning sunlight through the hall, decorating the spacious church with a multitude of colors during the opening hymn. When the music finished, the congregation sat down, the small band put down their instruments, and the choir took their seats behind the stage.

Everyone sat silent as Matthew approached the stand, a large Bible in hand. The white robe he wore was ironed to perfection, and free of any dirt or grime. He placed the Bible down and looked around at the crowd. He tried to summon affection for the group, but he had no love for these people. He never had. He enjoyed being their leader, but in truth he saw them as nothing but his personal servants. Not that he would never say something like this outright.

The news of yesterday morning's failure had put him in a sour disposition as well as leaving him exhausted. He had put in many hours dealing with the media, the police, and the followers who were put in jail. The money it had cost him in bail fees had put a thorn in his side, but it was a drop in the bucket compared to what he had amassed over the years.

Matthew forced a fake smile upon his wrinkled, clean-shaven face and raised his hands, greeting his people. He liked to keep up his appearance, even when he was distraught.

"A pleasure to see everyone on this beautiful morning. God has blessed us once again on this day." He spoke with authority and projected his voice, even though he also wore a microphone. "Today, I would like to speak to you about doubt. In the wake of yesterday's unfortunate events, there are some that have started to doubt our ways. I have heard the media speak slanders against our church, and question our motives. Blessed be those of you that are here now. You are the true faithful. You do not falter, no matter what lies are spread."

He looked around at the crowd for their reaction. Most of them were sitting silently and paying close attention. Although, he did spot a middle-aged woman he did not recognize. She seemed to be on edge. He noted her face and opened his bible.

"I would like to read you a passage out of the book of James today. James chapter one, verses five through eight." Matthew looked down and began to read aloud. "If any of you lacks wisdom, you should ask God, who gives generously to all without finding fault, and it will be given to you. But when you ask, you must believe and not doubt, because the one who doubts is like a wave of the sea, blown and tossed by the wind. That person should not expect to receive anything from the Lord. Such a person is double-minded and unstable in all they do."

Matthew finished his reading and closed his book once more. He took a step away from the stand and looked back at the congregation as he walked on the stage. "We all lack wisdom, in one form or another.

That is why we come together and ask the Lord. We must take everything he gives us without question and without doubt. In all ways, we must obey."

He began to smile once again, his wicked grin creeping across his face. "And I am here to interpret Gods meaning to you. Those of the general public that do not believe in what I've been teaching you are sinners. They have faltered from the light of God, and questioned his all knowing wisdom. I have tried to reach out to these people, but they are, as James said, 'like a wave of the sea.' They are unstable, and can be blown in any direction, whereas you all are like a rock because you do not question."

Matthew walked down a couple stairs to approach the first row of pews. He glanced around at the rows of people as he spoke, and recognized one elderly man, one that he has spoken to many times. That man was none other than George Armando, the same man Johnathen had struck many months ago at the restaurant.

"Brother George here has been with us since the day The Gathering opened its doors. He has been by our side through ups and downs, high and lows. In return, we have been with him every step of the way. Isn't that true, George?"

George nodded his head and smiled and Matthew continued. "It wasn't too long ago that George was confronted about his faith while having a peaceful dinner with his family. He was shamed in front of his wife, his kids, and others. He was attacked and beaten just like the saints of old! Why? Just for having faith. This abuse came from a man who has faltered far from

God's light, one that has committed the utmost sin of having relations with a man-made beast!"

George, aglow with the attention, nodded his head and the crowd murmured in agreement. Matthew turned and approached the stand once more, folding his hands behind his back.

"George knew that this man's decisions were wrong, as wrong as the decisions of any homosexual or interracial couple." Matthew put his hands on the stand and looked across the crowd once more. "These are the type of people who have heard God's word, and doubted it. They are lost, and without hope. They throw themselves into sin, even while knowing what they are doing is wrong. The result of their actions are violence, anger, and pain."

The middle-aged woman he spotted earlier began to stand in her pew, causing Matthew's bushy gray eyebrow to rise. He stood tall and watched her for a moment, worry starting to creep into his mind. She looked upset, but controlled, like she had something on her mind. "It seems we have a question from one of the congregation. May I ask your name, Miss?"

"My name is Sandra," the woman finally said. She clutched her hands into fists as she talked, clearly nervous but with something on her chest. "I… I have doubt myself. A lot of it to be exact," she began and cleared her throat.

Matthew tried to brush off the building tension with a calm smile. "Ah, Sandra my dear. There seems to be a lot on your mind. What troubles you?" He hoped that it was a typical easy question, one that he could answer with certainty to ease her mind. The emotionally distraught were always so easy, like lost sheep that need a shepherd to lead them.

"I have doubt that what you say is true." Everyone in the room turned to look at her, surprised by the woman's sudden confrontation in the middle of a sermon.

Matthew lost his composure, and for a moment he was visibly irritated at being called out in front of his congregation. He took a deep breath and put on his fake smile once again. "I only speak the truth. I interpret God's word to the best of my abilities for everyone to follow." Matthew said as calmly as he could, stepping down from the stage once again.

"I've seen you speak before, and the way you go about using God's word for your own personal gain is despicable," she said with anger in her voice now. Her hands were trembling as Matthew started to approach her.

"Sandra, you are confused."

"No! You say you teach God's word. You say that you have the best interest for your people, but what I saw last week made me realize what you are trying to do!" she shouted out.

Matthew's brow furrowed and he ground his teeth. It was becoming increasingly difficult for him to keep his composure. Everyone began to look at one another, muttering amongst themselves.

His eyes darted around as he realized that he was losing the attention of the people. "Dear, I don't know what you mean by any of these things. The events of last week were-."

"They were your handiwork! I know it. You wanted that fight to break out at the rally. The blond priest was preaching fascist beliefs! The people there weren't gathering for a peaceful sermon, they were there to riot!" she shouted once again, raising her voice above the crowd.

The ushers standing by the door stared directly at Matthew, waiting for a signal. Matthew opened his mouth to talk once again, but she began once more.

"Y…you just now lied to everyone, again! I researched what happened between George Armando and the gryphon's husband. George started the fight between them because he hated the sight of the gryphon in the restaurant! And that's exactly what the blond priest was preaching yesterday. Eradication, hate, and violence towards all minorities!"

Matthew pointed his finger at her and turned to the congregation. "What she spouts are lies and slander! She isn't a believer in God, she's a Satanist!"

The ushers began to walk down the isles quickly, causing the woman to panic. Everyone in the pew stood up to get out of the way as the ushers grabbed the shouting woman.

"I am not a Satanist!" she protested before the ushers grabbed her and dragged her out screaming. "You're a fascist! A Bigot!" she shouted one last time before being dragged out of the auditorium.

Matthew stood silent, shaking with anger at the sudden outrage. He closed his eyes and took another deep breath as the congregation continued to mutter amongst themselves. "My followers, I am terribly sorry for that outburst." Everyone fell silent once again and watched Matthew intently.

"That woman is clearly troubled and deranged. What she said was uncalled for, and certainty work of the devil's followers." He walked up to the stand and rubbed one hand over his bald head. "We will have to cut today's sermon short. I am afraid that I must deal with this personally."

He closed his bible and picked it up in his hands, holding it out for everyone to see. At once, everyone began to chant. "This is the word of God for the people of God! Praise be to God!"

Matthew bowed to everyone and put on a smile. "Now, go in peace."

The band began to play music as the congregation stood up and sang the last hymn of the meeting. One of the ushers walked up to Matthew quickly to accompany him out the door.

"Who the hell was that woman?" he asked the usher angrily as the door closed behind him.

"I'm not sure, Sir. We have put her in your office for the time being," the usher responded.

They walked down the hall towards Matthews's office. He handed the bible to the usher and threw open one of the heavy wooden doors. The woman sat, strapped to the chair with several large ushers standing around her.

"Had to end it early? What's the matter, couldn't take a little heat?" Sandra scoffed at Matthew as he walked in and took off his robe. Beneath it, he wore a white collared shirt and plain black tie with dark blue slacks. He did not bother responding to her, which only infuriated her more.

"Couldn't do it yourself, so you had to call your goons over to haul me away? What a big man you are!" She laughed hysterically and wrestled against the ropes that bound her to the chair. She stopped laughing and looked at him, increasingly becoming frustrated by his silence. "You know, tying me up is considered kidnapping by law! You better take me out of these bindings now or I'll press charges!"

Matthew hung his robe on a coat rack next to his immense oak desk and slowly turned around, glaring at Sandra. She grinned at his anger and spat on the wooden floor before him. The adrenaline had clearly turned this nervous lady into a wrecking ball.

"Who are you really?" Matthew asked in a low voice, now standing before her.

She chuckled a bit and looked up at him. "I told you before. I'm Sandra. You can say I'm something like a reporter."

She sat back in her chair, realizing that struggling was only making the bindings tighter. Matthew clearly was not entertained by her answer and sat down in the couch across from her. One of the men walked over and poured Matthew a glass of water from a pitcher.

"A reporter? For who? I know all the local reporters very well, and I haven't heard of you before." He took a sip of water while he waited for her response.

Sandra grinned a bit bigger and shook her head. "No, I don't work for anyone in this town. Those people you have in your pocket are despicable. I work with people that believe the general public deserves the right news."

Matthew chuckled at this and put down his glass. "Well, whoever is paying you to do this, I can easily double their price. You just have to give me a name."

"I'm not in this for the money." Sandra replied, staring back at him with contempt.

Matthew raised an eyebrow again. "Don't be stupid. Everyone has a price. Name yours and we can all leave this mess happy."

Sandra struggled at her bindings once more and clenched her fists. "Screw you and your dirty money!" she shouted. Both of the ushers standing next to her had to put their hands on her shoulders to keep the legs of the chair on the ground.

Matthew sighed loudly and sat back in the couch, rubbing his eyes in frustration. "Look, I've had a long week and I'm still trying to clean up the mess. I've met your kind before. You must be working with a group, or a faction."

"You got that right, bigot! I'm with The Gryphon Civil Rights Group and we aren't going to stop until you're brought down. We've got information and dirt on you. More than you know, and if you don't let me go now, kidnapping will be added to the charges!"

This got Matthew's attention. He had heard of this group. Online journalists and troublemakers. He sat up in the couch once again and stared dead into her eyes, gauging her bluff. "I doubt that. Besides last week's events, which got out of hand, I've been meticulous and careful in every step. I've hidden every track, and not left anything in the open. I doubt a couple of puny spineless nerds on the Internet could get anything on me."

Sandra shrugged her shoulders and leaned forward, meeting his gaze head on. "Believe what you want, old man, but we do have dirt. A lot of it. Do you think I would walk in here and try to stir up your followers without some kind of proof?"

Matthew rubbed his chin, considering what she was saying. He was detecting was a disconcerting amount of knowledge behind her words. She would have to be a fool to attempt such a demonstration without proof behind it. Either that or she was a fool and had a perfect poker face.

"I think it doesn't matter what you have and it won't matter if you suddenly went missing. I think your bluffing." Matthews's statement was met with a nervous laugh from Sandra.

"You think I wouldn't consider that you would have me killed? I had some of my colleagues take pictures of me walking in here this morning! That and the eyewitnesses of hundreds of people in your congregation that saw me dragged away would be evidence that this is the last place I was seen!"

Matthew only grinned at her words, which turned Sandra's confident expression into one of worry. "And…?" Matthew simply responded.

Sandra sat, dumbfounded by the one word answer. Did he not care what would happen if they made her disappear? Had she and her group drastically underestimated this man?

He chuckled. "So, you think that if your group starts putting out the information that one of you went missing, everything's suddenly going to change?"

"They will go to the police and..."

"I own the police around here! They won't do a damn thing," Matthew slowly stood up and walked over to her, sitting down on the coffee table in front of her. "As for the witnesses today, I'll just make something up like you had to be sent away for mental illness overseas and to have them pray for you."

Matthew looked up to the ceiling and raised his hands, impersonating himself in a sermon. "The poor girl was desperately ill! God sent her to us for healing, and we are blessed that she came! God works in mysterious ways, and now she is getting the help she deserves!"

"Does that sound good?" Matthew's impish smiled appeared again as he could see he was gaining the upper hand once more. Sandra's mouth was open, eyes tearing up with fear as she came to realize just how much they underestimated him. "No? Well I'll work on it a little more."

He reached out and wiped the tears off her cheek with a rough thumb, looking over her face. "There's no need for these, my dear. Don't worry, we won't kill you. We just want some answers and maybe, just maybe, we can convince you to join our side." Matthew looked her over again, waiting to see if she would respond, but Sandra simply stared at the floor, sniffling. Matthew stood back up and looked to the two burly ushers standing next to her. "Take her to purgatory. Make sure that she's taken care of and do get some answers out of her."

They both nodded and untied the bindings to let her free. Sandra suddenly got a second wind and started to fight back. She shouted and cried out, kicking her feet and squirming, desperately trying to get away from the two huge men. They dragged her out of the office and closed the door behind them, leaving Matthew and another usher to themselves.

The moment they were gone, Matthew grabbed the glass on the table and threw it across the room, shattering it on one of the many bookcases. The usher remained calm while Matthew snarled with anger and walked to his desk. He slapped one of the wooden crosses off his desk and sent it crashing to the floor before slamming his hand against the large bay window. Matthew stood there, staring outside in the afternoon sun, and recollected himself. “Usher, send for Daniel. Now.”

The usher perked up and went to the door, exiting it in a hurry. Matthew stood at the window, thoughts racing about what just progressed, and what he was going to have to do about Sandra. Despite the confidence he had shown her, having a kidnapped journalist to worry about was something he found incredibly disturbing.

Mumbling under his breath, he walked over to his leather desk chair and slumped down in it. He took a deep breath and rubbed his temples before reaching for one of the drawers. He pulled out a bottle of gin and a crystal glass, setting them down on the desk, then threw the top off to the side and poured a large amount into the glass. His hands were shaking so badly that some of it missed and spilled on the table.

The phone on his desk rang. He stared at it for a moment, and gulped down the gin before pushing the button labeled speakerphone. “Daniel, we need to escalate our plans. Come down here immediately!”

“Yes, Bishop Darnwall,” was all that Daniel said before hanging up the phone.

Chapter 4 Feeling The Burn

Thyra collapsed on the side of the field with a heavy sigh. Rachel and Antonio followed closely behind and grabbed their water bottles from off the bench.

"You did very well for your first skirmish, Thyra." Antonio pointed out, noting that Thyra's cream-colored feathery chest heaved with heavy breaths. He offered her a water bottle.

She took it from him gratefully and poured the cold liquid into her beak. Thyra had taken some hard tackles and made several catches. Her wings burned from flying air position in the second half of the skirmish, and she had struggled to keep them tucked in properly while on the ground. "Thanks, Antonio. I didn't know how I was going to do my first time."

Rachel, seemingly tireless, sat on top of the bench so that she was eye level with the other two gryphons. As usual, she talked nonstop. "Well, we all have a learning curve, but I think it comes naturally! Like I used to play with a couple locals in a small league in Chattanooga a couple years back. It was for fun mostly but the first couple times were a bit nerve-racking."

The corvid twins were talking amongst themselves as they approached the dugout, commenting on each other's performances and offering tips to one another. Rachel looked over Thyra's wing shoulder to glare at Nathanial as he approached, heading straight towards the small group.

"You got lucky today, Red-tail." Nathanial began, causing Thyra to turn to face him. She looked into his dark eyes and straightened herself up, hackle feathers beginning to rouse up in defense. He shrugged. "But, you weren't bad..."

Everyone blinked in astonishment, confused by the sudden compliment. Nathanial looked calm and collected compared to the way he had acted on the field just minutes before. The usual hothead had actually said something to her without yelling or screeching. He noticed their surprise.

"It better have been more than luck, though. I don't want you dragging us down." He snorted through his nares and brought up a forefoot to look at his talons casually. "I'm here to win, and this year, I'm going to bring the team to the first league. You better help out."

"You just wait, fish breath!" Rachel yelled out from behind Thyra. "She'll be kicking your scrawny butt in no time!"

Instantly, Nathanial's calm expression turned to anger as his bushy blond tail flicked with agitation. Rachel's voice was like a spark that ignited the fiery temper inside him.

"Who are you calling fish breath?! I should come over there and tie your beak shut, little runt!" Nathanial battered back at her.

Antonio rubbed his eye ridges with his fore talons and groaned. Everything had been going well for once. He had known it would not last for long, but there had been peace between them for just a second! Thyra stepped out of the way as Rachel jumped down off the bench and stomped over to Nathanial, still spouting insults back at him.

"This is going to be a long season…" Antonio said under his breath as Thyra sat next to him, watching the two angry feather dusters squawk at one another.

Coach Victor walked up behind Antonio and Thyra, sitting down with them momentarily to watch the other two go at it. "They both have a lot of spunk. I'll give them that." It was hard to hear his low voice over the screeching of the two gryphons even though his head sat right above Thyra's and Antonio's. "I'll let them hash it out for now. Just make sure they don't get violent. I don't want to deal with medical."

"Yes sir," Antonio responded and Victor turned around and headed off the field.

Thyra watched the great gryphon stop to say something to Jason, the golden eagle. They talked for a moment in private and she could see Victor point at her and the others with one of his gigantic gray fore claws. Jason seemed to laugh and nod his golden brown head before turning to approach the group.

"Hey, love birds!" Jason shouted at the arguing gryphons. Both Rachel and Nathanial stopped to glare over at the approaching golden eagle gryphon as he spoke. "Lunch time." Jason sat before the two gryphons, his chest puffed up to show authority. "Be in the training room in an hour."

Nathanial ground his beak. "Whatever! This ain't over, pipsqueak!" he said to Rachel, trying to get the last word in. His tail feathers flicked as he stomped away, leaving Rachel to steam and curse under her breath.

"You two make a great couple, you know," Jason told the tiny kestrel with a cheeky beak grin.

Rachel's nares turned a bright shade of red. "Whatever! As if I would ever date that dirty caracara!" She glanced over at Thyra and Antonio, who could not help but be amused at Jason's comment.

"Sorry, but you two do behave like pre-adults," Antonio said, which only added to Rachel's embarrassment.

Her gray feathers flattened against her body, making her seem even smaller than before. "Shut up. Let's go get something to eat."

Antonio nodded and turned to walk off the field with Rachel, still chuckling to himself.

"You all go ahead. I have to go find Addy. She brought me lunch today," Thyra said.

Antonio stopped and turned his head to look back over his burnt orange wing shoulders. "Addy is in the weight room, most likely. Do you know where that is?"

"I'll show her. You all go ahead," Jason said.

He stepped up next to Thyra and looked down at her with a smile on his sharp beak. He stood a full head taller than her, and had a more muscular build. He gestured for her to follow, then turned and headed the opposite direction. She suddenly felt awkward leaving with a gryphon she had barely even talked to, but walked with him anyway.

"So, Thyra! I understand this is your first gryphball team. How are you liking it so far?" Jason began, trying to break the ice. He spoke like a narrator, pronouncing each word in a deep and excited tone without any sort of accent. It took a moment for her to find her voice.

"It's good so far." She had to trot to keep up with him as his strides were far larger than her own. "Seems like everyone is nice."

Jason laughed in response and shrugged his shoulders. "It depends on what your definition of nice is, but they grow on you."

He led Thyra through one of the exits of the field and into a long brightly lit hallway. Jason's wing shoulders almost touched each wall as he turned down one of the corridors.

"It's a new experience for me. I haven't been around gryphons very much. There aren't many in my hometown," Thyra responded, which piqued Jason's curiosity.

"Well, this must be a huge culture shock to you. Where do you come from?" he asked, turning a corner to head up a set of stairs.

"Macon, Georgia. It's a little town an hour outside of Atlanta." Thyra stopped at the top of the stairs as Jason opened up one of the wide double doors into the weight room.

He motioned for her to step in first. "Can't say I've heard of it before."

The room was as big as a gymnasium. There was plenty of space to hold all the exercise equipment and large bay windows to let in the natural light. Modified treadmills, widened for gryphon use, lined the glass windows on the left side of the room overlooking the stadium field. Two gryphons were busy running on the treadmills. The loud thundering of their foreclaws and hindpaws trampling in a rhythmic motion echoed in the vast room.

Thyra took in the various machines and weight areas before spotting Aadhya on the far side of the room.

"Have you not been in a gym before?" Jason asked, noticing Thyra's lost look.

"No. Not once. I mean, Johnathen was on a health kick once and went to a local gym for a couple months, but I never went with him. He took some pictures of it to show me, but it was half the size of this!"

She watched as another gryphon leapt into the air from a platform and flew vertically towards the ceiling to ring a bell. It seemed he was wearing a harness of sorts with large weights tied to his chest.

Jason took a step past her and led her between all the weight machines. "I'll show you the ropes after lunch. Today is going to be cardio and wing day."

Aadhya spotted the two of them coming from the entrance. She had her massive wings outstretched and was pulling down straps attached to her outermost wing tips. She grunted and counted off another rep, pulling pulleys with weights attached to them up into the air. Thyra and Jason arrived as Aadhya held the weights in the air, straining to keep them up, then dropped them with a loud clang.

"Time for lunch, I presume?" Aadhya's white feathers seemed disheveled and she spoke with heavy labored breaths. She flicked her wings a bit to let the straps fall off and folded them in.

"Yeah. Victor said we have an hour." Thyra said and watched as Aadhya grabbed a water bottle before emptying it into her beak.

"Speaking of which, I better get going." Jason cut in and nodded to them both. "See you back here in an hour, and eat light, Thyra! Don't want you emptying your gizzard on your first day of weight training." The golden eagle turned and made his exit through the double doors.

Aadhya took another swig of water and put the bottle down with a loud sigh, finally catching her breath once more.

"So, what did you bring us to eat?" Thyra asked curiously.

Aadhya stood and began to walk towards the exit with Thyra following closely behind. "I have prepared a light meal, as I suspected today would be full of rigorous activity." The bearded vulture opened the door and proceeded down the stairs and turned to head down the corridor at the bottom. "To be exact, Salmon, sweet potatoes, and some fruit."

Thyra's stomach began to rumble at the thought of fresh fish. "You really went all out, didn't you?" she exclaimed.

The hallway was not wide enough for the two of them to walk side by side, and Aadhya had to turn her head to speak. “Apologies, what do you mean by ‘all out’?”

Thyra had to think for a moment for the response. “It’s, well, it sort of means that you didn’t take the easy way. Like you put a lot of effort into it.”

A big grin appeared on Aadhya’s long black beak. She opened the door to the empty locker room and walked over to a refrigerator sitting in the corner. “I like this. ‘All out’. When it comes to health, there is no other option than going all out.”

Aadhya grabbed opened up the refrigerator and grabbed a cooler bag by the handles to pull it out. “Where would you like to eat? I typically enjoy the west end of the stadiums roof. Allows for a good sunning after a meal,” the great bearded vulture said and shut the door behind her.

“That sounds good. I didn’t know if there was a cafeteria or something like that.”

“There is, but it is much too loud for my tastes. I prefer to eat my meal in peace. I would assume it is due to my ancestors living high in the Himalaya mountains. A little conversation with one or two others is nice, but not an entire room of gryphons.”

Aadhya grabbed the cooler bag handle with her beak to head out. They went back down the hallway and out into the stadium field once more before taking off into the air. It was a long climb to the top, but even after exercising, it seemed the ascension did not bother her in the slightest.

Most of the outer rim of the stadiums roof was slopped, but there was one spot where it leveled out flat. Thyra and Aadhya set down easy and overlooked the stadium bellow, autumn sun high in the sky.

"You're right. This is really nice." Thyra pointed out while Aadhya opened up the cooler, pulling out several plastic Tupperware containers.

"We are avian, after all. We naturally prefer high and isolated areas. Well, at least my own kind does." Aadhya said and placed a container in front of Thyra.

She wrestled with the lid for a moment, gripping the base with her foretalons and removing the lid. The fishy smell of fresh, uncooked salmon wafted into Thyra's nares, even in the steady breeze.

Aadhya already had a large chunk of salmon in her claws and was chomping away at the pink meat. Thyra did the same, letting the cold slimy fish slide down her throat piece by piece. She preferred the taste of cooked salmon, but thought it rude to complain since Aadhya had been kind enough to prepare lunch for the both of them. The sweet potatoes, however, were cooked with a nice seasoning and almost tasted like a dessert to her. She stabbed each slice with a talon and enjoyed the flavor of them much more than the uncooked salmon.

Aadhya finished her container and dug around inside the cooler bag once more to bring out a container of assorted fresh fruits. She offered the container after stabbing a couple slices. "Would you like some? I prefer the papaya and mango slices myself."

Thyra thanked her once more and skewered the soft yellow fruit with a talon. The sweet juices were refreshing on her tongue, and soon enough the container was empty. Aadhya lay down on her belly once she was finished and basked in the afternoon sun. She ruffled her white and pepper colored plumage, sending feather plumes up into the air before beginning to run her beak through her chest.

Thyra sat next to her, overlooking the stadium and listening to the gentle breeze blow past. Everything was calm and quiet for the moment, aside from the occasional car passing by. Aadhya stretched her massive peppered wings out and began to preen at the outermost primaries.

Thyra's mind wandered off as she overlooked the stadium below. There was so much that had happened the past week. She worried about Isabell.

Images of the small black gryphoness lying in the hospital bed with her wing wrapped up in a cast came to mind. The defeat in her blue eyes as she realized she might never fly again pulled at Thyra's heartstrings. Her red tail feathers flicked with agitation and her feline tail swished with a mind of its own. Aadhya folded in her wings now and let out a gentle sigh through her nares, pulling Thyra back from her thoughts.

"You seem distraught," Aadhya said softly, breaking the long silence between them.

Thyra looked down at her talons before responding. "I'm just thinking of Isabell."

"Your friend in the hospital? I pray for her full recovery." Aadhya said and sat back up now on her haunches. "A terrible thing."

"Yeah. I'm just pissed at the humans that did it to her." Thyra's voice grew low and graveled, becoming increasingly aggravated. “I want to find them and break their limbs for what they did.”

“I cannot say I agree with you. Violence is not the answer. Perhaps there are other ways in which to inflict justice.” Aadhya looked over to Thyra with her bright red and yellow eyes, seeking to mentor the gryphoness.

Thyra stared back, finding kindness and wisdom in the eyes, and realized that she was right. “I know it’s not right to hurt them, but it’s what I feel.” She looked away, watching a blue jay pass by.

Aadhya’s voice was calm and collected as ever. “Such feelings are natural. Just remember, every action does have a consequence. An eye for an eye leaves the whole world blind.”

Thyra closed her eyes and took a deep breath through her nares, knowing what Aadhya said was right. “I know.”

The corvid gryphons walked onto the field, chatting to one another. The sound of talking gryphons made Thyra’s eartufts perk up and eyes to open.

Aadhya stood and stretched out her hind legs. “Looks like our lunch break is over,” she said before gathering up the empty Tupperware containers.

“Time flies sometimes, doesn’t it?” Thyra replied as Aadhya leapt off the edge.

Thyra dove off with her, spreading her wings to glide down in a lazy spiral down to the field bellow. Both the corvid gryphons watched them approach as the gryphonesses landed near.

“Seems like a good place to have lunch!” Brandon, the yellow-eyed corvid said.

"May have to join you next time." Braden added in. Aadhya placed her cooler bag down on the ground and smiled warmly.

"You are most welcome, but the space is limited on the flat area on top," Aadhya pointed out, hoping they would take the hint that more company would be troublesome.

Both the corvids shrugged their wing shoulders together. "Maybe not, then! Sitting on a slopped area doesn't sound very comfortable." Brandon said.

"Yeah, and flying up there after all this exercise doesn't sound like fun, but thanks anyways!" Braden added in. Both of them wandered off to the benches while talking with one another leaving a bewildered Thyra and Aadhya behind.

More gryphons started to spill out of the entrance to the field, followed by Victor who started to corral the group towards the dugout. Antonio and Rachel soon followed and approached them.

"I didn't see you all in the lunchroom. Where were you guys?" Rachel asked.

"I have another place where I prefer to enjoy my meal." Aadhya responded.

"Well, where was my invite? I much rather hang out with you all than the rest of these guys! At least I had Antonio to talk to, or I would have eaten by myself."

Thyra chuckled and looked down at the small kestrel. "I'll text you next time."

Victor walked out in front of everybody, large gray crest feathers roused up to display authority. Everyone stopped talking at once and gave the coach their full attention. "Alright everybody. I hope you had a good lunch and rested a bit. For the rest of the day, everyone that was in the weight room will be out in the field, and vice versa." The team all nodded. "I will stay here in the field to watch this groups performance, and I trust those in the weight room will continue their scheduled exercises diligently." He looked over everyone with his dark eyes. "Clear?"

"Yes sir!" Everyone shouted at once.

"Good. Then get to it."

The mass of gryphons started to move around, heading to their appropriate places. Thyra stopped and turned to Aadhya. "Thanks for lunch again, Addy. We'll see you later."

The bearded vulture smiled warmly and nodded. "Not a problem. I am glad you enjoyed it."

"Red tail!" Victor's voice boomed, causing Thyra to quickly turn around as the massive harpy eagle gryphon approached her. "I see you have met Jason. He will be your personal trainer until you get into a regular training regimen, Listen to everything he tells you carefully, and do as instructed so you don't injure yourself. He has been weight training for many years, and he's very knowledgeable. It won't take you long to get into a groove if you do as your told. Clear?"

"Crystal, Sir," Thyra responded quickly and looked over to Jason who stood just as tall as Victor did.

"Good. He'll mold you quickly." Victor turned to look at Jason with a slight grin. "And don't go easy on her just because she's a gryphoness."

Jason laughed and looked deviously over to Thyra whose eartufts were pinned back. "I didn't plan on it, Sir."

Satisfied, Victor turned and yelled at the other gryphons, who quickly followed him to the center of the field.

"By the end of the day, you might hate me a little bit," Jason said and began to walk towards the exit of the field with Thyra close in tow. "As they say, no pain, no gain!"

She gulped nervously. "It can't be that bad, can it?"

Jason entered in the corridor once more and up the stairs. "Lets just say, you might be begging me to remove your wings by the end of the day."

Thyra froze in place at the front of the door. Jason opened it wide and motioned for her to enter the gym. "After you, madam."

Chapter 5 Discovery

Johnathen shut the car door behind him and locked it with his key fob. The bustling of cars in the busy city of Atlanta echoed off the towering buildings all around him. Even in the autumn, the city air was damp and hot.

He looked down at his phone to confirm his location and began to walk through the crowded streets. The radio station he was looking for was not a long walk away from the parking garage he had found. Soon enough, he was standing at the building that matched the address in his phone's map.

The sliding glass doors opened up before him and he entered the spacious lobby. Johnathen approached the help desk in the corner of the room. A bald man wearing a black vest with a logo of a security company sat behind it. As Johnathen stood before him, the man turned his head away from the computer monitor and looked up.

"Hello, Sir. May I help you with something?" he asked blandly.

"Yes, I'm looking for talk radio ninety-six. Google Maps said it was in this building," Johnathen said.

The man simply stood and pointed down a hallway. "It's on the fourth floor. Elevators are down there and to the left."

Johnathen thanked him and proceeded down the hallway to the elevators. Once on the fourth floor, he stepped out of the elevator and approached another front desk. The young blond lady who sat behind it smiled as he approached.

"Can I help you sir?" she asked politely.

Johnathen nodded. "Yes. I heard on the talk show this morning that you all were looking for information regarding The Gatherings intentions." Johnathen reached into his jacket pocket and pulled out a thumb drive. The woman arched an eyebrow at the USB stick. "This contains footage caught by the gryphoness who was severely beaten at that Gathering rally in Macon. She is in the hospital right now. The footage is shocking. It has everything you need in order to show the public what their true intentions are. Perhaps you could post the footage on your website."

Johnathen expected her to go and get one of the station managers and was surprised when the woman held out her hand, eagerly. "This is exactly what we're looking for! Here, I'll make sure it gets to the proper people and we will review it."

He gratefully handed it over and grinned. "I hope word gets out and you all can do some damage to them. I'm just glad that others are starting to realize that The Gathering isn't just another church. They're a cult."

She looked at the thumb drive and placed it on the desk. "Absolutely! I heard about it all this morning. They sound like terrible people. Mr. Ferguson will love to see this. We appreciate you coming in. What was your name again?" she asked, picking up a pen.

"Johnathen Arkwright," he responded, and she quickly scribbled his name down on a note pad. "Uh, that's spelled J-o-h-n-a-t-h-e-n. My parents were lousy spellers."

She smiled and fixed it. "Thank you again, Johnathen. I will hand this over to Mr. Ferguson He's in a meeting right now, but I'll get this to him and make sure he goes you a call when he's had a chance to go over it."

"Do you know how long it will take?"

"Well, he is busy. I can't guarantee he'll be able to get to it this afternoon. Maybe expect a call in a day or so," she assured him.

Satisfied, Johnathen thanked her and turned to the elevators to leave. Once he was out of the room, the woman frowned and picked up the phone to dial a number.

"Daniel… Yes. Someone came in just now and handed me a USB, claiming he's got footage from the rally that proves that the church is a cult … Mm-hm. Says it's some video taken by a gryphoness… No, he didn't say her name, but his name was Johnathen Arkwright … He just left… Ok, I'll get rid of it." She hung up the phone and picked up the thumb drive once again before breaking it in half and discarding it in the trash.

Johnathen left the building and walked back out on the street, pulling up the next address on his phone. This was just the beginning of a long day ahead of him. Even if this station didn't decide to use what he had given them, USB drives were cheap enough to pass out. He had multiple copies of the footage on different computers just to be safe.

Daniel hung up his cell phone and sighed. He leaned back in the large leather chair sitting across from Bishop Matthew's desk and rubbed his temple with a forefinger.

"What a mess," the blond man said, scrolling through the list of contacts on his smart phone.

The sunlight poured through the floor-to-ceiling glass window behind the desk showing the unkempt mess around the spacious office. The air was very still in the room and dust could be seen floating around in the rays of sunlight.

"Who was that?" Mathew asked, his attention still at the computer screen in front of him.

"The receptionist at Atlanta Talk Ninety-Six. Seemed our gamble of luring in people with information payed off," Daniel began.

Matthew's wrinkled eyes scrunched up more as he concentrated on the computer screen. "Go on," he said, pecking slowly at the keyboard.

"Seems Johnathen Arkwright has some video footage taken from the rally. He tried to hand it over to them just now." Daniel stopped scrolling on his phone as the slow sounds of keyboard clicks stopped.

Matthew looked up at him, cold eyes staring straight at Daniel. "Did he now? So, he just handed over this video?"

"Yeah. But it was only a thumb drive. He wouldn't hand over something valuable like that and just leave if he didn't have more copies." Daniel began to type a message on his phone.

Matthew's desk chair screeched when he leaned back into it. "So, you think he has more." The old man placed his fingertips together and began to think.

"I'm sure of it." Daniel's phone dinged as he sent a message. "I already have Cassie working on it. She's going to do a sweep of Johnathen's house and take his computer. Also, Jack is currently in Atlanta and I told him to trail Johnathen just in case he tries to go somewhere else. "

"Looks like you have everything handled," Matthew responded with a raised eyebrow, clearly impressed.

"You hired me for a reason. I plan on doing my job." Daniel stood and brushed his blond hair back with his fingertips.

Matthew went back to pecking at the keyboard. As Daniel turned to leave, Matthew cut in once again. "One more thing. Tell Cassie to trash his house. I want Johnathen to know how vulnerable he is."

Daniel opened up one of the oak doors and turned to Matthew in the doorway. "Do you want her to make it look like a random robbery, or leave a signature?"

Matthew peeked over his computer screen and replied, "Make sure he knows it was us."

Daniel nodded in response and exited the room, shutting the door behind him. His phone chimed again, alerting him of a message. He took the phone out of his pocket and looked at the screen. It was a message from Jack.

I have eyes on Johnathen right now. He just got in his Volvo and is heading towards the interstate. I will keep you updated.

Daniels leather dress shoes clicked with every step against the hardwood and echoed in the hallway as he walked. His phone buzzed again, this time with a message from Cassie.

ETA five minutes. How much time do I have?

He quickly sent a reply. *Jack says he's still in Atlanta, so you have about an hour. Also, Matthew wants you to ransack the house. Leave one of the bibles on the countertop too. He wants them to know that we were behind it.*

Satisfied, Daniel locked his phone and exited the hallway out of a side door into the parking lot. The bright sunlight caused him to squint his eyes. He pulled his black sunglasses out of his jacket pocket and put them on. He reached for his keys and pressed the keyfob, unlocking the doors to his mid-two-thousands Lexus. He opened the creaking door and sat inside before starting the car. The tan leather and exterior paint had sun damage from years of exposure, but the engine ran soundly. Daniel sat back in his seat, relaxing for a moment before his phone began to ring.

"Hey, hun… Yeah, I'm actually done with work for the day… It's going well! This guy is sort of a jerk but not as bad as the last client… You want me to pick up Kate from school? Ok then, I'll pick up groceries. Fish sound good?...Ok love you too."

He hung up the phone and put the car in drive. The vehicle clunked from the sloppy transmission but he was used to that and knew how to baby the car. Soon it coasted off down the road.

Daniel took the highway past the city and drove into the suburbs. He stopped at the local grocery to pick up fresh fish and other food necessities before proceeding to his house. He waived to the neighbors outside watering their garden. As he gathered his bags, he glanced at the browning grass and flower beds filled with weeds, noting that he should clean that up soon as well.

The quaint house had vinyl siding with the paint peeling in places. He opened the single car garage with a remote and walked around the various furniture and boxes piled within it to walk through the kitchen door. He was immediately hit by the stuffy heat inside. He really needed to get the air conditioning fixed.

He placed the bags on the kitchen counter and reached over to the sink to start filling it with water. He turned around and looked around the house for a moment. The carpeted floors were littered with brightly colored toys and dolls. There were papers and letters piled up on the small glass dining table tucked away in the corner of the living room.

Their little television sat crooked on its stand on an entertainment set in the opposite corner of the room. The channel hadn't been changed since he had left the morning and the local news was on. The weatherman was pointing at the screen and predicting colder weather the next few days. That was a relief to hear. He was tired of sleeping on top of the blankets at night.

Daniel turned off the water and took out a cedar oak plank from the drawer before placing it inside the sink to soak. He walked over to open the door to the back porch and left it open as he went outside, hoping some fresh air in the house would cool it down.

The grass was getting high in the backyard and was showing through the paver stones. He uncovered his stainless-steel grill and opened the lid. He turned the knob on the front, which clicked rapidly and ignited the fuel. After cleaning the plates with a grill brush, he stepped back inside and took off his blazer jacket, tossing it on the backside of the couch along with other articles of clothing.

Daniel withdrew a cutting board and a chef's knife from a drawer, and reached into one of the bags to retrieve a small sack of sweet potatoes. He chopped them effortlessly with practiced precision, dicing them into small cubes.

A cool breeze brought fresh autumn air into the kitchen while he placed the potatoes on foil and added brown sugar to the mix. With that done, he opened up another grocery bag and began to put away the contents in the older-styled white refrigerator. The sound of a car door slamming shut took his attention away for a moment, but he continued on.

The garage door began to rumble as it shut before the kitchen door flew open. Daniel smiled as Kate ran in. He quickly turned to pick up his little girl. "Hey pumpkin! How was school today? Did you have fun?" he asked,, and kissed her on the forehead.

"Yeah! We painted dinosaurs!" Kate responded and looked back to her mother.

"And how about you, Kathy? How was work?" Daniel asked as his wife shut the door behind her, carrying a little backpack decorated with cartoon characters and her leather purse.

She was dressed in black leggings and a woman's blazer with a T-shirt underneath. Her short dark brown hair was tied back behind her head with a hair tie. "Busy! But that's good for tips."

Daniel leaned forward to kiss her on the cheek as she rushed by to drop her things on the couch with a loud sigh. "Feels cooler in here. Did the AC repairman come today?" she asked curiously, looking with a furrowed brow at the dirty living room.

"No. Said they are booked till Friday," he responded before putting Kate back down on the ground. She ran to the opposite side of the room, and sat beside her dollhouse to start playing with it.

"Well, it's good the weather is getting cooler. These past few days have been miserable." Kathy took off her blazer and threw it on the couch next to Daniel's.

He grabbed the now soaked wooden plank from the sink and placed it on the counter. "I should've been an AC tech. Seems those guys make a lot of money during the season and there isn't enough of them for the demand," he said and began unwrapping the pink salmon from the wax paper.

"Don't you have to go to school for that sort of thing? Too bad you don't have the time and we don't have the money for that." Kathy walked over to the fridge and pulled out a bottle of wine.

"It's just six months, I think. Maybe a bit more. I'll look into it," Daniel said and placed the pieces fish down on the plank before throwing away the wax paper.

"You can do whatever you want, but I thought you liked being an advisor." She twisted off the cap to the cheap wine and poured it into a wine glass.

Daniel shrugged his shoulders. "It's got its ups and downs. Like this current client is an asshole. He's some sort of religious zealot that's in over his head and has his hands in too many places. I had to call in Cassie and Jack today."

Kathy took a big swig of the red wine and placed the bottle down on the counter. "So you're going to have to pay them out of your fees?" she asked as Daniel brought out some spices to sprinkle over the fish.

"Yeah. The client just wants too much from me. I can't handle it all myself." Daniel picked up the plank of fish and the potatoes before walking outside to the patio with Kathy following behind.

"But they're still paying you enough to cover everything this month and the AC bill, right?" Kathy asked with a little worry in her voice.

Daniel opened the lid to his grill and placed the fish inside. "Oh yeah, no worries about that. I just meant I wanted to put a little in savings and maybe remodel the kitchen," Daniel replied and closed the lid.

"Well, I can pick up an extra shift or two at the restaurant. We just had another waitress quit yesterday," Kathy said.

"You work enough as it is. Plus, we need you available. I never know when I can leave work and Kate needs to be picked up," Daniel said, reaching for the wine glass.

Kathy handed it over and let Daniel down the rest of the glass. Daniel's face soured slightly and he smacked his lips. The dry and flavorless taste of cheap wine was not ideal, but it was what they had.

"Well I was just being nice. I really don't want to be there longer than I have to." She smiled and walked back inside. "I'm refilling this glass. You want one too, hun?" Kathy called out from the kitchen.

"Naturally!" Daniel answered back and adjusted the heat on the grill. She came back out with two glasses this time and handed one to Daniel. They toasted to each other and sipped.

He grimaced again. "Maybe you could put on the charm a bit more and get some better tips so we can buy some better wine." He was quickly met with a playful slap on his shoulder.

"You're lucky I'm working and not just a housewife like the Stevenson's next door," Kathy said and grinned, sitting in one of the camper chairs next to the grill.

He chuckled and sat down next to her. "So, is Kate enjoying her new school? She seems happy." Daniel glanced inside, watching the little girl playing with her dolls.

"So far so good. The teacher is really nice. She says Kate has been getting along with all the other children too," Kathy responded, sipping from her wine glass again.

"That's good. I always moved around as a kid, so I know it's hard to adjust." Daniel put down his wine glass and stood up to open the grill, checking on the fish. “But I think it was for the better. City life in Atlanta didn’t really fit us, I think.”

“I like it here. It’s quiet.” Kathy agreed. “I just hope your client has work for you for a long time.”

Daniel shrugged. “We’ll see. But even after this dries up, there’s other places around here that probably need me.” He walked to the door and called inside. “You hungry Kate?”

The little blond girl looked up and smiled. “Yeah! What are we eating?”

“Fish,” Daniel said and grinned as Kate frowned.

“I don’t like fish though!”

Daniel laughed. “I think you will like this one.”

Kate stood up and folded her arms with a huff, throwing a little fit. “I wont!”

“If you at least try it, I’ll get you an ice cream. Sound good?” Daniel responded.

Kate’s fake frown turned upside down. “Ok, Daddy!”

Kate ran off into the bathroom to go wash up as Daniel walked inside and grabbed a couple paper plates. “I hope she likes it because the only other thing we have is mac and cheese. She’s eaten that two times this week already,” he said as he walked back outside.

“She’s a kid. What do you expect?” Kathy responded and watched as Daniel opened the lid back up.

“I know. I’m just trying to get her to eat different things, and something more nutritious than processed cheese.” Daniel sighed and flipped the salmon over. The aroma of spices and the sizzling of the fish wafted into the air, creating a pleasant smell over the grill. “Go ahead and get the table set, Kathy. These will be ready in just a couple minutes.”

Chapter 6 Story Telling

Thyra and the band sat silently next to the other gryphons on the field's sideline, intently watching Victor walk before them. The massive gryphon's cold black eyes looked over the multitude of colors before him as he sat down, readjusting his wings.

"A great effort from everybody today, as usual. I applaud you, but there is much progress to be made before tomorrow's game." The cool wind rushed through his tall gray crest feathers as the sun began to set over the stadium.

"Thankfully, the first game is against the Jacksonville Parrots and they have not played well the past couple of years," he continued and the gryphons began to relax a bit, letting their posture slump slightly. "Although, do not take this lightly. Just because the team did not perform great in the past, does not mean they have not improved." Victor warned.

The coach looked over to Thyra and her band of friends. "Again, I am confident with these new additions that we will defeat everyone in our way. Others may underestimate us, and it will be their downfall."

The great harpy's gray beak almost curved into a grin, and everyone began to trill in acknowledgement. Victors voice began to grow louder, like a rolling thunder approaching as he stood now to address his team. "We will not make it easy for them! We will train harder and better than any other team in the second league. And I will mold each one of you into superior athletes!" The whole team chirped in agreement, becoming riled up as their moods lifted. "Go. Rest now and prepare for tomorrow. You have a long day ahead of you. I want fresh claws and wings here at eight am. Clear?"

"Yes sir!" Came the voices of over a dozen gryphons.

Victor nodded to them all and responded. "Then go." At once, every bird stood and started to collect their things. Small groups of gryphons acquainted with one another began to gather, talking about what they would be doing after practice.

Thyra looked to the group of gryphons chatting amongst themselves and spotted a pair of gryphonesses talking to each other; an osprey and a peregrine. She had not seen them before, and watched as they chuckled and walked wing to wing.

Thyra turned to Antonio, Rachel, and Aadhya. "Who are those gryphonesses? I haven't seen them before." Thyra asked curiously. Antonio turned to look at the couple and saw he recognized them immediately.

"That is Priscilla and Viola. They are new comers from the third league. They have not practiced with us yet because they were finishing their league first. Their performance has been admirable, and Victor hand-picked them to be on the team," Antonio explained. Together, they began to walk towards the locker room along the field's edge, following the mass of gryphons.

"Do you all want to grab dinner together? I'm starving." Thyra asked. "But, somewhere nearby. My wing shoulders feel like a woodpecker has destroyed them."

Aadhya hung her head low to speak to them, black beard blowing in the gentle breeze. "There is one particular restaurant I favor in town. They have nice accommodations for gryphons, especially ones of my size."

Rachel darted in front of the three gryphons that towered over her and walked backwards as she spoke. "What kind of food is it? I mean I like all kinds of food to be honest but sometimes I don't have the right appetite for it. Like, there's times I can down a whole fried chicken and then there's other times I can't. Something like pasta sounds pretty good right now actually!"

"It is an Asian themed restaurant. Whole grain rice, sautéed vegetables, and meat selections," Aadhya responded as they walked into the corridor that lead into the locker room.

"I could go for some of that right now, actually!" Thyra responded gratefully. The thought of a nice hearty meal right now made her crop rumble.

"I second that," Antonio said, trailing slightly behind the rest of the band.

"Then it is settled. We can walk if Thyra is too tired to fly. It should not be but twenty minutes," Aadhya said and opened the door that led into the busy locker room. Everybody was chirping amongst each other and gathering their things. There were sounds of singing and water splattering across the floor in the shower as a couple gryphons washed themselves from the day's activities.

The band split up to their lockers and Thyra opened up her own to retrieve her satchel. She threw it over her neck and reached inside to retrieve her cellphone. It chimed to life as she turned it on, and immediately dinged with a new message from Johnathen.

Isabell is doing well. Says to tell you hi and says you need to bring her cigarettes, lol. Also I ran into Jimmie at the stand. Says he misses you and to see him soon. Hope you have a good night tonight and text me back when you get the chance. Love you.

She smiled and sat down on her haunches, opening the phone to the full keyboard and started to click away with her talons.

That's good to hear! I will visit her this weekend and Jimmie too. Today was good except it feels like my wings and arms have been torn off. I'm exhausted but it was a fun day overall. We're all going out to eat tonight. I'll let you know when I'm back in Addy's apartment.

By the time Thyra had finished the message, most of the gryphons had left the locker room. Aadhya and Rachel were carrying on a conversation, now wearing casual T-shirts and pants instead of their uniform. Antonio walked over, also wearing his casual clothes as well. He wore a brightly colored button up and a jean like material for his pants.

"You haven't changed, Thyra. Do you plan on wearing your uniform to the restaurant?"

Thyra looked up from her cellphone and flattened her ears in embarrassment. "I was such in a rush this morning that I forgot to pack anything else," she admitted. She put her cellphone away in its pouch before shutting the locker.

Antonio seemed lost in thought for a minute. He looked her over. "You seem to be relatively the same size as I, perhaps I could loan you some clothing?"

Thyra chirped in amusement at the thought of it. She had never worn another gryphon's clothing, and especially a male's before, but it was better than wearing her dirty uniform out in public.

She smiled at the kind gesture and seemed to grow a bit red in the nares. "Ah, sure thing. I mean it would be better than what I'm wearing."

Antonio noticed her blush and ruffled his feathers in response. "It is, as you say, no big deal." He turned to head to his locker and shuffled around for a moment before retrieving another brightly colored button down and pants. "I hope these will work," Antonio said and handed them over to Thyra.

She gratefully took them and observed the various patterns and designs printed on the shirt. "Yeah they seem about right. I'll be right back." Thyra threw the clothes over her shoulder and ventured into the shower room.

She placed the cloths on a bench and sat on her haunches to undo the zipper at her front. The spandex like uniform conformed to her body tightly, and was difficult to peal off. She rummaged for a minute, working it off in little steps and pulling her wings through the slots. She pulled the last bit off where it connected to her lower half, pulling her thin feline tail through the hole and stepped her hind feet out of it.

Finally free, she turned to look at the mirror and her eyes widened in shock just how much a ruffled mess her plumage was. She immediately walked to the shower nozzle and turned it on, feeling the lukewarm water splash across her feathers. The water beaded up, running quickly off her wings and back until it began to soak into her down. She ruffled up many times, sending water across the massive shower area, and preened vigorously at the stubborn feathers that would not lay down flat.

"You almost done in there? I'm getting hungry!" came Rachel's high-pitched voice from the locker room.

"Yeah-yeah! Just one minute!" Thyra responded and shut the water off. There were modified hair dryers on the opposite side of the room, made to air dry a gryphon in a minute. They had massive cones on the end to direct the airflow and get to the down quickly. She walked over and pressed a switch on the wall, causing them to kick on. It started slowly at first. Then the torrent of hot air caused Thyra's eyes to squint as it began to blow into her body. It felt as if she were flying head first into a hurricane. Feather plumes dusted the wet ground and the smell of drying down feathers filled the air.

Feeling mostly dry, she threw on the borrowed clothes. Thyra worked each wing into the slits and around her chest to button up with her agile foreclaws. She stepped into the pants and pulled them over her tail, finding the opening a bit large for her tail, but everything fit.

She looked in the mirror and chuckled at her appearance. She felt like a macaw in these things. Never would she consider buying brightly colored clothing like this, but it did look fine on her. If anything, the clothing made her average neutral coloration look that much more eye catching.

"Thyra!" Rachel called out again in a jesting manor.

Thyra grabbed her uniform and rushed out of the shower room to stare down the little gryphoness drumming her talons against the tile floor of the locker room. "I'm hurrying." Thyra said and threw her uniform in the laundry hamper next to the door before grabbing her satchel.

"You *finally* ready?" Rachel stated, huffing through her nares.

"Yeah! Lets go." Thyra said and Aadhya turned to open the locker door for them.

"Well good!" said Rachel. "I was getting so hungry I was thinking about having a chunk out of Antonio's side!"

Antonio turned to look at the petite gryphoness with curiosity. "You were planning on eating me?"

Rachel laughed as they walked down another hallway. "Naw. I bet you taste awful. And really chewy too. Maybe if you were smoked and drenched in BBQ sauce." Rachel said and bounded ahead of the other three.

Antonio opened his beak to say something, but clearly could not find anything to respond back with. Aadhya opened the door to the outside and the cool breeze blew against their feathers. They walked out into the parking lot and down one of the paved walking paths that led into the street.

The sun was setting beyond the horizon, casting a yellow haze on the buildings all around. Cars sped past them on the city streets as they walked together. Several people did double takes at the band of gryphons walking down the street. Seeing a couple gryphons around this area was not uncommon, given the stadium was nearby, but Aadhya's immense size was enough for anyone to give a second glance.

Rachel flitted about, chattering nonstop. "Hey Addy. How did you end up here anyways? I mean, your accent and species is like, from really far away. I know the south is great and all, but that's a pretty big move! Was it just for Gryphball or something more?"

The bearded vulture looked down at her with a faint smile. "Actually, yes. It was for Gryphball. I am from India, and I played in the first gryphball league there. There was an opportunity to come to the states, and so I took it. I have wanted to see the states ever since I was a gryphlet."

Aadhya turned a corner and continued down the street with the rest of the band in tow. "Not to say, that I do not love my country, for I do. But it was always my dream to visit the states. It was difficult to say goodbye to my friends and family, but I do keep in touch with them. Also, I go back on the holidays to visit."

She stopped in front of a building off to itself with odd-looking lettering on the sign. Rachel nodded, satisfied with the response. She was too distracted by the smells of food coming from the building to press further.

"This is it," Aadhya said and led them into the building. A dark-skinned man turned as the bell dinged at the door and smiled with open arms.

"Aadhya! Welcome back!" He said with a heavy accent, The server approached them wearing an apron with a T-shirt of the restaurants logo on the front. He pressed his hands together and bowed before Aadhya as she did the same. "I see you have brought friends!" He turned to the rest of the band and did the same bow.

"Yes. We are all famished from practice today." Aadhya responded.

The man stood back up and motioned with his hands to a booth at the back of the restaurant. The table was elongated and had massive pillows that look very comfortable for any gryphon to lie on. "Then I shall bring out a platter at once! Please, take the seats."

Aadhya thanked him and led the others to the table in the back. The rest of the room was garbed in traditional Asian decorations hanging from the walls and ceilings. The lights were dimmed down and a TV in the far end of the restaurant played some sort of foreign game show. The server ran off to the back to shout something at the cook in what Thyra assumed was mandarin while they all took their seats.

Thyra sat comfortably on a soft red cushion in the middle of the table and looked around. There was enough room for every gryphon, and they had plenty of space, even Aadhya who sat at the end of the table. The aromas of spices and cooking meat filled the room as the sounds of sizzling meat erupted from the kitchen.

"I guess you come here often?" Thyra asked to break the silence between the gryphons that were all busy looking around the room and being transfixed on the smell of food.

"Yes. The food here is nice, it is not far from the apartment, and they treat me well," Aadhya stated as the same waiter walked up once again with a pen and note pad.

"Hello, feathered friends of Aadhya. While the platter is cooking, what would you like to drink?"

"Sweet tea, please!" Rachel chirped without hesitation.

"A water would be fine." Antonio added.

"Yeah, same for me. I should cut out the Cokes." Thyra said.

"And would you like your tea, Aadhya?" The server said after he finished jotting down their orders.

"Yes, please. No sugar." Aadhya nodded to the server as he left in haste.

Rachel drummed her talons along the hard wood table, impatient as always. She focused on the vulture. "So, how old are you Aadhya?"

Aadhya, Antonio, and Thyra all shot a glance at Rachel, surprised by such a sudden question.

"This year I will be fifteen," the great vulture responded.

Rachel chirped in amusement and perked her small eartufts. "Oh wow! I would have thought much older. But then again I think the oldest gryphons are in there twenties, right?" Rachel asked once again looking around the room to the others.

"Yeah, actually the oldest one is twenty, well, was twenty. The labs opened up at the turn of the century." Thyra stated and looked down at her talons. Her expression changed, thoughts racing through her mind as she began to think back. Both Aadhya and Antonio both caught Thyra's mood change but it did not seem to register to Rachel.

"So, how old are you Thyra?" Rachel asked again.

Thyra remained silent for a minute. The cheerful mood started to break as Rachel finally caught on and folded her eartufts back. Her stone gray feathers flattened against her body as she opened her beak to say something. The waiter cut in and placed their drinks before all of them and quickly left, sensing they were discussing something.

"Thyra, I didn't mean…"

"I just turned nineteen," Thyra answered back. Everyone was silent once more, staring intently at Thyra. "The first gryphon's name was Anfang, it's from a German word that means beginning. Though he was the first gryphon to be created, he was not a complete success. He had, issues," she said, still staring down at her talons as the others intently watched on.

"I remember meeting him in the labs. He was a redtail, like me, but…" She paused for a moment and swallowed. "He was disfigured. His wings were not completely shaped, and he had spots where feathers would grow through his fur. His beak was… hideous, for lack of a better word. It was half formed, somewhere between the looks of a lion and a beak.

"He couldn't speak like as I could. He didn't pick up language very well and he tried to attack me the first couple times we met. But, over time, we became friends. They watched us and observed us. I translated what I could to English and they had us interact every day. He was confused, most of all. He wondered what he was, and why he was always locked away in a single area while I was free to explore.

"At the time, I didn't know what I was either. I was just, there. Alive. Living day by day. But he didn't understand that. He was stuck somewhere between being self aware and lost like a feral animal." Thyra reached for her glass and took a sip of water before continuing.

"The doctors explained to me that he was not well. Mentally or physically. He was always breathing heavy and struggled to walk. But he was alive none the less. He told me he hurt; he understood pain enough to express it into words. The doctors tried to take care of him as best as they could and ease the pain. I only saw him for the first six months, and then one day, he was gone. I learned later that he was alive, but I could not see him. I tried to track him down, but since the labs were long closed, I didn't know of anyone I could contact to see where he was.

"I didn't think about him for a long time. But then one day I had the most vivid dream about him. Since then, every once and a while I would think about him, and how that could have been me. I was so close to his age and in the same lab as he was. And then, just recently, I got a letter in the mail. I don't know who it was from, but inside it was a picture of Anfang smiling and a letter. It said 'Anfang has passed away. He went easily into the night and is now at peace. He lived well and remembered you always.'"

She stopped for a minute and wiped her eyes with a wing tip and sniffled, starting to choke on her words. "We were only a year apart, but they apparently tweaked some chromosomes or something. That next test was me."

Thyra finally looked up from her talons, eyes a little watered from the old memories flooding back to her brain. She took a deep breath. "I'm the second gryphon ever made. Or so I think. It… it's frightening. Not knowing how long we live. How long we have. Or what is going to become of me."

Aadhya moved to sit next to Thyra, wrapping a huge peppered wing around her friend to comfort her. Thyra leaned into her, burying her beak into Aadhya's warm plumage.

Thyra began to cry.

The band was silent for some time, watching their friend shake and sniffle inside Aadhya's wing. The waiter came walking up with a large metal plate of sizzling meats, and vegetables along with many bowls of white rice. He stood next to the table and opened his mouth to say something, but was quickly met with six pairs of concerned avian eyes. He quietly put the plates down and made his exit as swiftly as he could.

"S..sorry," came Thyra's scratchy voice from under Aadhya's plumage. She pulled her head back and chuckled in a dizzy state, tears still dripping off her beak. "I guess I'm just exhausted."

Aadhya wiped Thyra's beak clean with one of her massive talons and smiled to her friend. "That is ok, little one. Here, let us eat, and if you wish to continue, we will support you." Her red and yellow eyes looked around to the other gryphons. They all smiled and nodded in response.

“So, is anyone going to take the steak or can I have it?” Rachel asked and pointed to the biggest piece of meat on the platter.

Thyra preened gently on Aadhya’s neck feathers and trilled. “That’s yours, if you eat the whole thing.” Thyra retorted, now finding herself again.

The gryphons’ feathers roused up as the mood lifted at once.

“Oh you just sit back and watch me. I’ll devour this whole thing

Chapter 7 Upside Down

Johnathen's eyes glanced back up to his rearview mirror, seeing the headlights of the Mercedes van once again. It was the same van that had been following him ever since he left Atlanta. Now it was turning off on the same exit towards the center of Macon. It was either a very weird coincidence, or he was being followed.

Most of the time, the van would stay a few car lengths back, but now it was right behind him. He couldn't see the driver through the tinted front windshield, and there were no front plates for Johnathen to see where the van was from.

"I'm being ridiculous," Johnathen said to himself. True, he had just dropped off video proof that incriminated The Gathering, but there was no way for them to know. He was all the way in Atlanta. Surely their roots did not reach out as far as that.

Johnathen came up to a red light off the freeway and turned on his right blinker. He watched in the mirror as the van did the same. The light turned green and Johnathen turned left instead, then watched as the van suddenly turned across traffic to follow him.

"No doubt about it," Johnathen said to himself. He gripped his steering wheel tightly, palms sweating and his hands started to shake. What should he do? He could try to outrun him. The Volvo was certainty more powerful and agile than the large Sprinter Van. Or, he could confront him. Whoever it was would not pick a fight in the middle of a crowded street. Would they?

Johnathen made a sudden right turn down a city street and watched as the van followed. His eyes narrowed and he pushed the gas pedal down firmly. The gentle whine of the turbo spooling up filled the cabin as he accelerated down the city street. The bright xenon headlights started to fade in his rearview mirror and he made a quick right down another street before pulling into a gas station.

Johnathen put the car in park and watched the rear view mirror. Every second that ticked by felt like a minute. His breathing was heavy and heart pumped fast with a little adrenaline flowing through his body. To his relief, he saw the van speed by the street he was just on. Quickly, Johnathen put the car in drive once again and turned out of the gas station.

He took a deep breath and let out a sigh, letting his nerves calm somewhat. *Who was that?*

Johnathen's phone dinged with a new message as he pulled up to another red light. He pulled out the phone and checked the message. It was from Isabell.

Don't forget about me. I want a greasy burger. And a milkshake, please.

"Well, at least she said please." Johnathen could not help but grin at the message and looked up as the light turned green. He pulled down the road and thought about the restaurants on the way to the hospital. The hamburger place he liked most was on the way there. A bright light flashed in his rearview mirror and he glanced back up to see the high beams of the Mercedes' xenon headlights ficker at him. Johnathen's eyes opened wide and he gripped the steering wheel.

The other driver wanted Johnathen to know he had found him again. Fear slowly started to turn into anger as he drove down the street with the Mercedes close in tow. Johnathen looked around the car for anything he could use as a weapon if he needed it, but all he had was his suitcase. He was no fighter. He knew he would never win in a full brawl if one broke out. He only hoped this man following him would not fight him outright in public.

Johnathen took a deep breath and slowly eased into the parking lot of the burger joint and waited as the Mercedes did the same. His nerves went crazy and he mentally prepared himself for a confrontation. Just how bad it would get, he did not know.

Johnathen threw open the door just as the Mercedes parked and he quickly walked over to it, his eyes narrowing to see if he could see inside. The van's driver window rolled down to reveal a man in his forties. His head was shaved bald except for a single short stripe running from his forehead to the back of his head. He took off his sunglasses and calmly put them down in the seat next to him as Johnathen approached.

"Ya know, speeding is dangerous, son. 'Specially around these parts," the man said. He was clean-shaven and his eyes were droopy, either from lack of sleep or just exhaustion. Johnathen was struck by the sudden calm comment and stared at the man from a couple feet away.

"Why are you following me?" Johnathen asked, trying not to shout or let his voice crack.

His hands were balled into fists and his body trembled with adrenaline once again. The stranger simply looked at him, as if Johnathen was the one becoming an annoyance and not the other way around.

"Look here. All I was hired to do was follow ya. I ain't here to cause no trouble." The man's tired eyes stared directly at Johnathen, and he could tell this man was being legitimate.

"W…who hired you?" Johnathen asked, his posture relaxing a bit now seeing that the man was not a threat. The man simply sighed.

"Can't tell ya that. Professional courtesy, ya know," the man responded.

Johnathen frowned at the answer. "Was it The Gathering?" Johnathen insisted, more demanding now.

The man's expression did not change one bit. "Can't tell ya that either."

"Well? What can you…"

"Son. I ain't here to play twenty questions with ya. Would you so kindly go back to your business so I can continue mine?" The rumble of the diesel engine on the Mercedes started back up again, implying that he was done talking.

Johnathen became increasingly annoyed and angry with him once again. His voice began to rise. "What is your business exactly?!"

The man rubbed his eyes with his forefingers. "I told ya already. To follow you. Now go on and get. I would love to get home before dark," the man replied and pulled out his cellphone to start typing a message out.

Johnathen stared at him for a few moments. He wanted to rip the man out of the Mercedes and beat him until he got his questions answered. The man stopped typing and looked over to Johnathen standing there and raised his eyebrow. "Well?"

Johnathen let out an exhausted grunt and turned around to go inside, turning his head once to watch as the man simply played with his phone. His hands were still shaking as he opened the door to the restaurant and walked inside. At least this guy didn't seem to be a threat of any kind. He apparently was there to observe and report, nothing more, but report to who? He did not seem like the kind of man that worked for the Gathering. He was too laid back and informal.

"Can I help you?" a girl from behind the counter asked curiously. Johnathen realized he had been standing in front of the counter staring out the window for a couple seconds now and it had put the woman off edge.

"Oh! Sorry, just thinking about my order." Johnathen responded, putting on an easy-going smile.

The woman smiled back before responding. "Well the burger of the day is the New Bacon-ings burger. Comes with thick slices of bacon, if the awful name didn't tip you off."

"As far as burger names go, I think it's clever. I'll take two of those. And a chocolate shake." Johnathen replied and pulled out his wallet. The server tapped away at the screen and took his credit card before disappearing to the back. Johnathen walked over and sat down at a chair near the counter where he could see the van.

"Thyra," Johnathen said out loud to himself and pulled out his phone, quickly typing a message to her.

I don't want you to worry, but there's something weird going on. A man in a Mercedes Sprinter Van has been following me ever since I left Atlanta. I confronted him and all he told me was he was hired to tail me, but wouldn't tell me who. Just keep a lookout.

Johnathen sent the message and locked his phone. The sounds of a machine whirling to life made him look up quickly. The woman behind the counter was blending the milkshake and looked over to Johnathen, noticing the sound startled him.

"Um, sorry. Do you want whip cream on top?" she asked and poured the contents into a container.

"Sure. Sounds great," Johnathen responded. The sound of a bell from the kitchen rang through the small restaurant and the woman disappeared into the back again. He looked back out the window to notice a lighter in the Vans window, followed by a puff of smoke.

"Sir? Order's ready," the woman said. Johnathen grabbed the bag and the shake, thanked her, and left the building. He walked over to his car and looked at the man smoking a cigarette with the window down.

"Those will kill you, ya know," Johnathen said, mocking the man for the earlier comment.

"Yeah? So will those burgers," the man responded and watched as Johnathen got back in his Volvo. He started the engine, and backed out of the parking space as the Van did the same. Johnathen stopped and looked in the rearview mirror again and the man motioned for him to go. They pulled out of the parking lot together, like friends following one another home.

The drive to the hospital was a short ways away. The sun hung low in the sky and the streetlights flicked on as he drove away from the city. Soon, Johnathen pulled into the hospital parking lot and got out of his car as the Van pulled up next to his car. He rolled down the window and leaned out, looking to Johnathen and then to the hospital.

"Thought you were heading home. Here to visit that gryphoness?" He asked, carrying on the conversation like they were buddies.

Johnathen frowned and narrowed his eyes. "What do you know about her? If you harm one feather…"

"Take it easy. Just asking. I just know about her from the news." He looked down at his watch and sighed then back up at Johnathen. "You plan on being here long?"

Johnathen threw up his hands and looked away. "Yeah. I don't know. A little while at least. Not like it's any of your damn business."

"No need for cursin', son." He stared at Johnathen with the same expressionless look he had worn the entire time. "Well, I guess I'm going to call it a day. I'll see you tomorrow," the man said and started to drive off.

Johnathen's mouth opened in disbelief at what the man just said, but before he could retort, the van was gone. "What the hell…"

Johnathen had never been so confused in his entire life. How could someone who was caught doing something so wrong be so calm about it? The man acted like it was just another day at the office and what he was doing was completely natural. Johnathen stood in the parking lot and watched the Van drive off down the road. He turned and noticed a couple of black Harleys parked off to the side of the hospital. He immediately recognized them.

They were Saul's and Carl's motorcycles.

Johnathen headed into the hospital with a newfound energy and took the elevator. Once he was on the right floor, he could hear bellowing laughter come from down the hallway and the sounds of a gryphoness chirping in amusement.

Johnathen smiled and knocked on the door, peeking in to see the two heavy-set bearded men standing next to Isabell's bed. They both looked up and smiled, still wearing the same leather jacket with cut off sleeves as they had the last time he had seen them.

"Well I'll be damned! It's Johnny!" Saul shouted and walked over to give Johnathen a big bear hug.

"Yeah, good to see you too!" Johnathen wheezed and squirmed in the tight hug as Carl and Isabell laughed. Just as soon as Saul put Johnathen down, Carl picked him up in a tight hug as well.

"Isabell told us you were a comin'!" Saul said as Carl put Johnathen down.

"I promised I would bring her dinner," Johnathen said and looked over to Isabell.

The gryphoness seemed more like her perky old self, feathers preened and eartufts perked up with excitement. She still lay in the same place, wing being suspended out to the side and cast wrapped around several joints, but she had a smile on her beak.

"And it's about damn time! I could hardly choke down the lunch they gave me," Isabell responded and held out her human-sized foreclaws. Johnathen opened up the bag and pulled out a foil wrapped burger before handing it over. "I hope that's my milkshake too!" Isabell pointed with a talon at the cup in Johnathen's hand.

"Yeah. With whipped cream also." Johnathen placed it down on the nightstand next to the bed.

"What happened to you last week?" Saul asked and sat down on the couch opposite of the bed. Johnathen realized that he hadn't spoken to them since the mess at the rally.

"After I distracted the cops, I just ran," Johnathen responded while pulling out his own burger from the sack.

The sounds of scrunching aluminum foil filled the room along with the greasy aroma of bacon and beef. Isabell sighed happily and stared wide-eyed at the burger in her claws before biting down quickly. She chirred deep in her chest and closed her eyes, savoring the taste. Everyone looked over and smiled, watching the cheerful gryphoness enjoy her meal.

"This is a godsend. I've only been here for a week, but damn, I've been craving a good burger ever since I woke up," Isabell said, grease dripping off her beak.

"They didn't try to follow you or nothin like that?" Saul pressed, his gaze still firmly pressed on Johnathen..

Johnathen unwrapped his own burger. "Just for a couple blocks, but I guess the commotion of the rally kept them from sticking with me."

Johnathen bit down into the cheesy and succulent meat. It had been a while since he had a grease bomb like this, and he was just as satisfied with it as Isabell seemed to be.

"I went to the planned meeting spot afterwards, but I never saw you guys again." Johnathen had to cover his mouth as he spoke with his mouth full. A rude gesture but he knew no one here would care.

"Yeah, everything went kind of…south, to say the least," Saul said, and looked over to Isabell, who was too distracted munching on her meal to hear them at the moment.

The group watched Isabell chow away, not caring about the crumbs and mess she was making on the bed sheets. "Carl actually found her, laying in the street. She was unconscious and mangled up somethin fierce." Saul started in a low voice, starting to choke on his words a bit.

"I thought she was gone at first," Saul began while looking at Isabell, his expression on his rugged face changing from worry to optimistic. "She's just a little thing. I picked her up easy enough and when I felt her heart beat I've never been so relieved in my entire life," he finished as Isabell gulped down the last of her burger with a contented sigh.

"Hey, you got a little…" Saul motioned towards his mouth as Isabell looked up, flecks of beef and grease shined brightly on her beak.

Isabell laughed and crumbled up the aluminum foil. “I bet I do. You know I’m a messy eater.”

Saul stood up to grab a tissue from the side of the bed and handed it over. She placed the foil on the counter and grabbed the tissue, wiping it across her beak and face.

“What were you all talking about? I was a bit busy.” Isabell asked and placed the tissue down.

Saul shrugged his shoulders. “Just bullshitting with Johnny over here. So how do you go to the bathroom? They got one of them things up in ya or somethin?”

Johnathen nearly choked on his hamburger but Isabelle didn’t seem to mind. “Yeah, it feels awkward as hell! But luckily, being avian, we…”

“I’m trying to eat!” Johnathen exclaimed with a light blush of his cheeks.

The rest of the group bellowed with laughter. “Oh come on Johnny! It ain’t nothin!” Saul said. Johnathen could not help but smile at their brashness.

Isabell picked up the milkshake cup and tore off the lid, looking over to Johnathen. “They give you a spoon by any chance? You know I can’t use a straw.”

Johnathen finished up his burger and crunched up the foil before looking through the bag. “Yeah! Here you go.” He stood and handed it over before taking the discarded lid to put into the bag.

Isabell took the spoon into the still thick milkshake and licked the contents up. “Much better than the chocolate pudding here.” She took another spoonful. “You talk to Thyra any today?”

He realized that she had not texted back yet, and immediately felt a knot form in his stomach. Was she ok? Did someone else get to her? He started to panic, fearing the worse. The group all stared at him for a minute as Johnathen thoughts raced in his head.

"Johnny, you all right?" Saul asked curiously.

"Y…yeah. She's good. Been at gryphball practice all-day and last I heard, she was going out with her friends to eat. Said she was really exhausted." Johnathen sat back down and put on a fake smile again. This time, it did not work.

"Somethin' is eatin' at you. What's the matter?" Saul leaned forward, looking generally concerned.

"She's fine. I know she is." Johnathen began. He tried to think of simple reasons why she hadn't replied.

"But?" Saul pressed on. He was apparently really good at reading people and knew there was something more bothering Johnathen.

"Well, I had a weird run-in today," Johnathen began. Isabell stopped eating her milkshake to look at Johnathen with everyone else. "I went to Atlanta to turn in the footage that Isabell caught. The girl at the front desk for the radio station gratefully took it, and said they would review it."

"So, you found her bag with the camera in it then?" Carl asked now and Johnathen nodded in acknowledgment. "Yeah. Made a couple copies of it at home. Anyways, I left the station and noticed a Mercedes Sprinter Van, you know those?"

"Yeah. One of our guys has one for transporting bikes to the workshop." Saul confirmed.

"Ok, well they are hard to miss. This one followed me from Atlanta all the way here. I tried to get away from him but I guess he was too good," Johnathen said and watched Saul's face turn angry once again.

"I finally confronted him outside the place where I bought burgers, and all he would tell me was he was hired to follow me. He didn't seem to care I confronted him, and was relaxed about the whole thing, like, it was just another day to him. He even followed me here, and told me he would see me tomorrow."

"Do you think he's part of The Gathering?" Saul asked seriously.

"I think so, but I'm not sure. I mean, he has to be hired by them or at least related, but he didn't seem like the kind of person that was part of the group," Johnathen responded. The room was silent for a minute except for the ticking of the clock on the wall.

"Don't worry about that guy. We will deal with him." Saul said reassuringly and Carl nodded in agreement.

"He knew about Isabell too. Said he only knew about her through the news, but I don't exactly believe him," Johnathen added and looked over to the gryphoness. Her eartufts were folded back and she ground her beak. "I just want someone here with her to make sure no one tries anything funny."

"I'll get someone here to watch over her. But what about Thyra?" Saul asked next.

"I haven't heard from her since I sent her the text an hour ago. I think she's just busy out with friends or her phone is dead." Johnathen said to assure himself.

"But if she doesn't answer me before midnight, I'll drive to Athens. She told me where she's staying."

"Do you want me to send someone up there? It's no problem." Saul answered back.

Johnathen shook his head. "No, that's fine. She has a lot of gryphon friends now. And she's staying with that bearded vulture, Aadhya."

"The one on the news that was standing with her?" Saul asked curiously.

"Yeah. I don't think anyone would try anything with that particular gryphoness in the way," Johnathen replied.

"If you think she is big on the television, you should see her in person. She's easily three times my size." Isabell chimed in while digging out the rest of the milkshake with her spoon. "An angry gryphon the size of Aadhya could probably tear a car door off its hinges if she wanted to."

"Yeah. No worries there." Johnathen said and stood up. Isabell held out her empty cup and Johnathen took it from her. "Well, I'll keep in touch and swing by tomorrow."

"I'll keep a look out for that Van. You just tell me when you see him and we will deal with him personally," Saul said with a stern look.

Johnathen nodded in response. "I'll let you know."

"Hey, thanks for the food," Isabell chirped as Johnathen walked towards the door.

He turned around and smiled. "No problem. But I can't feed you burgers every night or the nurses will have my ass."

Isabell chuckled gently and smiled back. “Just hide it under a salad or something next time.”

“See you later, Johnny,” Saul said, and Carl gave him a friendly wave. Johnathen waved back and left the room, heading back to the elevators. Just then his phone dinged with a message from Thyra.

Yeah everything is ok here. Are you ok?

Johnathen sighed and his shoulders slumped as he let out the tension he had been carrying. **Just a little shook up, but I'm fine. Just saw Saul and Carl in Isabell's room. They said they would take care of the guy tailing me.**

He exited the elevator and he walked out the front door of the hospital to his Volvo. Johnathen started the engine and drove out the parking lot en-route to his house. His phone dinged with a new message from Thyra again.

Ok. I'll keep a look out but I doubt anyone can tail a flying gryphon. Plus Aadhya is here too. I don't think anyone wants to mess with her.

Johnathen grinned and concentrated on his driving. The sky was growing dark as he pulled into the neighborhood and his headlights turned on automatically. The lights were off in the neighbor's houses, and all was quiet. Johnathen pulled up to the house and he suddenly slammed on his breaks. The dull light of his front door was on and he could see the door wide.

His heart skipped a beat. Johnathen drove around to the side of the house and opened the garage door. The garage light shone brightly across the boxy shape of his Mustang, which gave him some relief. He pulled into the garage and got out, looking around for anything out of place, but nothing had been touched.

Johnathen opened one of the drawers to his toolbox and stared down at the small Ruger pocket pistol that resided inside. It had been a gift from his grandfather from years past, and he kept it in the toolbox for safekeeping.

He quickly retrieved the Ruger and pulled the slide back with a loud mechanic clink as a nine-millimeter bullet loaded itself into the chamber. He threw open the door to the kitchen and his eyes widened with shock, looking at the mess that was inside. He kept the Ruger held down at his side as he looked around the room.

The contents of every drawer had been thrown out on the ground. Things were scattered across the wooden floor. His heart raced faster, and his hands shook as he observed the mess inside.

He did not hear any sound besides his own breathing and the soft rustling of leaves in the wind outside. Among the chaos along the kitchen counter, he spotted something foreign, a large black Bible. Johnathen put down the pistol and picked it up the Bible, squeezing it tightly in his hands. On the front of the Bible was inscribed, Church Of The Gathering. Johnathen screamed with anger and threw the Bible against the wall.

His mind raced with anger and he grit his teeth. His home had been turned upside down. Not only that, but the Gathering wanted him to know that they were behind it. They had invaded his privacy, his sanctuary, but for what reason? Why now after all these years?

He froze in place and could think of one thing only, the footage. He raced down the hallway and into his study, finding every book from the bookcase scattered across the floor. He searched his desk, but his computer was gone. He collapsed in his office chair and stared at his empty desk, eyes wide in disbelief.

"That's what they were after."

Chapter 8 A Cold Wind Blows

"Thyra," called a gentle voice.

The gryphoness lifted her head from her pillow and looked across the white room to see a man standing in the doorway. She concentrated on his face, but saw nothing but a blur. She could just make out that his glasses shimmered in the light and he wore a smile along with his white coat. Yet, even with his face out of focus, she felt comfortable around him. She felt she knew this man well enough to trust him.

"I didn't mean to wake you. How are you feeling today?" The man stepped inside carrying a clipboard and shut the door behind him.

Thyra slowly stood and stretched and looked down at her talons. They were much smaller than normal. She opened her beak to respond, but suddenly she couldn't remember how to speak. The man walked closer and sat in a chair, adjusting his glasses.

"Thyra?" he asked once again.

Her eartufts perked up as a few simple words slowly came back to mind. "I feel…good," she said, but her voice seemed alien to her.

The man smiled and nodded his head. "That's wonderful to hear." He jotted something down on his clipboard, then asked curiously, "You remember my name, don't you?"

Thyra stared at the man for a moment before his name suddenly rose in her thoughts. "Anthony."

"That's right! It's been a week since I've seen you. I'm glad you still remember my name." Anthony scribbled something down again while Thyra looked around the room.

The walls were decorated with framed paintings of mountains along with talon paintings she had done. She glanced out the window and watched gentle rainfall streak down the glass. A white board stood in the corner of the room with several simple math problems written on it. Some of the math problems had been solved by her own chicken scratch foreclaw writing, while others remained unfinished.

Anthony looked over to the board and then back down at Thyra. "It seems you were able to solve some of the problems."

Thyra nodded and held up her foreclaws again. "Some numbers…too high," she said out loud and once again her voice sounded unfamiliar to her. It creaked and rolled off her tongue in notes like a hawk calling into the wind.

"Don't worry. We will work on them together. But today, I thought you would like to go play with Anfang," Anthony said.

Thyra's feathers roused with excitement and her tail twitched. She could feel the corners of her beak pulling up in a smile. Anthony put down his clipboard on the table and leaned forward, putting his hands on his knees, his eyes hidden behind his glasses.

"Does that sound like fun?" he asked.

"Fun," she responded, nodding her head again.

He motioned for her to approached him. She did so a bit unsteadily. Her head felt jumbled as she thought about Anfang.

"Anfang feel good too?" Thyra questioned as he reached out and ran his fingers through her crest feathers.

He seemed surprised by the question and chuckled with amusement. "Ah, you are concerned about him. That's good. That's very good." He leaned back and jotted down something else on the clipboard. "But yes. Anfang feels good today." He stood back up, looking like a giant to her the way he stood on only two legs.

"Good," she responded and readjusted her wings.

Anthony grabbed his clipboard and turned towards the door. "Follow me, please," he commanded gently, but paused as he reached the door. He turned to look back at her a little more sternly now, making Thyra's ear tufts slick back with submission. "Remember, do not run off. Stay right behind me."

"I will follow," Thyra said and watched as he pressed the intercom button. Several seconds later, a loud buzzing noise sounded above the door and Anthony opened it, revealing a long white hallway.

He held the door open for her and began walking down the corridor. She followed him through another set of metal doors that opened up into a room. Many people walked around in the open space, carrying odd-looking tools and instruments. Thyra looked at each one of them, but only saw blank faces that paid her little attention as they continued to their duties.

"What do they do?" Thyra asked, and paused to look through one glass window. Inside she saw a woman wearing a mask and blue gloves, looking through a device on the countertop.

Anthony moved next to her and peered through the window. "That is called a microscope, Thyra. People use it to see things that are really small."

"Mic…microscope." Thyra repeated the word and watched as the woman continued to stare through the device.

"Very good," Anthony assured her and walked on, turning his head to make sure Thyra followed. He waved at a couple other people in white coats as they passed by, each one seeming to smile at Anthony.

"Everyone likes Anthony?" Thyra asked.

He chuckled gently and opened up another set of doors. "Everyone is being extra nice because I just got back from vacation."

Thyra walked past him and looked up into his glasses again, head tilted with curiosity. "What is, vacation?" she asked.

Anthony looked down and ran his hand along her head once again, making Thyra trill gently. "You are stunning. Simply my most perfect creation," He said under his own breath. He leaned down and she caught a glimpse of his own green eyes. They were kind, and bright with admiration.

She repeated the word. "Creation."

Anthony nodded and walked down the next hallway. It was bare white just like the one in front of her door. He threw open a pair of metal doors and approached the last one at the end of the hall. He stopped and pressed the intercom button on the side.

"Anfang is very excited to see you today," Anthony said as the door buzzed loudly. He opened the door and gestured for her to go inside. The room was similar to her own, a couple windows and many paintings decorating the far side of the wall. There was no table or chairs, nor was there a whiteboard and puzzles.

At the far end of the room, a creature sat on his haunches, staring out the window. His mangy gray tail slowly moved behind him, clearly concentrated on something outside. He had no wings to speak of, simply deformed stubs protruding from his back. Brown feathers and white fur were mixed together randomly through his body, with bare patches of pink skin showing in spots. His one feline ear twitched as Thyra entered and he slowly turned to look at her.

The gray light from outside shined across his upper gray beak. The deformed lower part of his mouth was a cat-like muzzle. His tired green avian eyes searched Thyra blankly for a minute until she saw them spark with recognition.

"Thyra!" Anfang chirped and slowly stood up. His body trembled weakly as he stepped forward, balancing on his four avian feet. "Y..you come play?" he asked in a mix of chirps and trills. His mouth was constantly agape as he was unable to close it completely due to the protruding lower teeth scraping across the sides of his beak.

Thyra smiled and walked to him, running her beak across the top of his head. "Yes. They told me I could come see you," she responded. The words flowed more fluidly as she carried on. "They told me you are feeling good today." Thyra sat down before him, looking across his deformed face, concerned for him.

"Yes, yes. I want to see friend," Anfang said and roughly nosed his beak portion against her own, a small rumble beginning in his chest. He was happy when she was around.

"I wanted to see you too," Thyra said with a smile and nipped at his beak playfully. Her heart ached when she was with him, but that never stopped her from wanting to see him. He laughed and ruffled what feathers he had, sending plumes into the air.

"They gave me new toy!" Anfang exclaimed and turned to limp to the other side of the room. Thyra followed after him and watched as he dug around the bright blue bins with his claws until pulling out a bright red rubber ball. "See?" Anfang said and held it out for Thyra.

She picked up the ball and squeezed it gently in her foreclaws as Anfang walked a distance away. He held out his claws and Thyra smiled, knowing what he wanted. She practice tossed the ball a couple times, watching his eyes follow it each time. She underhand tossed it to him, and Anfang caught it with a cheerful squawk.

He held it happily and tossed it back to Thyra. The ball fell a little short from her foreclaws. "Can you stay forever?"

Thyra caught the ball on the second bounce and looked at him, trying to keep her smile. "I don't think they will let me," Thyra answered before tossing the ball.

This time, Anfang did not attempt to catch it. The ball bounced past him as his cheerful expression flickered out. His beak frowned and feathers pulled close to his body.

"W..why?" Anfang asked. Thyra's eartufts folded back, realizing she accidently upset him. The room started to shrink in her vision, and the lights dimmed. "I don't know. Maybe.."

"Why do they keep me here?" He screeched now, making Thyra wince at his sudden outburst. She opened her beak to try to talk him down as she saw tears starting to pool around his eyes. "Why they keep you from me!"

She felt herself reach out towards him, and her heart ached even harder.

A door flew open and three men stepped in to grab Anfang. He twisted and swiped at one of them, screeching out. One of the men screamed and fell to the floor, clutching his bleeding arm. "I don't want to go! Thyra!"

"Anfang!" Thyra screeched, feeling tears pool from her eyes as well. She tried to rush towards him, but a gigantic pair of talons rose up from the ground and gripped her.

Every muscle on her clenched, trying to pull away from the strong talons gripping her body, but it was no use. The men began to drag him out an arched exit that suddenly appeared in the background. The large doors creaked open slowly, and Thyra watched helplessly as the men dragged Anfang into the darkness inside.

"Thyra! Don't leave me, Thyra!"

"Thyra!"

"Thyra!"

Her eyes jerked open to see Aadhya standing next to her, watching with concern. Thyra's chest heaved quickly with deep breaths, and her beak was wet with tears.

"Thyra, you were having a nightmare," Aadhya calmly said and pulled her white-feathered foreclaw away. Thyra rolled off the couch and stood, glancing outside to watch the rain pitter against the window. Aadhya's eartufts folded back. "You called out for Anfang."

"I had a dream about him. Maybe it was a memory. I-I don't know." Thyra glanced over at the clock. It was still really early in the morning. "I'm sorry I woke you up."

The vulture shook her head and stood to walk into the kitchen. "It is no matter. Here, let me make you tea to calm the nerves."

"Thank you." Thyra let out a sigh and sat down on a cushion in front of the coffee table.

"Would it help to talk about it?" Aadhya asked, filling up a teapot with water before turning on the stove.

Thyra looked down at her foreclaws, remembering how small they had seemed in her dream. “Maybe, but I don’t want to keep you up even more.”

“If I wanted to sleep, I would not have asked if you wanted to talk,” Aadhya said and selected some tea bags out of the cupboard.

Thyra’s eartufts pinned back at the comment and she realized that Aadhya was right. She could have simply stayed in bed and not even come out to check on Thyra, yet here she was, making tea in the middle of the night for her friend.

“It was about Anfang,” Thyra began. Aadhya perked her long white eartufts and walked out of the kitchen, her attention fully on Thyra now. “I don’t know how much of it was real, but I was dreaming about seeing him again. I the labs. I remember that they used to let me visit him every now and again, but I think this dream was about the last time I saw him.”

Thyra looked up into Aadhya’s striking yellow and red eyes as she continued, “I was young, maybe around two at the time…I would visit him almost every day by this point, but there was one day he lost control. I don’t know what happened, but I remember him screeching wildly, and people dragging him off. I never saw him again after that. They probably deemed him unfit for visitation.” Thyra looked down at her claws again, trying to remember more.

“How long did you know this gryphon?” Aadhya questioned.

“I don’t really know. Everything is just so fuzzy. I could have known him for a couple months, or maybe even a year. I was too young to really remember.” The teapot on the stove slowly began to whistle.

Aadhya walked into the kitchen to turn off the stove. “You said you received a letter about Anfang’s passing recently. That must indicate someone took care of him all these years,” Aadhya pointed out and stepped out of the kitchen, clutching the pot in her beak and walked on three legs to carry the cups.

“Yeah. Somebody had to take him in. And I want to find out who they are.” Thyra took the cups from Aadhya to set them on the table.

The vulture sat before her and poured the tea with ease into the cups using her foreclaw now. “I am sure you will be able to find them.”

Thyra nodded in response and took the cup, gently blowing over the surface of the hot beverage. The earthy herbal aroma filled her nares and lungs, calming her slightly. “That wasn’t all I dreamt,” Thyra continued, staring down in her cup. “I had a dream about a caretaker that was there. His name was Anthony.”

Aadhya sipped from her cup and placed it back down on the table. “You remember a name? That is a breakthrough. Most of us do not recall much from the labs, and remembering a name is quite rare. Is that the first human you remember the name of?”

“So far, yeah. His face was the most clear too. And I remember he had bright green eyes, like mine. Usually people I dream about have a blurry face,” Thyra said and sipped from her own cup. Her face scrunched at the bitterness of the tea, causing Aadhya to chuckle gently.

“I forgot the sugar, let me get you some.” The vulture went to stand, but Thyra stopped her.

"No. It's alright. I should cut back on the sugar anyways. Plus, I think I'll start to like it more if I don't always load it down with sugar."

Aadhya nodded and sat back down, relaxing again. "Was there anything else you remember?"

Thyra thought for a minute, and took another sip. "Actually, there was a lot more. He was teaching me the names of different things in the labs. He was really pleased with how quickly I was learning and called me his perfect creation."

Aadhya stopped and put down her cup, now looking intently at Thyra. "He called you his creation and he had the same eyes as you. Thyra, that was not a caretaker. He had to be the lead scientist and perhaps your human donor." Thyra's eyes widened at the discovery they both just made. She put down the cup and stared back, crest feathers rousing up.

"You mean, I dreamed about my fath…" Thyra stopped and thought. "My creator…"

"I believe you have. Also, you now have a name. It may not be much, but it is better than nothing. Many of us never found out who created us. Much of the documentation was lost in the early years," Aadhya added in. She drained the rest of the cup into her beak and swallowed. "Maybe we can find him. I am sure there are not many scientists named Anthony in the field of Genome Editing." She looked to the digital clock on the counter before standing up onto all fours once more. "But for now, we must rest."

Thyra nodded her head in agreement. They did not have much time until daylight and they needed the energy. "Yeah. It's my first real game tomorrow and even though I'm on the bench, I still need to be prepared. Thanks, Addy."

Aadhya smiled and flipped off the kitchen light. "I hope you sleep well. Goodnight."

"Goodnight." Thyra watched as Aadhya walked down the hallway and shut the door behind her. Thyra climbed back onto the couch. She lay on her back and stared up at the ceiling once again. Her mind was still racing with questions from her dream. It all felt so real but distant at the same time, like a mix of memories, and made up fantasy in her head. She closed her eyes and took a deep breath through her nares, trying to replay the images in her head again, but came up blank.

Thyra laid still for a minute more, and then sighed in defeat. She rolled over to her side and pulled the blanket over her body. Maybe the memories would come back to her in time. With that final thought, she drifted off into a dreamless sleep.

Chapter 9 Opening Act

Thyra and Aadhya landed gently on the soft grass patch next to the side entrance of the stadium. Thyra folded in her wings and looked at the vast parking lot covered with cars, her eyes searching the parking lot for Johnathen's Volvo. She spotted it towards the front of the lot and grinned. She was so excited for him to see her play.

"Looks like we're going to have a crowd," Thyra pointed out. There was already a long line of people in front of the main entrance waiting to go through security checks.

"Yes. Typically, the first game of the season brings a good crowd. They want to see how we do." Aadhya approached the door and typed in a code on the keypad mounted on the wall. The door unlocked with a loud click and Aadhya pulled it open, letting Thyra go first. She followed Thyra inside and they walked down the long corridor.

"I bet it's because of all those fantasy leagues they have online. I wonder if I'm even on one of them." Thyra chuckled to herself and turned a corner that led to the locker room. She remembered playing in a fantasy league or two over the years. The first games of the season were important for trading players around and guessing the outcome as well as making bets on who would make it to the finals.

Thyra opened one of the double doors that lead into the locker room. There were a couple of gryphons putting on their uniforms, but it looked mainly empty. Thyra wing-waved at the corvid twins who were conversing between themselves and walked to her locker.

"Where is everyone else?" Thyra asked Aadhya.

"We all have routines before a game," Aadhya began while opening up her locker. "Many warm up by working out in the gym, and others enjoy long relaxing flights." The bearded vulture took her uniform off of its hanger and looked it over carefully.

Thyra pulled her locker door open and saw her freshly-cleaned game uniform hanging up as well. She took it down and held it in her talons, looking over her name on the back. Thyra watched Aadhya pull the spandex uniform over her head, working her gargantuan wings through the openings in the back. Thyra did the same, but with less grace.

She struggled with pulling her wings through the openings, and felt the helping talons of Aadhya assist the wings through the slots. "You will get a hold of it with time. This elastic material can be tricky, as it is designed to conform tightly to our bodies," Aadhya said and pulled the rest of it down to Thyra's rear.

"Yeah, you should have seen me the first time I tried to put it on! I looked like a flailing catfish on land," Thyra admitted.

Aadhya let out a soft chuckle and nodded. "You can imagine I did the same. I lost my balance and fell over a bench in front of my new team." The large gryphoness took her gloves from the locker. She slowly pulled the modified gloves over her foretalons and tugged the Velcro strap tight with her beak.

The door opened behind them and gryphons began to pour into the locker room. Thyra turned to see Rachel and Antonio in the midst of the ruffled group. Many made their way towards the showers while Rachel and Antonio approached her.

"You didn't want to join us for the pregame workout?" Rachel asked, ruffling her coat of feathers. Her nares dripped and her beak was wet with saliva.

Thyra shook her head and closed her locker. "Not after all the exercise I've had the past couple of days! If Coach has me play today, I'll need all the energy that I can get," Thyra admitted.

"That is alright. Eventually you will have energy to spare," Antonio said and grabbed a towel from the clean pile before slinging it over his back. He looked over his wingshoulder to watch coach Victor walk into the locker room.

"Redtail! Corvid! Front and center," Victor commanded. Thyra felt her feathers fall flat from the harpy eagle's boisterous voice. She left the group and walked over to Victor, Braden walking next to her. Victors tall gray crest feathers rose up as he looked between the two.

"Yes, coach?" Thyra asked.

"As you know, you two will start on the bench along with two others. Depending on the performance of your teammates, I might substitute you in. I want you to be prepared nonetheless," Victor said and looked to the rest of the gryphons putting on their uniforms or getting out of the shower. "I want you to have game time experience, as that is the only way for you to get better, but only if we are clear for a win."

"I understand, Sir. Whatever's best for the team," Braden chirped. Thyra nodded in agreement.

"Good." Victor looked up to the other gryphons again and screeched loudly for all to hear. All the eartufts in the room perked to attention and everyone turned to look to Victor. "Meeting in five minutes. Get a move on!" Victor walked over to the showers. "Caracara! Finish up and get dried off! This isn't a beauty pageant!"

Thyra could not help but laugh at the comment and watched as the team quickly scattered to their lockers to put on their uniforms. The locker room doors opened again and Thyra saw a brunet-haired woman peek her head in. She was wearing a headset and carrying a clipboard.

"Thyra?" the woman said.

Thyra made eye contact. "Yes?" she asked curiously.

"Your husband is here to see you."

Thyra quickly walked over to the doors and stepped outside the locker room to see Johnathen standing there with a smile on his face. Thyra got up on her hind legs and wrapped her foretalons around the back of his neck to rub her beak against his face.

"So glad you could come!" Thyra smiled and pulled back to look into his brown eyes. Johnathen laughed and ran his fingers through her almond brown cheek feathers before placing a kiss on her beak.

"I wouldn't miss it for the world. I'll always be here to support you," Johnathen said.

"I mean I may not even play today. I'll just be sitting on a bench probably the whole game," Thyra said.

Johnathen shrugged his shoulders and played with one of her eartufts. "And you'll look beautiful doing it. But I don't care if you sit on the bench all season. I'll still be here every game."

"I hope I don't have to, but thank you," Thyra replied and gestured back at the brunet. "How did you convince her to let you back here? I told coach you would probably stop by, but I didn't know who else to talk to."

"I had to show this lady my ID because she didn't believe me when I told her that I was your husband!" Johnathen said with a chuckle. "She just kind of looked at me like I was crazy."

"Well, she's not wrong. You are crazy." Thyra beak grinned and brushed his long black hair back with her talons. He shrugged and tugged playfully on her beak.

"Yeah. Crazy for you," Johnathen said. Thyra huffed through her nares and took a step back to sit on her haunches.

"You're being overly sappy today! Is everything ok?" Thyra jested and noticed Johnathen freeze up for a minute. She raised an eye ridge at the sudden break in his mood and grew concerned. "John?"

"Yeah! Yeah, everything is fine. Just a bit tired, and it kind of sucks sleeping by myself, but everything is fine." Johnathen rubbed the back of her neck. She could see dark circles under his eyes and his stubbly beard was misshapen. He was lying.

"Redtail!" Caracara! Let's go!" Victors booming voice rang out, interrupting Thyra's train of thought. She stood up again to get another kiss from Johnathen and looked him over one last time.

Thyra smiled and backed away. "Ok. I'll see you after the game."

"I will. Good luck!" Johnathen waved as she trotted towards the door.

Thyra wing-waved one last time and entered the room, finding the gryphons all gathered around Victor. She wondered what had happened to have Johnathen flustered, but she could just be overthinking things. Victor gave her an admonishing stare as she sat between Aadhya and Rachel. She forced herself to concentrate.

"This is our first game as a team. I want to see a strong start to this season and put our name on the board. No mercy," Victor said as he paced back and forth in front of the team. "If we can keep them at zero the entire game, then we do it. I want the league to know we mean business. We are not here to play around. We are here to win." Victor said and sat down in front of them. His black eyes looked to each player before him before spreading out his gigantic gray wings. "We are the Redtails! We will bring victory to this city and our fans. We will destroy any and all that get in our way!"

The team screeched in agreement and stamped their foretalons on the ground. Victor looked around the room and nodded approvingly at their excitement. "Well? What are you waiting for! Get out there!"

Every gryphon stood up and started towards the door, pouring out of the locker room. Thyra followed Aadhya out the door. She could hear heavy electronic music playing over the stadium speakers as they walked down the hallway.

The announcer's voice came across the speakers. "*Good evening ladies, gentlemen, and gryphons alike, it's gryphball time here in Athens*!"

The team stopped right before the exit of the hallway, and Thyra could see out into the field with the stands in the background. She took a deep breath as nervous tingles filled her body. Rachel nudged a wing against Thyra's side.

"It's exciting, isn't it?" Rachel asked, her tiny wings twitching with excitement. The cat-sized gryphoness moved in place, unable to keep still.

"Yeah, I haven't felt this nervous and thrilled in a long time. Not since my wedding," Thyra admitted and roused her feathers, forcing her tail to keep still.

"Can't say I know what that feels like, but if its anything like this, then I'm going to love it!" Rachel squawked out as Victor walked past them all to stand at the front of the group, Jason moving up next to him.

"*Let's meet this year's Athens Redtail's, led by coach Victor himself!*" The announcer said, and Victor led the march out onto the field. The crowd cheered and clapped their hands as the team ran out towards the center of the field.

Thyra looked out at the crowd and saw many seats empty but, there were still hundreds of fans in the stands. She had always wondered what it was like to be down there on the field surrounded by excited fans, but she would never imagine it would feel this good.

The announcer began to call out each of the players one-by-one as they ran across the field, waving a wing to the audience. Thyra glanced around the front rows until she saw Johnathen standing and waving to her. She smiled, immediately feeling more confident with her husband's support at her back.

The gryphons grouped up in the center of the field as the announcer gave quick backgrounds for each of the players. "*...and this year there are four new players to the team! Aadhyea, number three. Bearded vulture and rear air guard. She played in the Middle Eastern league before transferring here. Antonio, number eleven. Harris hawk and air center. He was best known in the South American league where his team took the red amulet home in 2019, 2020, and 2021. Rachel, number eight. American kestrel and air forward. Best known in Tennessee as the fiercest and fastest Kestrel in the state. And last but not least, Thyra, number thirteen. Redtail hawk and reserve air center. She's a complete rookie without previous experience in gryphball, but rookies have shocked me before! Let's hope this is the case for her.*"

The crowd cheered for their team as modern electronic music played over the stadium's loudspeakers. Now that the announcer had finished up the introduction, Victor led the team over to the dugout. Thyra and the rest followed while the announcer started to call off the players from the opposite team.

A small portion of the crowd cheered for the away team while they walked onto the field. Thyra did not recognize any of the names. They all seemed to be the average run of the mill gryphons from other gryphball teams, more redtails, such as herself, a couple eagles, other hawks and falcons.

Once in the dugout, a young human male with short red hair walked over to the starting with an open case. Thyra watched as Rachel stood up on her hindlegs and took a small teardrop shaped device from the human. She sat down and started to fit it to her eartuft, making sure it was snug.

"How does your earpiece fit?" Aadhya asked while fitting her own. Rachel flicked her eartufts a couple of times to test it.

"Perfectly! I was worried it was going to be too big, but it looks like they got the measurements right." Rachel reached up and pressed a talon to it. "Testing, testing. The quick brown gryphon jumps over the lazy dog."

"I hear you. Unfortunately," Nathanial chimed in as he walked by. He huffed and flicked his tail, then grabbed a water bottle that was offered to him by the young human and downed the contents before tossing it to the side. "Your voice is even more annoying through a speaker."

He grabbed a gryphball to tuck it under a wing and walked out onto the field. Rachel clicked her beak with agitation but did not retort back.

"What? You don't have anything to say?" Thyra asked curiously. Usually she always snapped back to him.

"Nope. I'll just show him how good I am on the field. That will show him." Rachel replied and headed out onto the field with him. She took to the skies and chirped down to him. Nathanial tossed the ball up and let Rachel swoop down to catch it. They repeated the throws, getting their muscles warmed up before the game.

"Their tongues are sharper than their talons. I think they will play well together," Aadhya said.

Thyra watched them continue their practice throws and nodded. "Yeah. They are just both hotheads." Thyra looked up at the bearded vulture. "Kind of made for each other, don't you think?"

Aadhya let out a gentle chuckle and adjusted her wings. "I agree. Perhaps we will see them grow closer together over time."

"*And the clock is ticking down! Grab your drinks and hot dogs, we have three minutes until launch*!" the announcer called out over the loudspeakers. Victor whistled to the gryphons and motioned with his wings for them to go ahead and take their positions on the field.

"Good luck out there," Thyra said to Aadhya and Antonio. Both gryphons looked back and thanked her before heading out onto the field.

Thyra sat down on the soft padding on the bench and looked at the other gryphons that were on the bench. There weren't very many: a peregrine falcon, a female osprey, and one of the corvid twins, Braden. All their eyes were on the field, except for the osprey gryphon Thyra was sitting next to. She had bright golden eyes that shone in the light. The top of her head was white with a black mask across her eyes that streaked down to her neck. The osprey looked in her direction, but did not make eye contact. Her chest feathers were a bright white that was decorated by streaks of shiny brown.

Thyra perked her ears and beak-grinned to the osprey, but the gryphoness flattened her eartufts nervously and puffed her chest feathers out.

"I'm excited for this first game, how about you?" Thyra asked the Osprey. For the life of her, she could not remember her name despite being introduced once. All she remembered was that she was quiet, and still remained quiet. "So what position are you going to play today? Well, if we get to play at all," Thyra joked.

The osprey simply looked away, putting focus on the field. Thyra saw her bright brown crest feathers rouse slightly in the wind, and she cleared her throat. She was incredibly confused, has she offended the Osprey or something?

"Don't mind her, she's just incredibly shy," the peregrine said. She had a neutral American accent and snow-white chest feathers with completely black eyes. Thyra reached out and shook the gryphon's yellow talons and roused up her crest feathers as the peregrine continued, "I'm Priscilla and that's Viola. She doesn't mean any disrespect, but it might take a while for her to warm up enough to talk."

"Well that's good! I was worried I offended her or something. I remember meeting all of you all at the beginning of training, but it's been a crazy month. Sorry, I'm just not good with names," Thyra responded and looked over the gryphoness.

The peregrine was relatively the same size as herself, but her body was less bulky. While Thyra had slight bulk and muscular structure to her, Priscilla was thin, built for speed instead of bulk. Black feathers dominated the top of her head and her beak was gray.

Thyra perked her eartfuts as a loud buzzer went off on the jumbotron overhead, signaling for the players to line up. She watched the team walk into their positions, getting ready for the launch.

"Not at all. She may be quiet now but don't let that fool you. She's one hell of a player, isn't that right, hun?" Priscilla said before leaning over to preen the ospreys white crest feathers. Viola slowly closed her piercing golden eyes and emitted a low happy trill in acknowledgement. Priscilla looked back up at Thyra and sat up straight once more. "I've seen you practicing around the field the past couple weeks. You're pretty good!"

Thyra shuffled in her seat as she took the compliment and readjusted her wings. "Ah, thanks! I've been really training hard to try to prove myself. I know I'm a rookie and have a lot of ground to cover, but I hope to be a good addition to the team."

Priscilla chuckled and nodded her head. "I understand that completely. I was the same way when I started my first gryphball team. Well, you have a lot of talent! Don't let anyone tell you that you cant do it. Keep at it."

The announcer cut off their conversation as his voice boomed over the loudspeakers. "*I hope you all are ready because it's time for the launch! Let's count it down! Three, two, one*!"

The sound of a large air cannon shook the stadium. The fans stood to their feet and cheered as the white egg-shaped gryphball flew across the field. The opposing team's rear air guard caught the ball and started to advance through the sky towards their goal.

Immediately, Thyra could tell that there was a big skill gap between second league players such as themselves and the first league teams she had watched all her life. They tossed the ball clumsily to their air forward who fumbled the ball in their talons. Rachel easily read into their movements and tackled one of the air forwards to steal the ball from them.

"*An easy tackle and possession from Redtails' eight*," the announcer called out. "*That kestrel hit him hard enough to make his wings flail like spaghetti! And away she goes*!"

Rachel easily out maneuvered the rear air guard and tossed the ball down to Nathanial, who was left wide open. Nathanial tucked the ball under his wing and advanced towards the ground goal.

"*A clean pass from air to ground*."

The opposing team's goalie landed hard on the ground and spread his wings, trying to guard the goal. Nathanial feinted one direction, causing the goalie to lose his balance, and then tossed the ball to the opposite corner of the goal. The ball soared into the net and the stadium erupted with cheers.

"*Ground goal for the Redtails! They made it look almost too easy! The Parrots have to pull out their A game if they want to stand a chance against the Redtails*."

Thyra watched Rachel swoop down to touch wings with Nathanial as the team turned to head back to their side of the field. "It looks like they have it in the bag," she commented. "We may get to play if they keep this up."

Another loud whistle went off as the thundering sound of an air cannon echoed in the stadium. Thyra watched the gryphball fly through the air, only to miss the talons of one of the rear air guards. The white egg-shaped ball bounced off the ground until it was caught by the Parrot's goalie.

"Judging how they are playing, it's going to be an easy win," Priscilla agreed.

They watched coach Victor snort at the other team's performance and clap his talons together when the team held off another pitiful offensive attempt. The Parrot's coach was a human in his earlier years, about the same age as Johnathen. He was stomping back and forth in front of their dugout, swinging his arms and yelling loudly in anger.

"It looks like my brother is getting bored out there!" Braden pointed out. The other corvid twin was sitting down on his haunches in front of their goal, adjusting his gloves as the jumbotron blasted its sirens to signal completion of the first quarter.

"I don't think he's had to move the whole game so far," Thyra agreed, and watched as Aadhya tackled one of the Parrot's air forwards. "And I don't think he's going to have to."

"*Man, these Parrots can't catch a break! Another firm tackle by Redtail's three and a pass forward*!"

Thyra watched Antonio carry the ball past the first air guard, and maneuver down to pass the ball to Jason. She did not need the screen on the jumbotron to see who it was. Her eyes were strong enough to see the feathers on his back rustle in the wind as he swooped down. Jason caught the ball with ease and dodged a rather poor tackle attempt by a ground guard.

"*Redtails' twenty-two wide open for a ground goal attempt*," the announcer commentated. Jason grabbed the ball from under his wings with his left foretalons and threw the ball past the goalie to score yet another ground goal. "*And it's good! Another ground goal for the Redtails, and with ten minutes left in the first half! Those Parrots sure are in trouble*."

"So, Thyra," Priscilla said, interrupting Thyra's concentration. "I read about what happened to your hometown a couple weeks ago."

"Oh, did you?" Thyra asked, turning to look at the peregrine curiously. The conversation had sparked the interest of Viola and her bright yellow eyes were focused on Thyra.

"Yeah. Are those cult members still in your town? Are they still trying to preach about white supremacy and all that noise?" Priscilla asked in a low voice as the crowd cheered on. Thyra glanced up to the field to watch the action for a second, and then looked back at the two gryphonesses sitting next to her.

"Sadly, yes. Johnathen, my husband, and a couple others of us have been trying to open the public's eyes about it, but they don't seem to mind The Gathering at all. They put on too much of a good guy church front. Though their last rally and putting my friend Isabell in the hospital did help somewhat as far as waking up the public, it's still not enough."

The crowd cheered and then sighed as the Redtails missed another air goal. Thyra watched the team fly across the field to take their defensive positions once more. Priscilla's talons intertwined with Viola's as she thought.

"I watched your interview on the news. It was moving. Especially for us." Priscilla looked over to Viola and they rubbed beaks against one another's. "We face somewhat of the same thing back home, but without the cult element. It's just a bunch of shelled-up minded people. People really don't have respect for gryphons, and lesbian gryphons especially. They see it as completely unnatural."

A sudden air gust blew across the gryphons faces as Antonio flew swiftly by right in front of the dugout. They all peeked their heads out to watch him bank up with the gryphball in his talons and toss it far across the field. Rachel rose up and caught it high in the air earning another round of cheering from the fans.

"Unnatural? Yeah, that's what they say about Johnathen and I." Thyra replied.

"Have you ever thought about moving?" Viola suddenly asked. Thyra blinked her eyes as the quiet osprey finally spoke up.

Her voice was so soft and gentle that Thyra had to replay the question in her head. There had certainly been times when they had wanted to pack up and leave everything behind, but they had never been able to bring themselves to do it. "We have. But I don't think we ever would. I mean it's our home, and I want to change the town. I don't want to run, I want to stay and fight."

"I understand that. It was hard for us, but we had no choice. We moved here to start a new life hoping that another city and a fresh start would be good for us, especially with the promise of playing gryphball together. We hope maybe if we become famous gryphball players, people will respect us more. And hopefully it will give other gryphons like us a voice to speak up," Priscilla explained.

A loud siren interrupted the both of them as the announcer came on. "*And that's it for the first half, folks! The Redtails are up eleven to zero*."

The team made their way towards the dugout as Victor walked to the sideline. He called for everybody to gather around with his wings. Thyra and the others stood up from their bench spot to join the rest of the team around Victor. The rear guards and Brandon, the goalie, seemed just as rested and relaxed as the minute they left the bench themselves.

Victor looked around to all the team members as he praised them. "This is fantastic. Exactly what I wanted to see. They brought out lambs for us to slaughter today, and we are making fools of them all. Provided, it doesn't make a very interesting game for the crowd, but I'm not too concerned with that right now. Since we are far ahead, I'm going to put out the reserves this next half," Victor said looking over to Thyra and the others. "Everyone needs game time. So air centers and guards, take a break this half. Let your teammates help carry the ball to victory for the day."

Thyra felt her hackle feathers rise up with excitement at the opportunity to play. She looked over to Antonio, Rachel, and Aadhya with a beak grin before receiving it back.

Victor looked down to the reserves. "With that being said, you let them get too close to scoring a goal, and I'll pull you out. Understood?"

“Yes sir!” they called out. Victor nodded his head and picked his clipboard back up.

“Good. Now everyone get a drink and get ready. You’re on in five.”

Chapter 10 Confrontation

Johnathen switched on the television which was now hanging crooked on the wall. The coffee maker beeped loudly as the weatherman talked about an incoming storm. Johnathen took one of the non-broken cups out of the cupboard and filled his mug with coffee.

The morning sun beamed in from the kitchen windows, shedding light on the littered kitchen. Various items from the drawers were scattered across the floors and countertops. He walked over to the refrigerator, avoiding the broken dishes and cutlery decorating the ground, and retrieved the creamer.

Johnathen placed the mug down and poured the creamer into it, stirring it in while staring blankly at the television. "Why do we even have weathermen anymore?" he wondered to himself.

He picked one of the barstools up off the floor and sat down, then sighed and rubbed his tired eyes. All the commotion from the break-in and having to drive to Thyra's game yesterday had left him exhausted.

He hated not telling Thyra about the break-in yet, but she had enough to worry about going to practice today after yesterday's game. He had been happy to go to her first game, and even more excited that she was able to play the last half, although she barely had possession of the gryphball during that time. The opposing team had played so poorly in the second half that the team's defenders were barely needed. In the end, the Redtails utterly destroyed the Parrots twenty-two to zero. Thyra had been able to make a couple passes and one solid tackle, but most of the game involved her hovering in place more or less.

Johnathen took a sip of the hot coffee and let the roasted fragrance calm his nerves. A knock came from the door, causing Johnathen to look up. He went to the door and moved the chair that he had wedged in front of it to keep it closed.

"Johnny! You look like hell," said Keith with a slight smile on his face. He stood on the front porch with his hands in his suit pockets.

"Yeah, no shit." Johnathen shook his head and stepped to the side, inviting him in. "And looks like you finally shaved that stupid mustache."

Keith's black hair was cut close to his scalp, much shorter than the last time he had seen him, and the scruffy mustache he usually sported was gone. Although, he had not done anything about his bushy eyebrows.

Keith laughed and slapped Johnathen's shoulder before stepping inside. "Kayla told me it had to go. Wasn't too fond of it anyways." Keith took a look around at the carnage and whistled. "Man. They really did a number on this place." He watched as Johnathen pulled the chair back in front of the door to hold it shut. "Did they take anything?"

"The computer," Johnathen said, and kicked some books out of the way as he walked into the kitchen. "Coffee?"

"Sure," Keith responded. "At least they didn't take the coffee maker. It wasn't the cheapest birthday present, ya know." He looked around the kitchen and frowned. His more playful demeanor faded as he saw several photo frames busted on the hardwood floor. "Why would they do this?"

Johnathen found another intact coffee mug and inspected it. "I think they found out I had incriminating evidence on them," he stated while filling the mug with coffee. Keith gratefully took it and sipped.

They were both silent for a minute, staring at the television as a reporter went on about a car crash from last night. "You made backups, right?" Keith asked seriously.

Johnathen shook his head. "No. I never got the chance to put them on a hard drive."

"Well, sorry to hear that. Let me know what I can do to help," Keith said and put down his coffee mug. He walked over and picked up a busted photo frame off the floor. It was a picture of Thyra and Johnathen walking in the park. Keith handed the photo over to Johnathen "I remember taking this picture. It was from the company picnic, remember? You and Thyra won the game of tug a war, which wasn't fair by the way, and won that free gift card."

"We never used that card either. It's probably still around here somewhere." Johnathen looked at the scattered mess around the kitchen and sighed. He put the photo down on the counter.

"Well, how about this. I'll help clean up but the first one to find the gift card gets to keep it. How about that?" Keith said with a little smile which made Johnathen chuckle. Keith stuck out his hand and Johnathen shook it.

"Ok. You got a deal," Johnathen said with a little more enthusiasm in his voice. Keith always had a way of turning a bad situation into a bearable one. Johnathen went into the laundry room and came back with a couple of brooms and dustpans and handed one to Keith. "So, what do you mean the tug a war wasn't fair?"

"Come on, Johnny! You know it was cheatin'! Thyra's strong as an ox!" Keith exclaimed, and began to sweep up the broken dishware, glass, and trash into a pile.

Johnathen grabbed the trashcan and moved it over to the middle of the kitchen floor. "That's not cheating. Nothing in the rules said you couldn't have a gryphoness," he pointed out as he grabbed a couple cookbooks off the floor.

Keith laughed and filled a dustpan before dumping it into the trash. "That's a lawyer for ya. Always finding a loophole to win." He looked around and raised a bushy eyebrow. "Speaking of Thyra, where is she?"

"At gryphball practice by now," Johnathen replied, picking up what dishware was salvageable.

"Does she know about this?" Keith asked.

"No. I didn't want to bother her or make her worry. It wouldn't do her any good."

"The longer you wait, the more mad she's going to be," Keith prodded.

Johnathen sighed. He was right about that one. "I'll call and tell her tonight."

Keith shrugged and went back to cleaning. They worked in silence, picking up dozens of items from the floor, and throwing away whatever was broken. They moved into the living room and continued their work.

"Well I've got some good news at least," Keith said.

"A bit of good news right now would really help," Johnathen replied as he replaced books back onto the bookcase next to the television.

"Overheard the boss talking about you. Said something about getting the paperwork together to hire you back fulltime," Keith said with a smile.

"Really? That is some good news then," Johnathen said, finally smiling back as he finished stacking the rest of the books.

Keith pointed to Johnathen's beard and wild hair. "But, you can't go back to work looking like a hipster," he said and laughed when that earned a middle finger from Johnathen. Keith threw the cushions back onto the couch. "You look like you belong in some progressive indy rock band."

"At least I can pull it off. Plus, Thyra says she likes it," Johnathen pointed out and followed Keith to the front door.

Keith leaned down and inspected the damage, looking at the inner doorframe that was split open. "Guess I can't argue with that. You know they always say, 'happy wife, happy life.'" He moved the chair out of the way to open the front door. Then he opened and closed it multiple times to check for other damage. "At least they didn't break the hinges. Just split the frame where the deadbolt was latched." Keith stood back up. "You got screws and a drill?"

"Yeah, in the garage." Johnathen walked back into the kitchen, then out the door into the garage. He flicked on the light, which illuminated the immaculately clean and organized room.

Keith followed and looked into the garage. "And they didn't touch the mustang," Keith pointed out. "I can't imagine what you would do if that happened!"

Johnathen handed Keith the drill. "I would probably be in jail for burning down that damned church," he responded, pulling out some screws and drill bits from one of the toolbox drawers. They continued back to the front door and Keith crouched down in front of it.

"Did you tell the cops that you know who did it?" Keith looked over the drill bits. He sized one up against the screws before putting it inside the drill.

"Yeah. They said they would look into it, but I doubt they will. Mathew's goons wouldn't have left the bible behind if they were worried about evidence." Johnathen pointed out and leaned against the sofa, watching Keith work. The drill fired up in a whirl before boring itself into the soft wood. Keith made multiple pilot holes through the doorframe and put the drill down once more.

"You got a point. Maybe they paid the cops to look the other way, or maybe they have a fall guy ready to take the blame." Keith pulled the bit out and replaced it with a Phillips head. "Or Matthew just don't care. He might be slipping." Keith lined up the first screw and pulled the trigger. The wood pulled together nice and tightly as Keith went down the line

"Maybe." Johnathen frowned. "And if he doesn't care anymore . . . that has me worried. It would mean he's being reckless now. Probably tired of hiding in the dark, pretending to be a righteous figure. Could be he's starting to realize his goals aren't being met. He is nothing else but driven, and that could be dangerous."

Keith finished the last screw and checked his handiwork. He stood up and closed the door, watching as it latched back into place again. "The only thing we can do is watch and wait." He gave the handle a tug and nodded when it did not move. He handed the drill back to Johnathen. "There ya go. Now you have a door that closes, at least."

"Thanks for the help, but I could have done that," Johnathen said and placed the drill on the table.

"Not without splitting the wood even more. I've seen your so-called craftsmanship," Keith sniped. "Like when you started that back deck for Thyra by yourself, and you..."

Johnathen huffed. "Alright! Alright, I get the point." He looked out the window and nerves shot through his body as he saw the same van from yesterday sitting outside on the street. A puff of smoke bellowed out of the window, and Johnathen could make out the man's face.

Keith noticed the sudden anger rising in his friend and turned to look outside. "Is that him?"

"Without a doubt." Johnathen quickly opened the door and walked down the front steps. Johnathen felt the same nervousness and anger he had felt yesterday and he clenched his fists as he approached the van. He looked to his right, and saw his neighbor outside watering the flowers. He could not make a scene right here.

The man in the van must have seen him coming, because as he drew near the window rolled down fully. Johnathen walked up to the passenger window, and saw the man calmly sitting in his car, smoking a cigarette and playing with his phone.

"Morning, Johnathen," the man said without even bothering to glance up. Johnathen grit his teeth as Keith walked up beside him to peer inside.

"Take your good morning and shove it up your ass," Keith responded.

The man looked up and sighed, staring at the two men standing at his door. The bags under his eyes were dark and he looked even more tired than he had the day before. He put down his phone. "Before y'all start yammering away, I didn't have nothin' to do with the break in." He took another drag of his cigarette and flicked it out his window.

Johnathen's eyes narrowed as he stared him down. "Then how did you know about the break in?" he asked, hands gripping the window seal.

The man looked him over before responding. "The boss ordered it, but I didn't do it."

"So your boss is Bishop Matthew," Johnathen replied, his voice rising in volume.

The man shook his head and waved him off. "That insane bigot? No. I can't stand him."

Both Keith and Johnathen were incredibly confused by this comment. They looked at each other and then back at the man. "Then what?" Johnathen began.

"Listen, you're not far off. My boss works for Matthew. Well, works with Matthew. He's not too fond of the priest either, but it pays the bills right now. I don't know what you got yourself mixed up in, son, but that guy really doesn't like ya."

"No, you don't know what you got yourself mixed up in," Keith retorted, staring at the man.

The man turned his attention to Keith and raised an eyebrow. "I've been in this field for twenty years now. I know exactly how to handle myself."

"And what field is that, exactly?" Keith asked.

"Let's call it, private investigating," the man joked with Keith, almost grinning at his own comment. This just irritated Keith and Johnathen more and the man could see it. He raised his hands. "Boys. It's not me your angry at, it's Matthew. So, if you're feelin' froggy, why don't you go down and confront him instead?"

Keith grunted and backed up. He put a hand on Johnathen's shoulder to pull him away. "Let's go back inside. This asshole isn't going to give us anything more."

Johnathen let go of the car door and looked at the man one last time. "At least tell me your name. You owe me at least that."

The man looked over Johnathen and thought for a minute. "Jack," He finally answered.

"Well, Jack, I guess I'll see you around," Johnathen said and started to walk away.

"Unfortunately for both of us, you will," Jack replied.

The moment they were both inside, Keith shut the door behind Johnathen and turned to him. "We should call the police!"

Johnathen shook his head and slumped down in his couch. "It wouldn't matter. I'm sure the Macon Police know Matthew is tailing me. They were probably paid off to turn a blind eye. That's why they barely wrote up a report for the break in." Johnathen sighed, but suddenly a small smile grew on his lips. He pulled out his phone. "But, I might have some other friends that could do something about it."

* * *

"Come on Thyra! Ten more seconds!" Jason yelled loudly.

Thyra groaned in protest, but kept her shaking wings outstretched. She was standing in the open area of the weight room, and had weights attached to her wing tips. She stood in a wide stance, breathing hard and straining to keep her wings vertical. They began to droop towards the ground.

"Keep them up! Don't let them touch the ground! Five more seconds!" the golden eagle gryphon yelled. Thyra screeched and somehow found a new energy welling inside of her. She pulled them up straight again, still trembling. Jason grinned and waited even as the seconds past. "Five more!"

"Come on!" Thyra exclaimed, but still held her wings outstretched for a few seconds more. Suddenly they collapsed to the ground and Thyra flumped down onto the mat, breathing heavily.

Jason laughed and patted Thyra on the back. "There you go! Take a minute breather, and then have a go one more time." He handed her a water bottle, which she took gratefully.

Her wing shoulders burned and protested. She felt like they had been stabbed with red-hot knives. She took a heavy drink of water and huffed through her nares. "You said that was the last time."

"Yeah, I did. But I lied," Jason said with a smile. He grabbed the water bottle from her and she struggled up on her feet one more, wings drooping on the mat.

"Ready?" He asked once more. Thyra nodded in response. "Begin!"

Thyra lifted her wings off the matt and held them out straight. She was shaking already, wings trembling with exhaustion. Thyra cursed under her breath and strained to keep them in the air. She looked over and saw Rachel approach. A towel was slung over the tiny gryphoness' back and she was carrying a water bottle in her small beak.

"Looks like you're having fun!" Rachel teased and sat down next to Jason. Thyra shot Rachel a mean glance, which only earned a chuckle from the small gryphoness.

"Keep your wings up! Twenty more seconds!" Jason shouted as Thyra's wings began to droop once more. He looked down at the Kestrel next to him and nudged her playfully. "And you, if you antagonize Thyra again, I'll make you do the same exercise but with more weight." She quickly shut her little beak and nodded.

Thyra screeched and strained again, but no matter how hard she willed it, her wings continued their slow decent towards the ground. Jason shouted at her again, but it was no use. Thyra collapsed on the mat once more and let out a loud sigh of exhaustion. She trembled, lying splayed out on the mat with wings outstretched.

"Very good, Thyra. That's it for today," Jason said. He walked over and worked off the Velcro strap holding the weights to the end of her wings.

"Thank the skies…" Thyra muttered in between her labored breaths. Rachel looked over at the weights and grinned then back at Thyra.

"You're only using ten pounds? When I do that exercise, I use twenties at the least!" Rachel taunted. Thyra scoffed and slowly got back to her feet once more.

"Yeah, it's because your wings and half as long as mine are! It's about leverage, not weight." Thyra replied and winced as she tried to fold her wings back in. She tested her wings again, slowly unfolding and folding them back again.

"Go down to recovery and make sure someone puts some ice on your wingshoulders," Jason said as he put away the weights on a weight rack. "Rest up, drink plenty of water, and be back here ready to go again on Monday."

"Have a good weekend, Jason," Thyra said and started walking towards the opposite end of the workout room. Rachel padded up alongside her, still full of energy even after working out for hours.

"I'll show you were medical is! So, what are you doing this weekend?" Rachel asked and followed Thyra out the door.

"I just want to be at home and do nothing, honestly. If I can even fly home," Thyra said. They continued down the stairs and turned left. Rachel led her down the hallway and stopped at a pair of double doors with a red cross on the front. "What about you? Going back to Chattanooga?"

"Of course! There's a music festival in town this weekend, and I want to go to it." Rachel opened up one of the doors.

There were a couple of massage tables off to the side, and giant metal bathtubs on the far wall. A human female with short red hair stood at one of the massage tables where Nathanial lay stretched out on his belly. He groaned as she opened his wing and pressed between his wingshoulders.

The woman turned to look at the two as they walked in. "Hey Rachel. Is this the new player?" she asked curiously as she folded in Nathanial's black wing.

"Yeah! This is Thyra. She needs some ice for her wingshoulders and maybe a massage, but not on that table since it's probably infested with feather mites now." Rachel stared back at Nathanial, who ruffled his hackle feathers with agitation.

Nathanial huffed through his nares. He stood up on the massage table and jumped off, settling his wings and staring at the two with his pure black eyes. "I don't have feather mites! You're the one that's infested, fish breath," he retorted. "Why don't you get Carol to spray you down, while you're here."

With that, he raised his head up high and walked between the two, making sure to shove past them as he walked out the door. Rachel turned around to watch Nathanial leave, eyes not leaving the gryphon until he was out of sight.

"What, no smart comment back?" Thyra said and noticed Rachel staring. "Wait, were you just checking him out?"

Rachel turned around quickly with a blush on her nares, staring back at Thyra. "No! As if…" Rachel huffed which made Thyra chuckle with amusement. Carol stood at the table, confused by the sudden exchange and cleared her throat politely.

"If your wingshoulders are in pain, then hop up on here and I'll take care of you," Carol said and patted the soft cushions on the massage table.

Thyra walked over and hoped up on the table before lying down on her belly. Carol carefully took a wing in her hands and stretched it out, making Thyra wince.

"So, how long have you been playing Gryphball?" Carol asked while slowly opening and closing the wing. Thyra grit her beak and took a deep breath.

"Just this week." Thyra responded.

Carol was shocked by the response and stopped for a moment, then placed a hand on her left wingshoulder. She pressed down gently, extended the wing out and gave it a sharp tug.

Thyra cursed under her breath. “I thought this was supposed to make me feel better.”

“It will, trust me. I’ve studied gryphon anatomy for eight years now,” Carol replied and tugged hard, making Thyra’s claws dig into the cushions. “So, you’ve never played gryphball before this week?” Carol asked again and folded in Thyra’s wing.

“Not really. I’ve been a fan as long as I can remember, but there weren’t any other gryphons in Macon to play with.” Thyra watched as Carol walked around to her other side and placed a hand on the opposite wingshoulder. “But I guess I have natural talent for it. That’s what Richard said.” Thyra winced again as Carol pulled on the other wing now, keeping firm pressure on her back.

“It is what your kind was created for, after all,” Carol responded and tugged again. “Being a red-tailed hawk means you can adapt to many different situations. So it’s no surprise you can play well in any position, really.” Carol slowly folded and unfolded Thyra’s wing a couple of times, inspecting the primary flight feathers for any damage.

“What about you? What did you do before this, whatever this is?” Thyra questioned. She rolled her head over and watched Carol stroke her fingers through the secondaries.

“I was a veterinarian, specialized in avians. When I graduated school, I worked for a vet hospital for a couple years and watched as the first gryphon species were created.” Carol released Thyra’s wing and walked over to a stainless freezer to retrieve a blue bag of ice. “I was mesmerized by the first pictures I saw, and immediately I wanted to work with them. I know I couldn't afford to go back to medical school to get another degree to work in a hospital, so I decided to be an athletic therapist for gryphons."

Carol placed the cold pack of ice on Thyra's wingshoulders and pressed firmly. The sudden chilling sensation caused Thyra to rouse her feathers.

"The Gryphball league quickly realized there was a huge lack of athletic therapists that understand animal anatomy, and there were job openings everywhere for them." Carol pulled out a small flashlight from her white coat pocket and turned it on. She pulled up Thyra's eartufts and peered inside. "They just saw I was experienced with avians and had a vet degree, so they pulled me in. It wouldn't be so easy nowadays. Now, they have specific degrees and courses for this type of thing."

"I guess I never thought about it," Thyra said.

Carol walked to her front and hold out a finger in front of Thyra's eyes. Carol shined the light towards her eyes and she followed the finger.

"Nobody seemed to think about it. In the beginning, sick gryphons were administered to vet hospitals. People quickly found out that gryphons are extremely more complicated than your basic avian or mammal." Carol reached forward and grabbed Thyra's beak. She pulled out a tongue depressor from her pocked and motioned with her mouth for Thyra to open her beak. "We all just adapted as quickly as we could." Carol pressed the tongue depressor into Thyra's beak and glanced inside with the light. Satisfied, she clicked off the light and threw the wooden stick into the trash.

"I thought I was in here for my aching wingshoulders," Thyra said, feeling like a lab rat once again. The sounds of running water made Thyra's eartufts perk up and she glanced over to the back. Rachel was running a bath in one of the metal tubs, testing the water temperature with a foreclaw.

"You are, but since I don't have any medical data on you yet I want to get a baseline reading on you. They really should have made you come and see me on day one of training. I've told them over and over," Carol said. She looked over Thyra's beak again and ran her finger over the curve. "You could use a beak coping. I can do that for you too, if you want."

"No, I like to have my husband do it. Sort of our thing, you know?" Thyra responded. Carol raised her eyebrows and smiled.

"Oh, well isn't that sweet. Never seen a gryphon cope another gryphons beak," Carol responded.

"Actually, he's a human. His name is Johnathen," Thyra said. Carol paused for a minute and picked up her clipboard, seeming intrigued.

"Is he now? Well that is something. Can't say I've heard of a human and gryphon couple. Congratulations." She looked down at her clipboard and began to scribble some information down. "Do you have any allergies?"

"Not that I know of," Thyra responded. She relaxed on her belly and watched Rachel climb up over the tub and lower herself into it.

"Good. Are you on any medications?"

"No."

"How many alcoholic drinks do you consume in a week?" Thyra paused for a minute and Carol glanced up from her clipboard. "Three? Four?"

"Um… Maybe four. Depends." Thyra said.

Carol nodded and scratched some more on her clipboard before putting it back down on the table. "I'm going to take a blood sample from you." Carol reached into a drawer and pulled out a package.

"Really? Come on," Thyra protested. "I hate needles."

"I'm sure you do. Seems most gryphons do. Probably because you were poked and prodded for years in the labs, but this will be quick and it will just be a little prick," Carol said.

She unwrapped the package and pulled out a syringe with a couple glass tubes. Thyra sighed and held out her arm. Carol ran her fingers up the gryphoness' scaled forearms and parted the feathers around her elbow. She held the needle steady and slowly pushed it into Thyra's skin. She bit her beak and closed her eyes.

"See? Not so bad. I'll give you a lollypop afterwards for being such a good girl," Carol teased and twisted on the glass vial. It immediately began to fill with dark purple blood. "Maybe you can tell me how many licks it takes to get to the center of a tootsie pop."

"I'm not an owl, so I don't think I could tell you," Thyra retorted.

Carol laughed and pulled off the full vial before twisting on another one. Thyra lay still for a minute more and winced as Carol withdrew the needle. She put pressure on Thyra's upper arm with a bandage and taped it down.

"There. All done." Carol said and labeled the blood vials before placing them in a rack. She removed the ice packs and set them on the counter before picking up her clipboard once again. Thyra slowly stood up and stretched out on the table before hopping down.

"Try to keep your wings moving this weekend. Stretch them out periodically through the day and ice them before bed. Keep flying to a minimum and don't overstrain yourself. You should be good as new by Monday," Carol instructed.

Thyra opened and closed her wings a couple of times and found that they felt better already. "Well looks like I'm not flying back to Macon today."

"I would advise against that, but I can't stop you." Carol put down the clipboard and opened up a drawer to pull out a lollypop. Thyra looked up and laughed.

"I thought you were joking," Thyra said and took the lollypop from her.

"Usually I am, but I did take some blood. The sugar will help you from feeling lightheaded."

"Thanks." Thyra unwrapped the lollypop and stuck it into her beak. She looked over to Rachel who was relaxing in the tub and waved to her. "See you Monday!" Thyra called out.

Rachel lazily waved back as Thyra left through the doors. She walked down the hallway and into the locker room. There were some gryphons leftover from practice, discussing their weekend plans and gathering up their things.

Aadhya walked out of the shower room and looked over to Thyra. “Ah. How was your weight training today?” She opened up her locker and gathered some casual clothing.

“It was good I guess,” Thyra replied. “Jason kicked my tailfeathers. I feel like my wingshoulders have been clawed out. Carol told me not to fly home today, so I have to ask Johnathen to come drive me home.”

She opened up her locker and withdrew her clunky cellphone before turning it on. Aadhya threw on a shirt over her head, and worked it over her wings until they were through the openings on the shirt’s back.

“You plan on going home this weekend then,” Aadhya said with a little disappointment. She started pulling on a pair of slacks, working one foot in and then the other.

“Yeah. I just want to be at home with Johnathen. What are you going to do this weekend?” Thyra asked curiously. Her phone booted up and began to ding with missed text messages. Thyra scrolled through the messages, there was one from Johnathen, and another from Isabell.

“Cooking and cleaning mostly. I need to go to the grocery store, and perhaps a bit of reading. Nothing exciting.” Aadhya shut her locker and walked over to Thyra.

“Sounds about what I’ll be doing.” Thyra responded and opened up the text from Johnathen first.

Call me whenever you’re done with practice.

Thyra closed the message and opened the one from Isabell.

Hey! You better visit me this weekend. And bring me another one of those burgers Johnathen had. I can't stand to eat another damn sloppy joe.

Thyra chuckled and locked her phone, then looked up at the bearded vulture. "Well, if you want to come over for dinner, just call me. I'm sure Johnathen would love to talk to you. You two didn't really get to meet last time."

Aadhya smiled warmly and bowed her head. "That would be delightful." She stood to leave. "I will be available. Please do give me a call."

"I will. Bye, Addy." Thyra watched her exit through the door and picked her phone back up. She dialed Johnathen and put the phone to her ear.

"Hey hun… Yeah it was good! But I'm so sore. The therapist here told me not to fly much this weekend… I don't want to make you drive all this way but I do want to come home. Ok! Well I'll see you in a couple hours…. John, you sound upset, is everything ok?... Why can't you tell me right now?... Ok, we can talk when you get here then…. Love you too." Thyra hung up and looked at her phone, confused. "I wonder what's going on."

Chapter 11 Lashing Out

"Johnny! What's up… what? That asshole, again?...Yeah, we'll take care of him… Jack's his name? Got it…Alright, we are on the way." Saul hung up the phone and flicked his cigarette butt into a butt bucket.

A cool autumn breeze blew through his long, graying beard and made it whisk about as he stood up from a bench and looked up into the clear afternoon sky. He rubbed his tired eyes and turned to walk back toward the hospital's entrance.

Saul and Carl had spent the past couple of nights at the hospital with Isabell, making sure she had company and was kept safe. Saul was fairly certain that no one would try to harm Isabell in the hospital, but it was precautionary. He walked through the entrance room and into the elevator. A couple standing inside looked at him strangely as the big biker joined them and Saul gave them a polite nod. He left the elevator after reaching the second floor and proceeded down the hallway to enter Isabell's room.

"You smell like cigarettes," Isabell commented. The small black gryphoness flipped through the television stations. "I would kill to get out of this bed and have one."

"Maybe this hospital stay will help you quit. Lord knows I need to," Saul replied and looked over to Carl. "That dude in the van is back at Johnathen's house. We need to go pay this man a visit."

Carl looked up from his phone and stood up, giving him a nod in reply.

Isabell's eartufts pinned back against her head and she glanced over at Saul. "Well, teach him a lesson and hurry back. You know I don't like to be alone."

"I'll have one of the other boys come keep you company," Saul said, and opened the door for Carl as he smiled warmly to Isabell. "We'll be back tonight. If you want us to pick up anything, just give us a holler."

"Alright. You all be careful." Isabell said, beak grinning back as the two left the room. The loud stomps of their boots echoed in the hallway.

"We ain't going to rough him up. We're just going to have a polite and civil conversation," Saul said to Carl. The big man nodded his head again and went into the elevator. "But, if he doesn't seem too keen on having a conversation, we'll have to find another way to get our point across . . . without violence."

Once the elevator reached the ground floor they both exited . The bikers walked outside and adjusted their leather jackets embroidered with their crew's name. "Just follow my lead."

Saul and Carl put on their half helmets and mounted their Harleys. Both bikes fired to life, causing an eruption across the once quiet hospital parking lot. They took off down the street, engines roaring and echoing between the buildings. They turned onto the highway and rode side-by-side, heading towards Johnathen's house.

A short time later, the bikers pulled into the neighborhood and spotted the white Sprinter van parked outside. They pulled up in front of it before shutting their bikes off. Johnathen and Keith came out of the front door when they heard the sounds of their motorcycles.

Saul did not look over at them, but instead focused on the man sitting inside the van. Confrontation came easy for Saul. He could be intimidating and still keep his composure under control, for the most part. The burly bikers dismounted their Harleys and walked over to the van window.

Jack rolled down the window and glanced over at the approaching men before letting out a deep sigh. "Afternoon, fellas."

"Afternoon, Jack," Saul remarked. Carl stood next to him, and folded his arms together, making him seem even bigger. Saul took of his half helmet and tucked it under his arm. "It seems you are bothering my friend over there," he stated clearly in a deep tone.

He looked over the man, seeing how small he was in comparison. Surely, just the presence of two bikers that were twice his size would be enough to scare the man, but Jack just stared back with emotionless eyes.

"I ain't done him no harm. Just doing my job," Jack replied. He ran his hand through the short buzzed strip of his brown hair. "I guess you fellas are here just to back him up. I'm kind of surprised. Wouldn't have guessed Johnathen hung out with bikers."

Saul grinned slightly and leaned forward on the window seal. “It’s not exactly that. You see, a gryphoness friend of ours has really taken a liking to Thyra and Johnathen. So that makes us friends by association.” Saul reached into his pocket and withdrew a cigarette pack. “Mainly, we like to look after those that can’t look after themselves. We like to think of it as a kind of charity. Helpin’ those that need protection.”

Saul handed Carl a cigarette and light one up himself. He took a deep breath and blew the smoke into the cabin of the van, but Jack did not seem fazed. He glanced back and saw Johnathen and Keith walking in their direction, and held up a hand to stop them.

They halted before reaching the van and Saul gave them a serious look. He did not need them to come over and start yelling at Jack. It would only stir up more trouble.

Jack looked up to Saul and then to Carl. “Does your friend talk much?”

Saul glanced at Carl, before turning his attention back to Jack. “None, actually. I asked him why, once. He told me, for the first and last time, he doesn’t believe words are greater than actions. And that was it. Hasn’t said a word since.” Saul took another drag of his cig and blew it into the cabin once again. He stared directly into Jacks black eyes. “Now, I don’t want to let him express himself the way he knows best, so I was hopin’ you and I could come to an agreement.”

After a couple of long seconds, Jack leaned back in his seat and gave him a nod. “Listen. I was just hired to watch Johnathen and report what I saw. I’m not here to stir up trouble.”

Saul nodded. "I get you. And I can see your quandary. Your problem though is that, in our opinion, following our friend around and reporting his business? That's the very definition of stirring up trouble."

"I understand." Jack reached for his keys and clicked the ignition on. The diesel engine grumbled to life and Jack put the car in drive. "The pay ain't worth dealing with you fellas. I'll take my leave."

Satisfied, Saul stepped back from the vehicle. "I appreciate you going quietly."

Jack glanced back over and rolled the window back up. The van slowly drove away, leaving Johnathen and Keith to gawk at the two bikers.

"Really? It was that easy?" Keith asked.

Saul shrugged his shoulders and put his helmet back on the bike. "The Carl speech works most of the time. Somethin' about a big man that doesn't speak unsettles people. But honestly, Carl is a big teddy bear. He wouldn't hurt a fly." Saul stuck his rugged hand out to shake Keith's hand. "Don't think we've met yet. I'm Saul, and this here is Carl."

Keith shook his hand and went to shake Carl's. "Nice to meet you. Uh, how do you know Johnathen?"

"Well, as I said to Jack, we are good friends of Isabell. And since Thyra and Isabell are pretty good friends now, Johnathen just ended up lumped in with em." Saul laughed and walked over to Johnathen, giving him a rough slap on the back. Johnathen tensed up from the slap and Saul chuckled. "Oh, I'm just kidding. We've grown to like Johnathen, even though he can be a stick in the mud."

Saul flicked his cigarette into the street and looked over to Carl. "Well, seeing that our work here is done, we're going to go get some shuteye." Carl nodded with agreement.

"You all don't want to come in for coffee?" Johnathen asked.

Saul turned around to look back at Johnathen. For the first time, Johnathen noticed the dark bags under his eyes. Clearly, the biker was extremely exhausted.

"Gonna take a rain check on that, pal. We've been with Isabell all night, and I'd like to take a shower and sleep in my own bed."

"Hey, I really appreciate it," Johnathen stated.

"Any time. Let us know if that fella comes back, but I don't think he will." Saul smiled and walked with Carl towards their bikes.

Harley engines exploded to life with a fury of sound as they took off down the once quiet neighborhood street. Moments later, the sound of a hawk scream came from Johnathen's pocket and he pulled out his phone.

"You have Thyra's text tone as a hawk scream?" Keith asked with a slight chuckle.

Johnathen shrugged his shoulders and began to type away on his smart phone. He finished up his text and locked his phone. "Thyra's done with practice. She said she had to go to the team's therapist because her wings were sore and now she can't fly home."

"So, is she staying up in Athens again?" Keith asked and followed Johnathen back inside the house. He shut the door behind him and deadbolted it shut.

"No. I'll go get her. Plus I would rather tell her about all this mess in person. She's not going to be-." Johnathen was interrupted by a phone call. He glanced at his phone and then showed the screen to Keith. It was their boss, Dean Homer.

Excitement grew in Keith's eyes and he motioned for Johnathen to answer. With a deep breath, Johnathen answered and put the phone to his ear.

"Mr. Homer… I'm well, how about you?...So they finally dismissed the case?... Yeah, that is really good news… I would love to… See you Monday then?...Alright, have a good weekend." Johnathen hung up the phone and pumped his fist in the air. "I'm back on the job!"

Keith laughed with him and threw his arms around Johnathen in a quick hug, slapping him on the back. "Hell yeah! What did I tell ya!"

Johnathen let out a sigh of relief. "Thank God! It's about time. Funds were starting to get pretty low around here. I mean, all I did was punch that guy in the face. I didn't know it would turn into this. But I'm just glad to be back."

Keith walked over to the dry bar and pulled out two crystal glasses and a bottle of whiskey. "Well this calls for a little celebration." Keith popped the cork off and poured a generous shot for the both of them.

"This early in the afternoon?" Johnathen teased and took the glass that was offered.

Keith chuckled and clanked their glasses together. "Its five o clock somewhere."

"True." Johnathen downed the shot and put his glass back down on the bar top. "Alan Jackson always did know best."

Keith took the glasses and started to pour another one. He gave Johnathen a questioning look. "I always thought it was Jimmy Buffet."

Johnathen quickly shook his head and pulled his empty glass away. "Only one right now. I have to go get Thyra." He put his glass in the sink and turned to Keith, who slammed back another shot and let out a content sigh.

"Fair enough. Well, maybe we can grab dinner tonight," Keith suggested before walking out to the garage.

Johnathen followed behind him and nodded. "I'll talk to Thyra. She may be too tired, but we'll play it by ear."

Keith gave a thumb up and opened up the door to his black BMW. "Sounds good. If nothing else, I'll see you Monday."

* * *

"What do you mean, 'they ran you off?' Did they pull you out of the van and beat you? Did they try to chase you down and you fled?" Daniel ranted and rubbed his temples.

Jack leaned against the Van and took another drag of his cigarette. Clouds began to roll over the empty church parking lot, followed by a cold breeze.

"Like I told you, these bikers made it clear that I wasn't to be around them anymore." Jack looked over to Daniel expressionless and shrugged his shoulders. "It ain't worth the pay to deal with a biker gang."

Daniel thought for a minute, standing in silence. "Matthew isn't going to be pleased, but you're right. Just lay low for a while and I'll see what we can do."

Jack dropped his cigarette butt on the ground and stomped it out. "Sounds like a plan." He opened the door to his van and hopped inside.

Daniel walked back towards the church building as the van drove away. He entered through the double glass doors and into the welcome hall, then proceeded down the long hallway off to the side that led back into Matthew's office. Letting out a sigh, he knocked on one of the sturdy wooden doors.

"Come in," came Matthew's voice from the other side. Daniel stepped inside the low lit office and shut the door behind him. The old preacher didn't look away from his computer monitor. "Do you have an update for me?"

Daniel sat down in the one of the chairs opposing the desk. "Yes. The cops were called last night, as expected."

Matthew turned his attention fully on Daniel and folded his wrinkly hands. "And?"

"The report was a simple house burglary with minimal damage. Nobody will look further into it," Daniel assured him. "I spoke to the police chief to make sure it wouldn't get any further than that."

Matthew nodded and leaned back into his leather chair, causing it to creak and moan. "Chief

Adams is an easy one. He usually accepts the bribes without hesitation, as long as the pay is substantial enough to fit the crime."

"My tail man reported that Johnathen went to visit the gryphoness, Isabell, in the hospital. If that is worth noting," Daniel went on.

Matthew waved his hand off and snorted through his nose. "I still can't believe they let those filthy creatures into the hospital with regular human beings. It's insufferable. Anything else?"

Daniel twiddled his thumbs and nodded. "Yes, it seems my tail man ran into some trouble today. He was confronted by a biker gang."

Matthew raised a curious eyebrow to this. "A biker gang? What business did they have with your man?"

"It would seem they are friends of the gryphons, and Johnathen," Daniel explained.

"You need to get rid of them, especially if they are the same ones that assisted in the rally," Matthew said in a serious tone. "I do not want them to gather more disbelievers and spread lies to slander this church."

Daniel sat for a minute, trying to figure out what to say next. "How do you suggest I get rid of them? Because if you are insisting on physical harm, that is something we are not prepared to do."

Matthew slammed his fist down on the desk and pointed a finger at him. The look of rage that instantly came over the man's face caused Daniel to freeze in surprise. "If you can find another way of getting them to back off, then so be it but you will do what I ask! I hired you to deal with this. Do not force me to find your replacement."

"Yes, of course. I'll find a solution to this," Daniel responded quickly.

Matthew's wrinkled angry face returned to its usual passive state once again. He sat back in his chair and waved Daniel off. "Then we are done here." He turned his attention back to the computer, ending the conversation.

Daniel stood up slowly and turned to leave.

"Do not fail me," Matthew warned one last time.

"Yes, Sir," Daniel replied and closed the door behind him.

"Asshole." He muttered under his breath and pulled out his phone. This was not what he had been hired to do. Sure, he was used to the job changing from time to time depending on what the client needed, but inflicting harm was going too far.

Daniel thought for a minute and pulled out his phone. He would have to go consult with the bikers himself. Scowling, he walked out of the hallway and through the double doors before starting a text message to Jack and Cassie.

Matthew wants us to 'get rid' of the bikers. I told him what he was saying was ridiculous, but he demanded it. I don't know what else to do besides going to talk to them. We need to see where they hang out at, and approach them there.

This was all becoming a huge headache and Jack's words came back to him. Daniel repeated the phrase out loud to himself. "This isn't worth the pay."

Not only that, but he was being asked by a crazed man to do whatever necessary to get rid of innocent citizens.

Daniel sighed and unlocked his Acura before getting a message. He sat down inside and pulled his phone out to check the message from Cassie.

Fine. I'll assist. You will need a pretty face anyways, but this doesn't go any further.

Soon after, a message chimed from Jack.

Same. This is getting to be too much. I'll find where they hang out, but I ain't speakin' to them fellas again.

Daniel locked his phone and sat back in his seat, rubbing his temples again. The only thing he could hope for is this conversation going over smoothly. It would be unlikely these bikers would take a bribe to abandon their friends, but it was worth a shot. It was the only angle he had.

Chapter 12 Beasts In The Lord's House

"What!" Thyra screeched in the cramped car. Johnathen winced and covered his right ear as the piercing sound vibrated inside. "They broke into our house?!" Thyra's hackle feathers rose up in irritation. She clicked her beak and stared dead at Johnathen. "Why did you not tell me yesterday?"

"I didn't want to distract you from the game and worry you. I just…"

"They are the ones that should worry! I swear to the skies I'm going to rip out their damn throats! Every last one of those Gathering creeps is dead!" Her beak clicked again as she huffed through her nares.

Johnathen reached over to stroke Thyra's neck as they drove down the interstate. "As much as I would like to see that, I don't want to see you in prison for the rest of your life."

He felt Thyra pull away from his hand. She stared out the window. The sun was slowly setting in the cloudy sky, casting a dark shadow on the rolling hills. "And they have a tail on you too? Watching everything we do?"

Johnathen nodded. She huffed and ruffled her feathers, slumping back into the seat.

"This is ridiculous!" Thyra said, then grumbled something and closed her eyes to calm herself. "We have to do something. We can't just let them step all over us like this anymore." Thyra exhaled and leaned into Johnathen's hand and rubbed her beak along his palm. "They've gone too far."

Johnathen rubbed along Thyra's beak for a moment before returning his hand to the steering wheel. He turned on the turn signal and merged over to take the next exit. "Well, I got Saul and Carl to scare the guy off anyways. I don't think we'll see him again."

"How can you be so sure?" Thyra questioned.

He hesitated for a couple seconds, focusing on the road. The car came to a stop at a red light off the exit ramp, and Johnathen closed his eyes. "I can't."

He drove on down the road as the light turned green. The car was silent for a couple minutes more as thoughts raced in their heads.

"I'm going down there tomorrow," Thyra said, breaking the silence.

Johnathen shook his head. "No. That's not a good idea. We need-."

Thyra's voice quickly turned into a screech once more. "We've tried everything else! What the hell are we supposed to do now?! Roll over and let them stomp on our throats? I'm tired of it!"

Johnathen grit his teeth and clenched on the steering wheel tighter until his knuckles turned white. "NO!" he yelled.

Thyra pulled her head back and stared at him blankly. He never lost his temper with her. She narrowed her avian green eyes and stared back at him as he glanced over.

"I said no," he said more calmly. "I'm not having you go down there and stir up more trouble with that bastard."

"Damn it, John! That's why they walk all over us! We act so weak and..."

Johnathen pulled the car over to the side of the road and slammed on the brakes. She gasped and the seat belt tugged at her chest, making her wince. Johnathen looked over to her and bit his lip, pointing at her with a finger. She realized that his expression wasn't filled with anger, but with fear.

He laid his hand on her foreclaw and sighed before looking back up into her eyes. "I...I don't want anything to happen to you. I can stand to lose my job, our house, and all our possessions, but I can't lose you." He touched the wedding ring on her finger, then brought his hand up to cup her cheek. "I don't know what they are truly capable of, and if you waltz into his sanctuary, his home, the territory he controls most, I don't know what he will do."

Thyra looked back at him, and her eartufts folded back against her skull. Her brown and white plumage sank close to her body and she looked away for a minute. "I don't know either. But we have to do something."

Thyra took a deep breath and looked back over to Johnathen. He gave her a nod and put the car back into drive to proceed back down the road.

"We will figure it out. But we can't go marching into there." Johnathen turned into their neighborhood and putted down the road. "It would make us seem desperate too," he added as he pulled into their garage. They both unbuckled and threw the car doors open. "Let's just drop it for now and enjoy a nice dinner. Sound good?"

Thyra's beak slowly curved into a smile and she nodded. "Yeah. It's just nice to be home with you."

She followed behind him, talons clicked along the concrete floor as they entered the house together. It had felt like ages since the last time she been in her home. The familiar smell of cinnamon filled her lungs from the automatic fragrance dispenser that was always plugged into the wall.

The house was spotless and the granite countertops gleamed from the light. Thyra looked around. "I guess I figured this place would still be a mess."

"Keith came over to help me out the next day. They didn't break too much, but it still took all day to put everything away again." He opened the stainless steel doors and pulled out a package of steaks, wrapped in brown paper. Thyra perked her eartufts as he unwrapped them. "I went to Zach's butcher shop today and picked this up for you." He said, changing the subject.

"How is Zach, anyway? I haven't seen him in a couple weeks." Thyra said, her beak already watering.

"He's good. Cracking jokes and always laughing, as usual. Asked how his favorite beast was. Told him all about you getting the position for the gryphball team and he gave us these steaks to me as a congratulation present." Johnathen said.

"Well that's nice of him. I'll have to go by the shop and say thank you." Thyra replied.

Johnathen pulled out a pan from the cupboard and turned on the oven, setting it to his desired temperature. He threw butter into the pan and Thyras eartufts perked at the sound of sizzling butter in the hot pan.

"I'll be back. I'm going to go shower," Thyra said and Johnathen nodded.

She passed through her bedroom into the spacious bathroom. Thyra sighed and looked at her disheveled appearance in the mirror. Her crest feathers were sticking out this way and that, along with the ragged looks of her wings.

Thyra went over to turn the shower on and sat back down in front of the mirror. She pulled her cellphone out from the pouch around her neck and opened up the sliding keyboard. She began typing out a message to the Aadhya, Antonio, and Rachel.

I am going to confront Matthew tomorrow. Can anyone back me up?

She sat the cellphone down next to the sink and started to work the spandex uniform off of her feathered form. It was a struggle to get out of, as usual. The gryphon had to mind her wings and work the uniform off without cutting it with her talons. By the time she was done, her feathers were a heaping mess. She threw the well-worn uniform into the laundry basket and looked over to her phone to see it light up with another message.

It was from Aadhya. *I will be there. Tell me time and place.*

Thyra smiled, knowing she could count on her any time. She opened the keyboard back up and typed in the response. *Noon. Macon city hall.*

Thyra closed her phone again and saw the steam building up on the glass in front of her. She quickly hopped in the shower and made it quick, not wanting Johnathen to wonder what was taking her so long. She cut off the shower and hopped out with a ruffle of her feathers. She felt like a whole new bird once again. As she dried off with a towel, the phone vibrated again, this time with a message from Antonio.

I will also be there. Although, I must ask if you have a plan.

Thyra took a deep breath, thinking once more. No, she really did not have a plan. She just wanted to show Matthew that she was not going to tolerate being walked all over anymore, by any means necessary. She wasn't going to admit that, though. *A little bit of a plan, yeah.*

She closed the phone. Thyra walked back out into the bedroom and into the kitchen. The heavy smell of pan-fried meat was thick in the house, which only made Thyra's beak water even more.

"It smells amazing," Thyra commented and stood next to the island where Johnathen was cooking.

"Yeah it does. Zach marinated these for twenty-four hours. What he puts in the marinade is unreal," Johnathen replied.

He picked up a pair of tongs and flipped the meat over in the pan, causing the sizzling to grow louder. The oven beeped as it reached temp and Johnathen pulled out an iron skillet from the cupboard.

He picked up the sizzling steaks with his tongs before placing them in the iron skillet. "I didn't have any sweet potatoes, so I just had to whip up some instant potatoes."

The meat was slightly charred on each side, with a lot of raw pink showing through from the sides. Thyra could eat them just like that and love every bite, but he always insisted they were better once they were medium rare. He put a generous helping of butter on top of the strips and threw them in the oven. "And I forgot the green beans. So it's just meat and potatoes," Johnathen added and wiped his hands off with a paper towel.

"You know I don't like vegetables anyways. I wish I could just eat nothing but meat," Thyra said as she took another deep breath of the rich scent clouding the air.

The smoke detector suddenly started to scream loudly which made them both curse. Thyra ran over to the one detector chirping and started to fan a wing towards it. Johnathen opened up a window and a cold breeze blew in, bringing the fresh smell of leaves and quickly approaching fall. Within seconds, the smoke detector stopped its annoying siren.

Thyra rubbed her eartuft, still hearing the ringing. "I hate these stupid things!"

Johnathen shrugged and moved the pot of instant potatoes off the burner. "Yeah, but I would hate not to have them when we needed them." He pulled the wooden spoon out to taste test the potatoes. He thought for a minute and opened up the fridge to retrieve sour cream. "And I hope we never do need them."

Johnathen scooped out some sour cream and dumped it into the pot, giving it a good mix. “Anyways, how has practice today?”

Thyra shrugged her wing shoulders. “It’s alright. A lot of a hard work! Just glad to have the weekend off before the next game on Monday. My wings are so sore, and I’m exhausted every night, but it’s still a lot of fun. Everyone seems nice and wants to work as a team. They have been helping me out a lot.” She watched as he finished up and went back to the fridge. “I’m hoping I can start and not be a bench warmer by the end of the season, but I am new, so we’ll see.”

“You know I’ll be there to cheer you on.” Johnathen opened up the fridge and put the sour cream back before retrieving two bottles of beer. He handed one to Thyra, who quickly jerked the cap off with her beak. He smiled and grabbed a bottle opener to crack off the top of his beer. “Do you think you can get extra tickets? I’m sure Keith would love to go too.”

Thyra poured the light beer into her beak and swallowed, considering the question. “Honestly I don’t know. I’ll call Victor,” she replied.

The beeping from the oven interrupted their conversation. Johnathen put on an oven mitt and reached in to pull the smoking skillet of meat out. The heavenly aroma filled the air once again as he put the skillet down on the stovetop.

“Your first game was amazing. You did so well! It was nice to have front row seats to see my wife kicking ass and taking names.” Johnathen smiled and looked over at Thyra, who quickly beak-grinned back.

"I really didn't do that much! We were so far ahead that the Parrots just felt completely defeated. They barely crossed the half field line while I was out there. But who knows? Hopefully next game I can kick really some ass for you."

"Now that's the gryphoness I know," Johnathen said before putting the steaks on plates. "So, in other good news, Keith told me when he was helping me clean up that work wants me back since all charges were dropped."

Thyra's eartufts perked up at the good news. "Oh! That is awesome! I'm so happy to hear it." She grabbed the steak with her talons and brought it to her beak to tear off a chunk of juicy flesh. She swallowed it quickly and let out a gentle trill as the flavors rolled across her tongue. "Skies, that is good."

"Told you. That marinade Zach has been trying lately is killer," Johnathen said.

"But I know you have been going a little crazy without a daily routine. You happy to go back?" Thyra asked.

"Yeah! You know me, a workaholic." Johnathen stood at the island counter with Thyra. He opened a drawer in front of him to retrieve a fork and knife. "It sucks that I lost some of my current cliental, but I don't think my reputation took a detrimental hit. I should have clients again by the end of next week," Johnathen said before slicing into the rare steak. He brought the piece up to his eyes with the fork and looked it over, watching the blood drip down onto the paper plate.

The sound of ripping flesh brought Johnathen's eyes up to see Thyra rip into the steak again. Her beak shined with the butter and juices. Much to Thyra's relief, any expectation for manners had gone out the window long ago.

She found it troublesome to use cutlery, and Johnathen always found it amusing to watch her try to eat 'normally.' Johnathen placed the piece in his mouth and slowly chewed, savoring the taste while Thyra devoured half the steak in a minute.

"Clients by the end of the week? Not with the shape you're in now," Thyra said while motioning with a dirty talon to his scruffy beard and long hair. She let out a gentle chuckle. "You look like a progressive rock band player. I mean I like it, but it's not very professional."

"You know, Keith said the same thing!" Johnathen laughed and cut up another piece before pointing the knife at Thyra. "Fine, I'll book an appointment with Manny at the barber shop tomorrow."

Perfect. Thyra thought to herself. She needed him away for a while. She did not want him to know she was going to confront Matthew. "Good. I'll book him for you after we finish dinner."

* * *

Thyra looked over her wingshoulders and banked gently in the cool air. She had to beat her wings more frequently from lack of the warm thermals keeping her afloat. She stretched out her long white and almond brown wings, testing them. They were still sore, but she could fly on them now that she a good night's sleep.

Johnathen had gone out to buy a new suit and get his hair cut for his first day back to his job and left her alone at the house. It had been perfect. Now she could meet her friends and confront Matthew without him knowing.

She looked down at the bustling little city bellow. There was a market going on in the town's center where the fight between the Gathering and the protesters had erupted not long ago. Cars decorated every parking space available on the streets and the trees were starting to show their brown and orange colors. She spotted a small crowd of people around the city hall as she approached, and realized what the commotion was all about.

Aadhya and Antonio both stood at the city hall's steps, talking to each person that seemed to want to converse with them. She felt a bit of panic at first, bit from afar, it did not look violent or any way negative. After all, Thyra's friends had also been in the news on the day of that rally. Not only that but they were growing in popularity among those that followed the Second League gryphball teams.

Thyra landed softly a couple yards away from the crowd, which caused a couple of them to turn and look at her. A young man smiled and ran over to her, holding a smart phone up. "Thyra! We saw you playing for the Athens Redtails in the first game of the season! What can we expect out of you in Friday's game?" the reporter asked and held his phone out towards her beak.

Thyra blinked her big green eyes and looked surprisingly at the brown haired guy. "Y…yeah. I was excited to get to play in my first game with the Redtails.

I felt fortunate to have Coach Victor's confidence in me. I, uh, hope we have a good game on Friday and I hope to perform well for my team." Thyra nervously swallowed hard and forced herself to beak grin back to the reporter.

He pulled his phone away and clicked something on the screen before putting it back into his pocket. "Thanks for the comment! You don't mind if I publish it, do you?"

Thyra shook her head. "Not at all. Go ahead."

The reporter smiled and thanked her before making his exit. The small crowd slowly dispersed from around Aadhya and Antonio after getting their comments and pictures. Thyra walked over to the other gryphons.

"I didn't expect that at all," she said.

"You will see more of this as the season begins to heat up," Antonio replied and sat down on his haunches. He was wearing a casual colorful button up top and a pair of khakis. Aadhya was sporting an informal red top, which covered most of her body besides the long white feathers around her feet.

There was a long silence between them as the group watched everyone else leave. "Thyra, are you sure about this?" Aadhya questioned, breaking the silence. The great bearded vulture looked down at Thyra with her bright red and yellow eyes.

Thyra looked back up and nodded. "Absolutely. The reason Matthew keeps on threatening us and walking around on us is because we seem weak. I want to go there and let him know that I've had enough."

Thyra said, feeling more empowered with her friends at her side.

Both Antonio and Aadhya looked to one another and then back down to Thyra. "Does Johnathen know about this?" Aadhya asked in her smooth steady tone. Thyra shook her head.

"No. When I told him I was going to do it, and he got really angry. So I lied and said I wouldn't," Thyra replied and gave them both a determined stare. "Trashing our house was the final straw. As long as we don't get physical, I don't think this can come back to haunt me. I think we can scare him a little bit. The stupid old man's never faced three gryphons at once."

"Or this could anger him further," Aadhya pointed out. She was always the voice of reason, but Thyra had made her mind up.

"Yeah, but I don't know what else to do, and we are already here, except Rachel, but I think that's for the best," Thyra said. She took a deep breath. "Are you all ready?"

Both gryphons nodded. Thyra turned around and ran with her wings outstretched. With a hard wing beat, she was in the air, Antonio and Aadhya following close behind.

The Gathering's church was towards the outer edge of the city, and would be a short flight. They flew side-by-side, and conversed about what little plan they had. Soon they were landing in the large and mostly empty parking lot outside of the church. There were a few cars parked close to the entrance, but that was it.

Thyra took in the extensive structure before her. Already, her blood had begun to boil and her hackle feathers rose with irritation. Matthew had disguised this cult so well; painting the hatred it hid inside with a fresh coat of white paint. The hypocrites had erected large crosses outside in the front lawn, making them seem as harmless as any other church.

She clicked her beak with agitation and drew in one more deep breath through her nares before walking forward. The double glass doors to the main entrance were open, allowing access into the main spacious greeting room. The gryphons' talons clicked along the tile floor, echoing in the chambers.

Just being inside the church made Thyra's crop sour. She felt nauseous and her feathers tightened in against her body. The band stood silently, looking around for any sign of movement.

"Thyra, there is a sign that says offices this way," Antonio said quietly, pointing out with his foretalon. "He could be back there, if he is here at all."

"I know he's here. I can feel it!" Thyra hissed gently under her breath and turned down a hallway where the sign pointed.

She stopped at a set of doors and gently opened them, peering inside. They were at a side entrance to the main chapel room. Light poured in from the stain glass windows from the opposite wall. The room was eerie even in the colorful light. Pews sat empty in perfect rows in a half circle facing the stage. Thyra stepped back and let the door slowly close on its own.

"It seems to be just the same as any modern church." Antonio commented, also getting a look inside.

"In a way, I find it disturbing," Aadhya observed.

"Tell me about it." Thyra said and continued back down the hallway.

Her heart began to beat faster in her chest, thinking that anyone could come out at any time. The claws and talons from the small group of gryphons clicked and reverberated in the cramped confines of the corridor. Aadhya's wings touched either side of the walls and scrapped gently against them as they walked. Thyra's eartufts twitched as she stopped at another door.

Aadhya and Antonio both stopped with Thyra and perked their eartufts as well. "Do you hear that?" Thyra asked. The sounds of metal chain scrapping along the ground and a gentle groan came through the door.

"Yesm" Both of them responded, thoughts racing as to what was behind the door.

Thyra reached for the door handle, and tried to open it, but it was no use. They were all so concentrated on what lied behind the door that they did not hear the footsteps of two men approaching.

"Beasts," one of the men said.

They were both wearing black suits and ties. All three gryphons turned their heads and stared directly at the two men. They stood calmly before the gryphons, and showed no sign of a threat, despite the aggressive nature of the comment.

"Come with us." The same bald man spoke again.

"Where would we be going?" Thyra questioned, taking an assertive step forward and pushing her chest out. Both men looked at her without flinching.

"To see Bishop Darnwall." The men began to walk away from them, leaving the gryphons behind.

Thyra turned to Antonio and Aadhya, who both nodded in agreement. The band began to follow the two men down the curved hallway.

"This is what we came to do, after all. They are leading us straight to him." Antonio said as he continued to watch the men.

"Yeah but how did they know we were here?" Thyra asked the two of them.

Both gryphons shrugged their shoulders in response to Thyra's question. They came to a stop in front of a set of large wooden double doors. The two men stood on opposite ends of the doors and opened them. Thyra stopped and glared at the two men who simply motioned for them to step inside.

"I don't like this…" Thyra said out loud. She gathered up her nerves and walked past one of the men to step inside Matthew's office with Antonio and Aadhya walking at either side of her.

The first thing she noticed was the back of Mathew's head rising over the top of his chair. He was staring out the massive bay windows covering the outer wall of his office. Thyra turned her head as she heard the doors being closed behind them with a loud creek.

"And what do I owe the terrible company of you hideous abominations?" Matthew demanded, breaking the silence between him.

His words were like the hissing of snakes to Thyra's ears, and immediately it caused her hackle feathers to rise in anger. Even calm Aadhya's eyes narrowed at such a cruel and racist greeting.

"You forced my talons this time." Aadhya spoke up, forcing her voice to remain steadfast.

She took a couple of steps forward as Matthew turned around in his chair to face the group. His eyes widened slightly with shock seeing that one of them was a rather massive gryphon that was already becoming angered. They all stood before Matthew's desk and looked into his cold dead eyes.

"And what do you plan on doing? Kill me? I hope you know it would be the worst mistake you could ever make," Matthew said and leaned on the meat of his fists. He glared to Thyra, then to Aadhya and Antonio with his bushy eyebrows raised, waiting for one of them to make a move.

Thyra snorted through her nares and shook her head. "As much as I would enjoy ripping your disgusting tongue out of your mouth, I'm not going to." Thyra paused for a second. "Yet..."

Matthew's eyes narrowed as he stood up, visibly clenching his fists on his desk and looking down at the three. He was becoming afraid, and trying to make himself look bigger to them. "You putrid animals dare come into my house of worship and threaten me?!"

His gravelly voice rouse higher with each word. It carried around the office and suddenly the doors behind them opened up. The three gryphons turned to look at the two same men as they entered the room, checking on the sudden commotion. Matthew looked up at them and then back down at the gryphons.

"I dare you make one more racist remark, Bishop " Aadhya said, her voice growing dark and deep.

She took a couple steps forward, looking directly into Matthew's eyes. She grit her beak as she roused her white feathers and unfolded her black peppered wings. "Go ahead, human. Make one more remark and I will tear your spine clean out of your body. I will devour your bones as a snack, and leave this place unharmed." Aadhya continued and pressed her great curved beak close to Matthew's face. "You think these two men will stop me? I think not."

Matthew's eyes grew wide once again, staring back into the yellow and red eyes of the gryphon. He had been putting up the strong guy act for as long as he could, but took a step back as Aadhya came in closer.

"What do you want?" he finally asked.

"You will not bother Thyra or Johnathen ever again. You will cease these fascist speeches and go about your own business. If you do not comply, I will personally see to your head on my dinner table." Aadhya cocked her head and clicked her beak once more. The two men on the opposite side of the room froze, waiting for a command or to act quickly. Aadhya glanced over to them with a wicked chuckle and then back at Matthew. "Do we have a deal?"

Thyra and Antonio stood silently, staring wide-eyed at this new Aadhya they were witnessing. The usual calm and collected gentle giant they knew was long gone in that instant, replaced by an angered feral beast. Matthew took a step back again and waved his hand to dismiss her and the other gryphons.

"Fine. Deal. Now get out of my sight!" Matthew turned away from them and tucked his hands behind his back, staring out the window, defeated. Aadhya put on a smug smile.

"I'm glad you came to your senses, human." The great bearded vulture turned away and walked between the two men, shooting them both a glance. All though they were both armed, she still was able to strike enough fear into them that they took a step back. Thyra and Antonio quickly followed behind Aadhya down the corridor and out the front doors.

Thyra let out an excited laugh once they were in the parking lot, her nerves started to settle as she bounded up next to Aadhya. "I can't believe that! Where did that come from?"

Aadhya took in a deep breath and chuckled to herself, wings shivering slightly. "I am not sure. Something came over me," she responded and looked down at her gigantic foreclaws. "I could not let that man talk to us in such a demeaning tone and I know of all the evil he has brought upon you and gryphon kind." Aadhya turned to the other two gryphons and beak grinned once more. "Also, I knew he was afraid of me. It is exciting to use my natural size and intimidating looks to my advantage, every now and then."

"I was beginning to believe he was going to collapse from fear!" Antonio chimed in. Thyra gave them a nod and rubbed her beak against Aadhya's.

"I don't know how to thank you." Thyra commented. Aadhya shook her head and bumped her shoulder against Thyra playfully.

"No need to thank me. Although, some of Johnathen's cooking would be a start."

Chapter 13 Pleading

Daniel looked down at his phone and checked the location. He was sure it was the right bar. Neon signs displaying various domestic beers flickered in the windows and multiple motorcycles decorated the parking lot in a perfect line. He brushed his blond hair back with his fingers and sighed before turning off the ignition. Daniel opened up the car door and slammed it shut, standing in the dimly light parking lot. Crickets chirped all around as his phone dinged with a message. It was his wife, Kathy.

What time will you be home?

I have some business to take care of. May be an hour or more, Daniel quickly responded before stowing the phone in his pants pocket.

He walked across the parking lot and opened the door. He was immediately greeted by a cloud of cigarette smoke and loud classic rock. Billiard balls clanked against one another from the far end of the room, and a long-haired blond waitress looked to him from behind the counter.

“Have a seat wherever you like, hun. I’ll be with you in a minute,” she said, gesturing to the tables.

Daniel thanked her and glanced around the crowded bar, looking for the two particular bikers he was looking for. He had been given a very rough description by Jack: two burly biker men, both with long beards and wearing leather cut off vests. There were several that met that description, but with the glancing looks he was already receiving as a non-regular, he decided to sit at the bar instead of blindly asking around.

The televisions behind the bar were playing the highlights from the latest gryphball games, many of them being the Redtail's recent games. Daniel knew Thyra was on the Redtail's team, and immediately brought his attention to one of the televisions.

A human commentator was talking to a well-dressed black gryphon sitting next to him. "*The Redtail's currently sit at the top of the second league, with eight wins and zero losses. With only two games remaining, I think they have a good chance at winning the finals and advancing to the first league. What do you think, Derek?*"

"Well, I'm impressed by their performance this year, especially with such a dramatic player change," the gryphon commented and moved the papers around on the desk before him. "If you look here at yesterday's game, you can see just how organized they are! I say they are first league material,"

The television played a compilation video of the multiple game winning goals the Redtail's had made over the past weeks, but only a few short shots of Thyra herself. The commentators went on as Daniel looked around again, trying to look less obviously out of place.

He spotted two men at a booth at the far end of the room. They were exact matches to the description he received. The two heavyset biker men sat together, smoking cigarettes while one talked and the other listened. They looked as intimidating as the men Jack had described.

A feminine voice broke his train of thought. "How you doing, hun? What can I getcha?" He looked towards the waitress and waited for a moment, but she didn't bother to hand him a menu.

"Um, what kind of merlots do you have?" He responded.

The waitress stared at him for a second and let out a loud laugh. She turned to point at the draft selection on the blackboard on the wall and looked back to him. "Well, fancy man, we have Bud light, Miller light, and Coors light. What would you like?" she asked with a grin on her rosy cheeks.

Daniel looked over to their slim alcohol and draft selection. *Typical for a dive bar*, he thought to himself. He typically was not a beer drinker, but anything to keep up the image of a paying patron was good enough. "A Miller light is fine," he said, defeated.

She turned and grabbed a frosty mug before pouring the golden yellow liquid into the glass. Daniel turned around again to survey the scene. Many different types of people sat in booths or at tall tables, carrying on in conversation and laughter. Billiard tables took up the center of the room and there were a couple groups of dart players towards the rear.

He returned his gaze to the two men in suspect and watched them for a moment. The talkative one seemed to look around occasionally as well, checking up on the people. Suddenly, they made eye contact.

Daniel froze for a minute and saw a change in the other man's face immediately.

"Here you go!" came the feminine voice once more. Daniel turned to see the full frosty mug of beer had been set before him. "So you want to start a tab?"

"Yeah, put it under Danny," he replied and picked up the mug to take a sip of beer.

She nodded and pulled out a small notepad before replying. "Would you like to see a menu?"

Daniel shook his head and placed his mug down. "No, but I would like to buy those gentlemen a beer." He turned around and pointed towards the far end booth. The waitress looked over to them and chuckled gently before nodding.

"You got it. Do you know Saul and Carl?" the waitress asked curiously, scribbling on her note pad.

"You can say we are acquainted," Daniel responded.

The waitress nodded and turned back to the computer to tap on the touchscreen for a moment before grabbing a couple mugs and filling them with beer. Daniel looked nonchalantly at the television in front of him as she brought the mugs over to their table. He waited for a moment before turning his head to glance over. The waitress was pointing directly at him and talking.

Both Saul and Carl listened for a moment before laughing and looked over to Daniel. One of them waved him over, inviting him to the table. He took a deep breath and picked up his mug before making his way over to the booth. His nerves were in full force. He had prepared himself for what he was about to say. He wanted to make this as civil as he could. After all, he was in their territory.

"Well! I appreciate the drink, buddy, but I don't swing that way," the bigger man said. Daniel laughed nervously and approached the booth.

"No! It isn't anything like that," Daniel said and took a sip of his beer. "You mind if I join you all?"

One of the men scooted in his seat to offer the booth to him. He look directly into Daniel's eyes. "Not at all. I'm Saul, and this here's Carl. But something tells me you already knew that."

Daniel sat next to Saul and placed his beer on the table with a shrug. "Not exactly, no. I'm new to the area and just trying to make friends," Daniel replied with a smile and lifted his beer mug to them. Both Saul and Carl clinked their mugs with his.

"You sound like you ain't from around here. Where are you from?" Saul asked.

"I'm from Atlanta. Moved down here for business and I've just been looking around," Daniel replied.

Saul laughed and motioned around the room. "Here? You moved down here of all places for business?" The big man leaned back and drew out a cigarette before throwing the pack on the table. "You got me curious now." Saul leaned forward again, making sure his eyes never left Daniel's. "You happen to wander into this dive bar of all the places around this town, buy us a drink, out of all the people here, because you want to make new friends?"

Saul lit his cigarette. His mood had shifted from one of casual enjoyment to serious questioning.

Daniel's fake smile turned into a stare as Saul dragged on his smoke.

"Well, buying fellas a beer around here can be taken in two ways; your either gay, which don't get me wrong is just fine but this ain't the place for it. Or it's just a friendly way of sayin' hello," Saul said with a chuckle and turned up his fresh beer mug. He finished and slammed it down on the table with a serious look on his face. "I don't buy either excuse."

Daniel took a sip as well and looked over to Saul for a minute. He could see that the man was serious. This was not the first time someone has approached him in this way. Daniel placed his beer mug down and folded his hands on the table, looking directly over to Saul as he leaned back in the booth.

"You two threatened one of my employees," Daniel said firmly.

Saul and Carl shared a glance for a moment and looked back over to Daniel. "An employee? You mean Jack, the fella watching Johnathen?"

Saul took another drag of his cigarette. He acted casual, even in the tense situation. Carl said absolutely nothing, simply giving him a firm stare. He understood why Jack had feared the both of them, especially the quiet man. He didn't let that stop him, though.

"Yeah, Jack. Listen." Daniel forced himself to exude calm while looking over to them. "I don't like this situation any more than you, but I can't do my job if my employees are being harassed."

This response seemed to anger Saul. He leaned forward with an imposing frown. "And exactly what is your job that involves our friends?" Saul and Carl both crossed their arms, waiting for an explanation.

Daniel considered his next words carefully. "As of right now, I've been just been hired to observe their movements and report back. I don't know what Thyra and Johnathen have done to warrant this kind of action, but frankly, I don't care as long as my employer doesn't ask for more than mere observation."

The looks on the men's faces turned stony. Saul looked over to a group of other bikers and motioned for them to come over.

Daniel slowly turned his head to see a small number of large men make their way over to the table. "I don't plan on harming your friends, if that helps."

"You know who you're working for, right? He's a white supremacist, disguising himself as a priest. You're being paid with dirty money. Does that not bother you in the least?" Saul picked up his beer mug and took another deep draw. "I would consider your next words very carefully."

The group of bikers pulled up chairs and sat down at the booth with them, all eyes on Daniel now. The lithe blond man, by comparison, was definitely feeling nervous. Jack was right. This was not worth the money. Still, he had no choice.

"Look, I don't like Matthew either, but he pays well and my family needs the money. Right now, this is the only work I have," Daniel responded while glancing over to the other bikers, casually sitting in their seats. The bar began to grow quieter as everyone turned to watch the small commotion. The smoky air was thin in comparison to the tension in the room.

"I want you to listen here and listen good, boy, because I'm only going to give you this one chance." Saul leaned forward again, and his brown eyes stared directly into his own. "Quit. Quit doing his bidding and get out of town, if you know what's good for you and your family. Next time, I won't let you walk away." Daniel stared back at him resignedly and picked up his mug with a sigh before downing the rest of his beer. Saul raised an eyebrow as Daniel continued to sit for a minute. "Do I make myself clear?"

"Crystal," Daniel finally replied. He stood up out of the booth, causing the other bikers to rise from their seats. They all said nothing as Daniel pulled out his wallet and placed a fifty-dollar bill on top of the check sitting on the table. "I was hoping we could reach some agreement, but it seems we can't."

"You're damn right we can't. We won't abandon our friends, ever," Saul stated and watched as Daniel walked away silently. Before he reached the door, the biker called out again. "You tell Matthew that too!"

Daniel glanced back and nodded in acknowledgement. Then calmly walked out through the doors. Once outside in the cool air, Daniel stopped in the parking lot, closed his eyes and drew in a deep breath. Those men could have easily put him in the hospital, or worse. He stared up at the night sky, staring at the full moon and lost in thought.

Daniel repeated Jack's words once again. "It ain't worth the pay."

He was tangled up in a bigger mess than he initially thought, one he doubted he wanted part of. In the past, he had run into similar issues, but ones that could be solved easily with negotiations and money.

This was the first time he had to deal with a group with moral conviction.

Daniel unlocked his Lexus and stepped inside, sinking down in the leather once again. He stared out the front windshield and watched as Saul's crew walked outside. Saul lit up a cigarette and leaned against the wall. Daniel turned the ignition and started the car, which earned a goodbye wave from Saul. As Daniel drove out onto the street, he pulled his phone out and searched his contacts for a minute. He put the phone to his ear and waited as it rang.

"Hey Jack. Yeah, I just left….No, not at all… Is there somewhere we can meet? Ok, I'll be there in twenty."

Chapter 14 From The Sidelines

Thyra sat in a crowded dark room, watching the projector screen play clips of past gryphball games. She had brought a notepad as instructed by Victor, and scribbled down notes as the game continued on. Victor sat at the front of the room, watching the screen looking for a particular moment. He paused it just as the camera zoomed in on a Bateleur Eagle after it scored an air goal.

“This is Phera. He was recently transferred from the South African Lions to the Asheville Jays. He was a first league player over on his old team, but got himself into trouble and was transferred here as punishment. He’s loud, fast, and very skilled. He doesn’t mind playing dirty, and has done so in the past.”

Victor’s large gray crest feathers rose up as he spotted Rachel playing with her phone the great Harpy Eagle gryphon’s voice boomed, “Kestrel! Pay attention!” His large black eyes stared her down as she compressed her feathers and put her phone away. “This gryphon can accidently kill someone your size.”

“Yes sir.” Rachel replied and straightened her back, her eyes now fixed on the screen.

Victor stared at her for a moment more, then took a deep breath and clicked the play button on the remote in his massive gray foretalons. “As I was saying, he is a formable opponent. In the Eastern First League they call him the Black Mamba. Fitting, for a snake eagle.”

The video played again, showing Phera move around impressively fast for a gryphon as large as he was. His dark red-skinned face and legs stood out from his black plumage even as the camera panned away to show a field view. His chestnut colored tail feathers were so short that Thyra could see most of his legs as he flew.

“Look how he maneuvers and memorize it. He’s going to be our main focus and we will have to adapt plays depending on his position. The other gryphons on the team are of no matter. The plays you have memorized will work for them,” Victor continued on while the video played.

Thyra winced as she watched Phera rise up underneath another gryphon at high speed and elbow his ribs. The gryphon buckled its wings, dropped the ball, and fell to the ground in a heap of feathers. The next scenes were of the refs stopping the game while the gryphon was carted off by human EMS. Another referee gryphon flew next to Phera and flashed a red card.

“This is just one instance of many when Phera went too far. That gryphon, Jifra, was out for the season after this. Multiple rib fractures, a broken radius on his dorsal wing, countless broken flight feathers, and torn ligaments in both foreclaws.”

In the video, Phera lashed out verbally at the referee and turned to glide off of the field. Once he was back in the dugout, the red-faced gryphon threw multiple objects around, which earned with many complaints from his fellow teammates. “The only reason he still plays, is because he’s good, and he knows it.”

Victor walked to the opposite side of the room and turned on the lights, causing everyone to wince. “Now, I have prepared a new playbook that I want everyone to read and practice before tomorrow’s game. I want you all to know them by memory. Most of the plays have remained unchanged, but there are a few that have been modified and renamed.” He pointed at the table stacked with binders. Each one of them had a gryphons name on the front.

“I’m sure everyone is tired from practice today, so go home early and get a good rest. I want everyone here tomorrow morning in top shape for the game. If we win, we will have a chance at entering the first league,” Victor said and turned toward the exit of the room. “You are dismissed. I will see everyone here tomorrow morning.”

With that, the great gryphon left. Immediately, everyone began to converse between themselves. Multiple gryphons stood up and went to the front of the room to sort through the binders to find one with their name on it.

“Thyra,” came Aadhya’s voice from behind her. The vulture stood and walked up next to Thyra. Quietly, she asked, “Did you ever tell Johnathen about our engagement a couple weeks back?”

Aadhya and Antonio had spent most of that evening with the two of them at her house. Johnathen had been surprised to see the other gryphons join them for dinner, and had made an extra trip to the grocery store for food. He made no complaint, though.

Quite the contrary, he had seemed excited to see them. They had a pleasant evening together getting to know one another, but Aadhya had noticed that the main purpose of them being in town was never revealed to Johnathen.

Thyra shook her head. “No, I never did and I don’t think he needs to know. All he needs to know is that hopefully they will leave us alone for a while. Then again, he rolled over pretty easily for you.”

Thyra replayed the scene in her head. She thought she knew exactly what kind of person Matthew was, but that understanding had been destroyed when she watched him all but crumble to his knees in front of Aadhya. Did Matthew actually hate their kind just because he was afraid of them? Or was it something else altogether? “We may have made things worse.”

“I thought it would have been more of a fight,” Aadhya replied and made her way to the front of the room. “He seemed quite submissive, which is suspicious. Then again, not even great kings challenged lions.”

She sorted through the binders and handed each of her friends their binder. Thyra, Rachel, and Antonio took theirs and flipped it open to glance at the first page.

“I did find it strange that he gave in so easy,” Antonio chimed in. “Perhaps it was a play. Something he has always suspected would happen and had planned how to react.”

They began to read the first page of their binder. Each opening page was directed to the individual player, relating to their starting positions, their positions in the field, and other notes Victor decided to throw in.

"Wait, what are you all talking about?" Rachel suddenly asked. She had been too distracted by everything else to realize what the group was chatting about until now. "Did you all hang out recently or something?" She ruffled her small feathers, feeling left out.

"Well, kind of. We did hang out," Thyra began "But…"

"But you didn't invite me?" Rachel said with a huff in her voice.

"You were all the way up in Chattanooga," Thyra replied. "Plus you said something about concerts and…"

"And whatever! I would have come down if I knew all you all were chilling out!" Rachel started again.

"AND it wasn't really hanging out. We went to confront Matthew," Thyra finally said. Rachel froze for a minute and looked to the other gryphons. Her small eartufts folded back against her skull.

"And you didn't invite me because I'm too small. You don't think I'm scary enough," Rachel said and grabbed her binder. She tucked it under a wing before walking out of the door. The rest of them followed behind quickly.

"It is not because you are not scary, it is because…" Aadhya paused, searching for the right words. Rachel continued to walk down the hallway.

"It's because you all were scared I would get hurt if something went wrong," she said with another loud huff through her nares.

"Rachel, we.."

Rachel suddenly stopped and turned around. One wing flared open and feathers roused on the back of her head. "Well don't worry about me! I'll have your back no matter what! I don't care what you're up against." Rachel's screech, caused other gryphons to turn and pay them attention. "I don't give two shits if it's against the greatest army in the world! I'll still stand by y'alls side."

The group stopped and stared down at the small gryphon. Thyra felt guilty for not bringing her along. She had known that Rachel would have been upset about not being there, but thought it for the best at that time.

"I'm sorry, Rachel. Next time, you will be the first one I call." Thyra promised. The little black eyes of the Kestrel gryphoness looked up at her seriously for a moment more before her beak curved into a smile.

"Good. I want to be there to tear off Matthew's face next time," Rachel replied and turned to head down the hallway again as did the other surrounding gryphons.

Thyra took a deep breath and followed after her. "That's what I was afraid of," she muttered as they entered the locker room. The sounds of gryphons conversing and lockers swinging open filled the room as everyone went about their business to end the day.

Aadhya walked up next to Thyra and sat on her massive haunches. "As much as I love Rachel, I am relieved you did not bring her along."

She was right. Even if Thyra did feel guilty about leaving her small friend behind, the scene would have escalated more so if Rachel was there. “Yeah, I thought that was a good call. She will get over it.”

Feeling better about her decision, she opened up her locker. There was a fresh uniform hanging up for tomorrow, already cleaned by the staff and ironed out. “But we have more important things to think about, like how we are going to kick ass in tomorrow’s game,”

Aadhya gave her a warm beak grin in return and nodded. “I can not wait to see how you perform. Have you already memorized most of the plays?” Aadhya asked and watched as Thyra removed her uniform from her body.

She twisted this way and that, struggling to take off the tight spandex material. Aadhya assisted, using a talon to bring the back of the uniform over Thyra’s wings and head.

“Yeah. I mean most of them are no brainers, just common plays used in gryphball, but I’m sure Victor has a couple curveballs in the book.” Thyra tossed the dirty uniform into the hamper at the center of the room. She withdrew her cellphone from the locker and turned it on.

“I was thinking of inviting the others back to the apartment tonight,” Aadhya said as she began to work her own uniform off. It tugged and pulled at her white and peppered plumage until she peeled the clothing from herself. “I began a stew inside the slow cooker this morning. There should be plenty food to feed all of us. We can study the plays and go over them together. That is, unless you desire for more peace.”

"No, I think that's a great idea! I'll run by the store and grab some beer," Thyra replied and started to put on her more casual clothing.

Aadhya looked to her with a raised eye ridge. "Do you think that is advisable? Alcohol can interfere with one's performance."

Thyra waved Aadhya's concerns off with a foreclaw. "I'll just buy a six pack. That won't do us any harm. Plus the extra calories will give us energy, right?" Thyra laughed and slammed the locker shut. "I'll get us something light."

* * *

"Bishop, sir, she is ready," a well-dressed man said as he stood at the entrance of Matthew's office.

Matthew looked up from his computer screen and nodded. "Very good. Just give me a minute."

He finished a message on the keyboard. His typing was painfully slow, pecking away at the letters on the keyboard as the man patiently waited by the door. Finally, Matthew stood from behind his desk and straightened his crinkly white button down shirt. There was a faint five-clock shadow on Matthew's wrinkled face, and his usually bald head had grown patches of short hair from lack of upkeep. He followed the man out of his office and down a hallway, hands behind his back.

"So, she finally agreed to talk?" Matthew asked his hired hand.

The well-dressed man nodded in response and stopped by a door that had a deadbolt on it. "Yes sir. Says she wants to negotiate,"

The man knocked three times. The deadbolt unlocked and the door swung open, revealing a small, dark room. Matthew entered and looked to the woman sitting in the corner on a sofa chair, restrained and accompanied by another well-dressed man. There was not much else in the room besides a lonely sofa, and another chair that had been placed directly in front of the woman. She looked rough, but not beaten and abused.

Matthew calmly approached and sat before her in the dim light. He took a deep breath and folded his hands while he leaned back, staring directly into the woman's eyes. "They have told me you wish to speak to me, Sandra?"

"Yeah. I'm tired of this shit. I don't care what you are doing anymore. I just want to go home," Sandra replied and straightened out her fingers. Her wrists were red from the restraints rubbing the skin. "You mind removing these?"

Matthew looked to one of the men and nodded. The man walked over and undid the restraints, letting them fall to the floor. Sandra immediately began to rub her irritated wrists and grabbed the water in front of her. There was silence for several seconds as she downed the water glass and sighed.

Matthew leaned forward now and watched patiently. "Where is your group?" he asked calmly.

"What group?" she snapped back.

Matthew's face turned into a frown and he slammed his fist down on the table in front of him. Everyone looked surprised at the unusual display of loosing his temper so easily.

"Damn it, woman! Don't play games with me. I want to know the name and location of your group!" he yelled before snatching another water glass and curling his long, bony fingers around it. "You said you wanted to talk. Don't toy with me."

Sandra took a deep breath and put her emptied glass down. "Ok. Fine. Ill tell you everything only on two conditions," she began. "First, you let me walk free. I forget about this, you forget about me, and I'll never go to anybody with this information. I give you my word and you can check on me if you want."

Sandra stopped to gauge Matthew's reaction. He sternly looked at her for a moment then nodded his head.

"Fine. What is your second condition?" he asked suspiciously.

"Second is . . ." She paused and bit her lip. Matthew raised an eyebrow at the pause. Surely she had been thinking about what she wants for her information. Why did she not want to say it? "Second, you don't harm the gryphon."

Matthew was stumped by this comment. He sat back in his chair and intertwined his fingers once again. "What gryphon?"

"The gryphon we are holding. He's, different. Not like the others," Sandra began much to Matthew's curiosity. He motioned for her to continue. "A month back, we found out there was a gryphon being passed between labs. He had never been free or had a life to live on his own. When we tried to dig for more information on him, we came up blank. He was a ghost, as far as the government was concerned. Finally, we found the last place he was being held. We broke in late at night, and what we found…" She took a deep breath and closed her eyes. "We found an abomination."

"What do you mean? All gryphons are an abomination of man," Matthew retorted. Sandra shook her head.

"No. Gryphons are just as much human as you and I. But this thing wasn't a gryphon. He's something halfway between a beast and a gryphon. He has the upper beak of a bird, but his lower jaw is like a deformed cat's. There are patches missing out of his fur and feathers too. But even with all that, he's still a sentient creature. We couldn't just leave him," Sandra continued. "We hooded him, snuck him back to our hideout, but once we removed his hood, he lashed out. I don't know if it was fear, hunger, or just primal behavior, but he killed someone in our group.

"We couldn't do anything about it. He didn't respond to any of our calls. He just kept saying, 'Food.' This creature dragged the carcass of our man into the confined area we had made for him and devoured the guy." Sandra looked down to her bare feet, clearly lost in thought. "After that, we didn't dare get close. We tried to talk to him, but he just kept repeating the same things, over and over again. 'I want friend' and 'I need food'."

This story piqued Matthew's curiosity. A feral beastly gryphon that would kill for whatever reason it wanted. He chuckled deeply, causing Sandra to look back up at him with worry.

"Do not fret. I have no plans on harming this… Gryphon… if it is one. But do tell me where it and your group reside. Again, I promise to do no harm to either party if you uphold your word." Matthew looked to Sandra once more, awaiting her response.

She sighed and closed her eyes. "Northeast of here. Old Clinton Historic District. There's an old abandoned warehouse off the exit of highway 129 and 18. That's where they all are."

Matthew clapped his hands together and stood before her. "Splendid. Thank you for the information." He turned to leave towards the door before Sandra interrupted him.

"Hey! What about letting me go?" Sandra pleaded. "I gave you what you wanted!"

Matthew stopped before the door and turned to face her once more. "You did, but I don't know if your information is correct. I'll release you as soon as I confirm this. Now settle in, hopefully you will only be here for one more night."

Matthew opened the door before Sandra began to scream at him. Both well-dressed men pinned her down to the chair and began to tie her bindings once more. He stepped into the hallway and put his hands behind his back with a smile.

"An insane murdering gryphon. This could be beneficial."

Chapter 15 Retrieval

Daniel pulled the slide back on his Glock and locked it in place. He pushed the magazine release and pulled the clip from the base of the weapon. “Remember, we don’t kill people and we don’t harm the gryphon either.” He checked the number of rounds in the clip and loaded it back into the Glock again. “We only return fire, but I highly doubt this organization of computer geeks are capable of handling a weapon. We only have these to invoke fear in them. If you have to shoot, shoot to wound.”

Daniel dropped the slide with a loud metallic clack and then pulled it back to check if a round was loaded into the chamber. He holstered the weapon on his side and turned to look at Jack. The short man puffed on a cigarette as he drove down the highway in the sprinter van.

Daniel turned to look at the five other men sitting in the back of the van. “Everyone understand?”

All of them nodded and checked their own weapons. Most had assault rifles of different makes, and all of them were fully loaded out with accessories. Everyone wore black ski masks, save for himself and Jack at the moment.

“Good. Because if you kill anyone, then you don’t get paid and you’ll never work for me again.”

Daniel said with a scowl to reinforced how serious he was. He did not want blood today, especially when he was going up against a group of innocent civilians who were just standing up for what they believe in. Daniel sighed and pulled out his phone to check the GPS again.

"I don't like this, Daniel," Jack said in a low voice. He puffed on his cigarette and threw it out the window. "First, it's 'Watch these civilians.' Now it's 'Scatter this Civil Rights Gryphon Group and steal this gryphon.' But then what?" Jack turned to look at Daniel with his tired eyes. They were permanently baggy and showed dark circles around them. "We're rushin' into this without any Intel besides a location. So after we do this, then what else is that insane preacher going to make us do?" Jack asked, his eyebrows knit together in concern. "I don't want this to get like it was in the war,"

Daniel stared back for a moment and then at his phone again. "I don't know what he'll want, but I won't let it go that far."

Jack huffed and ran his fingers through the short hair that was cut into a strip that began at his forehead to the back of his head. "I'm getting too old for this shit."

"We'll worry about it all later. Let's just do this. Get in, scare them away, take one for questioning, get the gryphon, and be home by dinner." Daniel phone dinged with a notification. "Get off the next exit," he told Jack.

Jack turned on his blinker and drifted into the right lane. "Fine. But if this goes south, then I'm done," Jack said and pulled of the exit.

"I understand. Now, take a right," Daniel directed. He checked his phone and then locked the screen. "Go straight for four miles."

"I still see that kid, Daniel." Jack said, his voice haunted.

Daniel looked over to Jack, worried that he'd see his friend breaking down. But no. His gaze was firm and unyielding as always.

"I see him, dead on the ground, lying in the dirty dusty streets," Jack continued, his mouth curving into a frown. "You remember what I said before we went into that village?" Jack looked over briefly, but Daniel was looking out the window. "I told you then, I don't like this, but you insisted it would be alright."

"I hate what we did too, but-," Daniel began.

"But what, Daniel?" Jack questioned. "Someone got too trigger happy, didn't they? And then what?"

When Daniel didn't respond right away, Jack put his focus back on the road. The van was silent save for the small chatter in the back from the other men. They were carrying on conversations between themselves and seemed to not listen to their discussion.

"Then what happened?" Jack questioned again more firmly.

"We ended up with a dead child," Daniel finally said in a soft voice. Jack nodded and glanced over at the blond man sitting there staring out the window. His phone dinged loudly once again, and Daniel pulled it out to check. "Turn right in a quarter mile."

"I just hope my gut feeling is wrong on this," Jack said, and turned right onto a small road in the state of disrepair.

Both of them were silent as they approached a clearly abandoned large metal structure. The sun was just starting to set on the horizon, hiding behind a small mountain in the background. There was a parking lot beside the building with a couple of what seemed to be working vehicles parked in it.

A chain link fence surrounded the building and the lot but one of the gates had been left wide open. Jack stopped the van a few hundred yards away from the parking lot and pulled off into the grass behind some trees. He shut the engine off and looked over to Daniel.

Daniel got out of the van. The crew in the back followed, sliding the rear door open and piling out to face him. He looked to the five men wearing black ski masks and took a deep breath. “Once more. Do not discharge your weapon unless we receive fire first. The objective here is to clear them out, destroy their evidence, and capture a gryphon. I will go in first, and everyone else follow.”

Daniel reached into the van and pulled out a backpack. He threw it at one of the guys. “Jack will be carrying the tranquilizer gun, but just in case it doesn’t work, it never hurts to have a backup plan. There’s a net inside. Use it to capture the gryphon if you have to.” By this time, Jack had climbed out of the van and was at the back, digging around.

The men all stood silently, watching Daniel and Jack put on their ski masks. Daniel turned to Jack and gave him a nod before turning to walk towards the building. He removed his Glock from the holster and began to jog across the mostly empty parking lot.

The other men formed around him as they hunched over in the cover of dusk and ran through the open fence gate. Daniel's heart beat fast in his chest, the same rush of adrenaline he'd felt again and again in his military days. He knew how to control the emotions within himself, but Jack was right, something did not feel right. The group pressed themselves against the building near a side door. Daniel's chest heaved and he looked to Jack who seemed to be breathing even harder than he was already. They had really let themselves go.

Daniel lifted a hand off his weapon and pointed to a window. One man crouched and moved to the window to peer inside. A couple seconds went by as he watched, and the man came back with a nod. He held up five fingers for the count of five people inside.

That matched the Intel he had. One of Daniel's hired hands had been scoping the place out for the past week. There were three vans that came and went frequently, and only two of them had an additional passenger. From what they could tell, the vans had no additional seating in the back.

They all moved over to the door and Daniel took another deep breath to steadyt his mind. He opened the door quietly and rushed inside with his men in tow. He brought his handgun up with both hands, sweeping the room as the others followed. Their footsteps echoed loudly in the vast open metal structure, but nothing stirred. There was a dim light coming from a room in the back of the building and Daniel motioned for everyone to move forward.

The men were careful to step over the various items scattered along the concrete floor, not wanting to make more noise as they approached. Nevertheless, there was a sound of something rolling across the floor, and Daniel motioned for everyone to stop. A man walked out from around the corner, and peered out into the vast darkness for a moment, waiting for his eyes to adjust. Daniel and the others slowly crouched lower, hoping the low light would hide them well enough.

The man's eyes widened as he saw the group, and Jack fired his tranq. A quick puff of air was all that could be heard before the man clutched his chest and then fell to the ground moments later. Men in the room beyond began to talk loudly in alarm as they ran over to help their fallen friend. It was time to move.

Daniel led the group forward as fast as he could, shouting, to the people gathering around their unconscious friend. "Get on the ground!"

All of Daniel's men clicked on their weapons' flashlights and scanned the room. The gryphon lovers quickly scattered, shouting in alarm and running towards the nearest exits.

Daniel had his men give chase, but the people seemed to have a quick evacuation plan in place. This was fine with him. He did not want to take more than one for questioning anyways. They would be long gone before the group could come back with reinforcements. He and Jack went to a window overlooking the parking lot, and watched as three vans escaped, speeding off down the abandoned road.

"Well, that was easy," Jack stated before removing his ski mask.

Daniel nodded with agreement and looked over to the unconscious man lying on the ground. "Yeah, they scattered like rats just as I thought they would." He removed his mask as well. "Did you see anyone carrying anything with them as they ran?"

"No, not a thing," Jack said and the other men shook their heads.

Daniel shrugged his shoulders and holstered his weapon. "Good. All right, you two take this guy outside and load him in the van. You other two, take any laptops you can carry and destroy the other computers." The four men nodded and turned to go do their assigned tasks. Daniel turned to Jack and the last guy with the backpack. "And you two are with me. We're going to look for the gryphon."

Daniel took out his flashlight and scanned the back room first. There were old metal tables scattered everywhere, and a couple of them were set up with running computers and wires going in every direction. The room dead-ended there, with nothing else more to see besides dust and old abandoned office furniture.

The sound of gunfire echoed in the empty structure, causing Daniel to tense up for a second. He looked over to one of the men aiming his riffle at the now shattered computers, riffle barrel smoking from the shots. He frowned at the unnecessarily loud method of destroying the efforts, but did not bother to reprimand the man. After all, he had not specified how he had wanted it done.

Daniel and Jack continued outside the room and began to search the other areas under the upstairs offices. He noticed a camping cooler in the distance and pointed it out. As they approached, he noticed a couple of cots, some more coolers, and some duffle bags. "Go check those bags," Daniel commanded the man with the backpack. He started to dig through one of them, tossing clothes and other personal belongings to the wayside. Daniel saw a cellphone lying next to one of the cots and picked it up. The background was of some guy with a woman, but the phone was locked.

Jack walked around the corner before calling out in a calm voice. "Hey, we got something here."

Daniel put the phone in his pocket and walked around the corner to see Jack standing in front of a large metal sliding door that was chained shut. More gunshots echoed in the building as the men went about destroying computers, but he could hear something else inside. There was a laughing voice coming from within.

"Do you hear that?" Daniel asked. Jack nodded and pointed to an open cooler full of red meat.

"I don't think these scraps are for the guys here," Jack pointed out. This had to be where they were keeping the gryphon.

Daniel put his ear up to the metal door and closed his eyes to concentrate on the sounds inside. He could hear the clicking of talons across the ground, and more gentle laughter. Then, the gryphon began to mutter something to himself, but Daniel could not pick its words out.

Daniel pulled his ear away and knocked on the metal door. Jack raised an eyebrow at Daniel's action, but then the gryphon responded, "Food time?"

"Yeah, it's time for food. Can I come in?" Daniel responded. They waited for a minute and heard the chuckle of the gryphon again.

"Yes. Yes. Please, come in," came the eerie voice. Daniel found it hard to understand, like he was listening to growls and a distant human voice mixed together. Daniel reached over to the chain and started to unhook it from the wall.

"Go ahead and get ready." Daniel looked over to Jack. His friend looked nervous, and unsettled for the first time in ages. Daniel watched him for a second, looking into his dark brown eyes. There was fear in Jack's eyes, and his mouth was curved into a frown.

"Are you ok?" Daniel asked, concerned

"I don't like this," Jack responded and swallowed. He lifted his tranq rifle and took a step back. "I've got that gut feeling again." Jack looked over to his partner and closed his eyes. "But, It's your call."

Daniel put his hands on the curved metal handle and stopped. He could hear the talons scraping across the ground as the gryphon approached the door. It was not chained up inside, free to roam as it wished. That meant it was not dangerous, right?

Daniel froze for a minute, thinking to himself and weighing his options. They could turn around right now, leave this place and tell Daniel they did not find the gryphon, but that would mean they left this sentient creature to its death. "We have to."

Jack took a deep breath and squeezed on the tranq rifle. He turned on the flashlight and gave a nod to Daniel. He slowly opened the door, rolling it across the wall while it screeched and moaned in protest. He had to struggle to open it all the way. Daniel took a step back and brought his flashlight up to peer into the darkness, but there was nothing inside.

His heart beat hard in his chest and everything was quiet save for their own breath. More shots rang out in the background, causing them both to jerk and turn their heads to the source of the sound. In that instant, a massive black mass of fur and feathers leaped out from the darkness.

Jack pulled the trigger, and the dart hit the gryphon, but it did not stop. It landed on top of Jack with its wicked foreclaws placed on his head and neck. The great gryphon hissed loudly and squeezed, talons digging into Jack's throat.

"Jack!" Daniel cried out. Fear had overcome his body and he froze in place. His flashlight shook as he brought it over to see blood pooling around the gryphon's talons from Jack's throat.

The gryphon slowly turned its head and gave a weak laugh, and now Daniel could see the deformed face of the hideous beast. It had the lower muzzle of a feline, and the top half of a beak. Its feathers were missing in patches around its face, and it only had one eartuft. There was still blood on its beak from the last meal. Jack wheezed under the gryphon and struggled under it.

Daniel's nerves organized themselves, and he immediately drew his Glock. Tears began to pool from his eyes as he flicked off the safety and put his finger on the trigger.

"Get off him!" Daniel cried out and took a step forward. The gryphon's feline green eyes dilated as Daniel's flashlight glanced over his face.

"Why? He is food, yes?" the gryphon said in response. "I eat, and then we play…We…"

The gryphon swayed gently and his eyes began to droop. He lost his balance and then fell over onto the ground as the tranquilizer finally took effect.

By that time, the other men turned the corner and shined their lights on the scene. They all froze as Daniel dropped his side arm on the ground and ran over to Jack. He fell to his knees and picked Jack's head up to look into his eyes, and the eyes looked back to him.

"Jack..." Daniel said in-between gasping breaths.

Jack's throat had multiple punctures from the giant talons of the gryphon and dark blood poured from each one. Daniel quickly withdrew a handkerchief from a pocket and placed it over the wounds, pressing hard in a futile attempt to stop the blood flow.

Jack reached up and gurgled a word that he could not understand. Then the fear and panic that Daniel had seen in his friend's eyes moments before were gone, and he looked to be at peace, staring up at him.

"I'm sorry Jack. I-I should have listened to you. I always should have listened to you. Jack, don't. Please, don't," Daniel choked out as tears fell on his friends face.

Jack stared up at him and smiled for a second, and then his hand fell limp. Daniel felt Jack's body relax completely and it seemed as if the color slowly disappeared from his friend's brown eyes. Daniel took in a deep breath and wept silently. The other men fell in around him to gauge in the scene, but none of them talked.

Several long moments went by, and finally Daniel slowly placed Jack's head on the ground. he closed his deceased friend's eyes with his fingers and stood up.

"Two of you, get the kit and clean up his blood. We can't leave any evidence behind." Daniel wiped his face on an arm sleeve and walked over to his gun. He picked up the weapon and holstered it before turning back to the five men standing before him silently. "The rest of you, get this... damned creature out of here. I'll take care of Jack."

Daniel watched as the men went to work. Two of them ran out the door to the van while the rest started to duct tape the gryphon's legs together. He looked over the gryphon again as they did so. Unlike every other gryphon he had seen in his life, this one had fur sticking out in patches between the feathers. It also had four avian legs, and the wings looked completely off. They were well-formed, but didn't look at all like gryphon's wings.

Daniel lifted one of the wings and ran his hands across them. They were leathery, like bats wings. He ran his hand down to the base and found massive scar tissue formed all around the joints. Daniel looked over the gryphon's bulky body with a flashlight, spreading its feathers and fur out with his hands. It felt coarse and wiry. He found small metal discs embedded in the gryphon's upper arm with ports in the center and questioned what they were for. There were more scars and marks all across the gryphon's body in intricate patterns, and Daniel winced.

"What did they do to you?" he asked the sleeping gryphon. Its chest heaved unevenly, like every breath was hard for it.

The other men came through the door with bottles of bleach, powdered chemicals and water. Daniel stood back up and walked over to Jack who was lying limp on the ground in a pool of his own blood. Daniel bent down and gently picked up his smaller friend.

The men poured the chemicals on the floor to wash away Jack's blood, and Daniel carried him out into the night. A cold breeze picked up and blew his blond hair as he walked across the parking lot. He looked down at Jack and choked back more tears.

"Do you remember that one day when we took care of your nephew? We took him to go see that scary movie because his mom wouldn't let him, and he had nightmares for weeks." Daniel sniffled and chuckled gently. "Your sister was so pissed at us. She wouldn't let him cover visit you for months. I wonder how Kevin is? How has he been?"

Daniel continued to speak to his dead friend as he made his way to the van. He looked into the back and saw that the guys had stretched out a tarp on the floor. Daniel leaned forward and groaned as he gently placed Jack inside.

He turned away from the van and bit his lip to fight back his grief. T. He was responsible for his friend's death. Daniel sat down on the bumper and put his face into his hands. His sadness was replaced by a feeling of dread that crept through his body

He was going to have to be the one to explain it to all to Jack's family. He should have listened to Jack a week ago. Jack warned him time and time again about working for this cult, yet he had continued to follow Daniel no matter what. His actions had killed the only true friend he had, and he was going to live with it.

Daniel looked down at his holstered side arm. It was starting to look very friendly to him. It would be easy to end it all himself. Then he would not have to deal with Matthew anymore, or have the guilt of his friend's death so heavy on his shoulders. They could go down together, just like they promised each other in the past. No one would know Daniel took the easy way out besides the five men with him.

He immediately repressed the dark urges and thought of his family, his wife and daughter. He had to get away from this life, and provide a better future for them.

"No more," Daniel promised.

Chapter 16 Game Day

Thyra's eartufts perked up as she heard another high energy song play outside, causing the lockers to rattle occasionally from the bass. All the gryphons on her team sat at full attention in a semi-circle with Coach Victor in the center. Everyone would have looked calm to human eyes, but Thyra could tell that their feathers were flattened down with nervousness. Of course, she was no different. She could feel butterflies flying around in her crop.

Coach Victor was the only one of them that seemed at ease, sitting calmly as the bass continued to pump outside. He held a clipboard under his wing and was wearing his own professional button-down uniform with the team's logo sewn into a breast pocket. Finally, he stood and gazed at the players with his dark black eyes.

"You hear them out there?" Victor asked. "Can you hear all the people waiting to see a good game? I can. And this is our home field. These are our fans. We don't want to let them down, do we?" Victor looked around and when no one replied right away, his tall gray crest feathers stood up and he shouted, "Do we?"

"No sir!" all the gryphons called out at once.

"That's right! They came here to see us win this semi-final. Sure, we are in the second league and the media only cares about the first league, but that doesn't mean we should care less. Last year, we were close to getting into the first league, but, this year," Victor paused and looked to the new gryphons on his team. "This year, it's different. We are going to go all the way!"

The gryphons screeched out with him in agreement. Many feathers began to ruffle as the nervousness turned into energy, an energy Victor was shaping and bestowing upon every one of his players.

"We are going to win this game just as we have won every game this season, and then we are going to win the final. We can beat anybody! I wouldn't care if we were up against the damn Ospreys, because I know this team could kick their tailfeathers. So, what do you all say? Are we going to go out there and show them who the true tiercel's are? Or are we going to be hens?"

"Let's kick their asses!" Nathanial shouted and stepped forward. His uniform was ship-shape, and his feathers perfectly preened. He had even painted his yellow cere with black paint. Everyone shouted in agreement and stamped their foretalons on the ground.

"That's what I want to hear! Get your featherbutts out there!" Victor shouted and pointed to the exit. Everyone chattered excitedly to one another as they made their way out the door and down the long hallway.

Thyra felt a nudge and looked over to Aadhya, who had dusted herself in the traditional rich red coloration of the bearded vultures. "You ready?" Aadhya asked calmly. Despite her smooth voice, she had a ferocious look in her yellow and red eyes, as if she was about to leave on a hunt. She looked positively devilish, and not like herself at all.

Thyra felt the energy in the hallway build up inside of her, silencing those annoying butterflies. "Yeah! Let's do this!"

"I, personally, look forward to taking on this bateleur eagle, Phera," Antonio said. "I've been studying him ever since we went home the other night. I believe I have all his moves memorized."

They came to a stop near the entrance and listened to the announcer as he began. "*Ladies, gentleman and everything in between, it's gryphball time here in this great state of Georgia! Welcome to the Semi-Finals of the Second League gryphball season where we have our very own Redtails here to once again, try for that trophy! Last year, they came so close, but this year, Victor Sousa says that he is determined to take that trophy home and make it to the First League*."

Nathanial made his way towards the front of the group with Jason in tow. Thyra saw the earpieces on the sides of their heads as they talked in a low tone, checking the connection.

The announcer continued as the sounds of a live marching band started to fill the stadium. "*Introducing, your Athens Redtails*!"

The crowd erupted as Nathanial led the group out onto the field. Thyra took a deep breath and followed the other gryphons out into the bright light. She had to squint for a moment to get used to the bright sunny day but as she looked around, she saw that the stadium was full with fans shouting and clapping.

Thyra had never felt energy like this before. Through the season, each game had grown bigger in terms of attendants. The energy was always there, but with the stadium completely packed, it was intoxicating.

The team gathered in the center of the field as the announcer called off players' names with quick backgrounds. "*...Aadhyea, number three, Bearded Vulture and rear air guard. You know her as the 'Red Brick Wall in the Sky,' the fiercest defender in the southeast. Antonio, number eleven, Harris Hawk and air center. Also known as the 'Hurricane of the Gulf.' Rachel, number eight, American Kestrel and air forward, the 'Speeding Bullet of the Gryphball World.' And last but not least, Thyra, number thirteen, Redtail hawk and ground forward, the 'Promising Rookie.'*"

"That's the nickname they gave me?" Thyra laughed to herself as the team sat together, standing before the crowd as they shouted and cheered for their team. It was another reminder that she was the least experienced player on the team, but she didn't let that bother her. Not today.

"*Now to announce the visitors today: the Asheville Jays! They had a strong run last year, but fell flat before the final eight. That just gives them all the more reason to strive for better this year*!"

The Redtails looked to their right to watch as the opposing group of gryphons poured out onto the field. As the announcer began to introduce each player, Thyra's eyes focused on the Bateluer Eagle running out front and center from the team. He was powerful and imposing. Even from afar, his eyes spoke of destruction.

"*...And Phera, Bateleur Eagle and air forward. He is most well-known for his success in the South African league as the 'Black Mamba'. He has quite a reputation there, and I for one, can't wait to see this eagle in action.*"

Phera approached the group with his team following behind. Nathanial walked up to the eagle and puffed himself up to make himself look bigger, but still was small in comparison by the large gryphon. Jason stood next to Nathanial and sized the Bateleur gryphon up for himself.

Phera looked around at the group and huffed through his nares. His voice was raspy and low as he spoke. "So, this is what they call a contending team in this league? Pathetic."

Nathanial's eartufts folded back as he growled and took a step forward. "Keep talking like that and we will put your beak in the mud."

"Easy, don't let him get to you," Jason said calmly behind Nathanial.

Phera waved them both off with a wing. "When I am done with your team, you will be praying to whatever god you worship here," came the eagles threatening voice once again.

Nathanial remained steadfast, not breaking his concentration from the opponent. The cheers and music never stopped throughout the exchange.

The referee, a tiny Aplomado falcon, walked up between the two and held his small foretalons up. He spread out his blue-gray wings and spoke as loudly as his little lungs could carry him with the loud ambient noise echoing in the stadium. The falcon's voice was very stern even when dwarfed by the team captains. "Alright, alright. That's enough."

He pulled a coin out of his leather striped black and white vest before holding it up between the two angered gryphons. "I don't want to see any broken wings, or excessive blood. If I see any uncalled-for violence, I will eject you from this game. Are we clear?"

"Crystal," Nathanial said without breaking eye contact. Phera simply grinned at his response and nodded.

With that, the falcon ref turned to Phera. "You are the away team. Call heads or tails in the air." The ref tossed the coin into the air.

"Tails," Phera called before it hit the ground.

The ref leaned over to look at the coin as it landed. "Tails. Away team has the ball first," he confirmed as a small portion of the stand cheered for their team.

Phera fluffed up his black chest feathers and turned to flick his spotted feline tail at them. "Begin praying," the eagle said as the rest of his team chuckled and turned with him, a small group heading towards the dugouts.

Nathanial snorted and turned to his team. "I'm going to kill his ass," he commented before moving into position. Jason sighed and followed behind Nathanial, calling out for the other gryphons to come along. Aadhya, Rachel and Antonio nodded to Thyra as they walked off, following Nathanial closely while he discussed strategy with them.

Thyra and a few others made their way back to the dugout across the field. She wished she could be starting as well, but she understood Victor's decision to bring her off the bench. Despite a season's worth of games, she was still new. Her time would come. Still, it weighed heavy on her heart. She wanted to be out there with her team at this moment.

"Thyra!" She heard a familiar voice shout from the front row of the stands and looked up to see Johnathen standing there waving at her, and immediately smiled to her husband. His friend Keith was with him, along with Saul and Carl, who were completely shirtless with "Redtails" written across their gargantuan stomachs. Thyra laughed as they raised their beers to her.

She moved to the bench with Braden, Priscilla and Viola. "Looks like it's going to be a tough game today," Priscilla said, watching the gryphons get into position.

"Yeah, I doubt we will get to play today," Thyra responded. With a game this important, that would only happen if someone got hurt or their team got far ahead. She hoped for the latter, but there was always a possibility that one player could be injured. She did not wish it, but she was more than prepared to substitute in if need be.

Braden watched his twin corvid brother take his position at the goal and trilled with excitement. "I don't mind if we don't. I know my brother can handle just about any goal attempt anyone can through at him." It was true, his brother was one of the best goal keepers in the second league. The whistle blew, interrupting their conversation. The game was about to begin.

"I hope everyone is ready because it's time for Gryphball!" came the announcers voice over the loudspeakers. The sound of a large air cannon firing off signaled the beginning of the game. The white egg-shaped ball flew through the air. "*And there's the launch*!"

Three gryphons on the opposing team took to the air with hard wing strokes. One of them, an Egyptian vulture gryphon, caught it in midair and began dashing towards the opposite end of the field. Rachel, Aadhya, and Antonio leapt into the air in defensive positions, ready to guard.

The crowd began screaming even louder, chanting "Defense! Defense!" in favor of the home team. Rachel was up front, and attempted an air tackle but was out maneuvered by the surprisingly agile Egyptian vulture. Phera swooped in low and passed under Rachel to head directly towards the goal. The Egyptian vulture passed the ball over to Phera, but Antonio dove to intercept.

"*And it looks like number eleven, Antonio, has intercepted! He's got good momentum to slide past their air forwards*!" The announcer yelled as everyone cheered.

Phera and the Egyptian vulture summersaulted and pumped their wings hard to attempt to catch up. Rachel swooped in beside Antonio and screeched something at him. She rose up high above the other players as the last air guard on the opposition beelined straight towards Antonio. Right before he collided into the guard, Antonio spun and threw the ball high in the air. Antonio hit the gryphon hard and barrel rolled off to the side to regain composure as the other guard did the same.

"*Ouch! A hard hit between Redtails' eleven and Jays' sixty-six! But it seems the Redtails' air forward, Rachel, is wide open for a goal*!"

Rachel dove with high speed and caught the ball, heading straight towards the goal. The goal defender leaped from the ground to guard the air goal, but it was too late. Rachel faltered right and then banked hard left, causing the goalie to adjust wrong. Rachel tossed the ball through the hoop as a large siren played over the loudspeakers.

The crowd went wild. "*Gooooooaaaaaaal! An air goal by the Redtails in the first minute of the game! Wow, what a play! Those Jays are going to have to adjust their defenses against the 'Speeding Bullet of the Gryphball World!'*"

Rachel screeched loudly into the air as Antonio flew up beside her to bump his wing against her own. Jason and Nathanial ran on the ground underneath them heading back towards their side of the field. Thyra yelled from the sidelines and jumped in place, flapping her wings in excitement.

"I've never seen those two work together like that!" Thyra exclaimed as the jumbotron played replays on the screen for the crowd to watch.

"Yeah, and they are just getting warmed up," Brandon yelled over the loud music shaking the stadium.

Victor paced down the sidelines, and Thyra could swear she saw a smile on his beak as well. He waved his foretalons and held the clipboard in front of his beak as he spoke into the headset, giving commands for their next offensive play. Aadhya, Antonio and Rachel glided down to set in with the ground team to take a breather. They bumped wings together and spoke for a moment before getting into their positions once again. A loud whistle blew moments later and the sound of the air cannon echoed in the stadium.

"*Here's the launch*!" the announcer said as the air group took to the skies.

Rachel let the ball pass her and fall into the talons of Nathanial on the ground. He tucked the ball under a wing and began sprinting across the field. He crouched down low and galloped in long strides as the ground guards rushed forwards. Rachel swooped in low above Nathanial and Jason went left around the first guard. Nathanial juked right to attempt to get past the guard, but was hit on his rear flank.

"*Jays' number thirty-two with a direct hit on Redtails' five*!"

Nathanial tumbled along the ground, holding the ball firmly under his wing, and rolled back to his feet. By then, both rear guards were running straight towards him. Jason screeched loudly and held his wing out before Nathanial tossed the ball into the air.

"*And a pass attempt, will it be good? It looks like Jays' sixty-six is hot on the tracks*!"

Rachel turned to look at the Phera going in for an interception, but Rachel barrel rolled and struck him under the chest with her foot, causing the eagle to falter.

"And a good defensive play from Redtails' number eight! That fast flying kestrel really does pack a punch for such a small frame."

Jason caught the ball and turned to face the last rear guard. The gryphon was already in motion towards him. Jason screeched out again, calling for Nathanial to get open, but the other guards surrounded him. Jason jumped at the last second to avoid a tackle and beat his wings once to gain enough distance between them. A loud whistle blew as the falcon ref swooped down and halted the game, earning boos from the fans.

Coach Victor threw down his clipboard and screeched. "Bullshit! He beat his wings once! Not twice!"

The small referee ignored him and turned on his mic before unfolding his wings. "*Offensive foul for Redtails' twenty-two, carrying in air, start at center*," the small ref said.

The booing continued as the teams made their way to the center of the field. Phera seemed to say something to Rachel as she passed, and she responded with a middle talon. Victor groaned and picked up his clipboard before speaking into his mic again while all the players took their positions on the field.

"An unfortunate call for the Redtails. That really killed their momentum! It seemed like twenty-two had it there for a moment, but now they have to make all that headway up again."

The whistle blew again, and Nathanial instantly threw the ball up in the air. Rachel caught it and started beating her wings hard towards the opposite end of the field. When she saw Phera flying straight towards her, she dove and let the ball drop back down to Nathanial. Out of the sides, the Egyptian vulture swooped in and caught the gryphball before it reached Nathanial.

"*And an interception by the Jays fifty two*!"

Nathanial stopped in his tracks and started sprinting after them with Jason in tow. Rachel spun and beat her wings after the ball carrier, but the gryphon had too much speed already. Aadhya remained steadfast, floating steadily at the end of the field with her eyes locked on to the other vulture. She fell like a stone and spread out her great wings, as the carrier attempted to dodge, but was too late. Aadhya slammed into the carrier with a loud thud, earning cheers from the stands.

"*You know that had to hurt! Number three, the 'Red Brick Wall in the Sky,' isn't a force to be reckoned with*!"

The ball dropped to the ground and Bradon, the blue-eyed corvid gryphon, quickly picked it up and passed it to Antonio as he swooped low. Suddenly, Phera crashed into Antonio's backside, causing his wings to buckle. Everyone gasped in the stadium as he hit the ground hard and rolled. A loud whistle blew as the referee flew over to Antonio, who was still laying still on the ground.

"*That was completely uncalled for! An offsides strike by the Jays' sixty-six has sent Redtails' eleven crashing to the ground. He does not look good*."

Thyra watched with worry as Antonio attempted to stand but fell back to the ground. Suddenly, Aadhya tackled Phera out of nowhere and pinned him to the ground with her gigantic foretalons, screeching loudly in his face. A flurry of red, black, and white consumed the two. Talons slashed out and wings flared around in an attempt to gain the upper talon.

"*It seems like we have a fight! I can't say I don't blame Aadhya for lashing out.*"

Gryphons rushed over to the fighting as the crowd erupted in boos and cheers. They pulled Aadhya off of Phera and separated them. Thyra had never seen Aadhya in such rage. Her dusted red feathers were ruffled up, eartufts straight back, and a look of murder in her yellow eyes. She was still yelling and screeching at the enemy player as her teammates held her back. Aadhya pointed her curved talons towards Phera and he wiped some blood off his grinning beak.

"Damnit. Thyra, I think you're up. Antonio doesn't look good," Victor said softly, watching a group of humans run up with a stretcher.

They looked over him for a moment as Antonio struggled to stand with the help of the paramedics. The whole crowd began to clap as Antonio stood and limped off the field as the paramedics lifted under his wings. The ref walked up beside Phera and Aadhyea before flashing a yellow card in his claws.

Aadhya turned around and walked towards the end of the field, flicking her tail with agitation. Phera waved off the ref with a wing and begun walking towards the opposite end of the field.

"*A yellow card for the Redtails' eleven and Jays' sixty-six! I would have thought they would eject sixty-six from the game, but it looks like they are giving him his one and only warning!*"

"Get in there, Thyra," Victor commanded and turned to look at her. She nodded in response and stepped out of the dugout. "Be careful, but destroy that asshole if you can. I don't let gryphons that hurt my players on purpose get away without repercussion," Victor added sternly, his large black eyes narrowed.

"Ill do it," Thyra said with confidence and stepped onto the field. It was her time to shine.

Chapter 17 Insanity

Daniel pulled the van around to the back of the church and drove under an awning. The van door slid open and several men jumped out. Matthew and his two bodyguards walked out of the church through double glass doors and approached the van as the men opened the van's rear doors. Daniel jumped out and slammed the driver door shut, rage building inside of him as he saw Matthew's approach.

"Before you begin, my condolences. If I would have known-," Matthew began.

"Save your fake pity!" Daniel shouted, pointing at Matthew, his eyes still puffy and red. "You don't give a damn that my friend was just murdered. You just care that we actually got the gryphon that you want." He strode to the side of the van and watched as the men struggled to pull the limp gryphon out of the back.

"You're right. I don't care," Matthew said, crossing his hands behind his back. "He was your man, not mine. What happened was unfortunate, but I expected it was possible we could lose someone."

The bishop stood a couple feet away from Daniel, watching the men pull the gryphon out. Daniel turned around with his teeth clenched and hands trembling.

"I'm sure he was a good man..." Matthew continued.

It took everything Daniel had not to leap at Matthew and strangle him right then and there. If he caught them off guard, he could put down the old man and his two bodyguards within two seconds, but surely the others would retaliate. It would be a death sentence.

Matthew and his bodyguards saw the murderous intent in Daniel's eyes. They pulled back their jackets slowly and put their hands on their holstered weapons. Daniel did the same, reaching for his weapon.

"Daniel. Do not turn this into a bloodbath," Matthew said calmly. "Let us discuss this further." The men finished unloading the gryphon and all four of them struggled to carry the beast under the awning and into the church.

"Fuck your discussions! I'm done with you. I'm done with all your bullshit and whatever religious zealot endgame you have. I'm not doing this anymore." Daniel grit his teeth in anger. He turned to look inside at the tarp draped over the body of Jack. He huffed and slammed the two rear doors on the van.

"You can't quit. You're under con..." Matthew began.

"Watch me. You and your god can go to hell." Daniel quickly walked around to the driver's side and hopped in. He slammed the door shut and started up the diesel engine. The tires squealed as Daniel pulled away from the church and across the parking lot.

Matthew watched him leave and let out a sigh. "You'll be in Hell soon enough, Daniel," he muttered under his breath, then turned to head into the church with his men following behind him.

* * *

The small room Anfang was in was dark and shadowed. The creature could barely see his blood-stained and deformed talons. He stretched them out, noticing the chains binding his limbs together. His mind felt foggy, and he had a splitting headache that tore at the back of his skull. He flicked his one eartuft and looked around the room as his eyes adjusted to the darkness. "Wh…where am I?"

A door creaked open, letting in a blinding light. He hissed and squinted his feline green eyes. "I see you're finally awake," said a voice asked from within that light. "Anfang, was it?"

There was a click and a bulb above him flickered on. Anfang struggled to take in his surroundings as his eyes adjusted, revealing a rather bare room containing nothing more than a few chairs and tables stacked against the wall.

"Yes. Anfang I am," he replied, his voice croaking as he talked. He lifted his foretalons to rub his head with a low growl. "My head… It hurts," the gryphon complained and watched as the man grabbed a chair from the stack.

"I suspect so. Sedatives can have such a nasty effect. Especially ones as strong as the ones they used on you." The man placed the chair a safe distance from Anfang and sat down. "My name is Matthew. I'm here to help," he said as two other well-dressed men entered the room and stood beside him. "You killed one of my men. Why?"

Anfang sat up and stretched out his leathery wings. He looked to the bald man sitting before him, noticing the aging wrinkles covering his face. Anfang chuckled deep in his chest and shook his head.

"You humans so weak. You think killing so bad. Why? Why not kill what we want? Eat what we want? Play with what we want?" Anfang responded and looked to the two men standing beside Matthew. He noticed the weapons on their hips and let out a deep growl. "And I kill before I am hurt. I kill your man because he had gun. Those men, they have guns too."

Anfang got to his feet, causing the two men to place their hands on their holstered firearms. He tried to take a step forward, but something restrained him. He looked back to see his hindpaws chained to the wall behind him and clicked his jaws together again.

"You don't like guns." Matthew stated.

"No. They hurt me." Anfang answered.

Matthew paused for a moment considering the response. "They hurt you, do they? Have you been shot before?" Anfang nodded in response and pointed to a huge bare spot on his feathered chest that was covered in scars.

"Yes. Lots and lots. They hurt and sting bad," Anfang answered and gestured towards the bodyguards. "Tell them go away, then we talk!" he demanded.

To Anfang's surprise, Matthew decided not to press against his wishes for now. The old man looked to his men and gestured towards the door. Their eyes widened, but they turned to walk out of the room, leaving just Matthew and Anfang together.

"I don't want to hurt you. Unlike those other people, I want to take care of you. But, I need to know I can trust you." Matthew said, his gaze focused on the deformed gryphon.

Anfang chuckled again and hissed. "Trust. Trust. Trust. Why? Why should I trust humans? They want to hurt me. They want to poke me with tools and chain me and do it again…and again…and again. They hurt me so I kill them. You say you different. You want to help. But I am in chains still." Anfang's voice screeched slightly as he stared directly at the soulless eyes of the human before him.

Matthew sighed and sat for a minute more, considering his next words carefully. "What can I do to earn your trust?" he asked.

Anfang held up his deformed forearms and pulled at the chains. "Start with this. You say trust. Then trust that I not hurt you." Anfang's mangy lion tail swiped behind him. Matthew sat for a moment more and before he could say something else, Anfang chimed in again. "If I hurt you, those humans will kill me. I still no escape with rear legs chained."

"A valid point," Matthew responded.

He stood up from his chair and pulled a key out of his pocket. Anfang held his foretalons up watched him carefully as he approached. Matthew grabbed onto a scaled wrist and put the key inside the cuff, turning it and letting it fall off. He did the same to the other and held his breath for a moment as the gryphon's bloodied talons were now free.

Anfang trilled and rubbed his wrists. “Trust,” he said in a low tone as he placed his talons on the carpet. Matthew took a couple steps back and sat down in the chair once again.

“It is a start. Now, I have some other things to discuss with you.” Matthew sat back and crossed his legs. Anfang shook his head.

“I hunger. And you must make the head pain go away,” Anfang demanded. Matthew sighed and shrugged his shoulders.

“I figured as much. James?” Matthew called out calmly. The door opened slowly and one of the men from before peaked his head in. “Please fetch our friend something to eat, and bring some pain killers.”

He nodded and closed the door behind him. Matthew turned back to Anfang and looked at the metallic discs embedded in his upper arm. “I am curious as to what those are for.”

Anfang looked down at his arms and raised a talon up to scratch at the black metal ports at the center. “The people in white put them there. They put sharp things in it. I not know what for,” he responded while still touching them. He turned back to Matthew and put his talons back down. His one eartuft returned to its natural position and his mangy coat of feathers smoothed down as the gryphon relaxed. “I ask now. Who are you?”

Matthew placed his hands together and smiled. “That is a complicated question. Who exactly is anybody? I am simply a man of God seeking to help lost souls find their way in this world.” Anfang growled and spat on the ground, causing Matthew to frown.

"You humans with this God. I not understand. I not want to. Some humans try to explain, but it makes me angry." Anfang responded and looked away, staring at a crucifix on one of the walls. "They say things like eternity. We live. We eat. We die. That all."

"I'm not attempting to press religion on you. You asked who I was, so I simply gave you my answer," Matthew retorted, trying to keep the beast calm. "My turn for a question. Who are you?"

Anfang glanced over to Matthew, his green feline eyes looking over him for a second before glancing back at the wall. "I Anfang. A gryphon. They tell me I made for war. I made to kill. I follow orders. That is all I am."

"Made for war, you say? So, you mean the military made you," Matthew asked.

"I not know this word," Anfang responded.

Matthew thought for a second and nodded his head. "Well, I am curious. You seem to be angry at humanity and know pain. Also, I have never heard of a gryphon such as you… like..."

"A monster?" Anfang clicked his cat-like teeth against his upper beak again and hissed. "I hear humans call me this. All of them."

"No, I was not going to say such a word. You are simply different than other gryphons," Matthew pointed out. Anfang looked down at his talons and raised one to his beak to begin cleaning the dried blood off of them with a rough tongue.

"I not know this. I never be free. Only one cage to next cage. I only see one other gryphon. Her name was Thyra." Anfang stopped cleaning his talons for a moment, lost in thought.

Matthew's bushy eyebrows rose up at the mention of her name. Matthew leaned forward in his chair as Anfang took notice of his sudden interest. "Do you know Thyra?" Anfang asked.

"I do. Very well, in fact. And her husband, Johnathen," Matthew responded.

Anfang's eyes widened and a small smile grew on his deformed beak muzzle. "I want to see her!" he said excitedly. "It has been long time. Years and years!"

Matthew chuckled and shook his head, his curiosity doubling. "Don't worry, I'll let you see her very soon. How do you know Thyra?"

"We grow up together. Same lab when young. I miss her. She came to my room to play every day and we have fun," Anfang began, then suddenly frowned and looked down to the ground. "Then they take her away. They take me away. I…I was angry. I killed one of the humans. They hurt me and I wake up somewhere. They put me on table, hurt me, change me . . . and put me in cage for long time. Then I wake up somewhere new. I not see her again."

"Do not fret. I assure you that you will see her very soon," Matthew said gently. The door opened slowly, breaking Anfang's concentration. Matthew turned around to see James holding a plate of raw steaks and a small pile of pills "Ah, here you are, Anfang." Matthew said as James placed the plate on the ground.

Anfang's pupils turned into pencil thin slits at the sight of red meat. He quickly put his foretalons on a chunk and leaned his beak muzzle down to tear off a bloody piece. He smacked his jaws together and swallowed the piece whole. Matthew watched with disgust as the beast made quick work of several pounds of meat as if they were nothing more than an appetizer.

The sounds of tearing flesh echoed in the small room as the gryphon snapped the last piece up and swallowed it. His beak dripped with blood and he closed his eyes, savoring the last morsel while it descended his throat. Matthew sat for a minute more, watching as Anfang licked his talons clean.

Once finished with his meal, Anfang's pupils widened as the sentient part of his mind returned. He ruffled his coat of tattered feathers and fur before sitting up straight once more. He noticed the pills on the plate and picked one up to inspect it. "These help pain, yes? Not more?"

"Just painkillers, yes. I'm not trying to drug you. Remember, trust." Matthew responded. Anfang watched Matthew for a moment more, seeming to study him. Satisfied by the response, Anfang tossed them back and swallowed quickly.

"As you were saying?" Matthew pressed.

"I say I never free. Not free as human is. I say I want to be free. I want to see Thyra." Anfang gave him a firm stare. "You promise me I be free, and I do what you want."

"It seems we have a deal then. I can guarantee your freedom," Matthew said with a crooked smile. "But first, there is someone I need you to kill." He reached into his pocket and pulled out his cellphone. Matthew leaned forward and showed Anfang a picture of Daniel.

Anfang looked at the picture and cocked his head. “I remember him. He was there before I sleep. I can kill him. I good at kill. It is what I know. Why do you want Anfang to kill?” Anfang asked curiously. Matthew seemed to slightly confused by the question but answered.

“This man has done many bad things, bad things that shouldn’t go unpunished. As far as I’m concerned, he’s food. You do this for me, and I’ll bring you to Thyra?” Matthew replied.

“I can play with him? Eat him too?” Anfang asked.

“You can do as you wish with him. I don’t care,” Matthew responded and sat back in his chair. Anfang put on a toothy grin, clearly excited at the opportunity to kill again.

“I do it,” Anfang said with a nod. He pulled at the chains again still binding his hindfeet and turned to look at them.

“Here, let me get those for you.” Matthew stood and walked around the gryphon’s backside. He put his key into the cuffs and pulled them apart with ease. The chains made a loud thud as they fell to the floor, and Anfang slowly stood up.

Suddenly, Anfang turned around and swiped his foretalons out. Matthew did not even have time to react as the gryphon took him by surprise and struck him against the chest. Matthew coughed as he was flung back against the wall.

Anfang's talons sunk into the wall around Matthews throat, but not a scratch was put on him. The gryphon held him firmly against the throat, careful not to cut off his air completely. The gryphon stood on his hindfeet to tower over the small fragile man and spread his leathery wings out for measure.

"You listen now, yes?" Anfang craned his head down to press his wicked beak muzzle close to Matthews face.

His breath reeked of dead flesh and blood and his eyes glowed green in the dim light as he stared directly into Matthew's eyes. The old man realized that the beast was perhaps not as stupid as it had seemed.

Anfang saw the bishop's fear and chuckled deeply in his chest. "You think I stupid, but I smart. I know lies. You lie to me, and I will kill you. I will kill all of you. Listen, yes. Listen. I had humans in past lie to me. They think Anfang stupid, think they smarter, but they now dead. All of them." Anfang slurred, his words mixed with hisses.

Matthew placed his hands on the gryphons scaled foreclaws, trying to find purchase on them. His eyes were wide with fear, and he shook uncontrollably. "Who the one in chains now…?" Anfang held him there for a few seconds more before Matthew found his breath again.

"Yes! Yes I understand. No more chains and I promise I won't lie. You have my word," Matthew spat out.

Anfang watched and slowly pulled his head back along with his foretalons. Matthew fell to his knees and coughed loudly, holding his throat. Anfang sat on his haunches again, and watched as Matthew found his breath again. The door opened behind them as one of the men peeked in.

"Sir, is everything alright?" the man asked. Matthew looked up at Anfang and saw him staring back. He motioned his beak muzzle towards the door, pushing Matthew to respond positively.

"Yes. Everything is fine. I tripped while undoing his chains," Matthew said.

Satisfied, the guard closed the door again, leaving the two of them alone. He stood up and brushed himself off as the gryphon snorted through his nares. Anfang stepped aside to allow Matthew to pass and followed him to the door.

"You try anything like that again…" Matthew muttered under his breath.

"And?" Anfang quietly replied, following Matthew out into the hallway. Matthew clenched his fists and crossed his hands behind his back. The silence caused Anfang to chuckle deeply.

Matthew's men walked behind the bulky gryphon cautiously, watching his every move. Anfang turned to look back at the men, who remained unspeaking. They were trying to suppress their fear, but he could sense it. His beak muzzle curved into a toothy grin, knowing how helpless those men felt.

"You can wait here for a few minutes. I'm going to confirm Daniel's location and you can be on your way." Matthew stopped at a pair of wooden doors and opened them. Anfang looked inside at the room filled with bookcases and furniture. Outside the gigantic bay windows, the sun was raising high in the sky.

"I not know this place. How do I find this Daniel?" Anfang said as he entered the room. He looked around at all the books, and turned back to look at Matthew, who was still standing at the doors.

"We will guide you. But first," Matthew took a bracelet that was handed to him by one of the men. He held it up for Anfang to look at the armband, and his eartuft folded back with displeasure. "You must wear this. It is a tracker. It will tell us where you are."

"You want to leash me." Anfang growled deeply and looked over the metal band again. It looked simple and streamlined with a small screen at its center, nothing big and awkward to get in his way. The thin shiny metal was decorated to look almost like the watchbands he had seen humans wear, but without the dials in the middle.

"If you mean figuratively, then yes. You promised me to help me. I can't have you flying off as soon as you leave these doors." Matthew took a step forward and opened the band. Anfang sat for a moment and thought.

"Where is trust?" Anfang pointed out.

"A certain amount of trust is earned, not given," Matthew replied.

Anfang slowly lifted one scaled forearm and huffed through his nares, reluctant to accept the band but knew there was no other choice. Matthew put the band on and clipped it in place to make sure it was tight. He pressed a button on the side and the small screen lit up with numbers. "There. Now sit tight. I will be back in a couple minutes."

Matthew left and shut the doors behind him, leaving Anfang alone in the office. The gryphon glanced around, looking at the countless books lining the walls and then out the window once again. A small clock on the wall ticked rhythmically, counting the seconds as they passed.

Anfang walked over to one bookcase and sat, running his talons across the spines of the books. He could read simple words, and tried to sound out a couple of the books names. "Pride and Pre…pred…predju…" Anfang grumbled as his tongue ran across his sharp teeth. "Moby, Moby Dick… Ham…let."

He picked one out in particular and pulled it from the shelf to glance at the cover. "War…and P...Peace." Anfang held the book in his large talons and opened it up to a random page. He took a while trying to read the first sentence, and listened to the clock somehow growing louder with every tick.

His eyes strained until he shut them. His mind grew fuzzy and distant before remembering a similar clock in a white room. There were several men standing in front of him, dressed in white with masks over their faces. One was holding a weapon and was pointing it straight at him.

Anfang had hissed and tried to move, but he was bound to a wall. A loud noise had rang out and his ear rang as a sharp pain had lanced through his chest. He had screeched and looked down at the wound leaking with blood. One of the men walked to him and bent down to retrieve a piece of metal on the ground.

Anfang had struggled against the bindings, wanting to lash out and rip the human in half, but it was no use. The rest of the humans began to clap as the man placed the small metal piece on the tray and walked back to the group. Anfang had looked through an observing window, seeing two men garbed in intricate green clothing and wearing many badges. He could see them smiling.

Anfang shook the memory from his mind and roared before tossing the book across the room. It slammed against the clock and broke it into pieces before it fell to the ground. The wooden door suddenly opened as one of Matthew's bodyguards peaked in with a frightened look on his face. Anfang glared at the man, and he slowly closed the door behind him.

The gryphon turned to look back at the window to watch the trees blow in the wind. "War. No peace."

Chapter 18 The Hunt

Anfang closed his eyes as fresh air flowed into his lungs. The evening sun beat down on his brown and crème feathers, bathing him in pleasant warmth. The wind whipped across his scarred face, up over his back. and under his leathery wings.

He flapped once and felt the burning of exhaustion in his wing joints. It had been so long since he had flown free that he was out of shape. He beat his wings again and straightened them to glide.

His armband beeped and he lifted his foretalon to look down at the small screen. Matthew had explained how to use the device. At first, he had been confused by the concept, but he display was simple; just an arrow pointing towards his destination and the distance left to go. It had come to make sense to him with practice.

"Follow the arrow," Anfang repeated out loud and he felt his stomach rumble. It had only been a couple hours since last he last ate but his crop was empty

Another beat of his wings and the burning painfully reminded him of his inexperience at flying for long periods of time. When the device told him five miles to finish, he had no concept of what that distance meant. Was five miles far away or close? He hoped he would arrive sooner rather than later.

His task was simple, find Daniel and kill him. Matthew had made it clear he did not care if it was done quietly or if it was done in the presence of a crowd. Anfang smiled at the thought of having an audience for his show. The look of horror on the faces of humans as he dug his talons into hot flesh had always been a delight to him and well worth the punishments he received for it back in the labs. Only this time, there would be no repercussions if he performed it right. There would be no one to chain him and beat him for his actions. There would be no one to help this Daniel.

The band beeped again and Anfang looked down to see the words, *destination reached*. He saw no arrow anymore, and assumed his target was somewhere below him. Anfang banked and turned into a lazy spiral down, scanning the area for the best place to land.

There were a few buildings below him, each a short distance apart with trees surrounding them. He felt his curiosity grow as he scanned the buildings, wondering what the humans did with each one. Each had a parking area filled with multiple cars. He had watched television and understood concepts such as restaurants and grocery stores since that's where humans went for food, but everything else was a mystery.

Anfang landed roughly in a grassy area next to one building and folded in his aching leathered wings. He looked around, checking to see if any humans had seen him land, but found none. Anfang looked through the glass window on the side, and saw multiple tables, chairs and booths. He watched as people conversed while sitting across from one another, and eating food.

Anfang finally put it together. “A restaurant!”

It was interesting to see so many humans sitting in one room, eating and drinking together. A woman walked back and forth from one door, and each time she appeared again, she held multiple plates of food. He grinned at the thought of a human bringing him endless amounts of food and eating until he could not fit another bite into his crop. A blond man in the corner of the restaurant turned to wave at the woman bringing food and Anfang’s feline eyes latched onto him.

“Daniel,” he hissed under his breath.

Anfang could feel his heartbeat quicken, and his muscles tense up as his predatory instincts inside came to life. His muzzle curved into a toothy snarl and he chuckled to himself as endorphins rushed through him, giving him a high in the process.

He twitched his head to the left as someone stepped out of the restaurant’s front door and headed towards their car. A way in. Anfang walked towards the front door and opened it with his foretalons.

As he stepped inside, he focused on Daniel in the back, busy eating his food. Suddenly, the room fell quiet. He realized that every person was holding their breath, staring straight at the monstrosity that just casually walked in. He gave them his best toothy snarl.

“M-may I help you, sir?” a woman stuttered from behind the counter, clearly terrified at the beast before her.

Anfang's eartuft stood straight up and his feathers ruffled as he pointed to Daniel at the back. "Yeeesss. I've come for him," he said with a croak in his voice. Slowly, Daniel turned around and stared blankly across the room.

Anfang stared into Daniel's blue eyes, and the man turned ghostly pale. The hideous gryphon laughed and walked across the room, pushing tables and chairs aside with his massive body.

Daniel stood quickly, drew out his weapon and pointed the barrel at Anfang. "Matthew sent you, didn't he?"

Everyone in the restaurant screamed and went into a panic at the sight of the sidearm. The gryphon broke into a sprint across the restaurant, his wings flared. Tables, chairs and people scattered as the gryphon closed ground. Daniel fired.

Anfang winced as the familiar pain shot through his body. The bullets stung but they fell to the ground after hitting his body. His blood pumped and his ear rang as another shot was fired, yet the gryphon did not stop. A third shot was produced just as Anfang closed in. He swiped, and felt flesh tear against his talons.

Daniel was sent flying towards the front windows and hit hard, breaking the glass. He quickly sat up, clutching his chest as blood poured from the open wound. People screamed and rushed out of the building. Anfang watched the crowd leave, and turned back to Daniel. They were alone now.

Anfang slowly approached his preyl, his eyes wide and a permanent grin attached on his toothy beak muzzle. Daniel, lifted his weapon and fired again. This time, the bullet missed Anfang completely. The gryphon grabbed Daniel's wrist, and squeezed. A loud snap echoed in the quiet room along with Daniel's cries. Anfang trilled and perked his eartuft, savoring the sound.

"I sad everyone leaves. I want people to watch. I want them to see." He dropped Daniels limp arm and leaned his beak muzzle in close to Daniels face, staring into his eyes. He wanted to see the pure terror in them, but all he saw was anger.

"I'm going to kill you for murdering Jack, you bastard," Daniel spat out weakly. Anfang cocked his head, and sat on his haunches in front of Daniel.

"Jack? Oh, you friend! Yes. I no get to eat him. I was sad." Anfang responded. He saw Daniel grit his teeth in anger and reach for his weapon with his uninjured hand. Anfang let him almost reach it and then pushed the gun away with his foretalons.

"You think you so strong. But you so weak!" Anfang taunted and pushed a talon into a gaping cut on Daniels chest. The man yelled as Anfang dug around for a moment, and pulled the talon back. He ran his long salivating tongue across his talon to lick the blood from it.

The sweet copper taste made the insane gryphon shiver with pleasure as he watched Daniel stare helplessly up at him. Daniel looked at the bleeding wounds on Anfang, clearly confused how the gryphon was still standing after being shot multiple times.

"What are you?" Daniel asked and gripped his chest, desperately trying to stop the bleeding as it soaked his shirt.

"They call me a weapon for war. A killer. Yes, humans make me this way. It what they want. Death. War. Blood." Anfang took a deep audible breath through his nares as if to take in the smell of it all. "I know why you humans like it. It feel good. It taste good. Power and blood." Anfang reached forward with his gigantic talons and wrapped them around Daniel's throat.

The man wheezed and put his functioning hand on the gryphon's scaled forearms, desperately clawing at them with his fingernails. "P...please," Daniel choked as tears filled his eyes.

Anfang looked into his eyes again, finally seeing the fear and realization of his own mortality. Anfang laughed loudly and leaned his beak muzzle in again.

"Yes?" Anfang asked and squeezed firmly. Daniels mouth opened as he tried to suck in air. The gryphon waited for a moment, and tilted his eartuft to Daniels mouth as if to wait for a response. "I not hear you," Anfang taunted and pulled his head back.

Then he looked out through the broken glass window as bright flashing blue lights caught his attention. Daniel's body shook and his legs kicked wildly under the crushing talons. Anfang frowned as he watched several men hop out of cars and suddenly the quiet room erupted into sounds of explosions.

Anfang screeched out as several shots hit him square in the body. He fell onto his back and rolled to his feet, shivering with pain. His whole body screamed at him, and his vision faltered. He had to run.

Anfang turned to see Daniel gasping for air, lying on his side. No, he had to kill Daniel first. Anfang turned to lunge at Daniel, just as the front door opened violently and several men poured into the room. Several more shots rang out as Anfang crouched low and maneuvered behind a row of booths. He ran along the wall, and heard the men call out orders to one another. The gryphon slipped out low to the ground, and saw three men standing at the entrance, looking over to Daniel.

He seized the opportunity, and leapt with his wings flared out wide. The sounds of crushing bones filled the room as Anfang took one of them to the ground, talons digging into one officer's spine. The other two remaining men spun around to see the great beast pulling his talons out of their fallen comrade. Anfang lunged low and swiftly, swiping talons at the two men's legs. They both shouted in pain and fell to the floor.

Every movement he made was pure hunter instinct. The officers did not stand a chance against him. Anfang righted himself and bit down on one man's neck, breaking it in an instant. He stood over the last human, looked down at him as he cried out in anguish. Another round of shots rang from outside, whirling by his body. Anfang screeched and quickly turned his head to see more men standing by their vehicles, all opening fire.

Anfang crouched low again and ran towards the back, busting through a swinging door. He looked around quickly, his eyes darting back and forth at all the bright metal in the room. There was food scattered all across the shining tables, along with dishes broken along the tile floor.

He perked his eartfut as he heard the humans shouting at one another. Anfang chose a door, and slammed into it. He tumbled out of the building and darted across the back lot to the cover of the trees. More gunshots filled the air and he felt pain jab through his rear leg.

Anfang cursed and darted between the trees as fast as he could. He did not know where to go. He just knew he had to get away.

Anfang ran until his muscles burned, and then he ran faster. His bloodied talons sank into the moist earth with every long stride he took, his wings tucked in tight to his side. He had to find a clearing or somewhere where he could take to the skies.

Then he found it. The tree line broke into a vast open space. There were small people running around in the middle of the field, passing around a ball with other humans standing on the edges of the field.

Anfang spread his wings, and pushed with all his strength to climb into the air. He beat his leathery wings hard, fighting for altitude as the people below him shouted to one another. Anfang felt his chest heave as it struggled to take in enough air, but he pushed forward and flapped his wings harder. The humans below him became tiny specs as he ascended into the sky.

His mind slowly became clearer as cognition came back. He checked behind him, watching as the restaurant and the multitude flashing lights disappeared from view. Anfang began to laugh uncontrollably.

"Yes! What a rush!" He called out to himself and strained for another wing beat. "So much blood. So much."

Anfang smiled and rose higher into the air until he was almost touching the clouds. He set out into a steady glide, and let the air streams take over. His endorphins tapered off, and with that, excruciating pain rocked through his entire body. Anfang fought back the pain and ground his curved teeth against his beak.

"Daniel still lives…" Anfang hissed under his heavy breaths, cursing himself for toying with his prey too much.

He should have made it swift, precise, and calculated. It would have been easy to snap the man's neck or tear out his throat at any time during their whole exchange. He had just been having too much fun. Sure, maybe he would die from losing blood, but Anfang had wanted to watch him die!

Anfang looked down at his chest and ran his talons over it, finding multiple bleeding wounds. He ran his talon around one wound and retrieved a bullet still stuck halfway into his flesh. He flicked the round away and checked another wound on his chest. That one had barely scratched the surface but had left a huge blue welt in place.

Anfang glided and checked the rest of the wounds he could see, occasionally pulling out a bullet and tossing it away. He was lucky they hadn't used bigger guns. The humans had experimented enough with his altered flesh for him know that he wasn't completely immune.

Satisfied with his condition, he looked to his wings outstretched in the air. His muscles were exhausted. He tried to force another wing beat out of them, but only received a slight twitch in response.

His bracelet vibrated, and he looked down to see it flashing with a message. He cocked his head and tried to read the digital words. "L…Land… and hide. We will come… to you."

He clutched his front talons to his chest and looked around, noticing nothing but forest and a few sparse roads beneath him. Anfang looked to the sun and took note of how much lower it looked. He must have been flying for hours and not realized it.

In the distance, he could make out a small red structure at the end of a field. It looked abandoned and far away from any road he could see. Anfang slowed his momentum and made his descent towards the building. He felt his wings give out just as his foretalons touched the ground.

He tumbled across the grass and sighed as he lay on his back while the world spun wildly. He slowly forced himself to stand up on his quivering legs, wings drooping to the side. The building in front of him was in disrepair, old red paint flicking off of rotting wooden boards and the front door slightly open.

He limped through the door and forced his eyes to adjust to the darkness inside. The smell of old manure and animal hair stung his nares along with the musty air. Several stalls were open with moldering straw on the ground, and various rusting tools hung on the walls.

Anfang struggled to move forward, and saw a pile of soft-looking hay. His body ached to fall down into it and he did not stop himself. He collapsed and took a deep breath of the earthy scent, allowing his eyes to close. Then everything went black.

Chapter 19 Confidence

Thyra's heart beat heavily in her chest as she walked onto the field. She could hear the positive shouts behind her from Johnathen and others, giving her the confidence and energy that she needed. Antonio limped next to her with the assistance of the crutch under his wings.

"You can do it, Thyra," Antonio assured her.

Her crest feathers ruffled as she saw the spark of spirit in his eyes. He believed in her, even though she was inexperienced and nervous about failing her team in this important game. She looked to her teammates, who all smiled in reassurance. She was surrounded by great gryphons, and even in the shadows of negativity, they still smiled. Thyra approached Rachel and Aadhya first, and extended her wing to bump against their own as the opposing team got into their positions.

The personal foul meant they were staring on the Jays' side of the field with the ball in their hands. Thyra and hunkered down with wings spread, ready to leap at the sound of the whistle. The world seemed to slow as her senses were increased by excitement and nerves.

She assessed the opposing players, her eyes darting between them quickly. She mentally went over Victor's teachings on the new defensive plays as she looked to the other opposing players and tried to read their movements and think of corresponding actions against their defense. Then her eyes locked onto Phera's and anger rose within her. She was going to beat this gryphon fair and square.

The whistle blew, pulling Thyra out of her thoughts. Nathanial, the ground forward, hiked the ball into the air as Rachel quickly took the skies.

"And the game is on!" yelled the announcer.

Thyra pushed with all her might against the earth and beat her wings hard. She watched as Rachel clutched the ball in her talons, and avoided Phera's first poor attempt at a tackle. Thyra could see that he was overcome by his temper, and unable to think clearly. Rachel read into this as well, and easily avoided his hasty attack, leaving her wide open to progress down field. Thyra followed behind, having trouble keeping up with the much quicker falcon.

One of the air guards rushed Rachel, leaving her no choice but to pass the gryphball backwards to Thyra. Thyra's eyes widened and darted between the two, watching the ball fall in slow motion. She caught it and tucked her wings to avoid the air guard as he dove to intercept.

"*A smooth pass and Redtails' thirteen avoids the guard for the Jays*!"

Thyra looked down below, and saw that Nathanial and Jason were both covered by the Jays' guards. She flicked out her wings into a steady glide and checked her front; there was only the last guard and the goalie to take care of. Making her decision, she beat her wings hard and headed straight towards the last defender.

She heard a shout from below and looked down to Nathanial pointing to the right. An opening, if she needed it. She felt determination well up inside of her. She had the chance to prove herself in her first minute of the game. If she made a goal right now in this semifinal game, it would silence anyone that questioned her abilities.

Thyra's eyes narrowed as she approached the last defender headlong and braced herself. She rotated left, and felt the defender's beak slide along her chest, taking a couple feathers with it but ultimately the tackle had no effect. The crowd screamed in excitement at the near miss.

"*The Jays' sixty-eight guard missed the tackle! Redtails' thirteen is clear for an air goal! Can the goalie hold his ground, I mean air*?" the announcer shouted as she beat her wings hard towards the goal.

Her eyes focused on the hoop behind the hovering gryphon, and she remembered the strategy she was taught. Thyra dove, confusing the goalie and then faltered right. Clutching the egg-shaped gryphball in her talons, she brought it over her head and tossed it underneath the goalie.

The goalie tried to correct, but his talons missed the ball by inches. Everybody held their breath as the gryphball struck the side metal pole, then bounced in. A loud whistle erupted from the referee falcon, and the crowd went wild.

"*An air goal by the Redtails' thirteen! What a play from the rookie*!"

Thyra screeched with excitement. The band played as the fans jumped to their feet and yelled, clapping their hands and chanting. She flew a victory lap around the field, feeling the energy from the fans as they celebrated another goal.

"*With that score, it's Redtails six, Jays nothing.*"

Thyra wore a big beak grin and pumped her fist in the air to get the crowd riled up even more. She looked back Phera, and could see the anger on his red face. Laughing, she flew up to Rachel.

"I knew you had it in you!" Rachel yelled and bumped wings with her. They glided down together to their side of the field and landed softly. Jason and Nathanial jogged up, both looking very pleased with the performance.

"Not bad, Redtail. Not bad at all. You keep playing like that and I'll consider you a teammate," Nathanial said with a slight beakgrin. He bumped wings with Thyra as she took in the rare compliment from the caracara.

"You got it," Thyra replied. Nathanial turned to head towards the center of the field, talking to Victor in his headset.

Jason listened to the conversation in his headset and nodded in understanding. He relayed the instructions. "Victor says good play. Keep your formation and adjust with Rachel as needed. You'll be guarding the other vulture if they advance past midfield. Conserve your energy as much as you can, but take any openings you get."

"Understood," Thyra said as she watched the opposing team get into position. Above, Aadhya turned in lazy circles high in the air. She was looking down with a bright smile on her face.

"*Five minutes left in the first half, aaaaaand here's the launch*!"

A loud whistle went off and the sound of the air cannon shook the stadium. The crowd chanted, "*Defense! Defense*!" and stomped their feet with the beat.

Rachel and Thyra sprinted across the field before taking to the skies once again, the opposing air team doing the same. Rachel proceeded forward to intercept, but missed by a small margin. She flipped quickly and took off after Phera, who had possession of the gryphball. Thyra hovered in place, and then backtracked to adjust speed with the Egyptian vulture as he flew by. She kept pace with him as he advanced towards their air goal.

Rachel caught up to Phera and flared her wings out to stop his progression. He had to bank towards the outside to avoid her. Aadhya dove out of the sky, and Phera looked up to see her fast approaching. He dove and tossed the ball down towards one of his ground forwards.

"*Looks like Jays' sixty-six doesn't want to feel that tackle again! A pass to the ground. And it's caught*!"

A black gryphon wearing number eighty caught the ball and took off down the field, narrowly avoiding an interception from Nathanial. Jason moved in to block his progression, but the black gryphon passed the ball off to another ground forward who was open. A small portion of the crowd cheered for their Jays team.

"*Jays' eighty is wide open for a ground goal! Only the Redtails' goalie can stop him!*"

Brandon stood in front of the goal with a wide stance, his black wings unfolded wide. Jason screeched as he picked up the pace, trying to catch up with the gryphon, but it was no use. Number eighty was faster.

The ground forward scooped the ball out from under his wing and threw it with all his might. Everyone held their breath. Brandon leaped to the left and blocked the ball with a wing, stopping it dead in its tracks.

"*Incomplete! The Redtails have possession.*"

A loud cheer erupted as Brandon tucked the ball away quickly, and everybody turned to head back to the opposite end of the field.

Thyra let out a sigh of relief and banked to get back into position. Brandon looked to Jason and tossed the ball to him. The golden eagle gryphon caught it and tucked it under a wing, looking to his players and then to Victor who was holding his clipboard in front of his beak.

Rachel glided up next to Thyra and matched her speed for a second. "Formation Z. We're going for a ground goal before halftime," the small gryphoness relayed with heavy breaths. She flew off towards the center, following Nathanial who was jogging underneath her.

"Formation Z?" Thyra tried to remember her notes. It was a lot to take in for her first game, but when she saw Nathanial head up the middle and Rachel carve left, she remembered. *Air center up the middle for fallback. Advance with attempt for ground goal. Ground center right field*. Thyra repeated mentally.

She geared herself up as Jason broke into a sprint underneath her and headed right. Once he passed over the half line, the ground center gryphon went to intercept, but Jason out maneuvered the gryphon, making him trip over his own foretalons. The crowd went wild with laughter and applauded as Jason advanced.

"*Excellent maneuver from Redtails' twenty-two*!"

Jason moved towards the center of the field while advancing. Nathanial crossed paths with Jason and ran to right field, confusing the rear defender. Jason looked to the ground guard sprinting towards him, and crouched down low. They collided hard, sending feathers into the air. Thyra watched Jason roll out of the impact and proceed forward.

"*The Jays' tackle is no good! Can anyone stop this Redtail train*?"

The guard that was all over Nathanial abandoned him to intercept Jason. Jason saw the goalie get into position on the ground, and the last guard heading straight towards him. He looked up to see Rachel flying right overhead, right in position. He tossed the ball up, and she caught in her talons.

The goalie saw the move and quickly leapt into the air to defend the air goal, but it was a ruse. Rachel folded her right wing, and dove towards center as Nathanial moved to the ground goal. She tossed the ball down, and Nathanial hit it out of the air with a balled-up foretalon like a volleyball to send it flying into the unprotected ground goal.

This maneuver was the gryphball equivalent of a dunk. Nathanial laughed and flared his wings to showboat for the crowd. Everyone stood to their feet and yelled as the band began playing again.

"*Gooooooaaaal! Incredible! What a maneuver! Let's see that replay*!"

Thyra laughed while circling back and watched the giant jumbotron played multiple replays of Nathanial's dunk from different angles. The scoreboard changed from six to ten for the Redtails. Victor clapped his foretalons in celebration as the team did their victory lap. The timer ticked down to zero, and a loud siren erupted over the stadium.

"*And that's halftime! I would hate to be heading to the Jays' locker room. Their coach does not look happy*!" the announcer proclaimed as Thyra flew down to the sidelines near the reserve bench. Rachel was right behind her and landed with the rest of the group.

"Where did that come from, Thyra? I think you were just holding out on us all this time." Rachel chuckled and they began walking with the other players towards the fields exit. Aadhya, Nathanial, and Jason jogged up next to them and Thyra could see the cocky grin on the star golden eagle's beak.

"I just kept the ball moving. What about y'all and that play back there? That was incredible! It worked out perfectly," Thyra commented as Nathanial pushed past them.

"Yeah, you did a decent job. You all played good enough so I could steal the show. Plus those ground defenders are terrible! I've seen gryphlets run faster than them," Nathanial said and bumped wings with Jason as they made their way to the front of the group. "Those gryphons are nothing but overgrown feather dusters." The cheering behind them slowly died out as they walked through the hallway and piled into the locker room.

Rachel fluffed up her feathers and sat next to the larger gryphon. "You couldn't have done it without my awesome pass though! Don't forget about that, Nate."

The caracara huffed through his nares, but nodded his head. "Yeah, yeah. Have your moment there. But all the cameras were on me when I slammed that gryphball into their wide-open goal!" Nathanial made the motion again with his talons and laughed.

"And are you two just going to forget about my stunning offensive maneuver that made all of it possible?' Jason chimed in.

The three continued to compare one another's performance as Aadhya sat down next to Thyra and rearranged her long wings. The burly red dusted gryphoness joined her in watching the team compliment each other and celebrate.

"I do hope Antonio is ok," Thyra said.

"I know he will be, and I know that you have made all of us proud, Thyra." Aadhya said in a low tone, a warm smile on her beak. She looked so calm despite the events not a half hour ago. The blazing fury that Thyra had seen in Aadhya's eyes were gone, and she was back to her old caring self.

"He did look alright when I walked past him," Thyra said to reassure herself and turned to watch

Coach Victor finish his conversation with Carol, the therapist.

Victor walked out in front of the group to look at everyone with a stern face. The team fell silent and waited. Suddenly a rare beakgrin appeared on the massive gryphon's face and Thyra felt the mood in the room rise to a new high.

"Now this, this is what I am talking about! Great performance out of everybody. Good hustle all round. Not once did I see someone where they weren't supposed to be, and even when the play had to change, everyone adapted and overcame. I couldn't be happier," Victor praised as the group all ruffled their feathers.

"I want to point Thyra out in particular," Victor said with his large grey crest feathers rousing. Thyra felt a mixture of pride and fear as all eyes were on her. "I had high hopes for you and I thought it would take a little while longer for you to shine, but with the unforeseen circumstances, I had to put you in. You performed as skillfully as any seasoned player and the audience saw that. We all did. Let's all give her a round of applause."

Victor sat on his haunches and started clapping his foretalons together. The room applauded along with him. Thyra felt like her nares were about to catch on fire from blushing so much, and her feathers stuck up on end.

"Now, for the bad news. I just received an update on Antonio," Victor said, and everyone fell silent once again. "His injury is not as bad as it looked, but with his pre-existing wing injury, we need to be more cautious than usual. He's out for the game, but Carol assures me that he will make a full recovery. For the time being, Thyra will act in his place until he is fully healed. We will have to play it by ear."

Victor walked over to the large dry-erase board hanging on one of the walls and picked up a marker. He began to talk about new strategies and what they could do if the opposing team decided to become more reckless. The overall message was simple, conserve oneself, play it safe, and burn out the clock while maintaining the current lead. After going over the plans, he left the room to go back to talk with Carol, leaving the team to their own devices for the remainder of halftime.

The team chatted with one another again as the sounds of the marching band played in the field. Rachel walked back up to Thyra and Aadhya and mumbled something under her breath.

"What was that, Rachel?" Thyra asked and leaned her head down to the falcon. Rachel waved her off with a foretalon and shook her head.

"Oh, it's nothing. Nate just being Nate," Rachel huffed through her nares and turned back to look at Nathanial as he talked with Jason. "Nothing I can't handle."

"You know, you two do act a lot alike," Thyra teased which earned the response she wanted from the petite gryphoness. Rachel ruffled her feathers and clicked her beak.

"Do not! I'm nothing like that dim witted, two-toned, feather mite infested, short winged, stuck up piece of seagull poop!" Rachel steamed. Thyra held up her talons in defense as the little gryphon continued. “Don’t make me tackle you out there!”

“Ok, ok! Messaged received,” Thyra laughed and nudged into Rachel’s side playfully with her beak. “Now that I got you worked up, you ready to go back out there and kick some tailfeathers?” Thyra asked and saw that spark of determination in the kestrel’s black eyes.

Rachel sorted out her wings. “You know I am.”

Coach Victor opened the door to the locker room and held it open. “Times up! Let’s go, Redtails!” the immense harpy eagle shouted, and waved them over with his long foretalons.

The team chirped together and got up, hustling out the door. Victor shouted at them all and slapped them on the back as they ran out down the hallway. Thyra’s anxiety quickly came back as the music’s volume from the stadium increased with every second.

The team burst out onto the field in a roar of cheering and Thyra made her way to the center of the field. She looked over to where her husband and friends were sitting and gave them a wing wave. They were on their feet shouting and clapping for her, giving all the encouragement they could.

Thyra stood behind Jason and Nathanial as they faced off with the other team. She could see anger in Phera’s eyes as he looked over all of them. The balteur eagle must have been lambasted by their coach during halftime. Many of the opposing gryphons’ feathers were flat against their bodies, and eartufts lay back against their skull. Thyra’s eartufts instantly did the same.

"It seems their meeting did not go as well as ours," Aadhya pointed out, reading the same things Thyra had into the gryphons' body language. "This could be dangerous as they will not think correctly due to their temper and act out in aggression, or it could mean they are defeated inside and will perform dreadfully. Either way, do take caution," Aadhya warned from behind. Thyra nodded.

The aplomado referee flew down between the two teams and turned on his microphone. He could sense the tension as well as anyone else. "This will be your last warning to those who have been aggressive, I will eject you from the game if I see so much a talon scratch." The referee turned to look up at the gryphons around him. They all nodded in acknowledgement. Satisfied, he referee began again, "The Jays will begin with possession and each team will switch sides. Prepare for launch in two minutes."

The crowd began to cheer again as they geared up for the launch. Aadhya stared at Phera with a warning, and then turned to head to the back of the field. Aadhya's warning was clear, she did not care if she was ejected out of ten games. If Phera hurt another one of her friends, she would rip him apart.

Both teams lined up on their ends of the field as the countdown played on the overhead jumbotron, then the sound of cannon fire filled the stadium. Thyra leapt in the air to play careful defense, and was able to perform as planned. It seemed the Jays had not adjusted since halftime and continued to play as before, but Thyra was still cautious. Aadhya had read them like a book and knew exactly how they were feeling. She was a seasoned gryphball player, after all.

Minutes ticked by as possession of the gryphball rotated between the two teams multiple times, with the Jay's getting a lucky trick play out and scoring one ground goal leaving the Redtail's leading ten to four.

Thyra and her team heeded Victor's commands, playing safe and reserving themselves. They were able to fight off any attack that the Jay's threw at them, and only made an effort to score when the opportunity presented itself. Thyra was impressed with how reserved Nathanial and Rachel could be when they wanted.

Thyra flew back and forth, stressing her wings to the limits without rest as time ticked by. She began to feel her lungs burning with each breath, and her heart beat so fast that it thumped in her eartufts. She found it harder to keep up with Jason underneath her when they went on the offensive, and even more difficult to block the vulture when on defense.

Suddenly, a loud whistle broke her concentration and looked down to see Victor making a T with his foretalons. She thanked the skies for the break and looked up to see only five minutes remained on the clock. Had she really been flying for forty minutes straight?

Thyra landed on the ground hard a few feet from Victor and took in a large breath. She winced when she folded in her wings, feeling them tingle and burn with complaint. Her nares were wet with secretions from the strenuous flying and it took a lot of effort to jog over to the huddle. Victor waited for the rest of the team to gather around before he began.

"Alright, we have five minutes to go. I want to see one more air goal at least. Hustle up and pour out the last of your energy. Let's send them packing with their tails tucked between their legs!" Victor yelled and clapped his talons together, looking at every gryphon with his large black eyes. "Thyra, you're slowing down out there. Get it together and push through."

"Yes sir," Thyra replied with heavy breaths. She felt someone tapping on her wingshoulder and looked over. A male human in his early twenties stood next to her holding a water bottle out, and she quickly grabbed it from his hands with a thank you. She took careful sips from the bottle, making sure not to down the contents as much as she wanted to. She remembered her previous mistakes of drinking fast all too well.

The whistle blew again, and everybody turned away from Victor. Thyra handed the water bottle back to the human and jogged out to the middle of the field to take their positions again.

"Just stay above me and keep your flight steady," Jason said to her as she crouched to take flight next to him.

"I'll give it my best," Thyra responded before the whistle blew to start the game once more. She leapt into the air and forced her wings to beat again.

Nathanial sprinted across the field with the gryphball under a wing and attempted to get past their defense. They cut him off at every attempt, and he tossed the ball over to Jason who took it back to midfield. He burned out the clock by passing it between Thyra, Nathanial and himself until an opening presented itself. Nathanial took the opportunity, and rushed past the first guard as the crowd leapt to their feet.

"*We have an attempt on the ground goal in the last minute of the game! Can the Redtails do it*?" The announcer said as Nathanial tossed the ball up to Rachel. Thyra flew to Rachel's right, and tried to outfly the vulture air defender as he kept his pace with her.

Phera dove after Rachel, and she quickly tossed the ball to Thyra to keep from being tackled. Thyra was able to get open and caught the pass before feeling the vulture make a poor attempt at a slow tackle against her side. She rolled it off and kept a steady flight towards the air goal. She felt a sudden burst of energy as the goal was in sight with no one between her and the goalie.

"Go for it!" Rachel screeched, relaying Victor's commands. Thyra beat her wings with all her might and flew straight towards the goal as the crowd held their breath again.

She sought for an opening as she stared the goalie straight in his eyes, and then tossed the ball towards the corner of the goal. The gryphball slipped in her talons. She was helpless to watch as the ball went off course and bounced off the post before falling out of bounds. Thyra quickly carved to the left to keep from slamming into the goalie and hung her head in defeat.

"*It's no good! That was a great attempt from Redtails' thirteen, but the shot was just shy of the goal*," the announcer called out just as the clock clicked zero.

The stadium shook as a loud siren played over the speakers, signaling the end of the game. Thyra glided down to circle around the stadium and Rachel flew up next to her.

"Get your beak up! We just won!" Rachel called out.

Thyra had almost forgotten they were ahead. For a few seconds, she had felt like the game depended all on that shot, but it did not matter. Whatever defeat she felt in her heart left her as she watched Rachel perform various acrobatics for the crowd. Apparently, Nathanial could not handle her having the entire spotlight because he soon flew up to Rachel and started to show off for the crowd as well.

Thyra glanced over to see Phera gliding nearby to her proximity. He did not look the least bit amused, clicking his beak with agitation. He locked his black eyes with her and snarled. The Bateleur eagle came in close next to Thyra, causing her to slightly falter back to avoid confrontation. "That was just beginner's luck. You won't be so lucky next time."

Before Thyra could respond, the eagle banked away from her to join the rest of his moping team. She took a deep breath and forced herself to relax. The sound of fans cheering and applauding brought her attention to her showboating friends.

Rachel and Nathanial celebrated together, spinning around one another and dancing in the sky. The two latched talons and rose up into the sky. They separated and folded their wings to dive away from each other towards the ground. The pair flicked out their wings to glide out of the dive and barrel rolled around each other, screeching in glee.

Thyra was close enough to see a certain form of affection in their eyes, one that they had not shown to anyone else. To her surprise, she was certain that was something more going on between them; a connection that neither of them were yet fully aware of.

Chapter 20 Awakening

"I never had any doubt in this team. You all have performed perfectly this season so far," Coach Victor began as he stood at the head of a long wooden table.

Thyra was sitting next to Johnathen and the rest of the band, including Antonio, whose foretalon and left wing were in a sling, but he did not look to be in pain. A flash from the opposite side of the room caught Thyra's eyes as yet another person took a photo of the group, possibly to share it on social media.

Victor looked to every gryphon sitting around the table in the dimming light. Shadows drifted across the room as the sun descended lower from the floor-to-ceiling windows.

"Actually, I am not going to lie, some of you worried me, especially the caracara." The Harpy eagle grinned at his jest, and everyone joined in a low laugh. Nathanial frowned at the comment and folded his eartufts flat against his head.

The talking from other humans on the opposite side of the pub quieted as Victor's voice carried in the room. The televisions on the wall above the bar were tuned into the sports network channel showing a couple of well-dressed men and one gryphon around a table discussing the game's best plays. A server wearing a casual T-shirt and jeans walked over with a tray full of beers and started to pass them out to the team as Victor started again.

"We fought hard today, especially Antonio, but I want you all to know your hard work was not in vain. I want to thank you for your effort in the season so far. I know I have been hard on you, but the results speak for themselves. You have been with me the entire time, struggling, fighting, and training every day. But with this victory, comes one last challenge. We have been undefeated the whole season, and have one more game to play. If-," He shook his head. "No. *When* we win next week's final game, we will advance into the First League!"

The whole team erupted into squawks of celebration, causing the other pub patrons to cheer with them. Thyra looked from Victor to the other patrons in the bar, seeing they were all sporting Redtail's jerseys that matched the team's. It hadn't occurred to her before, but she realized the team's victories had not only made Victor and her loved ones proud, but also the whole city of Athens.

"Tonight, we celebrate our hard-fought battle. Tonight, we dine like kings and queens of the earth and land. Tonight, we join our fans and loved ones in victory. Be proud of the gryphon you are! Keep your beak up, eartfuts perked, and lift your mugs with me," Victor finished and grabbed the cold mug in front of him. His massive talons wrapped around the glass as if it was made for a toddler. He lifted his mug in a toast and every gryphon did the same. "To the Redtails!"

"To the Redtails!" the team and patrons of the bar shouted along with him before taking a swig of the icy blond lager.

Thyra let out a loud sigh and placed her mug on the table as the groups began to converse among themselves. She looked over to Rachel, who was already beginning a heated discussion with Nathanial about who had more screen time on the television replays.

"So, how did it feel?" came Johnathen's voice. Thyra turned to look at her husband with a confused look, and then it clicked.

"Oh! You mean actually playing a full half and scoring my first goal?" she asked. He nodded, smiling as he sipped his beer. "Amazing! I really can't describe it! I've dreamed of being on a gryphball team ever since I was a gryphlet, as you know. But I never thought it would feel that incredible! All those people screaming and cheering . . ." Thyra beamed and lifted her mug again with a ruffle of her feathers.

"I couldn't be more proud and happy for you, featherbutt," Johnathen said with a chuckle, which earned a playful bat of her tail against his side.

"Well, you two are a fitting couple," Victors low voice interrupted.

Thyra turned her head to see the great gryphon standing beside them. Thyra's eartufts perked to attention as she spun around to face him completely. "Thank you, Sir! We've been together for six years now."

Victor nodded his large beak and sat down on his haunches, extending a foretalon for Johnathen to shake. "So I hear. You must be Johnathen. Nice to meet you."

Johnathen looked at the gigantic talons extended towards him, and quickly clasped them with his hand, which was dwarfed by the gryphon appendage. "Nice to finally meet you as well. Thyra has talked a lot about you." he said with a warm smile.

Victor's gray beak curved in a wry grin. "I'm sure it was nothing positive," he responded and pulled his talons away.

Johnathen let out a nervous laugh and looked over to Thyra as he rubbed the back of his head. "Well! She does talk highly of you. She also says you can be an insufferable ass, but that's to be expected with a coach." Thyra frowned and flicked her tail against his side again.

Victor let out a deep laugh, causing a couple teammates to turn around and stare at them. Victor rarely laughed. "An honest man! I like that. Seems she has chose well, even it is a human." Victor grabbed his beer mug from the table and easily downed half its contents with one swig.

"As I said earlier in the speech, there's a good reason I'm hard on them. It's because I care. And your wife is no exception. She came to me a greenwing, fresh from the nest. And now look at her!" Victor motioned to Thyra with his gray foretalons. "Scoring against one of the best second league teams in the nation. I'm proud of her."

Thyra could feel the heat from her nares as she blushed, listening to her mentor speak so highly of her. The butterflies in her chest came back while her hackle feathers roused up from the attention. “Now you’re just being sappy, Coach.”

“You should enjoy the praise for once,” Victor responded. “I rarely give it out. Normally, I am the one dealing tough love, but I just want you all to know, it is love.” A few voices called out from the other side of the room and Victor looked away from the two of them. “Excuse me, seems they want my attention.”

Thyra watched Victor leave, heading towards a small group of men holding pens and photos. The huge gryphon began talking with them while signing various memorabilia and taking selfies with the fans.

“He seems like a good guy,” Johnathen said and threw an arm around Thyra to bring her in closer.

“Yeah, he has a lot of heart. And he’s very talented,” Thyra said while watching Victor interact with the fans. He was putting on a smile and shaking hands with the humans.

“Pfft! Back in his day he was maybe half as good as I am, but now I would bet he couldn’t outfly a pigeon!” Nathanial chimed in from across the table.

“Please! You’re about as talented as a wet rat with stumpy wings!” Rachel retorted back and laughed. “I bet he could still outfly you with one wing tied behind his back!”

Nathanial slammed his beer mug down and leaned across with his beak grinding against itself. “You runt! I’m gonna..!”

“You two, please use your inside voices,” Aadhya interrupted, placing her tea mug down gently. “If you must behave like gryphlets, then take it outside.”

Rachel and Nathanial sat back and looked away from one another with their feathers ruffled. Antonio could not help but smile as the hot head gryphons settled down.

Nathanial noticed Antonio's smile and frowned. "What's so funny, *amigo*?!" he asked, making fun of Antonios' accent.

"Nothing. Nothing at all, mi amigo," Antonio replied and sipped from his beer mug. Nathanial's head crest raised and flattened multiple times.

"Whatever. I'm going to the bathroom," Nathanial huffed and looked to Rachel quickly. He finished up his drink and stepped back from the bench.

Rachel watched him leave and then cleared her throat quickly. "Oh yeah, me too. I'll be right back," she said before following along. Thyra watched her speed up to catch Nathanial and watched them talk for a moment.

"They couldn't make it any more obvious, could they?" Jason said while walking up behind Thyra and Johnathen.

Thyra let out a chuckle and turned to look back at the golden eagle gryphon. "I was starting to wonder if I was the only one that noticed."

"You would have to be blind to not see it. Typical high school relationship right there. Not that I ever went, but I've watched plenty of movies. You know, the classics and such," Jason commented. He gave Johnathen a beak grin. "Well! This must be the lucky man. How goes it?" He reached out and took Johnathen's hand in a strong grasp.

Thyra could see her husband wince at the strong grip. "Ah, it goes well! Yeah, man, you played one hell of a game." Johnathen responded awkwardly.

Jason shrugged his shoulders and finished his mug off before setting it on the table. His nares were already flushed and eyes a little glazed. Thyra would have never pinned him as a lightweight.

"Good! Yeah, Thyra tells me you're a lawyer. That's pretty interesting!" Jason's wings flared out excitement, almost knocking over Antonio's beer mug. "I watch a lot of criminal investigation shows. Live PD stuff too. I like the intensity of a good court case! You ever have a good murder case? What's the best, most exciting case you ever had?"

Johnathen ran his fingers through his clean-cut black hair and laughed nervously again. He wasn't allowed to discuss the particulars of his cases, but he could speak in generalities. "Well, um, I had this one domestic violence case that was pretty interesting."

Jason's golden eartufts perked up and he placed a foretalon on Johnathen's shoulder. "No way! Was it the one in Atlanta where the guy murdered all three of his wives?"

Johnathen looked over to Thyra with wide eyes. She shrugged her shoulders with a chuckle and sipped casually from her beer. "I, um, no. It was divorce court actually. Something about the guy ripping the heads off of the wife's beanie babies."

Jason pulled his foretalon away and his eartufts relaxed. "Well, that's lame," he said, readjusting his wings to fold them back in.

“Yeah, I don’t handle any of the more serious stuff. It’s really rare actually. Now my partner…”

“Thyra???” Rachel’s high pitch voice broke the conversation from across the room. The whole team became silent and turned to look over at Rachel and Nathanial standing in front of the bar. Thyra saw worry in Rachel’s eyes as she glanced back up to the television, and the bartender turned the volume up.

A news report showed a female reporter standing in front of an old-fashioned diner. There was police tape all around the building with several cop cars in the background and the scrolling message at the bottom read, “*Maddened gryphon in Macon kills two officers, leaving two others in critical condition*.”

Thyra felt her heart skip a beat in her chest as all the conversation and celebration was pushed into the background. Johnathen and Thyra stood up from the table to join a group standing in front of the television. “They are talking about a gryphon in Macon that went on a rampage, but I thought you were the only one in Macon.” Rachel said as the other team members gathered around with them.

“I was. I don’t know who…” Thyra paused as the bartender turned up the volume loud enough for everyone to hear.

“*… Several witnesses described this gryphon to resemble a rabies infested wild animal with mange. Several report the gryphon had multiple scars across its body, patches of fur missing, and wings like a bat*.”

“No… it can’t be.” Thyra’s mind raced and her breath quickened, The description reminded of someone from her past, except for the wings. No, it could not be Anfang. He had stubs in the place where his wings should be. Besides, he was dead. She dismissed the idea out of her head, but something still ate at her.

The television showed an interview with a couple that had seen it firsthand, describing the gryphon exactly as the newscaster had but in a less professional way. Their voices were heavy with southern accents, but they got their point across.

"Thyra? Are you ok?" Johnathen asked, noticing all her feathers flattening against her body.

She shook her head as the next images on the television was a recording from a cop vehicle as it pulled up to the scene. Then she saw him. His deformed face clear as day in the window of the diner.

"No…" Thyra said.

Everyone watched the television silently as shots rang out and the gryphon darted across the screen. There were more shots, and they saw the gryphon leap at an officer before disappearing off screen. More yelling and screaming ensued before the images cut back to a still image that was zoomed in on the gryphon's awful face, his upper jaw a beak, his lower jaw a lion's.

"*This is the gryphon in question. If anyone has any information on this gryphon, please call the number at the bottom of the screen. He is considered very dangerous. If you see him, do not approach at any cost*," the newscaster said.

Thyra felt her legs tremble, and tears fell from her eyes. Her talons flexed at the ground as she sat back on her haunches, staring wide-eyed at the screen, shaking her head.

Johnathen got to his knees and grabbed her head with his hands. “Thyra? Thyra honey, what’s wrong?”

Thyra choked down her tears and shook her head again. “No! no…”

She fought to find her breath again. Everyone was looking at her, wondering why such a display had got her so emotional, but only her closest friends knew. They all hung their head low, unable to speak as Johnathen rubbed his hand across Thyra’s cheek.

“Please tell me, what’s wrong?” he asked.

Thyra trembled and shook, shaking her head to deny what she had just seen, but she was sure of it. After all the dreams she has had of him recently, there could not be anyone else. It was like seeing a ghost coming back to haunt you, but seeing it in a video recording. She knew the gryphon they described fit his description, and now not only was he still alive, but he was out murdering innocent people.

“It’s… It’s Anfang… He’s still alive!”

* * *

Daniel’s eyes slowly opened and a groan escaped his mouth. His vision blurred as he tried to look around the small room. He found himself on his back, lying on a bed with covers over him. The gentle beeps of a heart monitor rang out in the room, and the television on the wall played recaps of the latest gryphball game.

He lifted his hand to see his arm wrapped in a cast. When he tried to bend his fingers, they would not respond. His mind raced as he tried to remember what had happened, but the drugs had taken a strong effect on his mind. He slowly lifted the covers to see stiches covering his chest along with purple swelling around them.

The heart monitor beeped quicker as bits and pieces of memories came back to him. The beastly gryphon rushing at him. The look of murderous intent in those green eyes as he struggled for air. Searing pain in his chest as the talons tore into him. People running and screaming. The sound of gunshots. Daniel closed his eyes and took a deep breath, forcing himself to calm down. He was alive.

The door on the opposite side of the room slowly opened. A feminine voice spoke as a woman walked into the room, letting the door shut behind her. “I see you’re awake. How are you feeling? Any pain?”

Daniel blinked his eyes as everything began to come into focus. He could see black hair about shoulder length, a white lab coat, and dark skin complexion. “I’m alright. A little sore,” Daniel responded which earned a chuckle from the doctor. She walked over to check his vital signs and his IV bag.

“I would suspect that. After all you were in the operating room for three hours. You’re lucky to be alive, Daniel,” the doctor said and went to the foot of his bed to check the clipboard. “I’m Doctor Elisa and I’ll be taking care of you for the remainder of your stay.”

"How long have I been out? And where are my wife and daughter?" Daniel asked as he looked at the clock. It was 2:00 but he did not see a date.

"For about twenty hours and they are in the waiting room. I suspected you would be out longer after the extensive damage you received." Doctor Elisa put down the clipboard now and put her hands in her jacket pockets.

"How bad is it?" Daniel asked, and blinked as he took a closer look at Doctor Elisa. She was slightly heavyset, but wore no makeup and had a thin face. There were crow's feet outside her brown eyes.

"You lost a significant amount of blood and we had to do multiple transfusions. You have four deep lacerations across the chest, one in your leg, five broken ribs, the radius bone and wrist in your right arm is broken, and you have extensive bruising around the esophagus. We ran a CT scan to check for any possible brain injuries but all appears normal."

Daniel listened and remained silent. The sound of people cheering quietly drew his attention to the television as he watched a replay of The Redtails making the ground goal dunk. "That doesn't seem so bad."

"You're over the worst part and you should make a full recovery in time. But, there are police outside that would like to talk to you when you are able. Can you talk now?"

Daniel thought it over. He would have to give them a report of what happened, but he wondered if he should bring up Matthew and the church. After all, these police officers could be on Matthew's payroll, but if they were not, then he would have to also explain how he worked for Matthew and the criminal acts he had done.

"Daniel?" Doctor Elisa asked.

"Yeah, I'm fine. Go ahead and send them in," Daniel answered.

"Very well. I can bring your family in after they leave," Doctor Elisa said and opened the door.

Daniel could see a small group of uniformed people standing outside the door before it shut. He heard them converse with the doctor for a moment before two officers entered the room, a man and a woman. Daniel noticed right away that the well-dressed pair were carrying weapons under their suit jackets.

"Daniel Jefferson, glad to see you awake. My name is Detective Johansson and this is Detective McGee. We've been waiting to talk with you," Johansson began.

She had her brown hair tied to a bun behind her head and wore a black suit with blue pinstripes. Detective McGee drew out a notepad from his brown suit jacket pocket and flipped it open. He had short gray hair and a wrinkled face with a small grey goatee.

"Yeah, I'm glad to be awake too. Pleasure to meet you," Daniel responded and held down the button on his remote to make the bed sit more upright.

"Do you mind describing the events that led up to your assault?" Johansson asked.

"I don't mind at all. I was at Chrissie's diner after work when a maddened gryphon came into the restaurant and rushed at me. I feared for my life and for those around me, so I opened fired to dispatch the threat. I must have missed because I was struck by the gryphon, and the rest of it is all hazy," Daniel said and as he did so the memories came back to him even stronger.

He knew every round had hit his target squarely. He clearly remembered Anfang teasing with him, toying with his prey. McGee scribbled on his notepad while Daniel fought back the image of Anfang's crazed feline eyes staring at him as he struggled for air.

Johansson waited for McGee to finish his notes. "Can you describe this gryphon?"

"Yes. Uh, coloration similar to a redtail, patches of fur and feathers clumped together, scars on his body, missing one eartuft, and wings similar to a bat. His face was deformed, like a cats muzzle on the lower jaw and a beak for an upper jaw." Daniel watched the two detectives nod to one another. "I assume you've already talked to other witnesses?"

"Yes, we have received similar descriptions," McGee chimed in with his deep southern accent and made a note of it.

"This is the first documented case of gryphon assault we've handled. From what we can gather, attacks like this are extremely rare and gryphon's do not attack unless provoked. Do you personally know this gryphon?" Johansson asked, his expression curious.

Daniel shook his head quickly. "No. I had never seen that gryphon before."

Johansson nodded her head. "I understand that you have recently moved here to Macon, and started working for The Gathering as a consultant. Yet, you have a military background. Do you mind elaborating?"

Daniel froze for a minute as the conversation suddenly shifted to what he felt was an interrogation. The investigators could simply be curious as to his sudden job change, as it would look odd on paper, but they could also know about the shady activities The Gathering performs. He decided to play it safe and write it out as curiosity.

"When I got out of the military, I worked for a firm in Atlanta for three years as a security consultant. The Gathering offered me a better position here in Macon and I took it."

Johansson listened to his explanation and nodded her head again. "And what exactly did you do for the military again?"

Daniel frowned and shook his head, letting a little agitation show in his voice. "I'm sorry but what exactly does that have to do with this investigation?"

"Apologies. We're simply curious is all." Johansson stated.

Mcgee closed his note pad and put it inside his pocket. "Well I think that's all we have for now. Sorry for bothering you. I'm sure you want to see your family." Johansson pulled out a card from her blazer pocket and placed it on the nightstand next to the bed. "If you can think of anything else, please, give us a call."

"I'll do that. Good luck with your investigation." Daniel responded.

"We will be in contact, Mr. Jefferson," Johansson said and turned to leave.

Daniel watched them close the door behind them before letting out a sigh of relief. He could tell they did not believe his story. That was not going to be the last time he saw them. He looked to the television to watch more recaps of the previous game, noticing the camera focusing on Thyra's goal shot.

He felt worried for her and Johnathen all the sudden; despite never had met the two. They seemed to be good people, but for some reason, Matthew hated them. If Matthew was willing to kill one of his own men, his right-hand man for just quitting, then what was he about to do to them? He had to warn Johnathen and Thyra as soon as he could. He decided if there was one positive thing he could do, it was that.

The door flew open, interrupting Daniels train of thought. A little blond girl ran into the room followed by his wife, Kathy. "Daddy!" Kate called out excitedly and jumped up on the bed. Daniel grunted as she put pressure on his stitches and quickly moved Kate to sit down next to him.

"Careful! Daddy has some booboo's on his chest. Good to see you, Pumpkin." Daniel brushed the blond hair away from her face and smiled to his little girl.

Kathy walked up beside him and leaned over to give him a kiss on his cheek. She had dark circles under her eyes and her long blond hair was mussed, half of it coming undone from the scrunchy she had used to pull it back into a ponytail.

"And you look lovely, Kathy."

Kathy chuckled lightly and watched as Kate lay next to Daniel and watched the television. "I wish I could say the same about you. How..."

"Hey, Dad?" Kate interrupted. "My friend Alissa from school said you had a fight with a gryphon. Was he being mean? I thought you said fighting is bad."

Daniel shrugged his shoulders and rubbed along her head. "Yeah, just a little fight. And I know fighting is bad, but sometimes you have to."

"Like, when you were away fighting for us?" Kate questioned.

Daniel looked up at Kathy and watched her expression change to concern. He took a deep breath before responding. "Well, that was different. But fighting is bad. If we can talk to each other, that is much better, ok?"

Daniel turned the volume up on the television. He did not feel like discussing politics of war and morals with his little daughter, not that she would understand. Kate wiggled around on the bed and laid her head on Daniel's uninjured arm.

"Ok. But why did you fight the gryphon?" Kate asked again. Daniel thought for a moment and opened his mouth to respond, but the door slowly opened. The group looked over to see a small dark gryphoness standing in the doorway. Her beak was long and narrow like a corvid's, and she sported eartuft piercings. Her wing was in a sling as well and her bright purple eyes searched the room. Her plumage shimmered in the light.

"Sorry to interrupt," her singsong like voice carried easily in the room. Kate sat up from the bed and pointed.

"Look daddy, a gryphon!" Kate pointed.

Immediately, Daniel grabbed her hand to pull it down. "Now Kate it's not nice to point. I'm sure she has a name." Daniel smiled and looked to the gryphoness slowly entering the room. "No, you're not interrupting. Can I help you, miss…?"

"Isabell. Well, not really help, no. I heard about what had happened and just wanted to talk." Isabell said and let the door close behind her.

"Wanted to talk about what?" Daniel questioned.

He had not seen another gryphon around town, but recognized her from the news months before. This was the gryphon that had gotten injured during the Gathering's rally. He furrowed his brow, wondering if she knew that he was working for the Gathering and if that was what she wanted to talk about.

Isabell was silent for another moment. She opened her beak to speak, but looked to his family. "Well," she paused again and readjusted her good wing, trying to choose her next words carefully. "It's about the gryphon that attacked you. I believe his name is Anfang."

Chapter 21 Facing Old Demons

Anfang had woken in a daze and discovered that Matthew's men had found him asleep in the bard and transported him back to the church. The gryphon did not remember the trip at all, but his chest still hurt from the multiple bullet wounds he had taken in the restaurant the day before, and he still felt fatigued. A short time later, Matthew had visited and told him that he had not yet won his freedom. Daniel still lived.

Anfang snorted through his nares as Matthew ranted angrily, driving the point of his failure home. He turned his head, looking out the large bay windows in Matthew's office. Anfang tuned the human's ravings into a soft murmur. The last thing he wanted was to be lectured by this ugly human.

Matthew noticed his bored look. "Are you listening, bird-brain?"

The large grandfather clock in the corner of the room ticked as seconds of silence went by. Anfang turned his head to face the elderly bald man before him, pupils narrowing into thin green slits again.

"Yes. I listen. I hear. I make mistake. Are you done?" he said and readjusted his large leathery wings.

Matthew scoffed and folded his arms in front of his chest. "No, I am certainly not done. You did not kill

Daniel like you should have, and instead toyed with him! You almost got yourself killed, and you went too far!"

"Too far?" Anfang said.

"Of course, I wanted to stir up the public and make them realize what vile creatures your kind is, and in that particular interest, you have succeeded." Matthew went on. "But there was no need to kill the police!"

Anfang growled and bared his teeth at Matthew when he mentioned gryphons being vile creatures. "I do not need listen to this," he retorted and stood up.

"You certainly do! Now, sit down and listen. You have to fix this," Matthew demanded and walked over to sit on the couch across from Anfang. The great beastly gryphon raised his head up high and looked down at the puny male, perking his one eartuft to attention.

"Fine. Speak," Anfang said strongly.

Matthew reached into his pocket and pulled out his cell phone. "We have figured out which hospital and what room Daniel is being held in. Now, so far it seems he hasn't told anyone what really happened, but we can't trust that his silence will last long. Your task is simple."

Matthew placed the phone down on the table for Anfang to see. "You're going to fly into his window, kill him, and get out as quickly and quietly as you can."

Anfang picked up the phone and looked at the screen. It was a picture of the front of the hospital with one window circled. The beast snorted again and placed the phone down on the table. "This not fun. Kill him in his sleep? No chase. No fight. No food. Just murder."

"I don't care if this isn't fun for you. I'm telling you to do this," Matthew commanded. He picked up the cellphone and started to type something into it. "I'm sending the location to you now."

Just then, Anfang's watch beeped. He looked down at the screen to see the arrow pointing him in a direction and a number at the top of the small screen.

"How long I do these things for you?" Anfang asked, growing irritated by these tasks.

"As long as you want a safe place to return to and eat what you want," Matthew retorted and put his cell phone away.

Anfang's eartuft fell flat against his head and he frowned, snaggle tooth sticking out of his bottom jaw to rub along his beak. As much as Anfang despised this man, he was right. There was nowhere else safe to go.

"Fine. I do this and you tell me where Thyra is," Anfang said and rose up onto all fours. Matthew waved him off with a hand and nodded his head.

"You have a deal," Matthew responded.

Anfang stood for a moment more and stared at the back of Matthew's head. He could rip it clean off and be done with this human before he knew what hit him. IT was tempting, but he thought better of it. "Then I go."

"I do have one other task I want you to complete before you leave," Matthew said, raising a finger. Anfang snorted through his nares as he concentrated on Matthew. Yet another task in what seemed to be a never-ending list. “There is a woman I have in captivity that I want you to dispose of.”

Curiously, Anfang raised his head and raised an eye ridge. “You have human girl that you want dead?”

“Yes. I don’t care how you do it either,” Matthew slapped at the air dismissively and walked towards his office door. “I have no use for her anymore, and she’s starting to become a bother.”

Anfang followed the old out of the office and started down one corridor. The beastly gryphon’s chest rumbled with amusement, his stomach beginning to growl. “I can eat her?”

“As I said, what you do with her is up to you. In fact, it would be easier for me if you did,” Matthew looked back at the gryphon following him.

Anfang’s eyes narrowed into slits as a small smile appeared on his beak muzzle. His agitation was all but gone now. What had seemed like another chore at first now felt like more of a reward.

They stopped in front of a heavily-secured door with multiple dead bolt locks. The door itself looked to be sturdier and less decorative than the other doors in the hallway. “Her name is Sandra, not that it really matters to you. Now, listen. This woman is a liar and will tell you anything you want to hear just to save her own skin.” As Matthew fumbled around with the keys, sounds of chains scraping along the floor came from the other side.

When the last deadbolt was turned, Matthew threw open the door and stepped to the side, motioning for Anfang to proceed inside. He glanced at the small frail old man, but Matthew would not even look inside, or at Anfang himself.

It was obvious that Matthew was disgusted with his choices. The old man had backed himself into a corner and the only way to get rid of this woman now was to kill her, but he did not have the guts to do it himself or order his own men to do it. No matter, Anfang did not care. He would feel no remorse for eating this woman. All meat was food.

"W…whos there?" A weak feminine voice called out from inside. Anfang stepped inside the dimly lit room and gazed down at the middle-aged woman before him. Immediately, Sandra's mouth fell open as she began to back up and clutched her bound hands to her chest. "N…no. No! It can't be you!"

Anfang heard the sound of the door behind him closing and turned to look. His eyes quickly adjusted to the dimly lit area, and he scanned her face. He recognized her from the abandoned factory he had been held in, and let out a low growl. "Anfang know you, Sandra. You keep me caged. You and those other humans."

Tears began to roll down Sandra's face and she shook her head. "No, please no, Anfang. We were trying to help you! We saved you from…"

Anfang took a step forward and screeched loudly, cutting her off. "You lie! Matthew say you lie!"

"Matthew is the liar! Don't you see he's just using you?" Sandra yelled and stood up, her back against the wall. "We are the ones that saved you from the experimental military lab! Don't you remember?"

Anfang continued to walk forward until he was standing before her, but the growling stopped as he thought about what she was saying. He remembered that he had been in a cage inside the labs, and then the next thing he remembered was waking up in a new area, surrounded by a small group of people and her specifically. He had lashed out at one of them, and tore him in half. That's how he had ended up in the group's makeshift prison.

"Maybe Matthew use Anfang, but he give freedom. He make promise." Anfang narrowed his eyes. "And if Anfang keep promise, Matthew will too."

For just a moment, Sandra seemed to visibly calm down. Her posture relaxed and grew less ridged as she realized that he was letting her communicate with him. "W…what did Matthew tell you to do?" Sandra asked, swallowing hard.

"Get rid of you," Anfang said calmly. Sandra's face contorted as she began to weep.

Anfang reached up with one of his gigantic foretalons and wrapped it around her throat. Sandra shook her head and grabbed onto the forearm, beginning to struggle for air. Anfang looked into her eyes and slowly brought his beak muzzle closer.

"No cry. No. You will become part of Anfang. Anfang use you as fuel. You will sleep now. Sleep in peace." Anfang opened his beak wide, fitted her head in between his jaws, and bit down.

An few hours later, cool air whisked past his patchy body, causing him to ruffle up what feathers he could. The sun rose higher into the morning sky as he spread his wings far out to absorb the rays. With a heavy push from the ground, he was off into the sky, following the directions on his smart watch towards the hospital. His stomach was full from the meal he just consumed, and had to force his wings to beat harder against the air to climb into the sky.

Anfang reached a good cruising altitude and curved his wings to find a gentle breeze. He was beginning to realize that there was no end in sight working for Matthew. It was possible that he would become a slave to the insufferable man, and he knew that, but there was little he could do about it.

Anfang repeated Sandra's words. "Matthew is the liar."

The words ate at the back of his brain and he felt an unexpected tinge of remorse for his actions. What if she was not the one lying? Perhaps she had been the one trying to save him, like she had said.

He shook off the confusing emotion and aligned himself in the sky. It was too late now. He had consumed her piece by piece, She had been nothing more than food. Still, he could not help but think about what Matthew's true intentions were for the future.

He could run away and live somewhere in the woods perhaps, but he would surely be found over time or maybe starve to death if he could not find food. He had not lived without humans a single day of his life, and the thought of becoming weak and dying in the wilderness disgusted him, even more so than being a simple tool for Matthew.

Other birds passed Anfang by, shouting warnings to one another as he flapped his wings to keep his current altitude. Already his strength had returned, and he found flying easier than he had the previous days. It was amazing how quickly his body adapted, as if he was made for it.

He thought of Thyra, and how she must look at her current age. He wondered if she would still recognize him. He had been through multiple operations, and looked different than he once had. Also, how would she feel about him?

Thyra had understood him in the past, but even then they'd had their differences. Although they had been young, she was years ahead of him in her understanding, She had a greater grip on the world and all its interworking's such as society, what humans felt was acceptable behavior. He still remembered many of the lessons she tried to teach him.

As he thought over those old memories, he felt ashamed for a reason he did not understand. Thyra had been so innocent, so peaceful despite what naturally felt right. Would she understand the way he acted when he saw her again?

Not that he believed he was doing anything wrong. Sure, the humans who had taken him from the government facility had tried to tell him that it was wrong to want to kill humans, but in his mind, it was a natural part of being a gryphon. He had been trained and raised to kill. That was his purpose and acting on his instincts made him feel good. Besides, if his time in the labs had taught him anything, humans could be more vile and monstrous than he could ever be.

* * *

As the morning light shined through the open window Thyra groaned and pulled the covers over her face. She reached for Johnathen, but found his side of the bed to be empty. As her senses slowly returned, she could smell the fresh scent of cooking bacon, and hear the sizzling of the oil in the pan along with the drone of the television. She pulled back the covers and stared up at the fan spinning on the ceiling as the memory of last night came back into focus.

Thyra had told Johnathen everything about Anfang; her memories of him, their time in the lab, what she thought he was, and how they forcefully took him away one day to never be seen again. She had been worried that Johnathen would be upset that she had not told him about this sooner, but of course he was supportive.

She had cried during most of the car ride back, thinking about the pain Anfang must be in and how lost in the world he was. She had to find him and whoever was responsible for telling her that he was dead. Why would these people want Thyra to think he was dead in the first place? Who has been keeping him alive all this time? The questions raddled around in her brain, one after another.

The sounds of popping grease and a quiet curse from Johnathen brought her back to reality. Thyra threw the covers off and stood on the bed, stretching t with a loud yawn. The bed was covered with little tufts of down which drifted into the air as she hopped down onto the ground.

"You awake?" she heard Johnathen call out.

Thyra made her way to the cracked bedroom door and opened it up to see her husband standing at the island table with a pair of tongs in his hand. She walked over to the island table. She sat on her hindlegs and placed her talons on the counter, putting her head about even with his. "Yeah. I heard you cuss. Get burned from the grease?"

"I always do," Johnathen confirmed sourly and flipped the bacon again with the tongs. Thyra reached over to the heat dial and turned down the flame.

"It's because you run it too hot, dummy. I told you this a hundred times now," Thyra said as Johnathen rolled his eyes. The sound of the coffee maker caused her eartufts to perk. She turned her head to look at the coffee pot and then back at Johnathen. "Dark roast?"

"Of course," Johnathen replied. Thyra took a couple steps on her hindfeet over to the coffee maker. She grabbed her favorite owl mug from the cupboard and filled it with the stark black joe. "And I've got biscuits in the oven, the flakey kind."

"Thanks, hun." Thyra raised her mug to her beak, letting the bold aroma wash over her as she looked at the television. The police were still investigating Anfang's attack and were desperately asking people for more information. The interviews started out professional, but soon veered into actual gryphon bashing.

"*I always knew gryphons were dangerous! But everyone just keeps saying, 'Oh they are harmless! They are just like us and just let them live their life and we should be considerate!' But look how easily one could take out a fleet of cops with ease! I say…"*

Her hackle feathers ruffled with irritation. With a scowl, Thyra picked up the remote off the island counter and switched it over to the gryphball channel. Johnathen cleared his throat to bring her attention away.

"Looks like it's still bad," Johnathen began. "Anfang is—."

"It's not his fault. It's not the gryphon I knew. He's drugged, or confused, or someone is making him do this. He doesn't know what he's doing." Thyra turned to face Johnathen with a serious look in her green eyes. "He's out there, all alone, and with no one to turn to! I have to find him and clear his name." Her emotions overcame her and she slammed the coffee mug down on the counter.

"Honey, honey, it's ok. We will figure this out. But right now, breakfast is almost ready. So, let's just eat. Relax for a bit then we can discuss this," Johnathen pleaded.

Thyra looked over him for a second and then down at the coffee that had splashed on the counter. She took a deep breath and nodded.

"Ok. You're right. We have to think about this instead of just jumping right in," Thyra admitted and watched as Johnathen moved the cooked bacon to a plate. Her stomach rumbled, rudely reminding her of her hunger. "I think better with a full crop anyways."

"Yeah, you're not you when you're hungry," Johnathen said with a smile. Thyra nodded with agreement. He put on an oven mitt and reached down to withdraw the baking sheet covered with golden-brown biscuits. “Plus, you need to focus on tomorrow’s final game. You have a lot of homework to do today. Victor said you could skip their meeting today only if you studied his playbook and wants you there early to go over strategies and warm-ups. It’s going to be big day.”

“You’re right. I have to concentrate on that. It’s important.” Thyra grabbed her coffee with her beak and moved over to the living room.

Johnathen fixed two plates and followed behind her to sit at the couch. He placed the plates on the coffee table and turned down the volume on the television. Thyra picked up a piece of bacon and chomped into it. Pieces of the well-cooked meat crumbled as she let the greasy and salty meat slide easily into her crop.

“You’re going to work today, right?” she asked and picked up a biscuit.

“Yeah. I’ve only been back a week, but I have a couple clients already lined up for next week,” Johnathen responded and then looked to the television. “Hey, I recognize that beautiful bird.”

Thyra bit into the flakey and buttery biscuit, swallowing it quickly. She watched as the television played a couple scenes from the game, one of them being her flying with the gryphball in her talons. She felt a swell of pride at seeing herself perform and grinned. “It looks like the camera adds ten pounds though, especially at that angle.”

“I don’t think so,” Johnathen commented and scarfed down the rest of his breakfast. He looked down at his watch and picked up his plate before walking into the kitchen. "I'll be right back. Can't go to work in my pajamas."

"I thought Fridays were casual," Thyra commented and swallowed the rest of the biscuit.

"Not this casual, but I wish!" Johnathen said before disappearing into their bedroom. She heard shuffling around in the room as he grabbed the appropriate attire. "Thyra, your phone is ringing."

Thyra quickly stood up off the couch and walked into the bedroom to retrieve her phone, looking at the picture of Isabell on the front screen. "It's Isabell."

"Oh! Tell her I said hi and I'll bring her a cheeseburger later tonight," Johnathen said while buttoning his shirt in the mirror.

Thyra answered the phone and put it to her eart. "Isabell! Hey how are you?..." She listened for a moment and walked out of the room, hearing concern in Isabell's voice. "Wait, what's up?... Yeah, I've seen it. It's been on all last night and this morning… I know its him… wait, you talked to the guy who was attacked?... Well, yes I want to talk to him!...ok ok I'll be there in a little bit…Yeah?...No, they don't serve them this early! Just breakfast stuff. Johnathen said he will bring you one later… ok, see you in a bit."

Thyra locked her phone and placed it on the counter, mind racing. She had to get down there and talk to the victim. She had to know why he was attacked and maybe he knew more than what he leaned on.

"What did Isabell say?" Johnathen asked as he walked into the kitchen now wearing black slacks and a collared button-up shirt with a matching paisley tie. He grabbed his keys and wallet.

"Not a whole lot. Just asked me to bring her some lunch," Thyra lied and walked over to Johnathen. She stood on her hind feet and readjusted his tie for him before giving a gentle peck on the cheek. Johnathen returned the kiss and ran his fingers along her cheek feathers.

"I don't understand how she eats so much junkfood and stays so small," Johnathen commented as Thyra hoped down on all fours again.

Thyra shrugged her wingshoulders and looked at the keys still remaining. "Some gryphons are just engineered for it, I guess. You're taking the Mach today?"

"It's a nice day, so I figured, why not?" Johnathen commented and grabbed his briefcase.

"Well you have fun today and I'll see you later tonight!" Thyra said and watched Johnathen walk out the door into the garage.

Seconds later, the symphony of exhaust noise rumbled the house as the engine grumbled to life. Thyra walked over to grab her coffee cup and watched out the window as the grey mustang pulled down the street. "Finally."

She quickly walked over to the sink and poured out the rest of the coffee. She had to get to the hospital right away.

Chapter 22 We All Have the Hunger

Thyra landed at the hospital entrance and folded in her wings. She readjusted the gloves on her front feet and walked towards the entrance. The double sliding doors opened automatically to a spacious lobby with rows of seating all around.

The room grew quiet as Thyra walked in. She felt everyone's stares on her. They must have seen the news and were fearful the killer gryphon was walking in. She stood still for a moment until they relaxed and returned to their business. Still, it gave Thyra the feeling that she was unwanted, much like it had been in the past.

It was a reminder that the relationship between humans and gryphons was still tender. It bothered her that all the years of work between the races could so easily be upset by the foul actions of one gryphon. She approached the nurses station, and forced herself not to frown as the nurse backed away slightly from the desk.

"Good morning. I'm here to see Isabell," Thyra said calmly. She looked into the brunet nurses wide eyes and could see that the woman was uncomfortable with her presence, despite knowing she was not the murderer they had seen on the television.

"A...alright. If you would please fill out the visitor form..." the nurse said while handing over a clipboard. Thyra reached out with a foretalon and watched the nurse extend her arm as far away from her body as she could to hand it over. Thyra took it gently and thanked her before filling it out quickly. Once the paperwork was done, Thyra handed it back without a word and continued down the hallway.

She found herself met with similar stares and reactions from the groups in the waiting area. People moved out of her way quickly, acting as if she was a beast that could strike at any time. Thyra tried to ignore them, but the old feeling of being an outcast welled inside her crop. She entered the elevator alone, despite their being a line of people waiting for the elevator, and rode it to the third floor. She continued down the hallway and saw Isabell's room number. Thyra knocked on the door gently.

"Come in," came the familiar singsong voice of the gryphoness from the other side.

Thyra opened the heavy metal door and walked into the plain white hospital room. Isabell was sitting on the couch as comfortably as she could. The small violet gryphoness was holding her bulky shiny cellphone with one foretalon and flipping through the television channels with the other.

She looked up with a big beakgrin. "Well! If it isn't the famous gryphball player, Thyra!"

Thyra laughed and shook her head, letting the door automatically close behind her. "Well, not famous."

"Practically! You're going to have your big game tomorrow," Isabell said and placed her phone down on the small round table next to the couch. "You've had some good runs for a greenwing this season. Even though you've never started a game, every gryphball channel mentions your name in conversation as the most promising rookie in a long time."

"I was hoping to prove my worth before the end the season. I mean, I always did pretty well out on the field whenever I was substituted in, and I got to play in every game so far. But I am still new, so I know why Victor doesn't want me to be a starter yet." Thyra explained and shrugged her wingshoulders.

"Oh, quit being so modest. You're a gryphball star! But, It's good to see you though," Isabell said with a smile. Thyra walked over to Isabell and bumped her forehead with the other gryphoness in greeting.

"Good to see you too. Sorry for not visiting as much as I wanted to over the past weeks. How's the wing?" Thyra asked.

"Good! Docs say it should be fully functional by the end of the year. I hope it's good to go by Christmas," Isabell said and looked over to her bound wing. "I'm feeling much better now, but they want to keep me for a couple more weeks for tests and physical therapy. They've been kicking my ass. I feel like I'm training to become an athlete."

"Well that's not too awfully far way. Let's hope so. You know you're invited for Christmas dinner," Thyra said with a smile. Isabell returned the friendly greeting and hoped off the couch.

"So, about Anfang," Isabell said. The mood shifted as Thyra looked into gryphoness' purple eyes. "This guy, Daniel, knows about him."

"What all does he know?" Thyra questioned.

"He's the one that found him alive, but I'll let you two talk. You've only told me a little about your past with Anfang, but I think this guy knows more than what he's leading on," Isabell said and started walking towards the door. "I only talked to him for a couple minutes because his family was in the room."

Thyra followed closely behind as they exited the room and walked down the hallway. The humans did not seem to be bothered by Isabell as much as they were with Thyra, as she was easily twice the tiny gryphonesses size.

"Did this Daniel mention anything about how he found Anfang?" Thyra questioned as they made their way to the elevator. Thyra pushed the button and sat before Isabell, waiting for a response.

"No. I could tell he knew what I was talking about, but as I said, his family was present at the time." Isabell said. They entered the elevator and rode it up to the next floor. "I don't think he really wanted to talk to me about it, but he might talk to you since you knew Anfang personally."

The floor they stepped out onto was empty save for a couple of press members standing by Daniel's room door, all talking to the nurses. They suddenly stopped their conversation as they noticed the gryphonesses approaching them. One of the press workers, a young man, ran to them before anyone else could.

"You're Thyra, right? What do you know about this recent gryphon assault and how do you feel it impacts your community?" He shouted before holding the recorder in front of her beak. Thyra took a step back and looked up at the news reporter with wide eyes.

"I-I don't know who this gryphon is, but I feel he shouldn't be represented as a criminal until questioned for his actions," Thyra responded without thinking.

Isabell perked her eartufts and looked over at Thyra in surprise as members of the on-site security team started to push the press back.

"Thyra, Thyra! What do you mean! He clearly killed police officers! It was caught on camera," the press man called out as he was escorted away with the others. Thyra simply bit her beak down and decided to remain silent until they were alone.

Isabell looked over to Thyra and nudged her gently. "See? I told you that you were famous."

"More than I thought. I just want to get this over with and hopefully save Anfang," Thyra responded and knocked at Daniel's door.

"Come in," a voice said behind the door.

Thyra turned the knob and entered the hospital room. Daniel had the bed propped up and was sitting up straight, facing them. He immediately stared at Thyra and she looked back at him curiously, seeing recognition in his eyes, but more than just that.

His jaw worked. "Thyra, I..."

Both gryphonesses stopped at the entrance and watched Daniel as he struggled for words. Thyra could see tears forming in his eyes.

"I never meant for any of this to happen," Daniel began and Thyra was intrigued. Someone she never met was apologizing to her, but she could not tell why.

Daniel took a deep breath and stared directly at her. "I never wanted to hurt you, or cause any harm."

"What are you talking about?" Thyra asked, feeling the tension building in the room. She approached Daniel's bedside with Isabell and sat next to him.

"Isabell told me about how you knew Anfang in the past. I had no clue. I… I was just following orders. Trying my best to slide by and make a living. But…" Daniel stopped for a minute and looked away.

Thyra grew agitated at Daniel beating around the bush and clicked her beak. "What do you mean? What do you have to do with Anfang? I thought you were just a victim!"

"No… I met Anfang the day before he attacked me. We… how do I start this?" Daniel took a deep breath with his eyes closed, and then looked over to Thyra. "I used to work for the Gathering. More specifically, Bishop Matthew."

Thyra's hackle feathers ruffled on end and her eartufts folded flat against her head. She raked her talons along the tiled floor and moved closer to his bed. "You worked for that asshole? You better choose your next words carefully or I'll pull your larynx clean out."

Isabell's feathers fell flat and she took a step back, not knowing what to think. It was a shock seeing Thyra in such a rage. Daniel sighed and looked directly into her bright green eyes.

"Please, just hear me out," Daniel pleaded. "You have every right to be angry. Yes, I worked for that bigot. He offered me more money than my family and I've ever had I-. We were able to get out of a bad situation in Atlanta and start a new life here. But, I had no clue what he was, and what he was planning."

Thyra took a deep breath. "Fine," She said with a readjustment of her wings. "But my threat still stands. I'm tired of Matthew and all his self-righteous bullshit."

"And so am I. He tried to kill me. Well… he sent Anfang to kill me," Daniel began. Thyra raised an eyeridge at his comment. "Let me start from the beginning. I was first hired to be Matthew's right-hand man. Carry out his day-to-day business, or what I thought was normal business in my line of work. Then he had me put surveillance on you and your husband, but it wasn't enough. Next thing I know, he had me infiltrating a gryphon rights group hangout to capture a lost gryphon." Daniel paused and let the information soak in for a moment. "If only I had known what we would find. Anfang… he's insane."

Thyra's head spun as she shook her head. "When I knew Anfang, he was a lot of things, but he wasn't insane. He was just confused and lost!"

"Maybe, but the very first thing he did when we freed him was kill my best friend. I watched him die while Anfang taunted me about it. Called him food and a plaything," Daniel said before wiping away tears. "Nothing more than flesh to be eaten."

"No, he wouldn't do that." Thyra shook her head in disbelief. Her heart denied what she was hearing but her head told her that Daniel had nothing to lie about.

"But he did. That night I told Matthew I quit. Then the next day I'm sitting in that diner and suddenly Anfang's rushing after me. He toyed with me. He laughed at my pain. I shot him multiple times but my bullets didn't seem to do anything." Daniel continued to recount the story to her, describing the scene and watching her reaction. "I don't know who you knew back then, but he's not the same. He's a murderer, and he enjoys it."

"No! That's not him!" Thyra shouted in anguish.

Daniel lifted up from his bed and winced, holding his chest. "Thyra, I've seen people like him in Afghanistan. He's a monster!"

"He was just confused and-and he must have been under the control of Matthew!" Thyra screeched out with tears rolling down her face. Isabell wrapped a good wing around Thyra to pull her into a hug, but Thyra pushed her away gently. "He's not a murderer! He just doesn't know any better!"

"I hate to be the one that tells you this, but…" Daniel looked over to the window and froze. Thyra followed his eyes to the window and saw a brown flying object fast approaching.

She had no time to question what she was seeing, as the window of the hospital room suddenly shattered with a burst of glass. Thyra closed her eyes and felt glass shards scrape across her face. Her adrenaline spiked, her heart beating hard in her chest.

Thyra opened her eyes to see the ghost of her past standing before her, covered in bleeding wounds from the glass, the leathery wings that were new to her spread wide. His eyes were crazed like a feral animal's as he glanced at her before looking to Daniel sitting on the bed. She opened her beak to shout, but it was too late.

The great beast leapt, and was on top of Daniel before she could think to move. Blood splattered the white linens with a dark hue as Anfang tore his talons into Daniels throat.

It happened so quickly, all Thyra could do was shout out as she watched Anfang throw his talons to the side, painting the walls with a crimson splatter. The sound of Daniel gurgling on his own blood filled Thyra's eartufts as her muscles buckled, feeling frozen in time and space. Moments went by and the inside of the room went to a silence, the only sounds Anfang's heavy labored breaths.

Thyra stared at Anfang in shock and watched as his crazed green eyes met hers once more. Then something changed. His pupils turned from senseless slits into something more sentient. He paused and closed his wings as recognition and cognitive thought came back into his eyes. He stared at the gryphoness before him.

"Th...Thyra?" Anfang slowly spoke out in a rough voice. He climbed off of the corpse. "Is...is you?"

The deformed gryphon made his way to the ground, not daring to take his eyes off of her. She opened her beak to speak, but her voice was lost. Tears formed in her eyes and streamed down her face as she saw him for the first time. Saw him for what he had become.

"I....I missed you," Anfang said as he approached Thyra. She took a quick step back as he reached out his talons dripping with blood towards her face, and Anfang frowned. "What wrong? Not happy to see Anfang? I missed you, Thyra. I missed you so much!"

"Anfang! W..why!" Thyra shouted as she finally found her voice.

Anfang pulled his head back and folded his single eartuft, confused by her response. "Why, what?" He reached for her again.

Thyra cried out and slapped his foretalons away. "Why did you kill him!" she shouted. "Why did you kill all the police? Why are you here?!"

He pulled his talons back and sat before her, shocked that she had not greeted him with open arms. "I…I had to." Anfang's eyes glossed over as tears formed in his own eyes. "Thyra..."

Anfang searched himself for a moment, looking lost in his own actions. Suddenly, the door was kicked open and multiple officers filled the room. Anfang quickly turned his head and hissed, fanning his leathery wings as they pointed their weapons at him.

Both Thyra and Isabell screamed and fell to the ground just before the sound of gunfire filled the small room, causing their ears to ring. Thyra looked up only for a moment to see Anfang launch towards two officers, and strike them down with one foul swing. The distant sound of screaming filled the hallways as Anfang screeched loudly and looked at Thyra one last time. He extended his foretalons and looked at her with pleading eyes.

"Please… Please come with Anfang, he begged.

Thyra shook her head and saw the disappointment in his eyes. Anfang frowned and jerked his head to the entrance as more police filled the door. He hissed and turned his back, running towards the broken window and leaping out of it with a strong beat of his massive wings.

There was more gunfire as the police fired after him. Then the room was quiet besides Daniel's heart monitor ringing a flat line in the air. Thyra looked around the room, absorbing the carnage that had happened in the past minute. Her eyes were wide with horror upon seeing the blood splattered around the room, and looked down to her own crème colored chest decorated with red. Police, security and nurses rushed into the room, but none made more than a cursory attempt to check on Daniel. It was clear that he was dead.

Thyra found her breath and screamed in horror, collapsing on the ground. It was too much for her to handle. Isabell wrapped a wing around her and slowly led her out of the carnage, leaving the rest to clean up the mess.

*　　*　　*

Confused, hurt, and cast away, Anfang flew away from the one that he had been certain would understand him. Their conversation would have to wait. He did not dare look back as he beat his wings hard, getting away from that place. He felt tears fall down his face, but not because of physical pain. What he felt was something new altogether. His heart ached and it confused him. It angered him.

Anfang looked down to watch multiple police vehicles rush down the street towards the hospital and heard the thundering sound of a helicopter in the distance. Matthew had warned him of these helicopters, as they were quicker than he was and could track him in land and air. He quickly dove into the woods and found a high tree to take shelter in.

The birds around him squawked and fled from the tree as he found a good purchase on a thick branch. His heart thumped hard in his chest, and his breathing was labored, yet he remained as still as he could. From afar, he could watch police rush into the building and the surrounding woods as they frantically searched for the attacker, but they would never find him.

He rested in the tree, replaying the images in his head of Thyra. She had looked completely frightened by the gryphon she saw before her. He clicked his beak against the fangs protruding out the sides of his lower muzzle in agitation and confusion.

Why was she so frightened? How could she find his actions wrong? He had been raised to kill. The men in control of his life had made it clear to him that was his reason for living, and he felt no remorse for the ones that he had murdered. Violence was nothing more to him than natural feeling, yet the sight of Thyra's eyes confused him.

Anfang remembered his innocent early days with Thyra, realizing that she had tried to teach him the good aspects of humanity, and what it meant to choose between right and wrong. Regret for his actions started to creep into his heart. He had lost that part of him long ago, but Anfang began to realize what Thyra's eyes had been telling him. For the first time in his life he felt remorse for his actions.

The gryphon screeched in a mixture of psychological pain and confusion. His talons tore into the tree trunk as he realized what he had done. He had killed someone that he knew nothing about besides a name. Anfang remembered Daniel's speech the day before, begging for mercy because of his family. He didn't understand what it was like to have a family but knew he had taken Daniel away from his.

Anfang realized that he could not live this way, obediently killing others for those in command. He wanted to change, for Thyra. Perhaps if he could find her, she would understand.

The sirens grew silent after several minutes, and multiple cops began to leave while large vans with numbers pulled up to the hospital. Anfang watched people pour out of the vans and start setting up cameras in the parking lot. They grabbed humans walking out of the hospital and started to talk with them in front of the cameras. Anfang waited patiently for the commotion to die down, but then something else caught his eye. Thyra was walking out of the hospital.

Anfang came to his feet on top of the branch and watched as Thyra swiftly strode by the multitudes of people gathering around her. She didn't speak to them, but took to the skies and flew right above the treetops where he was hiding. He had to chase after her.

He ran along the ground for a short time until he was sure he was out of sight of any camera crews. Then, with a quick check of his surroundings, he jumped out of the trees and beat his wings hard to follow after Thyra. She rose higher into the sky, with Anfang slowly gaining on her.

For the first minute, Thyra did not notice. He was a noisy flyer, but the wind whipping by her face was even louder. As he approached closer, he shouted.

"Thyra!"

Thyra's body froze in midair as she turned her head to see him following after. The same fear that he had seen before returned to her eyes, and immediately she dove. Anfang cursed under his breath and tucked his wings to follow behind.

"Thyra! Please!" Anfang called out again. Thyra flicked her wings open and curved back up into the sky. Anfang forced himself to follow, but she was much more agile and quicker than he was.

After making a sufficient distance, Thyra turned around and hovered in the air. "Stop!" she shouted as loud as she could.

Anfang flared his wings and forced himself to stop as requested. He hovered, flapping his wings hard to keep himself afloat, but found it extremely difficult. "Thyra, I.."

"No! You don't get to talk right now!" Thyra interrupted. "You were dead! You were gone out of my life, and now…" Thyra choked on her words now, tears streaming down her face. "Now here you are. A murderer! I don't know where you came from or where you have been, but ever since you've been back it's been nothing but pain!"

"But… You my friend, Thyra! I do these things to find you!" Anfang called out into the wind. His lungs ached with each deep breath and his wing muscles burned deep into his back. He could not keep this up for much longer.

Thyra's eartufts pinned back, not knowing what to ask next. She was just as confused as he was. "What do you mean you did all this for me?"

"Matthew! He tell me I kill for him and he bring me to you! But I found you! I not need him!" Anfang spilled out.

His wings began to buckle as he started to lose altitude. Thyra noticed his struggle and slowly turned her back to begin gliding once again. But she was not running. She seemed to really stare at his leathery wings, looking over her wingshoulder, reluctantly inviting him to fly next to her.

Anfang evened his body out with a couple hard wing beats and quickly caught up to Thyra. She kept a short distance from him, but seemed to want to hear him out.

"When did you get those wings?" Thyra asked, still looking them over as if they were an illusion.

"I not know. I wake up one day and they there. Much pain for days," Anfang responded.

"Did Matthew have them grafted on?" Thyra asked sternly.

"No. I have them long time."

"And Matthew set you up to do it? All of it?" Thyra asked as they glided together on wing.

Anfang looked over to Thyra and his mind flashed back to images of her younger self in the labs. The way she had smiled to him in the past always made him feel much better, but he searched for happiness in her eyes now and did not find it. "Yes. Matthew make Anfang kill. But..."

"You enjoyed it though, didn't you?" Thyra finished the sentence for him.

He felt shame at her accusation, though he still didn't completely understand why. Anfang looked away from her and down at his blood-stained talons. His training told him that he had done was not wrong and yet, he knew she would disagree. He never wanted to hurt her or disappoint his friend, but he could not lie to her.

"Yes. I like it, but you like to kill too. We all do," Anfang responded, searching her face once again as he repeated what the humans in uniform had once told him. "Gryphons are meant to kill. It is nature. Humans same way."

She let out a sorrowful sigh. "It is natural to hunt, yes, but Anfang, this is different. We can't kill people."

"Why not? People kill people. People kill animal. People want to kill us. They hurt us. They hate us. Why…"

"Because we have to be better than them!" Thyra interrupted again, her voice filled with sadness and anger.

Anfang blinked and cocked his head curiously. Thyra took a deep breath and looked forward to the sky ahead.

"We are creations of man. So in that aspect, we are evolutions of them. Do you know what that means? Evolution is an improvement, something greater than what was. If we act like those who hate us, than we become what they loathe. Do you understand? It lessens us. An eye for an eye leaves the whole world blind."

Thyra looked to Anfang, hoping to see understanding. He was clearly confused, but something clicked in his mind. A spark of recognition went off and his eyes opened wide. He was starting to understand the philosophy she was trying to teach him.

She stared into his similar green eyes, the same way she used to years ago when they were back in the lab. "My friend Aadhya taught me that."

"Who is Aad…adha?" Anfang asked and saw a slight beakgrin appear on Thyra's face. Immediately, he felt better than he had in years. He wanted to see her smile all his life, and would do anything to keep her happy.

"A friend with a difficult name, but that's not important. Anfang, I…" Thyra's beakgrin disappeared as she thought hard for a moment. "I don't know what to do. I want to believe that somewhere inside you you're still the same gryphon I knew. The one that had heart and love for the little things in life. The one that would wake up every day with a new sense of adventure. I want to think you are just lost, and confused, but…"

"I am lost, Thyra. I need help…" Anfang pleaded, watching Thyra look to him with concern. "I not know what right, what wrong. I just want to be with you," he admitted and folded his eartuft against his head. "Please teach me."

Thyra thought for a moment. He seemed to understand what he was doing was immoral. Perhaps there was still some good in him. She sighed deeply and closed her eyes.

"Damnit! John is going to kill me."

Chapter 23 High Hopes

"Are you out of your mind, Thyra?!" Johnathen began with his voice rising. Thyra's eyes widened and she waved her foretalons in front of his face to quiet him down, then looked over her wingshoulders to glance at Anfang in the kitchen.

"Keep your voice down!" Thyra demanded in a whisper, relieved to see that that Anfang had not heard Johnathen. The beast gryphon was a too busy tearing chunks out of a well-marinated steak to notice their conversation in the living room. "Listen, I know I should have called you and told you, but…"

"Yeah, no shit! You know what you've done?" Johnathen exclaimed and motioned over to Anfang. "You brought a fugitive into our house!"

Anfang looked up from his steak and perked his one eartuft. "Fu..fu..gi...tive. What is this, Thyra?" Anfang asked curiously.

Thyra glared at Johnathen and then fake smiled at Anfang to calm him. "Oh, it's nothing! It just means…um… a finely cut steak." Thyra lied, not knowing what else to say.

Anfang pointed to the piece of meat he had in his beak and thought for a moment more. "So, this a fugitive?"

"Well," Thyra began.

"Honey? Can we talk outside in private?" Johnathen asked and strode towards the back deck. Thyra followed closely behind, but kept an eye on Anfang who had returned his attention to the steak.

Once outside, Thyra closed the door behind her and watched Johnathen pace back and forth on the deck. The sun was setting behind the trees in the back yard, casting a shadow on the house. He stopped in front of her and ran his fingers through his short black hair.

"What were you thinking?!" Johnathen began, trying to keep his voice level. She hadn't seen him this distraught since the night he had punched out that Gathering man at the restaurant.

"He needs help, John!" Thyra said, her crest feathers rousing up. "He's lost and Matthew made him kill those people!"

"It still doesn't change the fact that he killed those people. He's a wanted criminal! Not a single lawyer in Atlanta could get us out of this! If anyone found out we were even TALKING to Anfang, we would have the FBI shoving microscopes up our asses. But harboring him under our own roof?" Johnathen put his hands on his hips and looked up at the sky. "With the crimes he committed, including murdering two officers, he's going away for life and we could get five years."

"Well, what do you propose we do? He's already here!" Thyra pointed out and stood her ground. Johnathen looked down at her with a furrowed brow. They locked eyes for a minute, and Thyra watched the anger leave his. Johnathen let out a sigh and closed his eyes.

"And no one saw you bring him here, right?" Johnathen questioned.

"Not a soul, I made sure of that," Thyra confirmed. She looked over to the door and saw Anfang glance outside at them. He seemed curious about their conversation, and stared at the two of them for a moment before turning away. "We will figure this out after the final game tomorrow."

"What are we going to do about him in the meantime? I mean, can we just leave him here alone?" Johnathen pointed out. "He's basically an untamed animal!"

Thyra frowned at Johnathen. She hated it when people used that word to describe gryphons. Johnathen immediately changed his expression as she opened her beak to say something but a crash of something breaking made her eartufts perk up. Johnathen heard it as well, and quickly made his way to the door to open it.

Thyra stepped inside to see Anfang standing in the living room, looking down at a broken vase. There was a pile of gray ashes around the decorative vase, and immediately Thyra knew what it was.

"Tried to grab that book. But I break this," Anfang commented and pointed at the pile on the wooden floor.

Thyra looked up to Johnathen as his brow furrowed with anger. "John, he didn't know..."

"Get away from that, Anfang," Johnathen commanded and walked across the kitchen and into the living room. The great beast looked over to Johnathen as he approached and began to growl.

"You not command Anfang, human," the gryphon said and started to spread his leathery wings, readying for a fight. Apparently, Johnathen had already rubbed Anfang the wrong way, and his tone of voice was not helping.

Johnathen froze dead in his tracks and stared into his green cat like eyes, but anger over came his fear. "I said move!"

Anfang took a step forward and flexed his talons into the hardwood floor. It seemed the beast would leap at any second. Thyra ran up to get in between the two of them, putting her back to Anfang and looking up at Johnathen.

"John, please. Go outside. I'll take care of this," Thyra pleaded.

Johnathen looked down to her and then to Anfang. He gritted his teeth and pointed his finger at Anfang. "Fine. This is your mess anyways, Thyra. After tomorrow, he's gone!" Johnathen said harshly and headed back outside.

Thyra watched him slam the door shut behind him and pace on the back deck. She felt a pang in her chest as she realized that this was the first time she had seen him truly angry at her. Thyra turned around to see Anfang slowly relaxing himself now, his feathers laying back down flat and wings tucking into his side.

"I not like him. Humans, they the same," Anfang commented.

Thyra shook her head. "No. They aren't the same. Johnathen is good. He's just, upset."

Anfang did not seem entirely convinced, but perked an eartuft to what she had to say. Thyra took a deep breath, trying to figure out how to explain this. “That vase was very important to him. It contained his mother’s ashes.”

Anfang sat down and cocked his head slightly, not understand what Thyra was saying. He processed it for a moment more and pointed as the ash on the ground. “That was his mother? How?”

“When humans die, their loved ones sometimes burn the ones they loved to collect their ashes. They call it cremation. It’s what they do sometimes instead of burying one another,” Thyra explained softly. Anfang clicked his beak against his teeth again and picked up a small talon full of the ash.

“Why human do this? People die every day. Why so important?” he asked, letting the ash fall back to the floor.

Thyra stood up and walked over to the kitchen, grabbing a coffee from one of the cupboards. Anfang stood and walked with her, watching her every move.

“It’s a way they deal with death. They seem to do better knowing their loved ones can be visited, even though they are not here anymore.” Thyra emptied out the coffee into the trashcan and grabbed a small dustpan off the wall. Anfang followed her back into the living room and watched her scoop up a pile and place it inside the can.

“It sound stupid,” Anfang said as he watched Thyra clean up the mess.

She stopped for a moment and looked back at him. His eyes were cold, as they often were. He just did not understand the concept of death and what it meant to people.

"In a way, it is. You're right, in a way. But, over the years I have learned what they do is actually nice. It's a way of respect. And something we gryphons have to learn if we are to live in peace with the humans."

Thyra watched the words sink in Anfang's brain. His eartuft folded back against his head and he looked away for a moment. Thyra returned to her cleaning, sweeping up the last of the ash into the coffee can.

"Who say we have to live with humans. Why you live with him? He control you," Anfang said, breaking the silence. "Like a dog."

This took her by surprise. Thyra looked back over to the scared face of her friend and then back out the door where Johnathen sat on the patio. She had to consider her next words carefully.

"Anfang, it's not like that at all. It's not like he gives me commands and I obey him. We are a couple. Everything we do is decided together. We are partners." Thyra put the coffee can back up on the shelf and begun to pick up the broken pieces of vase. "I love him and he loves me equally."

"I not believe it. Human control us. Always have," Anfang said with a frown. He looked out the window himself and readjusted his leathery wings. "I want you, Thyra. I take care of you. We…"

"I can't do that," Thyra interrupted. Anfang stared directly at her and then looked down at the ground. He huffed through his nares and turned away, heading down the hallway.

"Wait! Anfang," she called out. He stopped in his tracks and looked over his shoulder, but not directly at her. "I care for you. You know that, right?"

Anfang's tail twitched in response. He seemed to weigh the words heavily and then continued down the hallway. She sighed as she heard his footsteps on the stairs heading to the guest room they had hastily prepared for him.

Thyra closed her eyes for a moment and took a deep breath before continuing to clean up the broken vase parts. She had to convince Johnathen to allow Anfang to stay for longer if he was going to have any chance to be introduced to society. Unfortunately, that would mean risking their own freedom.

For a moment, she considered if it was even worth it. Johnathen was right, Anfang was a convict on the run. It would be much easier and quicker if they just turned Anfang over to the police, but it would take years of lawyers pleading his case in order to get him set free. Even worse, the government might just have him executed. The best case would be if he pleaded insane, and was admitted to a mental institution, but that would take a lot of convincing for a gryphon that did not know the difference between right or wrong.

She would never be able to live with herself if that was his fate. He was practically family. Even though they did not share the same parents, they were two of the first gryphons born from science.

The closing of the back door called Thyra's attention from her thoughts and she glanced back to see Johnathen standing in the kitchen. She kept her back to him as she finished sweeping up the last of the vase parts.

"Where is he?" Johnathen asked calmly.

"Upstairs. I think I upset him," Thyra admitted and walked into the kitchen to empty the dustpan.

Johnathen shut the door behind him and seemed to relax a bit as he did not have to face the gryphon again right now. "And what did you do with my mom?"

"She's in a coffee can for now. We can go shopping for a better urn in a couple days." Thyra hung the dustpan back up and walked into the kitchen. She looked up at Johnathen and stood on her hindlegs to face him. "Listen, I'm sorry-."

"It's not your fault." Johnathen reached out and stroked over her cheek. "It's his. He doesn't belong here, and he can't stay here. He's…"

"An animal. You said that already, John." Thyra pulled her head back and returned to all fours once more. She let her voice grow louder, her head crest rousing with anger. "Then what am I to you? Just another animal like him?!"

Johnathen held his hands up in defense. "That's not what I meant-," he began, but Thyra interrupted.

"That's exactly what you meant! Yes, he's done a lot of bad in his life, but he doesn't know any better! He and I are the same kind. Deep down, there's good inside of him and I have to protect him. If you can't see that…" She paused and snorted through her nares.

"Then what?" Johnathen asked. They stood facing each other as her eyes searched his. "You're being unreasonable."

"Unreasonable?!" Thyra snapped and readjusted her wings. She growled and turned her back to him, heading to the refrigerator. “Just leave. I can’t deal with you right now,” Thyra said. She listened to the jingle of keys as Johnathen swiped them off the hanger next to the door.

“Already planned on it,” Johnathen said and exited to the garage, slamming the door behind him.

Thyra gritted her beak together and opened the refrigerator, pulling out another slab of steak. A loud rumble shook the house as his mustang fired to life and hastily left the garage. She looked out the front window as the taillights disappeared with the sound of screeching tires disturbing the neighborhood.

She slammed the refrigerator door shut and cursed under her breath as she heard the clangs of condiments falling over inside. Thyra could not remember the last time they had fought like this, but distance usually solved that issue. Maybe he was right, she was being a little unreasonable and hysterical, but she could not get past it.

“Thyra?” came Anfang’s croaking voice from down the hall. She turned to see him standing in the hallway, eyes gleaming from the kitchen light. “I heard fight.”

Thyra took a deep breath and forced her feathers to lay flat once again before responding. “Yeah. We had an argument,” she admitted.

Anfang growled deeply in his chest and walked into the kitchen, long untrimmed talons scraping against the wooden floor. “If he hurt you, I kill him.”

“No, you won’t. And he would never hurt me,” Thyra said while unwrapping the steak. She tore it in half with her foretalons and placed the other half on a plate. Anfang approached the other side of the island table and Thyra slid the plate over to him.

"That what you think. All humans lie. All hurt us soon." Anfang cocked his head and looked over to her. She watched him take the steak in his talons and tear a chunk out of it with his beak, but unlike her, he chewed before swallowing. "He will hurt you."

Thyra looked down at her plate, staring at the raw piece of meat before her as she took a deep breath. "Not all humans are bad. You have to learn that," she said before doing as he had, biting into the steak and swallowing a piece hastily. She let the flavor of raw meat and the feeling of it in her crop relax her. "I have to go early tomorrow to play gryphball, and Johnathen won't be home. I want you to stay here while I'm gone and don't leave the house. Do you understand?"

"Anfang understand," he said before chomping down the rest of the meat. She tossed her plate in the sink and walked over to her bedroom door, stopping for a moment. She turned around and looked at Anfang.

"Don't leave and don't hurt anyone." Thyra said. "Try to sleep. I'll see you tomorrow, ok?"

He raised his head and stared at her from across the room. She could tell the hospitality was unusual to him. He did not know how to react, and nor did she. Anfang readjusted himself and nodded.

"Yes. Anfang see you tomorrow."

*   *   *

"We're outside live at central hospital where another gryphon attack happened hours ago. The Sabertooth Slasher has struck again, claiming yet another victim and putting two other guards in critical care. The victim is Daniel Lions, the same man attacked just yesterday by this killer. It seems the slasher came back to finish the job.

"There is no video evidence of the Slasher's attack. But we do have an eyewitness report from Jordan, an on-site security member, who was there at the scene of the attack."

The video feed transferred to an interview with Jordan, his face at the center of the screen. *"The monster looked just like the pictures from yesterday. It had the wings of a bat, like a demon, and a scarred face with teeth hanging out of its beak. I ain't never seen a creature move as fast as it did. There was so much noise, and by the time we got into the room, the guy was dead and the monster was gone. It entered and left through the window in a minute's time. I don't know how we could have seen it coming. It was almost like it was a ghost."*

The image flickered to black as Matthew turned the television off. He leaned back in his office chair and tossed the remote on his desk. "It seems he did complete his task."

He thought for a moment and rubbed his chin. A single desk lamp was all that illuminated his dark office as he rocked back and forth in his chair. This was not exactly how he had seen his plan executed, but he had accounted for the fact Anfang might not return. After all, he had only been killing Daniel to earn his freedom.

A knock came from the far side of the room, breaking Matthew's attention. "Come in," Matthew spoke. One of the suit-wearing bodyguards opened the door and walked in.

"Bishop Darnwall, we have located the gryphon's whereabouts," he said before closing the door behind him. Matthew sat forward in his chair and leaned on his elbows.

"Go on," Matthew said calmly. The man walked towards his desk and placed a tablet down on his desk. Matthew picked the device up and tapped the screen, studying the map. A smile slowly appeared on his face as he recognized the area. "4214 Obar drive. Are you certain this is correct?"

The bodyguard stood up straight and held his hands behind his back. "As far as we can tell, this location is current. We have pinged the watch several times, and it seems to be moving slightly, indicating he is still wearing the device and it's currently operational."

Mathew chuckled and placed the tablet down on his desk. He leaned back in his seat "It seems our friend has reacquainted himself with his past. This could certainty work in our favor."

The bodyguard raised an eyebrow and looked down at him curiously. "Sir, I don't know what you mean."

"It means that we may be able to kill two birds with one stone." Matthew commented and looked up at the guard. "Is the new watch prepared for Anfang?"

"Yes sir. Our contact delivered it this afternoon. He has provided instructions on how to detonate it when you see fit."

"Very good." Matthew grinned evilly. "We will wait until morning to give our friend his gift."

Chapter 24 Deceived

Anfang sat at a window in Thyra's upstairs room overlooking the neighborhood, watching the sun rising higher in the autumn sky. He had heard Johnathen's car come home in the middle of the night and leave later that morning.

The house was now silent, except for the low noise of the television left on downstairs. It was an odd sensation to be left alone and for the first time, he felt relaxed. He readjusted his wings and watched as a bright yellow bus stopped at the edge of the street and multiple young humans boarded. Curiosity grew inside him, and he left the room to descend the stairs into the kitchen.

"Thyra?" Anfang called out, but the house remained quiet. She must have left with Johnathen to go to the game. Everything in this place was foreign to him, including the sizable strange shining box that he had seen Thyra open to retrieve food. He inspected it, and decided to pull on the handle.

It opened and the light flickered on inside. There were a variety of containers containing odd colored liquids and colorful plants inside. Anfang grabbed one of the containers with orange liquid inside and shook it around. He fussed with the end of the container, and it popped open with ease. He smelled inside and huffed through his nares as a strong citrus smell invaded his lungs.

The gryphon tilted it back and let the orange juice wash across his tongue. The odd flavor ignited his sense of taste, and made him click his tongue against the roof of his beak. His feathers ruffled. He could not parse out the sensation, but it was quite good. Anfang took another swig of the foreign liquid before placing it back in the refrigerator.

He decided to take a green plant out of the fridge and inspect it. He wondered why they would take something that grew outside and place it in this strange box with food. Anfang sniffed the plant and ripped a piece of green from the rest before putting it in his beak. His expression soured as he chewed on the leaf for a moment and spit it out on the ground. He did not like that. Anfang dropped the lettuce on the ground and looked inside the brightly lit box again.

He spotted a plate of meat inside with a film wrapped around it and immediately grasped it in his talons. Finally, something he recognized. He looked over the meat carefully and used his talons to pick at the clear plastic wrapped around it until it unraveled.

Anfang bit into the meat and swallowed a sizable piece with delight. All the foreign objects looked interesting and each one had tasted different, but what was the point? Why would they have anything else inside this cold box besides meat? Did Johnathen force Thyra to eat such odd things too?

He quickly dispatched the meat and closed the box before turning his attention to the television. He had seen these devices before. They displayed moving pictures with sound, usually giving humans news or some sort of entertainment.

"The Sabertooth Slasher is still at large and there are no leads to its whereabouts," said a woman with blond hair who faced the camera, seeming to talk directly to him.

He walked into the living room and sat down before the flat screen hanging on the wall. It was the biggest television he had ever seen and everything on it looked so life-like. He watched as images of himself attacking the police at the diner flashed on the screen, and growled deep in his chest. The image froze with a clear picture of him looking at the camera as the newswoman went on.

"It is still considered highly dangerous and a threat to society. It should not be approached by any means. If you are to see this gryphon, immediately call 911."

Anfang snorted and turned away from the television. The humans wanted to hunt him down like an animal, just as he thought. There was nowhere for him to turn. Surely, Johnathen would turn him in and he would be locked in chains once again. He felt anger rise within him and he snarled. Anfang lashed out at an innocent lamp sitting next to the couch, and watched it break into a hundred pieces as it hit the floor.

The sound of the front door opening brought him out of his anger. His eartuft perked to attention as he carefully walked out of the living room to look down the hallway. He crouched down as a familiar face entered the doorway. He stared into his eyes. It was Matthew.

"Why you here?!" Anfang hissed and his body swelled as he spread his leathery wings from wall to wall. Matthew held his hands up in defense and closed the door behind him.

"I'm not here to harm you, Anfang. I'm here to help you. Remember, you and I are friends," Matthew paused and stared into the beast's slitted pupils until Anfang slowly relaxed. He brought his wings back in, and forced his feathers to sit flat against his body. The old man took a calm step towards Anfang. "You didn't come back last night and I was worried about you. Are you alright?"

"Yes. Anfang find Thyra. Anfang happy." He took a step back into the kitchen cautiously. He watched as Matthew walked into the kitchen, taking a look around.

"I know this is where Thyra lives. It certainty seems like a nice place, but it's all a front," Matthew commented and folded his hands behind his back. He stood at the opposite end of the island table to put more distance between him and Anfang.

"A front? Not know what front is," Anfang said. He sat down on his haunches and looked over the counter at the old human before him.

Matthew rubbed his chin in thought and looked around again. "A front is something that is fake, something fanciful that is made up to hide the truth behind it. I know this is a difficult concept, but I believe you're intelligent enough to see what I'm talking about, Anfang." Matthew turned around to look at the coffee pot. The coffee maker was left on and the pot was half filled with the black liquid.

Anfang narrowed his eyes. "But why is all fake?"

Matthew walked over to a cupboard and began to open the doors, seeming to look for something. "Thyra, like most gryphons, is merely being used for her human's purposes. She's a slave, like you once were, before I rescued you." Matthew let the words sink in for a moment as he searched the cabinets. "Johnathen controls her, but she doesn't realize that he does."

Matthew found what he was looking for and pulled out a mug. He turned to look at Anfang, reading his face. The gryphon huffed through his nares and looked away.

"Johnathen angry at Thyra last night. Yelled at her. Yelled at me," Anfang commented and turned back to look at Matthew.

The old man wore a smirk for just a second, but quickly shifted to a neutral expression. He nodded and turned his attention back to the coffee pot. "Then I don't need to explain myself much further. You saw it first-hand. We humans are naturally greedy. We take what we want without concern for others wellbeing,"

Matthew poured himself a cup of coffee. "Johnathen is like every other human. He has taken Thyra for his own agenda, and uses her as he sees fit, much like a pet. I, on the other hand, want nothing but your happiness."

Anfang growled and dug his talons into the wooden floor as he let the bishop's words sink in. Matthew placed the coffee pot back on the warmer and turned it off. He looked back to the gryphon and raised his mug to gently sip on the coffee.

"Thyra belongs with her own kind, in the same way that humans should stay with other humans. They don't belong together. It's unnatural to think otherwise."

"Thyra belongs with Anfang, not Johnathen," the great gryphon said sternly.

Matthew walked around to the bar end of the island and sat down in a stool to face him. "Exactly, she does. But right now, she doesn't see it. Thyra has had the wool pulled over her eyes, and can't see the reality of the situation. She's been living a lie, and without even knowing it, she's crying out for help. Why else do you think she brought you here?"

There was silence between them for a couple of moments as Anfang searched the old man's eyes. Finally, he looked down at his talons. Matthew sipped his black coffee and placed the mug down on the table, waiting for a response.

"What should Anfang do?" the gryphon asked.

Matthew smiled and stood up from his seat. He reached into his pocket and withdrew a similar-looking watch to the one Anfang was currently wearing, though it was twice the original size. "Thyra is currently playing gryphball, a human invention to enslave your kind for their entertainment. Do you know this game?"

"Yes. Thyra said she must play today," Anfang commented and looked at the device Matthew held in his hand.

"Did you know that it is a very dangerous game? Gryphons fly and fight to entertain the humans. She could become gravely injured, all so that Johnathen can make money." Matthew held out the watch for Anfang to look over. "But you can stop it. I have programmed this to lead you to her. If you take this, you could save her and bring her away from all this. Will you help her?"

Anfang looked at the device reluctantly. He seemed to consider it for a moment.

Matthew shook the device and gave the gryphon a pleading look. "Remember, you can trust me. I haven't led you astray before."

Anfang's eyes gleamed as thought it over. It was true that Matthew had held up to his promises and treated him fairly, more so than any other human had in his lifetime. Anfang slowly raised his gigantic fore talon. "After this, you let Anfang leave?"

Matthew smiled and reached out to undo the old watch from the gryphon's wrist. "Of course. I only want to see you happy," he said with a slight chuckle.

He placed the old watch on the counter and secured the new one to Anfang's wrist. As he did so, the screen lit up with a familiar arrow telling him the direction to go in. This version was much bigger and bulkier than the one he had worn before but the weight was nothing of concern. "It bigger."

"That's because you have farther to travel this time." Matthew watched as the gryphon turned his wrist, looking the device over. "Well? What are you waiting for? Thyra is waiting."

Anfang stood up on all fours and looked to Matthew one last time. Without another word, he walked over to the back door and opened it to step outside. Matthew picked up his coffee mug and watched as the gigantic gryphon took to the skies, leathery wings flapping hard against the wind. He laughed under his breath and finished off the coffee.

"Good riddance."

* * *

"Don't let up, Thyra! I want you on that heron's ass before he makes a move!" came Victor's voice through the earpiece.

She cursed as the opposing team's forward outmaneuvered her and passed under. The Heron was impossibly fast with its great curved wings. She had never seen anyone maneuver so quickly before in her life. Thyra banked hard, then beat her wings to gain speed.

"*It looks like Redtails' thirteen couldn't keep up with Roadrunners' two! He's wide open*!" the announcer called out over the loudspeakers.

Half of the audience cheered loudly while the others remained silent, biting their tongue. The stands were completely packed with fans from both teams. It was the final match of the season, and the winner would take home the title and gain advancement into the first league. Everything rode on this game.

Aadhya moved into position to intercept, and the Heron threw the gryphball down to a teammate on the ground. A bright red gryphon caught it with ease and tucked it into his wings.

"This cardinal is too fast! I can't catch up! Nathanial, come at his right and slow him down!" came Jason's voice on the intercom.

Thyra knew he was right; the sleek cardinal gryphon could outrun any of them on the ground.

The cardinal gryphon glanced over and saw Nathanial rushing at him from the side. Nathanial leapt and threw his body squarely into the red gryphon's wide flank. It was a successful hit, but it seemed to have little effect on the muscular beast.

Thyra watched from above, still sticking with the heron as he doubled back to get open if needed. She was amazed this gryphon could take such a good hit and barely even be phased. The last time she took a hit from Nathanial like that, she had the wind knocked out of her.

"*A tackle attempt by Redtails' five, but it seems to have no effect on Roadrunners ninety-nine! He's clear for the goal!*" The crowd stood to their feet, screaming at the top of their lungs.

Brandon, the Redtails' corvid goalie, was all that remained between the cardinal and a ground goal. The black gryphon spread his wings out and hunkered down, staring down the opposing team player heading straight towards him.

Everyone held their breath as the cardinal jumped to switch the gryphball from under his wing to his foretalons, and threw the ball towards the left corner with great speed. Brandon maneuvered quickly and blocked the throw with a wing, causing the gryphball to bounce down on the ground and out of bounds.

Redtails' fans cheered loudly and a loud whistle blew in the stadium. "*A failed ground goal attempt by the roadrunners! The score still remains four to three, with the Redtails in the lead and twenty seconds remain in the game. Will the Redtails be able to hold them off long enough*?"

"Thyra, take the opposing corner and remain in position alpha. Aadhya, Rachel, do not let your air opponents get open. We will control the ground," Jason said across the intercom as he walked over to the corner of the field nearest to the goal.

Thyra circled around, looking to Aadhya and Rachel as they assumed new positions. Another opposing team gryphon took the ball in talon on the sidelines and waited.

The whistle blew again and the Roadrunners' team began to flutter about, trying their best to get open. The cardinal gryphon was the first to break formation from their defenses, and caught the ball as it was thrown to him.

Thyra looked to the sky and briefly caught a glimpse of a large bird flying towards the stadium, but as soon as she did, the Heron broke away from her. The cardinal gryphon on the ground tossed the ball skywards for the heron to take possession.

"Damnit Thyra, get your head out of your tailfeathers and block him!" Victor yelled into the intercom.

She screeched and quickly adjusted her to intercept. Thyra beat her wings hard, heading directly for the heron. She clamped her beak hard, put her wing shoulder in and collided with the heron hard.

Thyra's vision faltered as they collided. Her wings went limp as she spiraled out of control to the ground along with the heron. She tried to adjust her body to catch wind as she saw the sky, the ground, and sky again. Everything seemed to move in slow motion as she separated from the other gryphon and began to right herself.

Then a large dark figure flew in out of nowhere and slammed into the heron that was falling next to her. The sound of surprised shouts echoed through the stadium as the two gryphons hit the ground hard, sending the gryphball flying in the air.

Thyra flicked her wings out slow her decent right before colliding with the ground. She felt the impact of the earth against her and everything went black for a second. She gasped and winced as she tried to stand. Her vision was blurry, but she could make out the large figure standing above the heron. Anfang's talons were digging into the lifeless gryphon below him. The packed stadium yelled in disbelief at the sudden violent interruption.

"*Folks! I don't know what is going on! It seems another gryphon has come into play*!"

Anfang pulled his talons out of the dead gryphon below him and looked to Thyra. Her eyes grew wide, at first with fear, and then anger grew inside her. "What have you done!"

A loud whistle blew, interrupting the game. All the players paused on the field and turned their shocked attention towards the two. Thyra looked at the Heron, watching blood pour out of his torn throat and onto the green grass below.

"He try to kill you. They all do. They control you. Come with Anfang now, Thyra! I protect you!" Anfang shouted, his eyes turning into small green slits. Thyra took a step back and looked around the stadium, seeing the cameras focused in on them both.

"*Sweet Jesus, it's the Sabertooth Slasher*!" the announcer shouted.

Many in the crowd screamed with horror, but surprisingly these cries were overridden by a surge of yells and boos towards the killer gryphon. Anfang's eartuft lowered as he noticed multiple police offers beginning to pour out onto the field. He looked back to Thyra and took a step forward, extending his bloody talons once more.

"Please! I protect you!" Anfang pleaded.

"No! Get out of here, Anfang! Leave me alone!" Thyra shouted at him.

Anfang hissed and turned his attention back towards the cops surrounding him now, weapons drawn. Thyra noticed Anfang taking a defensive position, ready to strike.

She flared her wings and screeched for the officer's attention. "Don't! He will kill you all!" Thyra pleaded. A couple of officers turned to look at her and she could see the pure fear in their eyes. Even their weapons were shaking. "Anfang! Please don't kill them!"

Anfang looked between the surrounding officers and let out a low growl, turning around slowly to face each human. He heard Thyra's pleading, and remembered Thyra's conversation on wing just yesterday. Some form of recognition shown in his eyes.

One of the officers yelled and started to open fire on Anfang, causing everyone to scream. The beastly gryphon leaped towards the officer, but instead of going for the throat, he slashed the weapon out of his hands. The policeman fell to the ground clutching his bleeding hand and cried out; causing the remaining forces to take a step back, their own weapons lowering. They could tell their guns were useless.

Suddenly there was a flash of light and a loud explosion shook the stadium. Thyra dropped down to the ground and covered her face with her wings and talons. The stadium lights flickered, and the audience erupted into cries of terror.

Chapter 25 Chaos

Chaos filled the stadium as everyone fled. Time stood still for Thyra. She rose to her feet, beak agape with horror. Everything seemed to be a blur. There was a glow coming from the parking lot just outside the stadium and a towering plume of smoke rose above the bleachers, drifting into the air above the field.

She looked over to where Johnathen had been seated in the stands, and saw him being pushed out with the crowd despite his best efforts to resist. She could see the worry in his eyes, even from far away, but there was nothing he could do. He was a fish trying to helplessly swim upriver but he was dragged along with the current.

Power returned to the stadium and immediately sirens started to blare across the loudspeakers. The remaining officers on the field fled, heading towards the exit of the field.

"Thyra!" shouted multiple voices from behind her.

She snapped back to reality and looked to see Aadhya, Rachel, Jason and Nathanial flying towards her. She grit her beak and turned back to Anfang, staring at him with hatred in her eyes. He seemed just as lost and confused by the explosion as she was, but now anger overtook her.

"Why did you do this?!" Thyra screeched.

Anfang looked down at her with frown and took a step forward. Thyra stepped back and found the rest of her teammates standing next to her. Their protective demeanor angered Anfang.

"Anfang come to rescue," the great beast growled and took another step forward.

"No! You didn't! Look at the mess you made! What was that explosion?" Thyra asked as the other gryphons stood next to her, wings flared in defense. Anfang looked down to his wrist where the large watch used to be, and something clicked in his head.

"Matthew give me watch. I dropped it over there. I not need it . . ." Anfang began to explain. As he put the puzzle pieces together, he screeched with anger, now feeling betrayed. "He… meant to kill Anfang. Meant to kill us!" He looked at the other gryphons and hissed. "Move. I take Thyra to safety."

Aadhya was the first to step in front of Anfang. She dug her talons into the ground. "No. You will not touch a feather on her," the huge vulture said sternly.

Anfang looked to the group and spread his leathery wings out to make himself seem even larger. "Then you will die," he promised and rushed forward.

Thyra yelled for Aadhya to move, but it was too late. The two gigantic gryphons collided with one another, talons raised in the air. Anfang swiped a foretalon across Aadhya's side, sending her tumbling.

Thyra yelled again, tears pouring from her eyes, but that did not stop the rest of her teammates. They all rushed to move onto Anfang, but it was not enough. He easily shrugged off their attacks, and struck each gryphon down as they came within reach.

Thyra saw her friends on the ground as they groaned with pain. She clicked her beak and looked to Anfang now, seeing the murderous intent in his eyes. With a bellowing roar, Thyra leapt forward.

Her beak connected with his throat, and she clamped down as hard as she could. Anfang hissed with pain and rolled onto his back, using his hindlegs to kick Thyra squarely in the stomach. All her breath and energy left her as she was sent flying through the air, and hit the ground headfirst.

Anfang quickly maneuvered to his feet and looked over to the motionless Thyra lying on the ground. His pupils dilated as sentience came back to him. His beak fell open with horror at the realization he had hurt the one he loved. Anfang ran over to her, and placed a foretalon on her side, rolling her over to her back. She was still breathing, but clearly unconscious. The other gryphons started to recover, returning to their feet.

"L...leave her alone," Rachel coughed and struggled to stand. Anfang looked over to the small gryphon with a growl before reaching down to Thyra and scooping the limp gryphoness up with his foretalons. "Put her down!" Rachel pleaded, wings hanging limply next to her.

Anfang stood on his hindfeet, cradling Thyra in his massive foretalons, and jumped. The rest of the band watched helplessly as the great beast took to the skies with Thyra in his grasp, beating his leathery wings against the darkening sky. Rachel slammed her foretalon against the ground and squawked at Anfang. Aadhya, Nathanial and Jason all slowly rose to their feet, checking themselves for wounds.

"What do we do now?" Rachel asked in a panic. Her wing was damaged, missing flight feathers with a long gash running along the length.

Aadhya placed her talons on her chest, and pulled it away looking down at the blood. She was hurt, but not too badly. "I can fly," Aadhya confirmed with a stretch of her wings. Before anyone could argue, Aadhya pushed away from the ground and ascended into the sky. The rest of the team sat in helpless silence, watching the gryphons disappear from sight.

"Anfang!" Aadhya called out when she was within earshot of the flying beast.

He turned his head to look at his pursuer and snarled. Anfang picked up the pace, flying harder and faster. Aadhya matched his speed, despite the injury to her chest. The wound had numbed by now as adrenaline pumped through her body.

"Anfang, please listen!"

The stadium quickly disappeared behind them as they flew away from the city. The sounds of car alarms and sirens slowly diminished until there was nothing more than the rhythmic beat of their wings and the blood pumping in her eartufts. Yet, the monstrous gryphon would not listen. She gave chase still, and waited for him to calm down enough to be talked to.

After what seemed like ages of patient pursuit, his pace began to slow, giving Aadhya an opportunity to gain on him again. "Where are you taking her?" Aadhya asked as she flew up beside him.

Anfang snarled again and moved towards her to attack, but Aadhya easily dodged the slow strike. "What are you going to do?" she asked once more, forcing her voice to calm. Anfang looked over to her, and she saw the indecision in his eyes. He was scared, lost, and wanted only one thing, to protect Thyra. "I am Thyra's friend too. I want to keep her safe, just like you," she said gently, trying to level with him.

"Anfang want to save Thyra. Thyra is a slave. Slave to human. Slave to game," he finally responded.

His wings straightened out to catch the wind and began to glide. Aadhya rose up next to him once again and did the same, matching his speed. She looked at Thyra tucked into Anfang's massive foretalons, still unconscious.

"What has made you believe that is true?" Aadhya asked curiously.

Surely, he had been manipulated into thinking Thyra was miserable, but she wanted to get to the bottom of it. Anfang readjusted his wings as he started to lose altitude, his chest heaving from exhaustion.

"Matthew told Anfang that Thyra is slave to all. She unhappy. She is in danger. Thyra not belong with humans. Thyra belong with Anfang," he said under his breath, struggling now to keep upright. They had been flying for a while and she could tell the weight of carrying Thyra was getting to him.

Aadhya herself had started to feel the pain in her chest return. It was taking tremendous effort to keep concentration. She was more adept to longe didstance flying with her broad wings, and knew it would not be long until Anfang had to land. “But that is not true. Thyra is happy with us. She is happy with her life. Matthew has lied to you, Anfang. He is Thyra’s enemy.”

Doubt flashed across Anfang’s features. “Matthew try to kill us. Anfang threw away watch. Not need anymore, and it explode. Matthew want to use Anfang as bomb. Matthew lie.”

“Then you see if for yourself. Matthew has lied to you on every account. Thyra did not need to be rescued, because she was not in any danger. Well, not from anyone, but Matthew.” Aadhya was trying her best not to stir up more emotion for the hair-trigger gryphon. It was in her best interest to keep calm and he seemed to understand reason. Anfang’s speed started to slow once more, and he forced his wings to beat harder.

Aadhya knew this would not last long. “Anfang, let me take Thyra. You cannot hold her any longer. I can carry her home to safety.”

The bestial gryphon looked over his wingshoulder to face Aadhya. His eyes were no longer angry as he stared at the gryphoness for a moment more. He held out the limp Thyra in his foretalons and offered her to Aadhya. “We take her home. Then safety, yes?”

Quickly, Aadhya moved in, gliding next to him and carefully retrieving Thyra from his talons. She beat her wings harder to adjust for the weight shifting as Anfang did the same.

“Yes. She will be safe at home,” Aadhya responded.

She was not sure what Anfang's idea of safety was. He had always been moved from one cage to the next. He had no home or a place to go. Did he mean to take her into the wilderness, to live as ferals and never to be seen again?

She did not know, nor did she intrude on his thoughts. She had Thyra in her possession and that was all that mattered at the moment. The main goal was bringing Thyra to her home. She would wait for Johnathen. Surely, he would know what to do.

"Anfang…Anfang not mean to hurt others…" the gryphon said as he struggled to keep righted in flight.

Aadhya adjusted herself and turned her head towards him, curious as to his explanation. As far as she had observed, he had brought nothing but despair and death to all those around him. Yet he now displayed some form of guilt.

"Humans always hurt Anfang. Angry, alone, hurt. I not know how to act. Thyra says she teach Anfang. Learn how to be better. How to be with people." Anfang lowered his head and turned away from Aadhya. "But, I hurt you. I hurt friends of Thyra."

The gryphoness looked to Anfang, carefully selecting her next words. "I believe that you mean well, Anfang. You are lost, and you require help. Thyra has told me of your history or what she knows of you. I believe you can be a better gryphon, and become one of us."

Anfang looked over to her with wet eyes, ones that searched for redemption and recognition. "You think Anfang can be good?"

"Yes. I believe you can be good," she said, though she didn't think the rest of the world would give him that chance. "First, let us return Thyra home safely."

* * *

"A plague has been placed upon the non-believers of this town!" Matthew slammed his fist down on the preachers stand before him. The loud thump echoed in the great chapel room over the loudspeakers, and he adjusted the mic hanging from his ear to his liking.

"God has sent an archangel, a demon, into our midst. He has sent him to punish us for our wrong doings and not doing what is right for our community! This abomination has killed, maimed, and hurt many of our innocent townsfolk. Yet out there in the world, there will be many who call it a creature in need, one who simply needs help emotionally. They would treat this monster as they would any common man, but this, this thing is much less than that!"

The congregation remained silent in their seats, watching him with unbroken attention. Normally, the bottom rows of the chapel were packed shoulder to shoulder with most of the upstairs overflow full as well. Yet today, rows of benches remained empty in the great hall.

Over the weeks since silencing the female interloper that had hidden in the congregation, Matthew had noticed the crowd gradually becoming lighter than normal. He had hoped it was for simple reasons like illnesses or vacations, but as he looked over the small gathering for his usually busy Sunday night sermons, he began to grow worried.

Matthew stood straight and disregarded the butterflies in his chest. He folded his arms behind his back, and began walking back and forth across the stage. The white robe he wore dragged gently along the carpet behind him. His mic picked up his heavy breathing as he forced himself to calm down.

"I come to you asking, why? Why do we continue to let sin into our community? Why do we sit idly by as others try to change our tradition and spit on the grave of our ancestors, forefathers, and beloved past teachers? How can we allow this to continue when God Himself so belatedly tells us to take action against such injustice? To anyone who would treat this killer with mercy, I say no. This monstrosity does not deserve a trial. He deserves a swift death!" Matthew yelled out.

His outcry was met with more silence. Matthew had expected some applause or amens in agreement, but not a soul moved in the crowd. He looked over the people once again, noticing some shuffling in their seats, as if they were uneasy by this sudden change of sermon. Matthew had made an unexpected jump in the usual script.

Somewhere in his sermon, the subject of God's punishment had evolved into a hate speech against the gryphons once again, especially Anfang. He felt it was necessary, what with the fear in the community over resent actions the gryphon had taken. Not to mention, the more grievous actions that would appear on the news soon.

Surely, the bomb had detonated by now. Anfang would have blown up on the field of the Gryphball finals, taking Thyra and her other gryphon teammates with him. Perhaps there would even be human casualties. Either way, the world would have reason to fear gryphon kind once more and Matthew would be vindicated for his fight against them. Any moment he would hear the news.

"A swift death for the demon. That is what I call for action. His existence goes to show us that the demons live in each one of the gryphons. They are man-made living beings without a soul, without a purpose. They can become savage at any time, and their power is beyond what we know!

"We have flown too close to the sun, like Icarus before us, and now we must pay in blood. Unless we are to be rid of these mistakes, we are doomed to repeat history and fall farther from God's grace. And we know what wrath can be brought down upon us from above. I say to you!" Matthew raised his hands but a door opening from the side stage caught his eyes.

One of the well-dressed bodyguards came on stage and locked eyes with him. Everyone in the congregation began to mumble as Matthew hastily walked over to the man and faced him.

"What is the meaning of this?" Matthew whispered urgently, holding the mic with one clenched fist. His back was turned towards the congregation, and he could hear slight whispers between people as they began to murmur amongst themselves.

"It seems the plan has failed," the man said plainly.

Matthew's eyebrows raised in surprise and he turned his head to look back at the mumbling audience. People began to check their phones, showing the screens to one another and pointing at their devices.

"What do you mean, it failed!" Matthew exclaimed, his voice rising enough that the mic still picked it up. Matthew heard it over the loudspeakers and made a cut-off motion with his hands towards the sound guy behind the stage. A loud click emitted from the speakers as Matthews mic was turned off.

Hesitantly, the bodyguard pulled out a tablet and handed it to Matthew. "I'm not sure. The detonation was successful, but it missed its target and exploded in the parking lot. The stadium still stands, and there are news reports of Anfang interrupting the game."

Matthew quickly took the tablet from the bodyguard and watched a live news feed of a reporter standing next to the stadium, retelling the events that just unfolded. Next to the news reporter, a small gryphoness and larger gryphon stood, both wearing Redtails jerseys.

Matthew recognized them to be players of the Redtails, Thyra's friends. He recognized the harris hawk gryphon right away. It was one of the beasts that had been in his office when they threatened him months ago. Matthew shoved past the bodyguard and entered in the back hallway before turning the volume up on the tablet to listen in.

"I stand here with gryphball players Antonio and Rachel who have seen the action unfold before their very eyes. Rachel, what happened here tonight at the stadium?" The reporter asked and knelt down next to the small gryphoness. Rachel took the microphone into her foretalons and looked directly at the camera.

"Gladly, Sandra. A gryphon attacked us at the game tonight, and we know who he is. His name is Anfang. He… well, let's just say he's an old friend of Thyra's," Rachel began. Sandra spoke into the microphone

"You mean to tell me Thyra, a player of the Redtails, knows the slasher personally?" Sandra asked.

Rachel cocked her head. "Yes and no. Well, apparently they were made in the same lab together, but were separated long ago. Thyra found out he was still alive when she saw his attacks on TV, but he's not the gryphon everyone makes him out to be! Or, so she says. But he did attack all of us after the bomb exploded. Thyra told us that Anfang was being held hostage by Matthew, a preacher for the Gathering in Macon and I believe her."

"Matthew Darnwall, the bishop of the church?" Sandra said with a gasp.

The tiny gryphoness nodded. "He's always hated Thyra and all us gryphons. I think that Anfang has been forced or brainwashed into doing that bigot's bidding! He was forced to kill all those cops, all those innocents, and Matthew wanted this stadium destroyed tonight, but it think Anfang had a change of heart. Or he didn't know about the bomb. I'm not really sure on what's going on either. But from what Anfang said on the field, I know he was under Matthew's control. That old bastard is the one at fault!"

Sandra took the microphone back and looked at the camera as she summarized in her own, more professional words, her face white. "We seem to have a new story developing here at Chanel Ten News tonight! Allegations that Matthew, the leader of the Gathering, has just attempted a bombing at the Redtails' stadium tonight."

Antonio raised a foretalon to ask for the microphone next. "What my colleague has said is true. We have known about Thyra's past relationship to Anfang and he had never been this way before Matthew got hold of him. I am aware what he has done means he is a criminal, but it is due to the acts of the evil man controlling him."

The camera panned back to Sandra as she began to summarize and ask questions, but Matthew no longer wanted to watch. He threw the tablet down at the ground, roaring with anger. The device shattered into multiple pieces with a loud snap, causing the bodyguard to wince behind him. Matthew never lost control like this. He cursed under his breath and stared at the broken remains of the tablet on the ground as silence filled the hallway again.

"Where did he go?" Matthew snapped and grabbed the collar on his bodyguard's suit. The man shook his head and shrugged his shoulders, causing Matthew to grumble and drop his hands down to his side. A moment passed as Matthew ran his fingers across his temples, rubbing them gently. "I'll figure this out in a few minutes. Learn all you can about this while I finish the sermon."

As he finished that sentence, Matthew heard a commotion coming from the hall, and quickly burst through the door onstage. His eyes widened as he saw everyone standing to their feet and showing each other their phones. As soon as Matthew stood on stage, a series of loud shouts erupted from the congregation.

For the first time in his life, Matthew felt pure fear strike into his heart. These people that had once been his sheep were now looking upon him like enemies holding proverbial pitchforks and torches. Matthew held his hands up high, palms facing towards the crowd and tried to speak, but his words were lost in the outcry. His mic soon cut back on, but all he could do was stutter nonsense across the loudspeakers as he was shouted down.

"Liar!" "Killer!" "Antichrist!" were several of the words that Matthew could understand.

They began to pour out of the rows and started to make their way towards the stage. Matthew felt his heart pound in his chest, and he fled. He broke through the door and closed it behind him. The bodyguard stood next to the door with a blank expression, not knowing what exactly to do. Suddenly, the door burst open, and people began to rush through it

Matthew fled down the hallway, looking back to see his bodyguards being overrun by the enraged audience. He sprinted down the long corridor, faster than his aging legs had carried him in years, and burst out the back entrance.

His Jaguar was parked out back, hidden from plain sight far away from everyone else's vehicles. He hastily dove into the car and slammed the door shut, listening to his deep labored breaths as the interior lights dimmed.

The angry mob of once-obedient people poured out of the church in search of Matthew, but none knew where he was parked. He could see people moving about in the rearview mirror a good distance away, yet none approached him. Within minutes, the angry mob dispersed, and multiple headlights across the parking lot switched on.

Matthew had been exposed. Daniel had tried to warn him this could happen, but he had refused to believe it. His empire was in shambles and there was nothing he could do about it. Now, he was without backup. He was without his people, his contractors, and his religion. All he had left was fear, and anger.

Anger was the emotion that took over in this instance, as it would in most humans. He gritted his teeth, thinking of Anfang's failed mission. Thyra, and Johnathen's mocking faces rose in his mind. It was they who had started the whole fight between the common man and gryphon. They were to blame. He was sure of it. And he knew where they lived.

Matthew slammed his fist against the fine leather steering wheel and screamed out in anger. His head throbbed and his chest heaved with breath as his mind whirred over his options.

Matthew pushed the cylindrical button on the dash to release the glove box. The hatch opened revealing a small Kimber 380 pistol. The old man took a deep breath and grabbed the weapon in his shaking right hand. He pulled the slide back. A round cycled into the chamber and he dropped the clip, checking to see if it was filled.

Matthew chuckled to himself, madness in his voice as he placed the handgun on the seat next to him. He reached down, and pushed the start button to his Jag, causing it to roar to life. If there was nothing else he could do, he was going to make sure Johnathen and Thyra got what they deserved.

Chapter 26 Like Moths To A Flame

Aadhya adjusted her angle of flight as she recognized Thyra's neighborhood coming within distance. Despite only being to the house once in her life, she had a photographic memory for location, as well as a fine-tuned feel for direction, perhaps due to her avian genetic heritage. The lights and house arrangements told her that this was the place.

She looked down at the gryphoness in her talons as she glided in. Thyra stirred and Aadhya whispered to her. "Thyra?"

Thyra slowly opened an eye. She was clearly disoriented as she looked around, her eartufts whisking in the wind. Nevertheless, a sign of recognition sparked in Thyra's green eyes when she looked upon the bearded vulture.

"Aadhya?" she asked gently.

The bearded vulture smiled and nodded. "Yes. You are almost home,"

Thyra stiffened as she saw Anfang gliding within close proximity. Her feathers ruffled as she began to stir in Aadhya's foretalons. Surprise and fear entered her voice. "W...what is Anfang doing here?"

Clearly, she recollected the events of their encounter. Anfang saw that she was awake and folded his one eartuft back in shame. He slowed, starting to glide slightly behind the two.

"Do not fret, he wants to help. He did not mean to hurt us. He only meant to protect you," Aadhya responded calmly and began her decent.

Thyra looked up at the large gryphoness and relaxed slightly, knowing that she was in her trusted friend's grasp instead of Anfang's. Still, she did not know where she was. The breeze that pushed her feathers apart told her that she was flying, yet the way she was laying, she couldn't tell where they were.

Aadhya saw her uneasy demeanor and quickly readjusted her grip so that Thyra could look at the ground. "We are seconds away from home."

Thyra seemed to relax as she looked around and saw the familiar buildings of her neighborhood. She had flown home at night more times than she could count and easily recognized her position from the sky. Aadhya slowed her decent, flaring her wings wide and gliding into a soft landing in Thyra's yard.

Once on the ground, Aadhya placed Thyra on her feet, and took a step back to give her friend a moment to regain her mind.

Anfang landed nearby, but still kept his distance, clearly ashamed by his actions. "Thyra, I…"

"Why didn't you just stay in the house?" Thyra growled. Anfang avoided her gaze and looked down at his talons. "Why?! Why did you have to ruin my life!" Aadhya blinked in surprise at her outburst and moved in to put a wing over her, but Thyra shrugged it off.

"I just want to help," Anfang responded and folded his eartuft flat against his head.

"Well, you've done a terrible job at that. All you have done is stir up trouble and bring death and destruction to everyone around you!" Thyra took a step forward towards Anfang and flared her wings out, hackle feathers rising with fury. "What made you think that coming in to kill another gryphon during the most important game of the season was helping me?"

Anfang looked up into her eyes and grimaced, his beak muzzle souring into a frown. "Anfang think Thyra in trouble. Think you forced to play. I thought it was hurting-."

"Well you thought wrong," Thyra interrupted again. "I don't know how to forgive you after this, Anfang. I'm at the end of my rope here. I don't know what to do with you or how to help you. Everyone now knows there's a connection between us, and just that fact alone could cost me my position as a gryphball player or worse, get me arrested and tried for helping a fugitive."

"But..."

"No. You're going to listen to me now," Thyra demanded and approached him until her beak was close to his.

Her eyes were beginning to water with animosity and Anfang could see it. He cowered before her and lowered himself down, feathers falling flat against his body.

"After tonight, you're going to leave," she said. "I don't know where you're going to go, but you have to leave until I can figure out what the hell I'm going to do with you and how I'm going to clean up your mess." Thyra waited for a moment more and cocked her head slightly. "Do you even understand what I'm saying?"

"Yes. Anfang understand. I hurt you. Hurt you and friends. Cause bad things for Thyra," Anfang summed it all up simply.

He broke eye contact with her and looked down at his deformed talons again. Thyra took in a deep breath, letting her fury subside and as it did, she could feel the heartache building in her chest again. Anfang understood that Thyra was hurting but truly did not understand the consequences of his actions. He had never lived in the real world and the complex society that it held. It had been tough enough for her to adapt to the world even though she had grown up in it.

"Can I trust you for tonight at least? Just one damn night. It's all I ask." Thyra asked firmly. Anfang nodded his head as it hung low. Thyra glanced at Anfang with distrust, but before she could decide what else to say to him, Aadhya pointed towards the driveway.

"Thyra, I hate to interrupt, but who's car is that?" the bearded vulture asked.

Thyra followed her gaze and looked to the open garage. Johnathen's Mustang was still gone, and another vehicle was parked awkwardly in the driveway. She let her eyes adjust to the darkness, and felt a jolt of fear rise through her spine when she recognized the car.

"That's Matthew's car!" Thyra exclaimed. They looked through the windows of Thyra's home. There was movement in the dim light, which could only mean one thing.

"He's inside," both gryphonesses said at the same time.

Anfang was the first to rush up the steps. Wood splintered and a loud crack filled the quiet air as Anfang broke down the front door and burst inside. The dizziness that Thyra had been feeling left her body as she quickly followed.

As she surged into the dimly-lit living room, she saw Matthew standing there. The old bastard was in her own home, holding an upturned gasoline jug in his left hand. Liquid was pouring from the nozzle and pooling on the floor. The smell of fumes was chokingly strong.

Matthew's loud laughter filled the room and she saw a handgun in his right hand. He was pointing the muzzle directly at Anfang. Thyra's blood pumped quickly through her veins as she saw Anfang hunker down and hiss loudly to the despiteful human standing before him.

"The whole crew is here! I didn't expect you so soon," came the old man's mocking voice.

Her hackle feathers rose. In the low light, Thyra could make out a wicked smile, and his grey eyes were glazed over. When she had faced the man in the past, Matthew had always been composed and controlled, but his current demeanor was completely different. He had the crazed look of an animal pushed into a corner, with no other option left but to attack.

Fear shook her very form as he quickly dropped the jug. Matthew stepped back and flicked out a lighter, the flame burning bright in the dim lighting. She stood next to Anfang and looked up at the crazed human.

"Matthew! Please! Wait!" she pleaded.

Matthew laughed loudly and shook his head, pulling the small hammer back on his handgun. "It's too late for that, you feathered bitch! You.... You and your bastard husband are done. You have taken EVERYTHING from me and now I'll take everything from you!" His hand trembled, the lighter shaking in his hand. The flame continued to burn brightly, and Thyra took a step forward.

A gunshot rang out, barely missing her and striking into the wall behind her. Anfang hissed again and took a step forward, ready to lunge. Thyra held a wing out to hold him back as Aadhya stood in the background, frozen with indecision.

"The world was fine before your kind arrived!" Matthew snarled. "We were perfect. We were happy."

"We didn't ask for it either!" Thyra yelled out to him. Matthew's smile faded slightly as he narrowed his eyes at the gryphoness. "I didn't ask to be created! All I've done my whole life is try to fit in with humans! Even though Johnathen never asked me to, I've tried to prove myself, tried to act like a human. Yet all you can do is deny my existence and call me an abomination!"

Tears streamed down Thyra's cheeks, dripping down her beak as she closed her wings in close to her body. "I'm no different from any of you! All I want is a happy life and to live peacefully, but its people like you that hold me back!"

"No! You will never be the same as I!" Matthew yelled and held the lighter out further. He lowered his voice, his gaze fixed with determination. “You’re an abomination! I was made in God’s image with a soul to serve him. You come from human sin. The human sin of trying to create and become an equal with God, and I can never forgive that.”

Matthew tossed the lighter. The room erupted into a roaring flame, blinding Thyra and throwing her back. She hit the ground and rolled before struggling onto her feet again. Her ears rang painfully loud as everything in the room burned in a bright yellow light.

Adrenaline scorched through her veins, causing everything to move slower than usual. She could see Matthew clearly as he recovered back to his feet. Pure terror and fury filled her body as she watched her living room burn and the man responsible for it was standing before her.

She screeched and rushed towards Matthew, heedless of the fire between them. Gunfire rang out again and a sharp pain filled her leg. She fell to the ground a few inches from the flames.

Anfang screeched to the top of his lungs and lunged through the fire towards Matthew. Thyra watched the man’s eyes widen with fear as he emptied his weapon into the gryphon, but the bullets had no effect.

Anfang’s talons slashed towards his throat, catching the tender flesh and flaying it into multiple pieces across the living room. Blood splattered across the television as Matthew dropped to his knees and let the weapon fall to the floor. He clutched his throat, gurgling on his own blood, the deep purple liquid coating his hands.

Thyra rolled onto her side to get away as the fire caught quickly, turning the once dark room into a blazing inferno. She screamed at Anfang as he clasped his talons around Matthew's wounded throat and squeezed.

A snap echoed in the blazing room, and the human's head twisted at an unnatural angle. Anfang released the old man and he fell limp on the ground. His eyes glazed over as Thyra stared into them.

The shock of seeing her enemy dead filled her very soul, causing her crop to lurch in an unnatural fashion. She was sickened by the sight before her, but even more sickened by the satisfaction she felt at his death. She didn't even notice her tail catch on fire.

"Thyra! We have to go!" Aadhya called out as she rushed up next to her. Aadhya quickly used her own wings to beat out the fire that caught on Thyra's tail.

Thyra tried rising to her feet, but found the wounded leg unable to move. Aadhya saw this and quickly lifted the gryphoness. Thyra grimaced and clicked her beak at the pain, putting her weight onto her friend. By then, the fire had overtaken most of the living room and had spread to their entrance.

Anfang twisted around, flaring his wings out protectively over the gryphonesses as he looked for an exit. A loud crack rang out as a piece of structural timber fell from the ceiling. Anfang called out and began to rush towards the back. Thyra coughed while smoke filled her sensitive lungs.

Anfang lunged at the back door and broke it open to create an exit. Aadhya lifted Thyra and carried her onto the back porch, jumping over the railing to glide roughly into the back yard. They collided with the ground hard and let out a wince of pain as they laid breathless in the grass, looking to the burning house before them.

There was nothing they could do. Anfang, Aadhya and Thyra could only watch as the home quickly burst into an inferno, the fire swallowing it whole for fuel. Thyra put her beak into her foretalons and wept. The home she had come to love and feel safe in was now a burning wreck. All her possessions and the place where she and Johnathen had made so many memories, gone.

Aadhya held Thyra close in her wings, comforting her as best she could with gentle preens. Anfang sat silently, watching the fire blaze into the night sky.

Sirens in the distance broke their concentration while the sounds of neighbors pouring from their homes began to grow apparent. Anfang looked to the two gryphons, clearly worried and confused.

"Where we go?" he asked.

Thyra sniffled through her nares. "You can't stay here."

Anfang cocked his head in confusion. "I....I stay with Thyra. I protect you," he said gently as the sirens began to grow louder.

Thyra shook her head and wiped her nares with a spare wing. How could she explain? In a gentle gravelly voice, she said, "If they find you here, they will arrest you, maybe kill you. You can't be here. You can't be around me, or they'll arrest me too."

She looked up to the beastly gryphon with bloodshot eyes and saw his muzzle beak curve into a frown. They sat in silence, save for the crackling inferno before them and the sirens growing closer to them.

"Thyra… I.." Anfang started.

"You have to leave," she insisted. "I'll try to find you again, Anfang. I'll try to bring you help, but… But promise me…" She gasped and tried to find her words again. "Promise me that you will never kill another human again." Thyra gulped as tears continued to stream down her face. "If you do I'll never be able to forgive you. No more… this is it."

Anfang was lost in indecision. For the first time in his life he was free and yet, at that very moment he was more lost than he had ever been. "Wh-where I go?"

"Just get away from here, far away from humans," she said. "Hide. Stay in the mountains or the forest, just don't let yourself be seen or they will hunt you down."

Anfang nodded his head gently. "Anfang promise, but Thyra find me again."

Anfang stared intently into Thyra's green eyes with his own and she could see he felt remorse for all his actions. The flames had began to spread across the deck towards them, and she could feel the heat of them on her face, yet all she could think about was the hard road ahead of him.

"I promise," Thyra said in return.

Reluctantly, Anfang spread his great leathery wings and took one last mental picture of her before leaping into the sky. His form quickly disappeared against the black abyss as her eyes were adjusted to the bright flame before her.

Thyra took a deep breath and screeched out into the air, letting all her anger, emotion, and sadness go in one breath. Her body trembled hard against Aadhya, and the bigger gryphoness wrapped her tight in a constricting hug. They watched her home burn together as the flames spit into the air, the light catching on the surrounding trees and turning them into a flurry of orange.

"I don't know what to do, Addy," Thyra sobbed into her friend's comforting neck feathers.

Aadhya stroked across Thyra's cheek. "There is nothing left for us to do. Although, I can offer you my home, of course. You and Johnathen can stay with me. It is the least I can do."

This comforted Thyra slightly, knowing that there was a familiar place to go home to. She had a true friend, and right now, that exactly what she needed.

Their solitude was interrupted as the sounds of sirens pierced the air of the quiet neighborhood. Thyra's human neighbors visited, providing comforting words while the fire fighters arrived, attempting to put out the inferno. She thanked her neighbors gently, appreciating the words of support from the concerned humans, yet, Thyra couldn't help but feel that all was lost.

She wondered if they would be as passionate and forgiving as they were right now after they found out the truth. Would they reprimand her for taking a killer into her house? How would the general public react to that? Not only the fact that she knew and took care of Anfang, but when they found Matthew's body inside her house. She would surely be proven innocent of murder, but there were those that would think otherwise. She could be labeled as a killer for the rest of her life as well. It could be the end of her career as a gryphball player, and it could kill Johnathen's career as well.

As Thyra's thoughts darkened and she watched the firefighters continue to battle the raging inferno, she heard her name being called. Thyra lifted her head off of Aadhya's shoulder and looked around.

"Thyra!" came a familiar voice. She turned to see Johnathen ducking under police tape and rushing into the backyard.

"Johnathen!" She felt the fear and loathing leave her as he embraced her strongly. Johnathen fell to his knees, clutching his wife firmly in his hands, clutching her feathers tightly. Together they cried for a moment, holding one another as tightly as they could. She wrapped talons and wings around him to embrace him.

"I'm so sorry…I… I" Thyra struggled with words, chocking on her tears.

"Honey, honey it's ok. It's just possessions. It's just stuff. It can be replaced. But I could never replace you. I don't know what I would do if you were hurt." Johnathen replied and pulled back to kiss her beak.

"It was Matthew. He…" Thyra began to explain but Johnathen shook his head and rubbed along her eartufts.

"We can talk about it all later."

Johnathen was right. All of it was over. There was nothing left to do, nothing left to say. All that was left, everything she had in the world now was him, and she could not be more thankful.

Epilogue

Thyra sat at a table alongside her teammates as multiple flashes from cameras filled the small pressroom. The backdrop behind her had the Redtails logo imprinted all across the borders, amongst the symbols of multiple team sponsors they had for the season.

Media members stood with recorders and cameras, yelling and raising their hands as they desperately tried to ask their next questions. Coach victor pointed to one of the ladies in the crowd, and everyone grew silent.

"Victor! We all know the game was interrupted with only one minute to spare! How will the game be judged, and will your team advance to the first league?" the reporter asked, holding out her microphone.

"Currently, we are the victors, but it is under review. That is all I have in this matter," Victor responded in a rough and deep voice. Multiple people jumped up from their seats, shouting to get the next question in. He pointed to another gentlemen towards the back. "Yes? You with Channel Ten?"

"I understand Thyra was friends with the Sabertooth Slasher and is still a suspect in the murder of Bishop Matthew Darnwall. Will that have any affect on her position in the next league?" the man asked loudly.

Everyone began to mumble, and Thyra pinned her eartufts back. It was the same questions the public had been asking her all week. Not just the press, but multiple officers of the law too. She was not in chains, yet, but she could not shake the feeling that everyone blamed her for the multiple incidents.

As far as Thyra could tell from the news reports, there were some that believed Matthew was still a good man and his death was an unfortunate loss to the community, while some were believing the hard evidence coming up against Matthew and the Gathering itself. With so many in disagreements of what truly transpired, and no leader to run it, the Gathering was in shambles. It was unlikely the church could continue.

Despite that one bit of good news, the constant inquiries made her question her future in not just gryphball, but as in a citizen as well. Would she ever be looked at in the same way, or was she going to be forced to live her life as she did years ago? Would she spend her life as a cast out, a menace to society, and nothing more than a dangerous animal? Thyra sank down in her seat and glanced away from the reporters, unable to look them in the eyes any longer.

Victor cleared his throat again and gripped one of the multiple microphones before him. "Yes, I understand that Thyra knew the criminal, and Matthew was found in the rubble of Thyra's house, but she has yet to be accused of any wrongdoings. Next question, please."

Victor spoke casually as if it was a simple question, yet it weighed on not only her mind, but also the mind of everyone else in the room. It had been a week since anyone had seen Anfang, and since her home had been burnt to the ground. She was here for one reason only, to settle the matters between the gryphball matches.

Another man raised his pencil high in the air and was able to speak louder than everyone else. Victor acknowledged him with a beak tilt and the crowd grew silent once more. "Yes? Gryphball news network?"

The man had a slight smirk on his face as he held out his recorder. "I hear what you're saying, but regardless of how the allegations turn out, if your team advance into the first league, will Thyra be joining you? Are the owners willing to have that kind of publicity around the team?"

Everyone began to mumble under their breath again. Victor's large gray crest feathers rose with agitation. He slammed his fist on the table and leaned forward to point a great curved talon at the man who just asked the question.

"That's enough. I will not have any more scrutiny against my player in this meeting! Thyra is a damn good gryphball player, and a damn good gryphon with a heart of gold. She doesn't possess a single ounce of malice in her hallow bones, which is more than I can say for the lot of you! Hell itself would freeze over before she would commit any of those acts she's being blamed for and that's all I have to say about that matter."

The man shouted out asking for a follow up question, but Victor cut him off. "This press meeting is for gryphball. This isn't a courtroom. If anyone else touches on this subject again, I'll remove you from this meeting myself! Is that understood?" Victor shouted to the top of his lungs. The great gryphon's voice would have easily carried in the small room without the help of microphones and speakers, but it had an added affect of silencing the press before him. He puffed up his gray chest feathers and forced them down once more. "Good. Let us continue."

Another human stood and held his microphone high in the air. Victor pointed a foretalon to the press member, giving permission to speak.

"If your team is advanced into the first league, what will you do first?" the man asked him. Finally, a normal question. The whole team let out a sigh of relief as Victor began to explain his plan.

Thyra could not help but let her eyes wonder among the crowd. She had seen the same interviewers and media workers many times over, but one man in particular stuck out like a sore thumb. He did not bear any notepads, recorders, or clothing that resembled some sort of work attire. He seemed to be a simple businessman that somehow made his way into the team interview.

He was in his late fifties and wore a very simple gray suit. His hair was cut short and gray, but the gleaming green eyes he possessed drew Thyra's curiosity more than anything.

Victor went back and forth with several more interviewers, but his words became mumbles as Thyra continued to stare at the odd man. His eyes locked onto hers and a small easy smile curved on his lips. The smile felt familiar, and something about him comforted her. She somehow knew him, but she just could not put her talon on how.

"That's all the time we have for today," Victor said, ending the interview. Thyra snapped back to reality and looked around the room. Everyone rose from their chairs once more, but this time, silently. Satisfied, the press began to separate and head out of the exits nearest to them in the meeting room.

"Are you ok?" Aadhya asked gently.

Thyra looked over to her friend and saw the rest of the band watching with interest. Her friends must have noticed how dazed she was, but probably feared it was from the sore topics Victor had to answer. She put on a smile and nodded her head.

"Yeah, I'm ok. I'm used to getting grilled at this point. It's just been a really long week and I haven't slept much." Thyra responded. Her friends seemed reluctant to accept that simple response, but stood up with the rest of the gryphball crew.

"I have heard you talk with Johnathen well into the night. Perhaps I should pick up some herbal medicine and serotonin on the way home," Aadhya suggested. Thyra felt a slight stab of guilt. They had been staying at Aadhya's house while deciding what to do, and it could not be easy on her having all that added stress.

Rachel hopped up on the table and folded in her wings "Or we could all go out for dinner tonight! What do you say, Thyra? You could use a night out and I sure could use some tacos! What about that Mexican place we've been to a couple times? Las Mas! I'll buy the margaritas!" the small gryphoness exclaimed, trying her best to lighten the mood.

Thyra smiled and shook her head. "I'd like that, but not tonight, maybe tomorrow. John is probably already back at Addy's apartment with food for the night. He's been learning how to cook Indian cuisine and said he wanted to try something new tonight."

Rachel huffed and shrugged her wing shoulders. "Fine, fine. Rain check then. What about you Antonio? Tacos?" Rachel asked, cocking her tiny head at him..

Antonio could not help but chuckle at that offer and nodded his head. "Of course, ask the Spanish one if he wants tacos. Yes, as long as you are still buying the margaritas."

Excitedly, Rachel hopped of the table and proceeded down the hallway out the back. The band all followed each other, except for Thyra. She looked out into the dispersing crowd to see the same man with the green eyes still sitting quietly and staring straight at her.

Thyra froze as a sense of recognition flowed across her memory. She was still certain that had seen him multiple times before, but could not place the memory.

"Thyra? You coming?" Rachel stopped and asked. She looked over to the small gryphoness and waved her off with a wingtip.

"Yeah, yeah just a second. I'll be right there." Thyra responded. Satisfied, Rachel ducked behind the curtain with the rest and disappeared into the backstage.

Thyra locked eyes with the businessman once again, not knowing why she felt drawn to him. He stood and began to walk upstage, as she descended down towards him.

"Thyra," the man said gently. Immediately, she felt comforted by his voice, as such a person would feel when listening to a loved one. She flicked her wings and stood before him.

"Why do you seem familiar?" Thyra questioned carefully, looking around for anyone in the area. Everyone in the room had vanished, the interviews over. All that was left was him and her.

"I've known you all your life, Thyra," the man gently said.

Again, the familiar voice of a ghostly past washed over her. She felt her legs tremble as she looked to the man, and his face grew stronger in her mind. The connection happened and she took a quick step back, finally realizing who he was. It was the man from her dreams.

"You… You were there!" she cried out loud, feathers fluffing in anxiety and uncertainty. He held up a hand and slowly reached forward, eyes beginning to water as he observed her.

"I was, yes. Thyra…It's been so long," the man said and stroked along her beak. She usually did not allow strangers to show her such a sign of affection but this, this felt so right. It felt so comforting. Even his distant scent relaxed her as she locked eyes with him. "I'm glad to see that you recognize me. I'm Anthony, your creator. And I'm here to talk to you about Anfang."

Made in the USA
Columbia, SC
10 October 2020

22529078R00236